Fugitive

A King David Novel
Book Three of the Davidic Chronicles

Greg S. Baker

Fugitive

A King David Novel
Book Three of the Davidic Chronicles

by

Greg S. Baker

Copyright © 2019

ISBN: 9781701377394
Independently Published

First Edition

All Scripture quotations are from the King James Bible.

All rights reserved. No part of this publication may be reproduced or transmitted in any form or by any means, electronic or mechanical, including photocopy, recording, or any information storage retrieval system, without permission in writing from the copyright owner.

This is a work of fiction based on the Holy Scriptures as presented in the King James Bible. All characters and events resembling real people and events outside the Scriptures is wholly coincidental.

Other Books by Greg S. Baker

Biblical Fiction Novels

The Davidic Chronicles

Anointed
Valiant
Fugitive
Delivered
King

The Rise of Daniel

Crucibles of God
Children of the Captivity
Revealer of Secrets
Arising Wrath

Adventure/Fantasy Novels

Isle of the Phoenix Novels

The Phoenix Quest
In the Dragon's Shadow
Phoenix Flame
Rise of the Dragon Spawn
More to come…

Christian and Christian Living

- ***The Generational Warrior*** – *The Battlefield Manual for First-Generation Christians*
- ***Fitly Spoken*** – *Developing Effective Communication and Social Skills*
- ***Restoring a Fallen Christian*** – *Rebuilding Lives for the Cause of Christ*
- ***The Great Tribulation and the Day of the Lord****: Reconciling the Premillennial Approach to Revelation*
- ***The Gospel of Manhood According to Dad*** – *A Young Man's Guide to Becoming a Man*
- ***Rediscovering the Character of Manhood*** – *A Young Man's Guide to Building Integrity*
- *Stressin' Over Stress* – *Six Ways to Handle Stress*

www.GregSBaker.com

To King David.

Long gone from the earth, King David continues to inspire millions. His story is the foundation of this series. Acts 13:36 tells us that David served his own generation, but he has also served my generation. His love for his God continues to inspire.

Acknowledgments

As always, the time and efforts of others have a large impact on the finished product of any written work. This is no exception. My wife, Liberty, continues to lend her encouragement and support of my writing endeavors. My parents, Keith and Debbie, read and re-read this manuscript, pointing out errors and problems. Trent Cowling, always willing to talk "Bible" read one of the working drafts to help ensure biblical accuracy.

Thank you to all!

Author's Note about Biblical Fiction

What Is Biblical Fiction?

Biblical fiction can mean a variety of things, but essentially, for my purposes, it is similar in nature to historical fiction. In biblical fiction, the author takes the true events and people of the Bible and expands upon them into a fuller story of "what might have happened" that connects those events and people the Bible speaks of.

For example, David mentions to King Saul that he had killed a lion and a bear. The Bible does not describe those events, so in a Biblical Fiction novel, I might write the scenes surrounding those events as it might have happened while staying true to the biblical account. It is not to be Scripture or to replace Scripture. Instead, it is meant to bring to life a possible fuller picture of the characters and events that the Bible describes.

It is similar to what preachers do when retelling a Bible story from the pulpit. They embellish the story, add emotional responses or reactions to the characters, and extrapolate events and actions in ways that depict logically what might have happened or how biblical characters might have felt. It is fictional, but logical fiction.

In such a novel, I would bring together many of the historical facts mentioned in the Bible and present a possible fuller picture of what the Bible describes in a shorter context, often in just two or three chapters. An entire novel could be based on those few chapters, filling in fictionally all the blank areas.

Scriptural footnotes are added to show where a biblical fact has been incorporated into the story.

My desire is to ensure that the biblical facts are the mainstays and core of the story while the fictional aspects are forced to revolve around those facts to bring a cohesive narrative that remains true to the biblical record. Other biblical fiction tends to do the opposite in order to try and present a more entertaining story.

Again, to be clear, this is not meant to be Scripture or to replace Scripture of any sort. Except for what the Bible says, the rest of what I write is fictional—my best guess based on the information we have as to what might have happened.

These stories are meant to be fun and adventurous but remain true to the biblical account. These novels are not children's books, though they are suitable for children. I am writing for a more mature audience, teenagers and adults. I don't sugarcoat the men and women in the Bible. They were often thieves, liars, murderers, adulterers, and bloodthirsty warriors. I decided not to cheapen the violence and other horrible deeds that the Bible describes. I aim to show you an entertaining story, true, but also one that will hopefully inspire you to see the Bible stories in a broader sense. These were real people with real problems who made real mistakes but who lived real lives that God wanted us to study and know.

So, enjoy.

Map of Israel
At the time David flees from King Saul

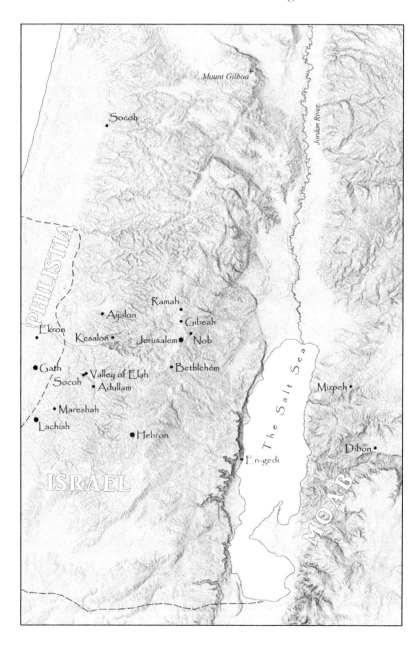

Prologue

The javelin slammed into the wall and quivered there angrily like a snake robbed of its victim. Before the shaft could settle into stillness, David had scrambled out the door, leaving two bemused guards to pick themselves up from where they'd been knocked to the ground.[1]

And King Saul raged.

Adriel, once David's armorbearer and now the king's son-in-law,[2] felt his heart drop into his stomach, and the metallic taste of fear stung his tongue.

His worst nightmare came true a moment later when the king's tall frame spun on him, his face livid and his bloodshot eyes bulging dangerously. In a voice shaking with fury, he ordered, "Take men and slay David!"

Adriel flinched, his face sagging in dismay. "My lord?"

"Does my voice not carry? Do your ears not hear? Go! Bring me his head by morning!"

Trying to still his slamming heart, knowing that his own life hung by the merest thread, Adriel dared say, "The city gates are closed, my lord; he cannot leave the city. He is likely fled to his house—"

---

[1] 1 Samuel 19:10.
[2] 1 Samuel 18:19.

1 Samuel 19:9-10

"All the better," Saul growled. "Go there and slay him!"[3]

His hands shaking against his will, Adriel continued, "And what then of your daughter Michal? Perchance she is in the house when we enter? Do you wish for us to slay her husband before her eyes?"

Saul muttered something inarticulate as his eyes darted every which way like a cornered animal. Finally, he slammed his fist against one of the walls. "Nay. Do not shed his blood in her presence. Set a watch," he ordered Adriel. "Take him in the morning when he leaves his house."[4]

Trembling, Adriel bowed low and turned to leave. He paused to glare at the Moabite ambassador, the instigator of Saul's most recent outburst against David. The dark-skinned man's eyes twinkled with triumph. If he had come to sow discord, then he had done his job well. Dismissing the ambassador from his mind, Adriel strode toward the door, selecting five guards to accompany him—guards who at one time or another had shown a measure of favor toward the son of Jesse. Adriel didn't want any overzealous or overambitious men who might overstep themselves. Taking David would not be easy, and one wrong move could end in more than one man's death.

He wished fervently that Jonathan had not been sent away. Tasking Jonathan with giving the Indebted their freedom was merely a pretext. He didn't need to do that in person, but even the king knew of his eldest son's love for David. Only Jonathan had a chance of turning away Saul's wrath from David. And he conveniently wasn't around. As it was, Adriel was left with little choice. He stopped just beyond the oak door as it closed behind him, his heart continuing to thud violently as his men gathered around him. Turmoil drained away his strength like a man who had lost too much blood. David was perhaps the closest person Adriel ever had to a brother outside of Jonathan himself. Killing him would be the same as killing himself.

---

[3] 1 Samuel 19:11.
[4] 1 Samuel 19:11.

— 2 —

He looked into the faces of the guards and saw confusion. They didn't understand. Adriel didn't understand. David was a national hero, the slayer of the Philistine champion Goliath,[5] and the man most responsible for routing the Philistines and protecting the people of Israel.[6] Of all the men of Israel, David had been most valiant for the LORD God and for Israel.

One of the guards, a wide-faced, pockmarked man with tiny eyes, licked his lips and asked, "My lord Adriel, are we truly to slay David?"

Adriel shook himself. Facing his men, he nodded, an action that cost him part of his soul. "That is the king's command."

"It is the evil spirit,"[7] another muttered, his face dark.

Adriel didn't respond, trying to think. The man was right, of course. The evil spirit had surely come upon Saul once again and driven him to do the unthinkable. All Israel loved David, and even those most loyal to Saul had come to accept David as their champion.[8] This discord between the two most important men in Israel did not set well with the men. Adriel understood, for he shared their disquiet.

But he dared not disobey. David would have to die by morning. Growing angry, Adriel snapped at one of the guards. "You, return to Saul's court and retrieve David's harp. Meet us in the courtyard."

The guard didn't ask questions. He turned and slipped back through the door as Adriel led the other four men down the hall. He snatched an idle servant by the man's tunic. "Find my wife and tell her to come to me in the courtyard."

The servant stammered a reply, "Me? Merab, my lord?"

Growling, Adriel pushed the man away. "Have I another wife, one of slow wit and dull of tongue?"

The poor servant swallowed hard and hastened away.

---

[5] 1 Samuel 17:50.
[6] 1 Samuel 19:8.
[7] 1 Samuel 19:9.
[8] 1 Samuel 18:5, 16.

1 Samuel 19:9-10

In the dark courtyard, Adriel's small squad of men gathered. Lamplight created a small pool of light around the men, and into this light Merab appeared, her jewelry tinkling about her as she hastened to her husband. Her presence comforted him somewhat. He looked upon her oval face and small, perky nose and found a measure of strength. Now that she was married, she no longer wore her virgin's veil. Her dark brown hair had been allowed to swing freely about her neck and was held away from her face by a golden tiara.

She looked anxious as she peered at her husband. "Here I am, my lord," she announced, a question in her brown eyes.

Adriel took David's harp from the guard who had retrieved it and thrust it into his wife's arms. Pulling her away from the others, he whispered, "Find your sister, and give her this. Tell her that David will be slain in the morning."

Merab's eyes widened. "My lord?"

Adriel sighed. He could relate to her confusion, but he could not ease it, nor did he have the time. "Go, my wife, and do as I bid. In the morning, I am commanded to slay the son of Jesse." He looked her sternly in the eye. "In the morning. Do you understand?"

His wife glanced over at the other five guards' stony faces, seeing them for the first time, seeing the weapons they carried, and the gravity of what they were about suddenly dawned on her. She swallowed and gave her husband a slight bow. "As you command, my lord." She hastened away, clutching David's harp tightly to her.

Adriel gave her as many heartbeats as he could to get well ahead of him. Taking a deep breath, he motioned his men to join him. He then issued some meaningless instructions before marching slowly out of the gate and into the narrow streets of Gibeah beyond Saul's house. Saul had built his house on the highest hill of the walled city, so from here, Adriel had a panoramic view of nearly the entire town. Dots of light marked the houses and rooftops as the citizens of the city prepared to bed down for the night.

How appropriate, Adriel muttered in the vaults of his mind. Murder and darkness were common bedfellows. He marched his men slowly through the nearly deserted streets. Their lamps only

— 4 —

penetrated the gloom so far, and furtive movement in the shadows hinted at the few citizens still about, scurrying to get out of the way of the grim-faced soldiers.

Most of the houses they passed were one or two-story structures. The walls were constructed of hardened bricks made of mud or clay. Adriel idly noted the contrast between the standard house of Gibeah and Saul's house built out of hewn stone and imported wood. Voices floated down from the roofs of many of the houses where families often either slept during the summer nights or were simply relaxing under the starlight. Many of these voices cut off abruptly when they heard the jingling sound of soldiers marching past.

Adriel gripped his sword hilt tightly as they neared David's house. This would undoubtedly be one of the longest nights of his life. The house of their quarry was a two-story building nestled between other houses on the main street that led out of the city. A small courtyard, bordered by a low wall, fronted the house. The door was tightly closed, but lamplight spilled out of an upper story window. Someone was home.

Seeing no sign of his wife and hoping she had already come and gone with her message, Adriel posted his men around the house. They obeyed silently, quenching their lamps and moving deep into the shadows. No one looking out their windows would see them.

Adriel would not act until the morning when the sun was fully up. He wanted to give David as much time as he could to figure out a way to escape. He prayed that David had already fled, that he was no longer in the house, but come sunup, he would obey his king's command. If he found David, the son of Jesse would be slain, and his head taken back to Saul.

1

David turned at the sound of his wife's frantic voice floating up from below. Michal's head popped into view as she climbed the ladder from the first floor. Her unveiled face was etched in consternation and something else—something David couldn't readily identify. In truth, his own emotions surged within him, like a storm lashing blindly at an uncaring mountain. King Saul had once again tried to kill him, and once again, David didn't understand why.

"David!" Michal cried again, scrambling the rest of the way up the ladder, awkwardly hauling his harp after her.

"You have my harp," he said, surprised. His heart lightened. If Michal had his harp, then maybe Saul had relented. Maybe the king's murderous attempt was but the product of the evil spirit and already the king grieved over his actions.

She froze, staring at him incredulously. "You rejoice in seeing the harp? This is nothing!" She tossed the harp bodily aside and David had to leap to catch it. The strings vibrated harshly as he caught it. She followed him and caught his hands in hers, urging him to lay aside the harp. He did so, but carefully. She then captured his eyes with her own. "If you don't save your life tonight, then you'll be slain in the morning!"[1]

"What is this that you say?"

---

[1] 1 Samuel 19:11.

"My father seeks to slay you, my husband. He has commanded Adriel to do the deed!"

David stiffened. "Adriel? He would not!"

Michal's voice filled with scorn. "Not even at the king's order? Do not be a fool."

"Hold your tongue, woman," David snapped, disliking her tone. "You know not of what you speak."

She laughed, a light mocking sound that set David's teeth on edge. "Do I not? I am a king's daughter, husband. I know the hearts of men and kings. My father does know that the LORD Jehovah has anointed you to be the next king of Israel.[2] You are more of a danger to him than all the Philistine hosts arrayed together. Nay, if you do not flee this night, you will be slain, even by the hand of your friend."

David licked his lips uncertainly. He had refused to believe that Saul truly wanted to kill him. Instead of hiding, he had come straight home after defeating the Philistine host, willing to give his life into Saul's hands if Jehovah so willed. Surely Saul's insanity was but temporary, sparked by the foolish Moabite ambassador, and gone just as quickly. He had hoped that once the evil spirit had left the king, then all would be well. But Michal's warning belied such a notion. Perhaps there was another way. "What of your brother, my wife? Would not Jonathan be a wall between me and your father?"

"Jonathan has been sent away," Michal replied impatiently. "You know this. He will not be back for at least several days. You cannot wait upon his return, for my father would not involve him, knowing that he loves you."[3]

She was right, of course. Jonathan might very well be able to blunt his father's fury, but not until he came back, and by then, David would most likely be dead. He would need to flee. The thought sickened him, but he could not see another choice. *But where? Where can I go?* To return to his father's house in Bethlehem would needlessly put his entire family in danger. So where?

His emotions knotted in his stomach, like a ball of tangled twine. If he fled, he would be a fugitive, an outcast from Israel,

---

[2] 1 Samuel 16:13.
[3] 1 Samuel 20:3, 18:1.

hunted and spurned by all. The king's word was law. Who would stay their hand when the king's command was so heavy?

Samuel.

David straightened as a desperate plan formed in his mind. "You are right, my wife. I will flee this place."

She regarded him fearfully, nibbling on a loose strand of dark honey-colored hair. David found her incredibly beautiful. Not as ostentatious as her older sister, Michal was more modest in her dress, disdaining jewelry for the most part and wearing her hair loose. Only a mole growing on the side of her long nose marred the perfect symmetry of her face. She looked up at him, her blue eyes steeling themselves for what must be done.

"Where will you go?" she asked quietly.

David ran a hand through his light-brown hair, his grayish eyes scanning every inch of his wife's face. "I will go to Samuel."

Michal's eyes narrowed, but she nodded shortly. "That is well. Samuel will know what to do." She glanced around, her lips pursed in thought. "But we must get you well away before morning."

David shared his plan.

From the upper window of David's house, the thrumming strings of a harp carried easily to the ears of the watchers around the house. David, his eyes closed and his breathing steady, let the chords wash over him in a vain attempt to quell his aching heart. Despite Michal's presence, he felt utterly alone. The moment he fled this house could very well be the last time he ever saw her. The ache in his heart spread so that he found his throat thick with emotion and his eyes brimming with tears.

He would flee, but he didn't understand why he must. Saul's unreasoning hatred pricked him to the quick, and Adriel's willingness to obey the king's command brought David more pain than he thought possible. In such times, he turned to the only One who might lend an ear, the only One who could save him, his God, Jehovah.

Words came easily to him at such times for they were less songs and more prayers. "Deliver me from mine enemies, O my God: defend me from them that rise up against me. Deliver me from the workers of iniquity, and save me from bloody men. For, lo, they lie in wait for my soul: the mighty are gathered against me; not for my transgression, nor for my sin, O LORD. They run and prepare themselves without my fault: awake to help me, and behold."[4]

Troubled, the tone of his psalm changed, and David prayed for God's wrath to be poured upon those who sought his life.[5] But toward the end of his prayer, his fear and anger expended, he besought his God with words of promise and thanksgiving. In near exhaustion, he sang softly, "But I will sing of thy power; yea, I will sing aloud of thy mercy in the morning: for thou hast been my defense and refuge in the day of my trouble. Unto thee, O my strength, will I sing: for God is my defense, and the God of my mercy."[6]

The words drifted off into the night, carried away by the last notes of the harp strings. David slumped over, his eyes red, his heart still heavy, but with a throb of hope and determination still residing in the core of his being. He would do as he promised and trust in Elohim to be his strength.

Michal had stood unmoving through the entire prayer. Her eyes regarded him with a mixture of wonder and awe. There had been power in his prayer as if God Himself had taken hand in the words he'd sung. David gave her a wan smile and pushed himself upright. "Is all in readiness?"

Numbly, she nodded.

David took a deep, steadying breath. "It is well. You know what to do."

"Aye." She glanced over to the bed where a mannequin lay covered with a blanket. A cushion made of goat's hair had been tucked in where a head would likely be.[7] It didn't much look like David, but it was the best they could do on short notice. It might deceive someone in dim lighting as they peered into the room from the ladder leading up to the second floor of the house. Maybe.

---

[4] Psalm 59:1-4, written when Saul sent men to kill David at his house.
[5] Psalm 59:5-15.
[6] Psalm 59:16-17.
[7] 1 Samuel 19:13, 16.

"Give me as much time as you can safely give," he said to her. He took her then and held her, mumbling inaudible platitudes. He didn't fear for her. She was the king's daughter, and she had the cunning of a snake. She was, if anything, a survivor. The embrace was more for himself.

He broke away and picked up his haversack, containing food, a wineskin, and a handful of silver shekels, and slung the leather traveling bag over his shoulder. He looked longingly at his sword and armor, but he put them firmly out of his mind. They would only hinder him for what he had to do, and he would avoid taking a Hebrew life if he could.

Michal moved close and kissed him on both cheeks in a farewell gesture. She looked meaningfully at the open window and the coil of rope tied to a beam of the house. He nodded. She then picked up the lamp and his harp and descended the ladder to the first story, plunging the upper room into an inky darkness. He settled in to wait, to allow the watchers without to believe no one remained in the upper level. Then, moving stealthily, David took the coil of rope and tossed it out the window that overlooked a back alley.

Below, his harp was thrummed idly as if someone was trying to think of the words to a song. Michal would keep the watchers busy while he escaped out the window.[8] Careful not to make even the slightest sound, he went out the window and dropped into the back alley between several houses. Only about three cubits separated the walls of the houses here, and he suspected that at least one watcher was stationed in the direction he needed to go.

While Michal continued to strum the harp loudly, he moved silently toward the alley entrance, picking up a stout rock as he went. He had to be careful where he walked for refuse often filled the alley, and it would be an easy thing to betray his presence with a misstep.

He took two more steps and froze. A half-moon hung overhead, affording scant illumination to his surroundings. Lazy clouds drifted across the sky, occasionally obscuring the moon. The shadows between the walls were dark and ominous. He couldn't see into the shadows there, but he'd heard the tell-tale sound of someone shifting position just ahead.

---

[8] 1 Samuel 19:12.

He counted his breaths until they slowed and his heart began beating at a more normal pace. Then he moved forward a handbreadth at a time until he judged he stood near the watcher still hidden in the shadows. Careful to make no sound, he tossed the rock out into the night beyond the sentry.

The clattering sound caused the guard to step out of the alley and into the street. The man peered into the darkness, hands tightly gripping his spear.

Silent as a shadow, David eased out behind the man and slipped into the darkness farther down the street. He froze there, careful not to move or make eye contact with the guard peering around for the source of the sound.

Finally, the guard stepped back into the alley and slipped from view. More watchers could be hidden anywhere nearby. He had to be careful. He waited. Suddenly, from his house came the sound of something shattering, a clay jug or bowl, along with an inarticulate cry of frustration. Acting quickly on the prearranged signal, David eased out of the shadows and into the dim light of the moon and casually walked away, dipping into the deeper shadows when he could.

Having lived in Gibeah for some time, he knew of several ways he could slip unnoticed out of the city. Soon, he was gone, heading northwest toward Ramah and the Great Seer Samuel.

At length, Michal set David's harp off to one side and blew out the oil lamp. She then sat silently in her dark house, idly wondering what Adriel and the other watchers outside would be thinking. Her brother-in-law's warning had been subtle, but abundantly clear. Surely, Adriel didn't believe David to still be in the house.

Not that it mattered now. She'd done all she could for her husband. He was on his own.

She sat in the stillness of her dark house, seething with anger over both her husband's refusal to stand up to her father and over her father's unreasoning fear and hatred of David. She pictured her husband in her mind's eye.

1 Samuel 19:11-17

No longer the boy, David carried himself like a lion, every step conveying lethal power and dominance. His muscles rippled with supple grace when he moved, and his gray eyes could pierce right to her soul with a keen intelligence that stripped away her emotional barriers with ease. Years of frontline battle had given his face a rugged, hard aspect made even more fierce by a scar that ran from his left ear into his beard—a gift from a now dead Philistine warrior. He kept his hair cropped short, so nothing of his chiseled features and strong, square jaw was hidden except for a dark beard. Standing several handbreadths taller than she, David was the preeminent warrior in Israel, the Hebrew champion who had felled Goliath and turned back the Philistines time after time.

And the Jehovah Elohim was with him.

Michal shivered in the dark. She knew as did her father that David would be king one day. But instead of accepting this end, her father sought to murder David and thus somehow usurp Elohim's will. Michal, instinctively understanding the futility of such a course of action, had decided upon another for herself—she had married David. She bit her lower lip. She did love David.[9] But her desire to be wed to him extended further than merely love. As the daughter of the king, it was her duty to help secure her family and being married to David accomplished that goal. So why couldn't her father just admit the inevitability and accept David as part of the family? Had she not been a dutiful daughter in marrying the son of Jesse? Had she not tied him to the house of Saul?

She fumed, her musings taking an even darker turn. She sat thus long into the night and took no notice when the darkness slowly faded as the sun began to poke up over the mountains of Moab to the east. Her reverie was shattered when a firm rap on the wooden door announced that the watchers had tired of waiting and had taken more decisive action.

"Open up in the name of the king!" a voice shouted from without.

Irritated, she crossed her kitchen to the front door, walking with sandaled feet across the hard-packed dirt floor. She yanked the

---

[9] 1 Samuel 18:20.

— 12 —

door open to see four men standing in the small yard that fronted the house. Adriel, her brother-in-law, stood foremost among them.

She studied her sister's husband with just a touch of disdain. Not as tall as David or as strongly built, Adriel still carried himself as a warrior should. His dark skin reflected the sunlight, giving him a momentarily ethereal glow. Michal sniffed, letting her irritation show. "What do you here, Adriel?"

"Fetch David," he ordered, his voice hollow. Dark rings circled his eyes, and it pleased Michal to think of him wrestling all night with the guilt of the task laid upon him. "The king commands it," he finished when she made no move.

Without thinking, she responded, "He is sick.[10] And I would not have you profane my house with your ill intentions. Begone from here." So saying, she slammed the door in his face and latched it.

A mirthless smile spread across her face. A woman's house was sacred and not lightly intruded upon. Plus, she was King Saul's daughter. The guards without would hesitate to force her compliance. She listened as the men outside moved off. She knew they would not go far as they waited while word was sent to the king for further instructions.

But not long afterward, the men once again stood without, and Adriel's voice carried through the window. "I'm here at the king's command, my lady. With your permission or lack thereof, I am bid to bring David forth and to carry him hence, even in his bed if must be."[11]

Michal considered for a moment and decided not to act. She sat upon a stool and waited, saying nothing.

Outside, she could hear the men muttering, and then she started when her door burst open violently and in tumbled two guards. One uttered an oath as he nearly fell flat on his face, and the other caught himself, blinking like an owl in the dimmer light as he studied his surroundings. He spotted Michal sitting on the stool near the kitchen, and he gave her a bow, managing to look sheepish and contrite.

---

[10] 1 Samuel 19:14.
[11] 1 Samuel 19:15.

Adriel strode in, his face carefully schooled to betray no emotion. He glanced around and then at the ladder leading up to the second story. "David," he called, "resist not, for we are bid to take you to the king."

Receiving no answer, he glanced suspiciously at Michal, his eyes questioning. She understood; he too hoped David would be long gone. She gave him an imperceptible nod.

Allowing a small sigh, he climbed up the ladder, his men following him. After a moment, the pillow of goat's hair used to mask the mannequin beneath the blankets of David's bed was tossed down the ladder to hit with a soft thud on the dirt floor. Adriel slid down to stand over it, his eyebrows raised. "He is not here," he stated flatly.[12]

Michal smiled viciously. "You're most preceptive, my brother."

He snorted softly at that, trying to hide a relieved smile of his own. "Then you must accompany us, my lady, to stand before your father. He will wish to understand this…deception." He nudged the goat's hair pillow with one foot.

"I am not some common wench to be ordered about by the likes of you."

"This is true," Adriel conceded, still struggling to hide a grin, "but the command comes from your father. Surely you will not defy the king."

No, she dared not disobey her father. She stood to her feet and straightened her white halug so that it came nearly to her ankles. "Come," she ordered imperiously, taking command, "you will escort me to my father."

Smothering another grin, he tried to look grave. "As you will, my lady."

They walked through the city at a sedate pace. Michal refused to be hurried, but as they neared her father's house, her worry grew like a boil within her heart. She'd witnessed her father's ravings and wrathful fits, and it would not be a stretch to imagine that he would turn on his daughter for having betrayed him and helping David elude his grasp. She might be able to hide behind the fact that she

---

[12] 1 Samuel 19:16.

was the king's daughter to others—but not before her very own father.

Suddenly, she realized her own life might truly be in danger. Fearful now, her steps faltered. Adriel noticed. "What ails you, my lady?" he asked.

Michal bit her lower lip hard enough to cause pain. When she spoke, she did so slowly, lest her fear be revealed. "It is nothing. The night was long, and I am sore tired."

Adriel grunted agreement. "I too look forward to the end of this business." He glanced around to make sure the following guards could not overhear. "I like not this strife between your husband and father."

"Aye," she agreed. "It bodes ill for Israel."

Adriel had nothing else to say, so the two fell silent as they walked the narrow streets of Gibeah. At length, they reached the top of the hill where her father's house stood. Ever before, it had been a refuge to her, but not this time. This time, she feared to enter the gates of her father's house and face his wrath.

She was escorted through the outer court and into the house proper. The long, cobblestoned hallway stretched out before her and for the first time she realized how bleak the cold, gray stones truly appeared. Even the wood carvings in the oak panels had taken on an ominous appearance, depicting as they did Saul's many triumphant battles.

Then before she could settle her emotions, she stood before her father in the king's court. His advisors, including Saul's cousin Abner, stood off to one side. Guards ringed the court, and not a single woman other than Michal was present.

King Saul's once powerful body looked frail. His brown eyes, once as piercing as David's, looked haggard and worn. His graying hair and receding hairline made him look older than he truly was, and more wrinkles than Michal remembered lined his face and hands. When those red-rimmed eyes, however, fell on Michal, a chill swept down her spine.

"What is this?" Saul said, standing up from his chair. Easily the tallest man in the room,[13] he seemed to loom over everyone like a

---

[13] 1 Samuel 9:2.

specter. "Why have you brought my daughter? Did I not command that the son of Jesse be brought before me in his bed so that I may slay him?"[14]

Adriel bowed. "We were deceived, my king. David has fled, I know not where, and a figure made to look as him lay in his bed."

Saul staggered at the news, one hand reaching out blindly for the chair to steady him. Michal wished fervently for her eldest brother. His being sent away did not bode well. There would be no one to vouch for David—or for her.

Recovering somewhat, Saul turned on his daughter. "You knew of this? Why have you deceived me, my daughter, and allowed my enemy to escape?"[15]

She heard no hint of mercy in her father's tone. Michal understood then that her life hung in the balance. One wrong word and her father would not hesitate to order her death.

Swallowing, she fell to her knees in supplication. "My lord, David surely threatened to take my life if I helped him not. He said, 'Why should I kill you?[16] Let me go that I may hide from the face of your father.'"

Saul's face turned livid. "The son of Jesse has shown his cowardice and his true face," he declared, sweeping the room with his eyes. "Behold, men of Benjamin and Israel, the wickedness of David. This affront must not stand, for he is doubly worthy of death." He strode over and gently lifted his daughter to her feet. "Fear not, my daughter. I declare this day that you are no longer espoused to David, the son of Jesse. You will return here to my house, and I will find for you a more suitable husband than David."[17]

Michal swallowed, knowing she dared not disagree. In one spoken sentence, her father had completely rearranged her entire life, divorced her from her husband, and promised to give her to another man. She couldn't think of a single precedent in Israel to justify his actions. She'd gained and lost a husband at her father's word. How could this thing be?

---

[14] 1 Samuel 19:15.
[15] 1 Samuel 19:17.
[16] 1 Samuel 19:17.
[17] 1 Samuel 25:44.

Saul noticed her troubled face. "Be at ease, Michal. David will be slain soon, and you will be free of your vows to him. Now tell me, do you know where he has fled?"

This was the tricky part. If she was to save her life, she had to tell the truth here. She nodded, trying to put as much meekness into her demeanor as possible. "Aye, my lord. David has fled to Samuel in Ramah."[18]

Her father's eyes widened. "Samuel?" He released his daughter and staggered back as if stricken. "They are in league," he whispered. "O Samuel, why have you done this to me?"

Looking around, he stood straight and something of the powerful man he once had been showed. He glanced at Abner. "Send men to Naioth in Ramah, for surely that is where the traitor will be found. Take David and bring him before me."

Abner bowed. "As you command." Turning, the wily and never-smiling general gestured to several of the warriors standing nearby and left the room on his errand of death.

---

[18] 1 Samuel 19:19.

2

Word of Samuel's gathering of prophets in Ramah had occasionally reached David's ears over the years. The old seer had not remained idle, despite having long retired from his habit of traveling a circuit[1] through Israel to judge the nation.[2] For now they had a king to judge such matters. Since his retirement from public service, the Great Seer had organized a school of sorts to train prophets of the LORD.[3]

When David trudged warily into Ramah early the morning after fleeing Gibeah, he immediately went looking for Samuel. The seer's home city was perched atop one of the taller hills of the region less than an hour's hard walk north of Gibeah. David marveled at this fact, knowing that Samuel and Saul had not spoken a word to each other in over five years while living less than an hour from each other.[4]

From the many flocks of sheep and vineyards David passed, he guessed that the hilly terrain was unsuited for farming. Ramah subsisted on sheep, goats, and wine. The small community of shepherds and vignerons offered David only a cursory look and

---

[1] 1 Samuel 7:16.
[2] 1 Samuel 7:17.
[3] 1 Samuel 19:20.
[4] 1 Samuel 15:35.

either waved a greeting or ignored him altogether. No one seemed surprised or suspicious of the stranger walking in their midst.

The houses here tended to be single-story structures and less packed together than in either Gibeah or Bethlehem. Many of the sheep and goats grazed on the sparse grass that grew between the houses. David got the impression that Ramah existed in a more secure world than did the rest of Israel. Perhaps the Great Seer's presence accounted for such a sheltered view. A wall around the small town did exist, but it seemed more an effort of controlling the roaming herds than as a means of protection against assault.

David hailed a shepherd standing nearby. "Which way to the Great Seer?"

The skinny man pointed to the north. "Samuel presides over the other seers at Naioth."

David paused, somewhat surprised. The word *naioth* meant "dwellings," or more specifically, "beautiful dwellings." "The seer resides no more in Ramah?" David asked.

"Aye, my lord," the skinny shepherd responded in deference to David's obvious quality of clothing and bearing, "this is his home, but the seers he is master over reside in huts at the base of the hill yonder." He pointed again over the hill to the north.

David waved his thanks and walked to the crest of the hill. From the shade of an ancient tree, he could see much of the surrounding terrain, including Gibeah to the south. He felt uneasy being so close to Saul, but if there was any one in Israel with the power to protect him from the king's wrath, it would be Samuel.

Looking down at the base of the hill, David saw a collection of huts near a meadow. Beyond, farmers tilled crops, contradicting David's first impression that the community didn't rely upon farming. The huts below were well ordered. Some of the more established structures were made from brick and looked large enough to house a score of men, but a few, perhaps because they had not yet constructed more permanent accommodations, were made from woven willow reeds,[5] imported from the wetlands located in the far northwestern portion of Israel.

Men, mostly young men ranging from fifteen or so to thirty years of age, scurried about the encampment on the performance of some duty or chore. Others knelt in reverence, eyes closed as if listening, and still others sang, the song blending in perfect harmony with nature, rising into the sky like a dove on a soft breeze.

They sang of the greatness of Elohim, the boundlessness of His mercy, and the greatness of His power. They sang in serenity, not in the frenzied, almost angry tones that the heathen often composed for their idolatrous worship, but a free-flowing song that ebbed and flowed with Elohim's creation. A subtle counter melody was added to the song, one that wondered at Elohim's love for Israel and that instilled a sense of profound awe in David's heart. *Truly, what is man that God would be mindful of him?*[6]

An old man stood near David, observing the activity of the young men below. His long hair, almost white with age, fell below his waist, an oddity in a nation where the men typically cut their hair.[7] He leaned easily against a smooth staff, but despite his age, he didn't appear to need the support. His hands were veined with age but possessed obvious strength. David recognized him immediately.

"My lord Samuel," he called, falling to his knees, a sense of utter relief washing over him.

The Great Seer turned, surprise filling his eyes. His white eyebrow arched questioningly. "Who comes here? Stand, young man, and let me see your face."

David rose to his feet and faced the prophet. The seer peered into his face with blue-gray eyes that radiated power and authority. A wide grin spread above that venerable beard. "David! Praise

---

[5] Also known as *osier*. Some contend that the name "Naioth" is derived from this willow tree, hence dwellings made of osier and thus the source of the name.

[6] Psalm 8:4.

[7] The Nazarite vow was specific—no razor shall touch the head for the duration of the vow. So, it would seem that cutting the hair was a Hebrew custom for men. See Numbers 6:5, Judges 13:5, 16:17, 1 Samuel 1:11, and Ezekiel 5:1.

Elohim! He has allowed me to look upon you once more before I die."

David started, taking a worried step closer. "Are you ill, my lord?"

Samuel chuckled, his deep voice tickling David's ears. "Nay, my son. I am merely old, and old men must one day die. It is the way of all flesh. I am content—now that I have seen your face once more. But I perceive you have not come here merely to speak to an old man. What ails you, my son?"

And as if a building storm had broken, all the emotions that David had pent up and hidden for so many months and years came gushing out. It was too much to bear, and now that he was in Samuel's presence, standing before the man who had started him down this path by anointing him those years ago, his strength left him all at once. He collapsed back to his knees as tears brimmed and then spilled forth. Heart-wrenching and uncontrollable sobs wracked his body. Only in that moment did David realize the totality of his own pain. For an enemy to seek your life is one thing, but when that someone is a friend—a loved one—the pain strikes deeper than can be imagined. In that moment, he wanted to die, to be rid forever of this pain and burden.

Then Samuel was there. He knelt beside the distraught young man, his hands coming to rest easily on David's shoulders. "Tell me what has come to pass," the aged seer said softly.

In broken sentences that struggled to make sense amidst his racking sobs, David told Samuel all that had happened. Samuel said nothing as he listened, his eyes betraying his own pain, for he too loved Saul and mourned the man he had once been.[8] At length, David finished, "And now the king seeks my life to take it away, for I have become an enemy in his eyes, and I know not how that came to pass."

Samuel heaved a sigh, and straightening his long robe, he rose to his feet, only a slight grimace of pain betrayed the effort it took

---

[8] 1 Samuel 15:35.

1 Samuel 19:18-24

for his aged muscles to perform the task. "Come. You are safe here. No evil can come to this place for it is holy. Only the praise of our God needs no leave to be spoken here. Come. I would that you meet a few among us that may do you service."

David rose to his feet, his body feeling utterly drained of all strength. He felt numb all over. The outpouring of all that pent-up emotion had taken more out of him than he believed possible. But strangely, he felt unburdened, lighter than he'd been in a long time. But then Samuel's offer penetrated his mind. "My lord, the king even now seeks my life. It will not be long until men seek me in this place. I would not put you in further danger. I pray, find me another place to hide."

Samuel's lips quivered in a hint of a smile. "My life does not belong to the king, my son. He can do nothing here. Come. You will see."

Together, the two men, one old and the other young, walked slowly down the hill to the small encampment where the song of the young prophets continued to rise into the air.

David recovered some of his natural curiosity as the song put him at ease. Looking around, he raised a question, "What do you here, my lord?"

Samuel's pleased smile erased years off his aged face. "This place is a haven, a refuge for those whose hearts God has touched. We prepare against the coming darkness."

"What darkness?"

"Our history has many lessons to teach, young one. The most important of which is that every generation must rediscover Elohim or risk the curses of our lack of faith. You know something of what I speak. Have you not seen the darkness fall upon the king? Have you not seen the result when the Spirit of the Lord is departed? The effect upon one man is evident, but what effect when the Spirit of the Lord departs from a nation? What darkness then must be endured? What loss?" Samuel paused, sighing deeply. "I spoke the words of the Lord to King Saul. And after the people chose a king, my task was to guide the king as he guides the people. I have failed."

David glanced up in alarm. "Not so, my lord!"

Samuel gave him a small smile. "I appreciate the comfort, my son, but King Saul no longer heeds my words nor listens to the Spirit of the LORD. So, here in this place I prepare the next generation."

"I don't understand."

Samuel stopped and pulled David around to behold the young men and to listen to their song. "The LORD has rejected Saul from being king[9] and has chosen you to become king in his stead."

A cold chill ran down David's spine. "Saul is the LORD's anointed," he protested. "I know well that you anointed me, but surely the LORD does not mean for me to raise my hand against the rightful king!"

"Nay, the LORD requires no such action. Saul's life is in the hand of the LORD. I say these words to prepare you. When you are king, you must understand the balance of power necessary to rule the kingdom. There are three, David, that Elohim has anointed with authority among men: the king, the priest, and the seer."

David looked intrigued. "But this was not always so," he argued. "For Israel had not always a king."

"Aye, I know this truth well. But harken. In time past, God raised up a judge to rule the people in His name. His task was to execute the law of the LORD, to be the shepherd's crook when the sheep strayed."

"What of the priest?"

"The priest stands between God and men. The priest brings reconciliation to the people, a means to stand before our God and seek His mercy and love. Without the priest, we would have no path out of the darkness, and through the priest we may speak to Elohim."

David thought hard on these words. "And the seer? What task has befallen him?"

Samuel glanced around and, finding that his lecture had drawn a crowd of young prophets, lifted his voice so that all may hear. "The

---

[9] 1 Samuel 15:26-28.

seer is the voice of Elohim. We, who are such, carry His word to the people." Samuel fixed his gaze steadily upon David. "And to the king. Harken David. Aforetime, when judges ruled, always the judge was chosen by the LORD's hand. Always was the judge raised up to deliver the people, to guide the people—but always by the hand of the LORD. That task of judgment now falls to the king, and not always will the king be a man that Elohim chooses, for a king may be a king by birth or by might. Thus, the seer must bring him the word of Elohim when he strays, when he no longer seeks Jehovah. This is the seer's task."

"You foresee a need to do thus?"

Samuel nodded gravely. "Such a time has come, young David. Men are prone to stray, and seers, priests, and kings are but men." Samuel beckoned to two of the young men standing nearby. "These are the ones I wished you to meet."

The first man to present himself had dark hair and nearly black eyes. He held himself with an aura of confidence, marred only by a boyish grin that nearly consumed his face. David took an immediate liking to him. "This unruly fellow is Gad," Samuel introduced.

Gad bowed deeply, his boyish grin made even starker by a black beard. "My lord," he greeted, "I am honored."

David, not knowing what to do, returned the bow. "As am I, seer."

Gad placed both hands upon David's shoulders and looked into his eyes. "We will meet again soon, David. The LORD has shown me this. I will bring the word of the LORD to you."[10]

Something in the prophet's confidence assured David that this would be true. "Then I am content," he replied politely.

Gad then did something extraordinary. He winked at David, still grinning. David blinked, unsure if he'd been insulted or not, for a wink was not considered to be a polite gesture.[11] But the young prophet stepped back, and another took his place. The second young man was not much older than a lad, maybe around thirteen years of

---

[10] 1 Samuel 22:5.
[11] Psalm 35:9; Proverbs 6:12-13, 10:10.

age. He wore a robe similar in cut to Samuel's, and his face had a somber cast that framed the hard features of someone who had seen much suffering.

"Nathan," he introduced himself simply, bowing slightly. He gave no surname.

David returned the bow, noticing that Nathan's right eye was completely white and the other icy blue.

Samuel noted David's curiosity. "A fire as a babe blinded him in one eye," he explained.

Looking closer, David could see scar tissue built up around the lad's right eye. His hair showed signs that the fire had stunted some of its growth as well. David had seen injuries like this before. When Nathan reached the age where he could grow a beard, David suspected that a white patch would grow where his face had been burned.

Nathan waved a calloused hand negligently as if to dismiss the tragedy behind the tale. He regarded David solemnly, saying nothing.

Samuel laid a hand on Nathan's head affectionately. "The LORD has shown me that He intends great things with this one, David. When I am gone, look to him—and to Gad. They will help you."

David frowned. "I little like this talk of your death."

Samuel smiled indulgently. "When you are my age, you think of it more often. It is the way of things. And for one such as I, not an unpleasant ending." Looking at Gad and Nathan, he asked, "What advice do you give the son of Jesse? The king seeks to take his life, for at the LORD's bidding, I have anointed him to be the next king of Israel. Come, what say you?"

Gad hadn't lost his grin, but his eyes shifted as he thought, giving him a mindless appearance. Nathan stood passively, revealing nothing of his thoughts. Finally, Gad refocused on David and began smoothing his beard before saying, "If this is the LORD's bidding, then it cannot be undone except you undo it. Only you have the power to thwart God's plan, David, for it is through you that Jehovah's hand is revealed. But if you remain a willing vessel of the

LORD, then He will see you through this time of trial. You merely must remain steadfast and unmovable in Elohim's will."

David sighed in relief. "Then you do not counsel that I lift my hand against the LORD's anointed?"

Gad shook his head. "Nay. Elohim will safeguard you without the need to act directly against our king."

Relief gave rise to the next question. "If the LORD is on my side, then who can stand against me? May I not return to King Saul and take my place at his side?"

Samuel shook his aged head. "Harken, David, for Gad gives good counsel. For in the day that you force Jehovah to choose between your life and Saul's, then the LORD will smite Saul and slay him."

David went cold all over. He vehemently shook his head. "That above all is what I do not wish. I would not bring harm to my king!" Everyone fell silent, watching David as he wrestled his way through this dilemma. There was a chance, of course, that Saul's attack on David's life was merely the result of the evil spirit that plagued the king. If so, then it may very well be that Saul had repented of his deed and would welcome David's return.

But there were two problems with that rationale. First, the evil spirit could still reside upon Saul, and the king would still be seeking David's life. Second, David had no way to know if the evil spirit was indeed driving Saul or if the king truly wanted him dead. He just didn't know.

In his heart, David suspected that Saul truly wanted to kill him, but he was loath to leave behind everything and everyone he had come to love. Jonathan, Michal, Adriel, and others stood near the king. And David loved Saul.[12] To bring any harm to the king was beyond David's ability. But could he also walk away from everyone else he held dear?

Seeing David's indecisiveness, Samuel glanced at Nathan. "What say you, young one?"

---

[12] 1 Samuel 16:21.

Nathan's expression hadn't so much as changed during the entire conversation. Now he looked steadily upon David with eyes far older than the youthful face. After a moment, he said, "I counsel that he abide here until we know the heart of the matter."

Samuel nodded. "That is wise, and it is my advice as well. Abide here, son of Jesse, for we will shortly know the king's mind. He will come here, of that I have no doubt, but no danger shall befall you, so take your ease, but prepare yourself to leave if the LORD bids."

Two hours later, the first of King Saul's men arrived to take David into custody. The fact that Saul had sent men to arrest him did not bode well for David's continuance at Saul's side. David was grieved as he watched the armed men move down the slope of the hill from Ramah, weapons at ready as if going into battle.

David watched them come, standing among the prophets who faced Samuel and his two acolytes. Samuel stood above the young seers, his voice lifting in song, and a mighty choir joined with him. David was immediately caught up in the song as the Spirit of the LORD descended upon all present.

David had felt the Spirit of the LORD upon him strongly at times, but always, it seemed, when battle was upon him. In those times, he became a different man, almost superhuman in his abilities. God had used David on several occasions to deliver Israel with a mighty hand. Goliath's death had been but the first of many victories for the young warrior, but this, standing here with Samuel and the prophets, was the first time he felt the Spirit of the LORD come upon him so strongly when there was no battle to be fought and death did not ride the winds.

He joined the young men and lifted his voice to the sky and sang praises to his God. David had often done exactly this while playing the harp, but never in such a company as the one in which he now stood. Every fear was washed away. Every care was set aside. The future mattered not. Only this moment. Only now mattered.

Vaguely, he was conscious of the fact that Saul's men, twenty hardened warriors of the tribe of Benjamin continued to descend the hill toward him. As they came, they spread out to cut off his escape.

— 27 —

He wasn't hiding. David was clearly visible standing among the prophets. But he was so caught up in the song of praise and finding himself in the comfort of the LORD's Spirit that he made no move to escape.

But as soon as Saul's men reached the company of prophets, they were swallowed whole by the Spirit of the LORD. First one, and then in mass, they slammed to a stop, looking surprised and awed. As if unable to control their own tongues, they took up the song. Hands fell away from sword hilts and spears. Daggers fell from limp, uncaring fingers, and rough, coarse voices joined those of the prophets as they sang and prophesied.[13]

A single man had remained atop the hill to watch over the operation to capture David. When he saw what happened to his companions, he slipped away. Doubtless, within the hour, Saul would know that David remained at large.

---

[13] 1 Samuel 19:20.

3

King Saul paced the length of his court, his hands clenched about the haft of his javelin and his face screwed up into a deep scowl that sucked the emotion from the room. "Soon," he muttered over and over. Soon his messengers would bring David before him, and he would personally wield the sword that would end the traitorous warrior's life. Never had Saul felt so anxious. He knew deep down that only David's death would free him from the evil spirit that constantly plagued him. With the son of Jesse's death, Samuel would have no choice but to intercede with the LORD on his behalf and restore Jehovah's favor.

And with the Spirit of the LORD once again upon him, his kingdom and line would be secure, and he could get back to the business of ruling. Too long had David thwarted him and defied his will. Too long had the son of Jesse stolen the hearts of the people. It had to end. "Soon," he muttered again.

The door opened, and one of Abner's warriors tasked with capturing David entered. Alone. Saul stopped his pacing and glared at the emptyhanded guard. Before he could say anything, Abner stepped forward and demanded, "Where is the son of Jesse, Phalti? Where are the rest of my men?"

Saul knew this man. Phalti was the son of Laish and a captain in Saul's army. The warrior bowed deeply to the king with a soldier's rigid discipline. When he straightened, his face was carefully schooled to reveal nothing. "My lord the king and my lord Abner, I alone have returned. For when we came upon Naioth at Ramah, the

— 29 —

prophets of the LORD did sing and prophesy. I stood atop the hill of Ramah and ordered those sent with me to descend into Naioth and capture the son of Jesse, for we could see him well, standing next to Samuel, the seer."

Saul hissed, his eyes narrowing. "Samuel gave safe haven to David?"

"Aye, my king, and still does. When we sought to take David, the seer caused another spirit to fall upon them, for they left off their duty and joined the prophets in their song. They abide there still. They heed only the Great Seer now. I alone have returned, having stood afar off to ensure that David did not flee where we could not see."

For a long moment, Saul simply stared at Captain Phalti, hardly believing the words. Then with a cry of rage, he spun around and used the javelin in his hand to smash his chair into kindling. Everyone in the room flinched and stepped back; fearful whispering spread among the king's advisers and commanders. Saul spun back around amid the splintered remains of his chair. "Hold your tongues!" he snapped.

Everyone fell silent, staring at the king.

Ignoring them, he strode over to Phalti. "Take more men and capture David," he commanded. "Do as before and go not near Naioth and Samuel yourself, but watch from afar as you did afore. I would know if this is Samuel's doing or some other power we may overcome. Warn your men. Have them harden their hearts against this evil, but bring David to me."

Adriel stepped forward from where he'd been standing near the wall. He bowed before his king, clearly asking leave to speak. Saul nodded, and David's former armorbearer asked, "And what of Samuel, the seer?"

Saul silently cursed, rubbing at his temples with one hand. Memories of Samuel swirled in his head. "Touch him not. It is he who anointed me king. I would that one day we two be reconciled." In his heart he knew this would only be possible when David was dead. His eyes snapped back to the captain. "Go now and return quickly." Not entirely convinced that his newest son-in-law hadn't somehow aided in David's escape from the city, he glared

— 30 —

suspiciously at Adriel. "I wish you to accompany the captain, Adriel. Bring David to me."

Adriel bowed low while Phalti answered, "Aye, my king!" The captain did an about-face and marched out of the room with Adriel but a step behind.

Saul stood in the center of his court, his eyes blazing with barely suppressed fury. He glanced over to where Abner stood stern-faced. The never smiling general gave no indication as to his thoughts on the matter. His bright-blue eyes remained, as ever, a closed book to Saul who prided himself on his ability to read the hearts of men.

He waved his cousin[1] to approach. Abner's coal-black hair didn't so much as stir as he stepped fluidly next to his much taller cousin. Abner gripped the pommel of his sheathed sword, a hand crisscrossed with battle scars, and the end of one pinky completely missing thanks to a chance sword swing by a Philistine warrior. "Speak your will, my king," he said in a gravelly voice that sounded as if he chewed rocks for pleasure.

"Where is my son, Jonathan?"

"He returns soon, my lord. He was only to see to the disposition of the Indebted. He should be returning shortly."

Saul chewed on his lower lip for a moment. The Indebted had been David's command, but Saul had long suspected that they were more loyal to the son of Jesse than they were to himself, so he had sent Jonathan to reward them with their freedom and to disband them—sending them home and scattering them throughout Israel. Saul worried about an uprising, but with the men most loyal to David scattered and focused on their families, there should be little concern.

"I would not that Jonathan know about David's death from any but me, cousin. See to it that he does not learn of these events. I know well that he harbors great love for the son of Jesse."

"This is true," Abner agreed carefully. "May I speak my mind, my lord?"

Saul felt amusement. Rarely was Abner so forthcoming. He was the most automatically obedient man he'd ever known. "Speak."

---

[1] 1 Samuel 14:50.

1 Samuel 19:18-24

"I confess that I do not understand your anger toward David, my lord. I know you believe him to be a traitor and believe he seeks to be king. But has he not served you well, my king? Have you not bound him to your family by marriage? He is your son-in-law."

Saul suppressed a flash of explosive rage. He needed to tread lightly here. Abner was an essential ingredient to Saul's power, and he dared not alienate the general. He placed a hand familiarly on Abner's shoulder. "It is true that David has served well and chastised the Philistines for us.[2] But what is that when held in balance with the future of our nation? Would you see Hebrew fighting Hebrew? Would you suffer a rending of the tribes of Israel? This is what I foresee if the son of Jesse lives—this and much more."

Abner's emotionless face never so much as twitched during that discourse. Whether or not he agreed, Saul would never know. The battle-hardened general simply bowed then and said, "As you will, my lord."

Frustrated that he couldn't elicit more of a positive response from his cousin, Saul tried to explain further. "There cannot be two kings in Israel. Samuel anointed David after he anointed me. But it was I who freed Israel from Philistine dominion, and it is I who am king by the will of Jehovah. We cannot have another contest for the crown, or we will bring the people low. I do what I do for our people."

Again, Abner bowed. "Aye, my lord." He straightened and looked steadily at Saul. "What would you have me do?"

"For the moment, nothing. Abide here. We will see if Captain Phalti can secure David. If not, I may have to take more direct means."

Moving away, Saul went to sit down and looked surprised at the shattered remains of the chair at his feet. *When had that happened?* Clearing his throat, he looked around until he spotted the newest member of his household staff. "Ziba, fetch me another chair." He then addressed everyone else in the room as the servant scampered out the door. "Now we wait."

Though Ramah lay close by to the north, it was a journey over rough terrain and a road that zigzagged often. It took a little less than

---

[2] 1 Samuel 18:13, 27, 30, 19:8.

— 32 —

an hour on foot to reach the city during ordinary weather. Therefore, about two and a half hours later, the doors to the court opened again and Adriel, followed by Captain Phalti, reentered. Both men looked deeply troubled, and once again, they came emptyhanded.

"Speak," Saul ordered from his new chair, lips tightening.

The captain and Adriel exchanged a glance. Likely Phalti had been elected to bear the bad news for he stood forth and bowed deeply. "Samuel and the prophets that stand with him remain yet in song and praise. The men you sent with me now number among the prophets."[3]

Saul could hardly credit his ears. "Surely, this cannot be!" he shouted. When no man answered him, he rose to his feet. "Will no man take pity upon me? Is it not evident that Samuel conspires with the son of Jesse?" Still no one so much as spoke a word.

Saul absently rubbed the golden armband that encircled the bicep of his right arm, the mark of royalty, and fell back into his new chair deep in thought. Fear gripped him, and he shuddered. He knew that the LORD was with Samuel and if the aged seer gave refuge to David, then the conspiracy to usurp Saul's throne was indeed strong.

He knew in his heart that he would have to personally go to Ramah if David was to be captured. Twice now, his own servants— men whose loyalties until that moment had never been questioned— had failed him. Somehow Samuel and David had persuaded his servants to betray him. He clenched his fist tightly around his spear dreading the inevitable confrontation with Samuel. How long had it been since he had last seen the Great Seer? Years.

But no. He dared not go personally. Not yet. Perhaps one more attempt would succeed where the others had failed. He held little doubt that Samuel had overcome his men by strange enchantments, but surely this power was limited. How often could the aged seer continue to turn the hearts of men loyal to the king?

He raised his gray-speckled head and fixed his red-rimmed eyes on Phalti and his handsome son-in-law, Adriel. "Go again," he said softly, voice cracking with emotion. "Take yet more men and bring David to me."

---

[3] 1 Samuel 19:21.

1 Samuel 19:18-24

Phalti bowed instantly, his armor creaking. "As you command, my king."

But Adriel stood forth a bit. "Have mercy upon me, O king," he said, obviously fearing to ignite the king's wrath. "Let me speak but once?"

Saul sighed deeply, but said, "You may speak."

"The Great Seer has made his power strong in Naioth, my lord. I fear all men will fall under his enchantment should they come within his borders. Sending more men may be folly, my king."

Saul considered the words, suppressing his instinct to leap from his chair and ram his javelin into Adriel's chest for daring to question his king. Yet Saul, while desperate to end David's life, was no fool. Twice now, his soldiers had fallen prey to Samuel's power. He understood Adriel's reluctance to go. But there was another advantage to sending yet a third squad of soldiers. If they too fell prey to Samuel's enchantments, then he would have all the justification he needed to bring the full might of his army down upon Naioth. The power of three was strong in the Hebrew psyche.

For the Hebrew, things often had to happen in threes for it to be considered immutable. The founding of the Israelite race rested upon three patriarchs, Abraham, Isaac, and Jacob. Three yearly pilgrimage feasts were commanded by Elohim.[4] And in each of the three feasts, every male would present himself before the LORD.[5]

A third betrayal was required for the Hebrew psyche to accept the perfidy of Samuel and David. Only then would Saul have a free hand to descend upon Naioth with all his might.

Saul shook himself and stood to his full height, head and shoulders above everyone else in the room. "Nay, my son," he said to Adriel, his deep voice carrying to all in the room, "we will yet send more men. Perhaps this is not of Samuel's doing. Perhaps this other spirit is none of Samuel's doing. But this third time will make it plain for all. If the men yet fall under the enchantment, then all shall plainly see that only by Samuel is this done, for the Jehovah Elohim will permit no man to raise his hand against His anointed." There

---

[4] Exodus 23:14.
[5] Deuteronomy 16:16.

— 34 —

was, of course, another explanation, but Saul steered carefully away from it.

He let those words sink in before gesturing toward the door. "Go. Bring me David."

With a silent bow, Adriel and Phalti departed. Their report, when they returned a few hours later was met with practiced stoicism. Once again, the men had fallen prey to Samuel's power and had joined with the young prophets in their religious fervor.

Rising to his feet, the king ordered Abner, "Muster the garrison, cousin, for we march on Ramah within the hour. It has fallen to me to end this rebellion."

Abner, ever loyal, saluted and gestured for Captain Phalti to follow him out. Adriel remained behind, standing uncertainly before his father-in-law. Saul's face betrayed none of the emotions that raged inside. Many years had passed since he had last seen Samuel. Once, long ago, Samuel had stood before God on Saul's behalf. The old man had tremendous power for he walked in the light of Jehovah. And once, that power had been wielded for Saul's benefit. No longer.

But somethings could not be easily dismissed. Saul genuinely feared Samuel, and the fact that Samuel was protecting David harbored nothing good as far as Saul was concerned.

"Attend me," he ordered those around him.

His closest advisers and two of his four sons moved closer to their king. He regarded his sons and son-in-law directly, even as he considered his next move. Ishui's long hair framed a thin, dark face of grim aspect. Saul's second oldest son was something of a disappointment to Saul. He simply did not have the wisdom necessary to rule. Jonathan did, but his eldest son harbored too much love for David to be trusted with this mission. Ishui was a weapon. He had to keep a tight rein on this son, but if he could point him in the right direction, he could cause the appropriate mayhem. "Ishui, prepare yourself. You will accompany me."

Ishui nodded shortly, a pleased smile that looked out of place, spreading across his thin features. "Aye, my father." He hurried out.

Saul glanced at the rest of his advisers. "You know your duties. I ask that you do them well during my absence." He dismissed them,

— 35 —

but hailed Adriel. "Stay, my son, and help arm me. For we must soon face a great foe."

Adriel said nothing as he began to help Saul into his armor. When the last strap had been tightened and his sword secured, the king hesitated only briefly before striding out the door of his own court. That single hesitation, however, shouted his fear louder than any words ever could, and more than one person in the court took note of it.

The well of Sechu lay at the converging base of several of the surrounding hills northeast of Ramah. A cistern that gathered rainwater from the hills, the well was a common source of water for several of the surrounding towns, including Ramah. Saul had taken a thousand men and had moved stealthily through the night, circling north of Ramah so that they could come at the Naioth encampment from an unexpected direction.

Most of his men had been sent a bit farther south closer to Ramah and carefully hidden from sight. Saul was determined not to give David and Samuel any forewarning of his intentions or whereabouts. With any fortune at all, David would assume that Saul remained yet in Gibeah. The traitorous shepherd would be looking south, not north. Saul smiled grimly in anticipation.

Several women, carrying large pitchers atop their turbaned heads, moved around the cistern in the early morning light. One of them looked to have come from the direction of Ramah. He and Ishui, Saul's second oldest son, stopped her as she approached the well. "Here now, good woman," Saul said cheerfully, "give, I pray you, your pitcher to my son and let him fetch water for you. I would have words with you."

The woman frowned at the highly unusual offer but gave a small shrug and handed her pitcher to Ishui. The battle-hardened young man gave his father a peculiar look as he walked away to fill the pitcher with water. Saul knew that Ishui thought the task beneath him, yet he did as he was told.

Saul turned his attention to the middle-aged woman before him. Like most Hebrew woman, she wore a coarse, brown halug that fell to her ankles. A scarf or keffiyeh had been tied over her long, graying hair, and she regarded the king with no recognition, for Saul had removed his royal armband and crown. He was but any other Hebrew warrior, though unusually tall.

The woman, made bold by age perhaps, looked him up and down, not a whit intimidated by the armed and armored man before her. Mercenaries and soldiers were not an uncommon sight. "You are right tall indeed," she said. "You could be a match for our king in height. Are you of the children of Amnon then? I hear they breed them tall in that country."

Saul swallowed a fierce retort. "Nay, good woman, I am a Hebrew, and all know that the king is head and shoulders above any other."

"Then our king must be of the sons of Anakims."

"Nay, for they are truly giants of unholy proportions," Saul said, seeing an opening. "Surely the Anakims are not to be feared, good woman. Did not David, the son of Jesse, slay one such?"

"Aye, he slew Goliath," she agreed. Her eyes turned suspicious. "How can you be a Hebrew and not know this?"

Saul waved her question aside. "I heard that David and Samuel are hereabouts. Where are they?"[6]

"They are at Naioth in Ramah," she said, squinting at him in the early morning light. "I have seen the son of Jesse there in discourse with the Great Seer."

Saul gave the woman a bow of respect. "I thank you, good woman. I will seek him out and hear the tale of the giant's slaying from his own lips."

Ishui came back at that point, carrying the full pitcher of water. The woman accepted it back, carefully balancing it atop her head. The woman's neck muscles tightened with the weight, but so often had she done thus, she seemed unbothered by the burden. "I know not if you will have opportunity to speak with the son of Jesse for he is in conference with the Great Seer."

"I can but try," Saul called after her.

---

[6] 1 Samuel 19:22.

Her voice floated back, "Aye. There is that."

When she was out of earshot, Ishui spat on the ground. "That is a vile woman. She didn't even recognize her king."

Saul turned a dark look upon his son. "We need strong women like her," he disagreed. "Show respect for her age."

The king's second son matched his father's scowl but nodded grudgingly. Saul knew it would be the only apology he would get. He turned away, saying, "We know now that David resides yet with Samuel. We will come upon them in less than an hour."

"We knew that already," Ishui said.

"Perhaps. It is still well to have the fact confirmed. Come. We must be away."

The two men took a little used trail up the side of one of the hills, weaving through trees and tall grass. Smoke from cooking fires of Ramah could be seen rising into the sky, and the city itself was clearly visible atop a hill to the south. The day promised to be clear and free of harsh weather. Perhaps Jehovah yet smiled upon him.

A thousand men were not easy to move in secret, but the Gibeah garrison was composed of veteran soldiers who had weathered hardship like most people handled a sore muscle. They made scarcely a sound as they followed Saul up a narrow ravine that approached Naioth from the northwest.

The king raised his hand, and every man came to an immediate and utterly silent stop. They were close now, and faintly, the melody of a song carried to their ears. Saul paused, and against his better judgment, strained his ears to hear. The song tantalized his mind, like trying to recall a pleasant dream, but where the specifics fled just beyond his reach. It left behind a vague sense of unfulfilled need.

He tried to shake off the feeling, but it persisted. Almost against his will, he moved closer to hear better. Behind, seemingly far away, a questioning voice rose, but Saul ignored it, trying to hear the song, to recapture that sense of elusive peace that hovered just beyond his grasp.

Before moving out of the ravine altogether, Saul heard someone say, "Back! Move back! The king is taken! Flee least we all likewise fall!"

The words meant nothing. Only the song mattered. Saul found his tongue loosening, and his voice lifted up in joy as he joined in the song of praise to Jehovah.[7]

---

[7] 1 Samuel 19:23.

4

"The king comes!" David, standing next to Samuel, left off singing to stare in stunned amazement. As Samuel had predicted, the king had personally come to seize David. Astonishingly, Saul came alone, staggering toward the young prophets as if being pulled roughly by an unseen hand. Saul seemed oblivious to those around him. His voice quivered in song and praise, his eyes looking only toward the sky.

Saul began stripping off his armor, almost frantic to divest himself of arms and armor. When the last of the armor lay scattered around him, he yanked off his royal tunic, and stood naked in his *kethōneth*.[1] He stood thus for only a moment before falling onto his back staring blindly into the sky. His mouth continued to move as if singing, but no sound issued forth. He never so much as blinked once, not even to wipe away the tears streaming freely down his cheeks. The Spirit of the LORD had overtaken the king.

The young prophet Gad, his mouth open in amazement, whispered, "Is Saul also among the prophets?"[2] No one answered, for no one had an answer.

---

[1] 1 Samuel 19:24. The Hebrews would consider any casting off the outer garments to be showing nakedness. The *kethōneth* was an undergarment, a long shirt-like garment that rested against the skin. This may be similar to Peter when he was naked while fishing—not totally bare, merely without an outer garment (John 21:7).

[2] 1 Samuel 19:24.

David stood uncomfortably over his king, his uncertainty growing. He looked to Samuel. The aged seer's eyes contained a vast sadness as he regarded Saul. After a moment, he shook himself and turned to David. "He will remain thus for a time, but you must go." He heaved a sigh. "You cannot remain here."

For a long moment, David stood rooted to the spot. The song of the prophets continued unabated, filling him with peace and comfort. He was loath to leave. He didn't know where to go.

Gad and Nathan stood beside Samuel watching David, presenting a wall between them that David could not penetrate. Finally, the youngest prophet asked, "Is not Jonathan, the son of Saul, counted among your friends?"

Of course! David gave the three prophets a deep bow, decision made. "I thank you. Your advice and care of me has helped renew my faith in my God. I will seek Jonathan, for if there is any who can tell me truly what is in King Saul's heart, it will be he." Looking hopefully at the prophets, he gestured to the entranced king. "The Lord's Spirit has taken him. Does this mean he may repent of his desire to slay me? May I yet find a place among his servants?"

Samuel shook his head. "I know not. It may be that the Spirit of the Lord will ease his fears and bring him to a place of reconciliation with Elohim. But this I know: God has rejected Saul from being king.[3] His kingdom will not last, and you, David, have been anointed to take his place.[4] This has not changed, nor will it." Samuel glanced at Saul, his eyes filling with a pain David did not understand. "In his heart, he knows this."

The king continued his silent muttering unabated, oblivious to everything around him. Embarrassment at the king's nakedness and helplessness reddened David's neck. "Can we not...cover him?"

"Nay," Samuel said, his voice dropping and thick with raw anguish. "This is of the Lord. We will not interfere." Seeing David's distress, he added, "But we need not stand over him as if carrion birds circling a battlefield. We will leave our king in peace."

Releasing his breath explosively, David hurried away with the three seers. At the edge of the encampment, the young warrior

---

[3] 1 Samuel 15:23.
[4] 1 Samuel 16:13.

— 41 —

paused to let the prophets' song once again wash over him. The words soothed his heart and mind, reminding him of the greatness of his God and the power of His majesty.

A thought struck David. "This is a holy song," he said, "it should be sung before the LORD's ark."

Samuel nodded. "Your heart is right, young David, and this thought is of the LORD. Say on."

David struggled to verbalize something that, up to this point, he had refused to acknowledge. He licked his lips, and slowly, he forced the words out. "When I am king—" There, he'd said it! "—I shall set singers and minstrels to play day and night before Elohim in His tabernacle and before His ark."[5] The last words came out in an explosive rush. He stood panting as if he'd run for half a day straight.

Samuel looked on in amusement. "Was that so difficult to utter?" His eyes twinkled. "You will learn, young one, that the LORD's will is not so easily thwarted. If Elohim has anointed you, then one day, you will be king. Only one thing can turn this end aside, even as young Gad has said: *you*. But if your heart and mind remain true to Jehovah, He will see it done." He turned and shouted, "Heman, Asaph, attend!"

Two young man around David's age, broke off from the company of prophets and moved to stand before Samuel. The moment they stopped singing, the song lost something of its power and heavenly melody. Their contribution to the song had weight, and David took instant notice of the two men.

The taller of the two wore a brown tunic, and despite his age, his receding hairline lent him a mature look that was bolstered by a firm chin and a somewhat stout nose. The younger-looking one was dressed in a white robe, cinched at the waist with a rawhide cord. Seeing that they sported the same black hair and the same brown eyes, David guessed they might be brothers.

The slightly older looking one bowed before Samuel. "Here we are, my lord." His voice held a musical quality to it that demanded to be heard, to be lifted up in song.

---

[5] 1 Chronicles 15:16-22.

Samuel placed a hand affectionately on an arm of each man and turned them to face David. "This is Heman, the son of my son,"[6] he said, nodding to the taller of the two. "The other is Asaph, the son of Berachiah. Take knowledge of them, David, for in due time, you must appoint heads over your singers. Consider well these two when the time comes to keep your vow. The LORD has endowed them with great skill."

David bowed in silence, acknowledging Samuel's words. He could scarcely believe his own vow or that he had spoken it. For the first time since the Great Seer had anointed him four years ago, he had accepted the truth of what Samuel had done. According to the LORD's will, he would someday be king.

Perhaps Nathan's youth allowed him to see what the others missed, for the young man, little more than a boy, put a hand on David's arm, gripping hard enough to force David to lock eyes with him. He saw understanding in Nathan's single icy-blue orb, and David knew as clearly as he knew his own name that one day this young prophet would stand at his side when he was king.[7] The thought sent a chill down his spine. He and this young prophet would be forever linked.

Nathan's blind eye wasn't in sync with his other one, but suddenly that white orb seemed to turn to David, and Nathan gripped his arm even tighter. "You must go," he intoned. "King Saul will remain here until the morning.[8] You know what you must do."

David nodded. Facing Samuel, he felt emotions surging within like a storm-tossed sea. "I will not forget your words, my lord. Pray for me."

Samuel nodded, looking wan. "As always, my son. Be well and go with Elohim. May He watch over your steps and be a light always to your path."

With a last wave at the young singers and prophets, David turned and began the trek back toward Gibeah. Absorbed in his own

---

[6] 1 Chronicles 6:33 (Heman), a grandson of Samuel (or Shemuel), through Samuel's firstborn son Joel (1 Samuel 8:2). Asaph is called Heman's brother, but his lineage is given differently. Possibly "brother" in this case is a distant family relation or merely a convention to explain that they shared similar professions and passions.

[7] 2 Samuel 7:2.

[8] 1 Samuel 19:24.

— 43 —

1 Samuel 20:1-24

problems and pain, he had failed to see the full depth of the tiredness that surrounded the Great Seer. It would not be long before the Great Seer's mantle passed to another.

No stranger to long marches and hardship, David easily made the trek back to Gibeah. He moved stealthily, for though Saul was held captive by the Spirit of the LORD back in Ramah, the king's other servants were no doubt seeking him still. But if there was one place on earth no one expected David to flee to, it would be Saul's city of Gibeah.

Disguising himself, he moved easily by the lax guards at Gibeah's gate and disappeared into the city streets. He considered going to his own house and seeing Michal, but he discarded the notion immediately. He needed to find Jonathan. Moving carefully, he made his way to Jonathan's house. He must be careful, however. His friend's dwelling was part of the greater compound of Saul's house and though the guards at the gate might be lax, David would surely be recognized if any of the soldiers or servants of Saul's house spotted him. Fortunately, one of Jonathan's windows overlooked a side street. Moving carefully, and being sure he was not observed, he pushed the wooden shutters aside and scrambled into Jonathan's house.

He closed the shutters and stood rock still, letting his eyes adjust to the gloom within. From his previous visits, David knew that Jonathan's wife spent much of her time in a small room near the kitchen. Listening, he could hear her singing and humming as she worked. He had made little noise and she seemed undisturbed, so his intrusion had yet to be detected.

Worried about startling her, he moved into the common room and then spoke softly, "Naarah, it is I, David. Please do not be alarmed." Her singing had cut off with a gasp the moment he had spoken her name. Moving slowly, he entered her line of sight. "I seek your husband, good lady. Has he returned to Gibeah?"

Jonathan's wife stared as if seeing an apparition, clutching a half completed woolen tunic to her chest. The whites of her eyes showed large in fright. David remained still, trying his best to appear less threatening. After a moment, she swallowed and seemed to relax somewhat. Standing, she put aside her weaving and came over to David. "He is not here, my lord," she said, keeping her voice low. "But I expect him to return this day."

David breathed a sigh of relief. If the good woman was planning on revealing his presence, she would have done so already. Still, hearing that Jonathan had not yet returned was discomforting. Seeing his frown, Naarah said, "Abide here, my lord. Word has reached me that the king seeks your life. My husband will want to help."

"I thank you," he said, feeling an easing in his muscles.

She pointed to the stairs. "I pray you, wait up there. It may be that guests will come to this house before my lord returns, and I would not that you were discovered."

Nodding, he walked up the stairs, a novelty in most Hebrew homes, and found a spot on the floor and sat, determined to wait. He waited long as the shadows shifted and began to grow long. Occasionally, Naarah would ask if he needed anything, leaving him a loaf of bread and a wedge of cheese to abate his hunger.

At length, David heard the door to the house open and Jonathan's strong voice announce, "Woman! I am home. Too long have you been idle, caring not for the..." he trailed off, and David heard some furious whispering, and then Jonathan was up the stairs and pulling David up to kiss him on both cheeks. "My friend! Why are you lurking about in the shadows and haunting my wife with this dark behavior?"

Not as tall as his father, Jonathan still loomed over David. His wide, weather-worn face was split by a grin that seemed to give mirth to his dark eyes.

David offered a tight smile in response, relieved to have his friend with him once again. "In truth, Jonathan, I fear for my life."

Jonathan's smile disappeared all at once, and his hands tightened on David's shoulders. "My father?"

"Aye, he seeks my life." He looked pleadingly at his friend. "What have I done? What is mine iniquity? And what is my sin before your father that he seeks my life?[9] I tell you truly, I understand it not."

---

[9] 1 Samuel 20:1.

— 45 —

Jonathan was already shaking his head. Pulling David forward, he guided the young warrior to a pillow around the low table where he and his wife ate their meals. "Sit, David." Once both were seated, Jonathan turned earnest eyes on David. "God forbid, my friend. You will not die. This I swear. My father will do nothing either great or small without telling me first."[10] He shook his head again. "He loves you, David. And if he does seek to slay you, why would my father hide this thing from me? I tell you, it is not so."

"Did not your wife explain what has happened?"

"Aye, but you know well what happens when the evil spirit is upon my father. It will pass. All will be well again."

David stared at his friend incredulously. Despite their close friendship, Jonathan had a blind spot. Jonathan could not believe that his father would seek to kill David. He would need to be convinced first. Biting his lower lip, David thought furiously. At last, he spoke, trying to put as much conviction in his voice as possible, "Your father certainly knows that I have found grace in your eyes, and he has determined that you should not know this, lest you be grieved, but truly, as the LORD lives and as your soul lives, there is but a step between me and death."[11]

Jonathan's eyes widened. He'd never heard David speak so, but David could still see the doubt in Jonathan's face. For a moment, friendship with David and trust in his father warred in Jonathan's heart. At last, Jonathan sighed. "Perhaps," he said doubtfully. "I can see you believe it to be true. Tell me what you want. Whatever it is, I'll do it."[12]

Having wrung that concession from his friend, David pointed to the ceiling. "Tomorrow is the new moon. As part of the king's household, I have a place at his table. When he returns from Gibeah, he will surely hope that I will be in my place, for doubtless he will do as you, and claim his rage is but the hand of the evil spirit. Instead, let me go that I may hide myself in the field unto the third day at evening."[13]

---

[10] 1 Samuel 20:2.
[11] 1 Samuel 20:3.
[12] 1 Samuel 20:4.
[13] 1 Samuel 20:5.

Gathering himself, David continued, "If your father at all miss me, then say that I asked leave of you that I might run to Bethlehem for there is a yearly sacrifice there for all the family. If he says, 'It is well,' then there is peace and know that you are right. But if he is wroth, then be sure that evil is determined against me by him."[14]

Jonathan hesitated, no doubt debating the necessity of these theatrics. Reaching across, David grabbed the other's wrist in a grip of iron. "I beg you, deal kindly with me. You and I have entered into a covenant of the LORD.[15] If you will not do this thing and you find any fault or guilt in me, then slay me yourself. Why should you bring me to your father?[16] I'd rather die at your hand."

The request startled Jonathan, and he shook his head vehemently. "Far be it from you." He sat up straighter. "If I knew of a certainty that evil was determined by my father upon you, then would not I tell you?"

"How will you get word to me? What if your father answers you roughly?"[17] David swallowed his rising fear. "The king knows of our covenant. Surely he will have you watched and followed."

Rising, Jonathan motioned for David to follow. "Come. Let us go into the meadow to the west of the city."[18]

Confused, David followed Jonathan out of the house. They made their way carefully through the city. Jonathan's presence averted much of the trouble that David would have normally run into, and since the king and his men had yet to return from Ramah, no one had any orders to apprehend or prevent Jonathan from leaving the city.

The sun hung low in their eyes as they proceeded toward the west and the meadows there. At last, Jonathan stopped and gestured to the field in front of them. "I swear by the LORD God of Israel that when I have sounded out my father sometime in the next three days, I will return here and tell you what I've learned—if there be good or evil toward you. The LORD do so and much more to me if I do not! If evil indeed is determined upon you, I will tell you and let you go

---

[14] 1 Samuel 20:6-7.
[15] 1 Samuel 18:3.
[16] 1 Samuel 20:8.
[17] 1 Samuel 20:9.
[18] 1 Samuel 20:10.

in peace." He hesitated as tears gathered in his eyes. "I pray that you may go in peace, and the LORD be with you as He hath been with my father."[19]

With tears openly streaming into his beard, he continued in a choked voice, "I know that the LORD intends you to be king after my father. I pray, that while I live, show me the kindness of Jehovah. Do not allow me to be slain when you are king. Do not cut off your kindness from my house forever. When the LORD has cut off your enemies—every one of them—from the face of the earth, remember me."[20]

David took a leather thong and bound their two wrists together tightly enough to scrape the skin. "I swear this to you, my brother. Your house shall not be cut off, and if I fail in this, then let my enemies rise up against me and smite me. Let the LORD require it at their hands."[21]

They hugged each other's necks, their tears mingling together in their beards. Finally, Jonathan pushed himself away and grinned. "Then it is well." He nodded to the field. "Tomorrow, as you've said, is the new moon, and you will be missed at my father's table." He pointed to the rocky pinnacle where David had once hidden within a shadowy crevasse while Jonathan had spoken to his father of the good David had done. His words had saved David's life, and he fervently hoped Jonathan could do it again. "I see you remember that spot," Jonathan said. "Three days from now, come to the rock Ezel and hide yourself there once again, for I will come out with a lad if perchance I am watched. Do not let the lad see you."

David nodded. "That is well, but how will you tell me of your father's intentions?"

"I will shoot three arrows as if I shot at a mark. I will command the lad to fetch the arrows and if you hear me say to the lad that he has passed the arrows, that they are between he and Gibeah, then come out, for as the LORD lives, there is peace toward you from my father." Jonathan paused, looking pained. "But if I say to the lad,

---

[19] 1 Samuel 20:11-13.
[20] 1 Samuel 20:14-15.
[21] 1 Samuel 20:16-17.

'The arrows are beyond you,' then flee, for the LORD has sent you away."[22]

David stared at Jonathan in consternation. The thought of being parted from his friend caused him physical pain. But he knew that if Saul did indeed mean him ill, then fleeing was his only option.

Jonathan reached out and grasped David's forearm tightly. David returned the hold instinctively. The king's son, his voice thick with emotion, whispered, "Do not forget what we have vowed this day, my friend. May the LORD be between you and me forever."

David nodded, his throat thick and dry. Jonathan let go and hurried away. David watched until the other was lost in the haze of the day.

Turning, he walked toward the rocky spire where he would wait for the next two or three days with only his own dark thoughts for company. No stranger to fear and death, David had come to terms with the possibility of his own demise. But never before had he felt so lonely. He struggled with the injustice and unfairness of it all, but before he reached the rock Ezel, his legs gave out as anguish and loneliness washed over him. He collapsed to his knees in the meadow grass, and with tears streaming down his face, he called upon his God, the only One he knew of a certainty would hear him.

---

[22] 1 Samuel 20:18-22.

5

onathan picked at his food, his appetite having abandoned him as the tension around him grew thick like cooling sap. It clung to everyone at the table, creating an unnatural silence and smothering the usual laughter and joy of the meal. Even when the king had recited the ritual Shema, few had found any peace or comfort in the familiar words of praise and worship to Elohim.

For David's place at the table was empty and given the king's volatile temperament toward his former armorbearer,[1] everyone wondered what King Saul would do. If any thought David would return of his own will, they were mistaken. But so far, the king had said nothing—not yesterday nor yet today.[2] In fact, other than some muttering under his breath[3] that Jonathan couldn't quite hear, the king seemed to have fallen into a pensive mood that belied the reported rage his father had shown toward David.

Strangely, the brooding gave Jonathan hope. He believed that his father loved David, and only the evil spirit that at times fell upon him had driven him to these actions of insanity. If the evil spirit had departed, then all would be well.

The king had returned from Ramah in a black mood, saying nothing about what had happened to him there. Jonathan had heard

[1] 1 Samuel 16:21.
[2] 1 Samuel 20:25-26.
[3] 1 Samuel 20:26.

the rumors, of course, how Saul had lain naked all night in a trance, uttering words of power and prophecy, how Samuel had stood above him intoning as thunder roared around the pair and lighting struck the earth mere cubits away from the two powerful men. The stories grew with each telling, and Jonathan hardly knew where the truth lay, but if his father could still be filled with the Spirit of God, then maybe there was hope. Perhaps the evil spirit had been driven away forever.

But as if thinking about trouble conjured it, Saul's eyes snapped up to fix upon his eldest son. Without preamble, he demanded, "Why is it that the son of Jesse comes not to eat meat, neither yesterday nor today?"[4]

Jonathan swore softly under his breath. His father's tone left little doubt as to his emotional state. He cleared his throat, meeting his father's eyes. "David earnestly asked leave of me to go to Bethlehem. His family offers a yearly sacrifice in the city and his elder brother commanded him to attend. He wished to see his brethren. It is why he comes not to the king's table."[5]

Anger contorted the king's features, and those already around the table seemed to shrink before his towering wrath. Slowly, as if it took every ounce of strength he possessed, the king stood to his feet, his eyes never once leaving those of his eldest son. Leaning forward past Abner, he glared at Jonathan. "You son of the perverse and rebellious woman! Do not I know that you have chosen the son of Jesse to your own confusion and to the confusion of your mother's nakedness?"[6]

Jonathan flinched, his face growing pale at the vileness of his father's words. He opened his mouth to refute his father, but Saul overrode him. "As long as the son of Jesse lives on this earth, you and your kingdom will never be established! Now send and fetch him to me, for he will surely die!"[7]

---

[4] 1 Samuel 20:27.
[5] 1 Samuel 20:28-29.
[6] 1 Samuel 20:30.
[7] 1 Samuel 20:31.

1 Samuel 20:24-42

Jonathan refused to believe his ears. He tried to hold his father's eyes, but something in them, some madness, rebuffed his efforts. Shifting in torment, he managed to ask, "Why must he die? What has he done?"[8]

With a primeval cry of rage, Saul snatched his javelin that always lay near to hand and threw it at Jonathan. Only Jonathan's training and battle instincts saved him from being impaled. He flung himself to one side and the javelin flew past to skitter along the cobblestone floor, the heavy iron head striking sparks as it slid away.

Those around the table began to shout and scamper back, trying to distance themselves from the enraged and shaking king. Jonathan had a fleeting glace of Michal, her white face shocked at the violence of her father's wrath. The sight of her snapped something deep inside the eldest son of King Saul. His own anger rose unbidden and soon became a match for his father's.

He stood to his feet, ignoring the spilled food and wine that had stained his tunic as he had dodged his father's javelin. He fixed his father with a steely look. "You do him and me shame, Father. I will have no part of this evil."

So saying, he turned and strode away, purposely knocking over a platter of meat as he passed to show his disdain for his father. All eyes watched as the heir to Saul's throne left. Some watched sadly, but others watched in calculation, knowing that in such strife, opportunity awaited.

Ignoring all, Jonathan hurried out of the room and outside. He spied a young lad who waited outside in case someone within needed something. "You, lad," Jonathan said, gesturing to him. "Attend me."

"Yes, my lord," the boy said, hurrying over.

The boy's eyes were wide and frightened. Doubtless, he had heard what had gone on within. Calming himself, knowing it would do little good to take out his anger on the lad, he asked, "Who is your father?"

---

[8] 1 Samuel 20:32.

"Ziba, my lord."

Ziba was one of his father's newer servants. "Do you serve your father well?"

"Aye." The lad looked suddenly sheepish. "I try, my lord. I have fourteen brethren, so my father has little time for me."

"Your father has fifteen sons?"[9]

"This is so."

"He is mightily blessed," Jonathan said somewhat sadly. He himself had yet to father any children, and after what had happened with his own father, he felt somewhat ambivalent about the matter of being a father.

The door to the king's court opened, and Jonathan's wife slipped out. Her eyes looked relieved when she saw her husband standing not far away.

He held up a hand, bidding her to remain silent. He turned back to the boy. "Harken then, son of Ziba. I have need of you on the morrow. At first light, be at my house. I must needs practice with the bow, and I will need someone to fetch my artillery. Can you do this?"

The boy's eyes lit up. This was a rare opportunity, and he knew it. "Aye, my lord! I will not fail you!"

"It is well then." Jonathan offered the lad a smile. "The task should not be too great, for I can but shoot no farther than a few cubits."

The boy's mouth gaped open, unsure how to respond to such obvious understatement.

Jonathan motioned for the boy to stay behind and attend those within should anyone require him. He then took his wife's hand and led her outside into the outer courtyard. The night sky blazed with twinkling stars. The vastness of the universe often made him feel small.

Naarah moved closer, her eyes clearly worried. "Is it well, my husband?"

---

[9] 2 Samuel 9:10.

1 Samuel 20:24-42

"I know not," he said softly. "I fear for my friend David, and I fear for my father. I understand not his anger."

"I beg of you, my lord, do not invoke the king's wrath further. His spear came close to slaying you."

Jonathan acknowledged her fear with a small nod and pulled her tightly to him. "It will be as Jehovah wills, my wife. Think no more upon it."

But he knew she would. So would he.

The next morning, the Sabbath, Jonathan met the lad in the main courtyard of his father's compound. "What is your name?" he asked the stocky boy.

"Johanan, son of Ziba, my lord."

Jonathan handed over a quiver of arrows. "Beware of the fletching, Johanan. They are delicate, and I would not have them disturbed."

The boy's face tightened in concentration as he handled the wooden quiver, careful not to touch the arrows. "Are the feathers then so important?" he asked.

Jonathan smiled as he motioned for the boy to walk with him. He didn't know if Saul would have him watched or followed, so the boy would be needed just in case. "The fletching helps the arrow to spin," he explained, "and this spinning keeps the arrow flying true. Aye, the fletching is important. In battle, it may be the one thing that saves your life."

The boy's eyes remained large as he took it all in. "And the bow, my lord? I have not seen one such as yours."

Jonathan glanced at his bow. The weapon was shorter than the typical bow, being a composite bow and constructed from several different types of wood glued together instead of the longer bow made of a single piece of wood. The composite bow, though shorter, was significantly more powerful with an effective range of three hundred and fifty cubits.[10] "This is patterned after the Egyptian

---

[10] Roughly 175 yards, based on a cubit being 18 inches.

bow," he explained. "They have used it to great effect against their enemies."

The boy puffed out his chest. "But not against Israel," he boasted.

Grinning, Jonathan nodded. "Aye, Jehovah Elohim is our shield. But see this?" He brushed back his brown hair to reveal a scar just above his right ear, barely visible and only noticeable if attention was called to it. "This was made by an arrow shot from this very bow."

If possible, the boy's eyes grew even wider. "Truly?"

"Aye, truly. I took it from the Philistine who wielded it for he no longer had need of it."

Johanan looked confused. "Did he cast it aside?"

"Nay, young one. He was dead. I slew him with my sword and took his bow."

The boy smiled. "It was a mighty deed, my lord."

"Perhaps. But remember this, son of Ziba, it is not one's ability to slay the enemy that makes one great. There are other...attributes." He trailed off, thinking of the contrast between his father and David.

"My lord?" the boy prompted, obviously perplexed.

Jonathan shook himself and ruffled the boy's hair before pushing him to a greater pace. "You will come to know what I mean when you are older. For now, we go to practice, and I need someone to fetch my artillery. Can you do this, son of Ziba?"

"Aye, my lord!" the lad exclaimed, his excitement mounting.

Jonathan kept a close eye out for anyone his father may have sent to follow him, but he saw nothing suspicious. Being the Sabbath, few people were out and about, and the market was closed, but he had little doubt that the king would wish to keep a close eye on his son, knowing the friendship that existed between Jonathan and David. For the moment, it looked as if he'd be able to slip out of the city without arousing suspicion and rendezvous with David without incident. It helped that the boy was along.

With each step, Jonathan's heart grew heavier. This day might be the last time he would ever see his friend. For today, he would

— 55 —

send David away. David would become a fugitive, and every hand loyal to the king would be against him to slay him.

Shaking himself, he realized they had already entered the meadow. With a quick glance toward the south and the rocky spire where David doubtless hid and watched, he took the quiver from the boy and fastened it to his side. Extracting an arrow, he set it to the bowstring. "Run ahead, Johanan, and find the arrows I shoot."[11]

The boy eagerly took off, bounding through the grass like a rabbit. Jonathan pulled back as far as he could on the bowstring and shot the arrow far over the boy's head. With practice ease, he quickly had two more arrows in the air flying beyond the boy.

When the boy came to the first arrow, Jonathan yelled, the prearranged signal he knew David would understand, "Is not the arrow beyond you?" The lad stopped and looked back. "Make haste! Stay not!" he shouted to the boy.[12] And with those words, Jonathan had effectively made his friend into a fugitive.

The boy gathered up the three arrows and bounded back to Jonathan who waited with ill-concealed impatience. "Return the arrows to the quiver," he instructed, handing the quiver back to the boy. "I am finished here. Carry them back to my house. I will follow shortly."

The boy said nothing, trying hard to hide his confusion and failing. Jonathan understood. They had just arrived and now he was sending the boy back. He placed a hand on the boy's shoulder and gently propelled him toward the city. "Away with you. But fear not. You have done well."

With a relieved nod, the boy ran away.

Jonathan watched him go until the rustling of grass from behind announced David's approach. Turning, Jonathan regarded his friend, tears already gathering in his eyes. Before he could say anything, however, David fell on his face before him, bowing himself three times in a gesture of great respect.[13]

---

[11] 1 Samuel 20:36.
[12] 1 Samuel 20:37-39.
[13] 1 Samuel 20:40-41.

His heart breaking, Jonathan dropped his bow and reached down to pull the younger man to his feet. "Nay, my friend. Do not thus." He looked around in worry. "What if I was followed?"

With tears falling into his beard, David said, "I care not. I would not leave without a word to you."

Jonathan tried to speak, but his words broke, and the two friends wept together, clinging to one another desperately and kissing the other's cheeks. Both knew that this could very well be the last time they ever saw each other.

A love existed between them, one born out of trial and tribulation. They were more than friends. They were brothers, brothers in arms, brothers in blood.[14]

After a time, Jonathan recovered enough of his poise to ask, "Where will you go?"

David shook his head, his haggard face betraying the pain he felt. "I have not yet decided. I saw men ride out this morning toward the south." He paused. "Toward Bethlehem."

Jonathan sighed. "I told Father that you were there. He must have sent them looking for you."

"I suspected as much. I cannot return home. My family will be watched."

"This I know," Jonathan agreed. "There are many in Israel who would betray you to gain favor with my father. You must be wary, and I will do what I can for your father and mother and brethren."

"I thank you." Indecision replaced David's gratefulness. It was etched along every line of his weathered face, and the scar on his left cheek turned whiter. "I...I have nowhere to go."

"Nay. Think not such. Jehovah Elohim is your refuge. We have sworn, the both of us, in the name of the LORD that He be between me and you and between my seed and your seed forever. Do you think this covenant lightly made?"

David found a smile. "Nay. It was not."

---

[14] 2 Samuel 1:26.

1 Samuel 20:24-42

"Then take heart, my friend. My father cannot prevail against this covenant for it is of the LORD."

His shoulders straightening, David nodded. "Then so be it." He kissed Jonathan's cheeks one more time. "This is farewell, my brother."

Jonathan's eyes shimmered with tears. "Only for a time. We shall see one another again. This I swear."

Nodding, David turned and began to walk away. Jonathan watched him until he disappeared among the trees at the edge of the meadow, and then with a deep sigh and a prayer to Jehovah, he turned back to the city.[15]

Whatever he could do to help save his friend, it would be by remaining at his father's side. *Someday*, he vowed silently, *David will stand once again at my father's side.*

---

[15] 1 Samuel 20:42.

6

David studied the tranquil city of Nob, feeling anything but tranquility. More of a village than a city, the small community had become known locally as the city of priests. The tabernacle, perhaps the holiest place in Israel, had been erected in the exact center of the low-lying village. Pens for sheep and oxen were erected around the town. The tithe was brought here so that the priests never lacked for a sacrifice or for food. A shifting breeze brought him the smell of the closely packed animals. All looked at ease. But from David's vantage point atop a hill, he had but to turn his head slightly to see Jerusalem to the south, and in the other direction, distant smoke from the north marked Gibeah.

He still hadn't made up his mind yet where he would go. Samuel had made it clear that he couldn't return to Ramah, so where then should he go? Bethlehem and home were out of the question. Saul would be expecting him there. He had no weapon, no provisions, and hunger gnawed at his stomach.

He had seriously considered trying to find his old companions from the Indebted. Adino, Shammah, and Eleazar would doubtless help him, but the men were scattered, returned to their homes and their families. David was reluctant to put their newfound freedom or their families at risk.

Unwillingly, he began to think that there was no place in Israel where he would be safe. King Saul would hunt him throughout all

— 59 —

the coasts of Israel, hounding him until he was captured or killed. And without any aid or resources, David feared he would not evade the king for long. That left only other lands, other people where Saul held no sway.

But if he had thought of it, then doubtless Saul had thought of it too. The main routes into Moab to the east and Amalek to the south were probably being watched. Going north meant traveling through a large territory that Saul had dominion over. To the south lay the scattered, but hostile tribes of Amalek, but that meant traveling through Judah, exactly where Saul would expect him to flee. Those directions were out. That left east.

The Philistines.

No one would ever believe that David would dare go there. Twice now, he had defeated their champions and had often routed their armies. His actions in harvesting the foreskins of two hundred Philistine warriors[1] had made him odious in their eyes, a living blasphemy and insult that had resulted in more than one assassination attempt aimed at David. Philistia might very well be the only place on earth where King Saul would not think to look for his former armorbearer.

David recalled the brief conversation he had had with the king of Gath before engaging three of the Philistine champions in combat. The heathen king had as much offered him employment if David would but betray his master and serve him. David would never do that, even if it cost him his life, but Gath might be the one place where he could hide and find a measure of safety. He could speak the Philistine language well enough, and Gath was the most cosmopolitan of the Philistine cities where Hebrews were not an uncommon sight. With a bit of Jehovah's favor, he could remain anonymous once he gained entry to the city.

He sighed, deeply troubled. Gath would be where he'd go, but first, he needed some food—and weapons if possible.

---

[1] 1 Samuel 18:27.

Moving to a better position, he studied the tiny figures moving about below. He couldn't see any sign of Saul's men. Many of the men and women he watched were Gibeonites, descendants of the race of people who had tricked Joshua into a lasting peace when the Hebrews had first invaded the Promised Land.[2] The Gibeonites were the closest thing to a slave race that Israel had. Joshua, angry at the deception, had enslaved the Gibeonites and made them servants to the priests to do much of the manual labor, freeing the priests of the tabernacle to focus on the things of the LORD.[3]

Wherever the tabernacle of the LORD had been pitched, there would be the Gibeonites—first in Shiloh, now in Nob.

David could see many of the priests moving about, wearing the ephod of their office. There was little activity, and David belatedly realized that it was the Sabbath day and little or no work was to be done. It was a day of rest, and indeed, everything looked serene, as it should be. So finally making up his mind and deciding that the best course of action would be to bluff his way through whatever objections the priests may offer at his traveling on the Sabbath, David stood up and headed down to the small town.

A middle-aged man of Gibeonite ancestry saw David striding into the village and bowed. "My lord, may I be of service?"

David nodded. "Take me to the high priest, Ahimelech. I would speak with him."

The man bowed again. "As you command, my lord. Follow me."

The man turned without any further questioning and proceeded to walk directly to the tabernacle. David had been here many times over the years, first with his father and then when his duties would permit. Three times a year, during the holy feasts, the men and boys of Israel would present themselves before the LORD at the tabernacle.[4] This would often be done over several days, and fortunately, Nob wasn't all that far from the core of the population,

---

[2] Joshua 9:3-27.
[3] Joshua 9:27.
[4] Exodus 23:17.

— 61 —

and so David had often made the journey as a boy to present himself before the LORD.

As always, a sense of holiness descended upon David when he entered the courtyard of the tabernacle. According to tradition, the tabernacle was always pitched longways east and west. They entered from the east side, the Gibeonite servant holding aside the heavy purple curtain of the gate for David. The walls all the way around were made of thick, waterproof material dyed in shades of blue, purple, and scarlet.[5] Goliath could have easily peered over the walls, but even Saul with his unusual height would not have been able to do so.

The first thing David saw upon entering was the bronze altar, upon which all the animal sacrifices were offered. Even now, the smell of burnt flesh lingered in the air from the evening's sacrifice. Beyond the altar stood the tabernacle proper. Also made of thick woven cloth, the building exuded holiness as it soaked up the faint sunlight that filtered through the cloudy sky. The cloth looked slightly damp as if it had been recently cleaned, making the colors darker to the eye.

A young man, younger than David, hurried up, nodding to the Gibeonite servant who took it as a dismissal and disappeared back through the courtyard curtain.

"I am Abiathar," the slender man greeted in a surprisingly deep voice while bowing low, "son of Ahimelech." David started to introduce himself, but Abiathar cut him off with a dismissive wave of the hand. "And you are David, son of Jesse." Intelligent, light-brown eyes carefully regarded the warrior before him, and David felt as if the young priest missed little and approved of less.

"Well met," David said, offering a bow of his own. While the prophets brought the Word of the LORD to the people, the priests had a much more solemn and sacred duty. The priests stood between God and His people, the true intercessors who invoked both the blessings and the mercy of Elohim upon the people of Israel. David

---

[5] Exodus 27:9-19.

studied the priest, noting the plain white robe, the close-cropped hair, and the gaunt cheeks—as if he'd spent too much time in study and not enough in eating. "It is your father I seek, Abiathar."

The man smiled enough through his perfectly trimmed beard to reveal perfectly straight and perfectly white teeth. "As is proper. Come."

He turned, and David followed the young priest around the altar and toward the tabernacle entrance where an elderly man washed his hands in the bronze laver set atop a bronze pedestal.[6]

Ahimelech turned at the sound of their approach and started, his eyes widening, at the sight of David. "My lord David, what brings you here?" His eyes flickered about, and seeing no one else other than his son, he added, "Why are you alone and no man with you?"[7]

David detected a note of fear in the older man's voice. For David to arrive on the Sabbath day when traveling was strictly forbidden could only mean an emergency of the gravest sort had compelled David forth.

He remained silent, casting a glance at Abiathar, hinting at secrets that only the priest should be aware of. Ahimelech waved a dismissal to his son. "Thank you for bringing him to me, my son. You may go."

Abiathar bowed to his father. "It was my duty," he said simply, seemingly unperturbed at being so dismissed.

David waited until the young priest was out of earshot and then stepped close to the middle-aged high priest. He hated what he was about to do, but he didn't see any real choice in the matter. He needed help, but he had to get it in such a way that the priests would be protected from Saul and not run off to inform the king of David's whereabouts. Clearing his throat, he said softly, "I am not alone, my lord. The king's business is secret and requires haste, and the others wait for me along the route of my journey.[8] What food do you have

---

[6] Exodus 30:18.
[7] 1 Samuel 21:1.
[8] 1 Samuel 21:2.

1 Samuel 21:1-10

at hand? I would be most thankful for five loaves of bread or whatever you have."[9]

"There is no common bread here, servant of Saul. Only hallowed bread." He fell silent, studying David from under thick, bushy eyebrows. David's stomach growled embarrassingly, and the high priest could not refrain from a small smile. "I will give you the hallowed bread—if the young men have kept themselves at least from women."[10]

"Of a truth, women have been kept from us these three days since we left." Well, it was partly true anyway. He hadn't been with his wife for the last three days—that much was true. Clearly, the high priest was assuming that David was being sent to oversee some battle and that his troops were waiting for him to arrive and take command. Hopefully, the deception would keep the high priest from any harm when Saul discovered that David had passed through Nob.

He continued, "The bodies of the young men are holy, and the bread is doubtless common now that evening has descended this day. Were you not soon to deliver it to your family for the Sabbath meal? Even if the bread were sanctified this day in the vessel, you would still eat of it, but do you not have bread ready to replace it before the LORD?"[11]

Ahimelech heaved a resigned sigh. "This is true, young man. Are you in such need as to require this bread meant for the priests?"

"I would not ask if it were not so."

The high priest considered a moment longer. "Wait here." He turned and walked sedately into the tabernacle.

David envied the priest. He wished more than anything to see what lay beyond the walls of the tabernacle. He knew what was in there, but he had never seen the holy furniture within. It was for the priests alone. How grand it must be to serve Jehovah in such a capacity. Even being the doorkeeper to such a holy place would be

---

[9] 1 Samuel 21:3.
[10] 1 Samuel 21:4.
[11] 1 Samuel 21:5.

preferable than what he was contemplating...to dwell in the city of the wicked.[12]

Eventually, Ahimelech emerged from the tabernacle and when the curtain was thrust aside, David caught a glimpse of the interior, spying the golden candlestick and the table of shewbread. He felt a thrill at spying such holy relics, and despite his impatience, a sense of peace stole over him. The only piece of furniture missing from the tabernacle was the ark of the LORD itself. King Saul had forbidden its return to the tabernacle, wishing to keep it nearer to Gibeah. David didn't understand and silently vowed that when he was king, he would reunite the ark with the tabernacle where it belonged.

The high priest handed him five loaves of the shewbread.[13] "I do not think it is enough for you and your men," he admitted, "but it is all that can be spared."

David nodded. "It will be enough." He hesitated, before asking, "Is there not now under your hand spear or sword? I have neither brought my sword nor my weapons with me because the king's business required haste."[14]

The high priest looked suddenly nervous and suspicious. "You have not prepared yourself for battle?"

"The business at hand requires haste, my lord. Time was not afforded me to claim my armaments."

David resisted the impulse to squirm. Up to that moment, his lies had been for the purpose of protecting Ahimelech in case Saul discovered that the priest had aided David. But this lie was purely selfish.

The priest gestured toward the tabernacle. "The sword of Goliath the Philistine, whom you slew in the Valley of Elah, is here wrapped in a cloth behind the ephod: if you will take that, take it: for there is no other save that here."

---

[12] Psalm 84:10.
[13] 1 Samuel 21:6.
[14] 1 Samuel 21:8.

1 Samuel 21:1-10

David's eyes brightened. He had forgotten about the sword that Jonathan had given to the custody of the priests. He said, "There is none like that; give it me."[15]

With a resigned look, the high priest returned to the tabernacle where he kept the ephod made by Moses for his brother, Aaron, the original high priest. He returned with a large sword held in two hands. David noted that the man's hands were shaking.

Almost reverently, David took the sword and tested its weight. Goliath's sword was longer and wider than what he was used to wielding. He removed it from the scabbard and examined the iron blade, noting that Jonathan had had his father's smiths hone it to a fine edge and hammer out the dents. He swung it carefully, gauging his ability to wield it in battle. Although much larger and heavier, he found that the years of warfare had given him the strength needed to handle the blade if necessary—though with a degree of awkwardness. Hopefully, it would not be necessary.

Returning the sword to its scabbard, he slung it over his back and bowed to the high priest. "Thank you, my lord."

Ahimelech never lost his frown as he regarded David. "Then begone from here. I do not approve of this breach of the Sabbath, my son."

David nodded, feeling guilty. "I understand. I beg your blessing. Please beseech the LORD on my behalf."

Ahimelech's dark eyes bore into David's. "If your way is righteous, then may Jehovah Elohim light your way and protect you from all harm."

David wanted to sigh, but he refrained. Naturally, the priest had to add a condition that David could not know the truth of himself. Was fleeing Saul the right thing to do?

Not feeling any better for the priest's words, he turned and walked quickly to the heavy curtain of the tabernacle courtyard. Pushing it aside, he slipped through into the fading light of evening. The Sabbath was nearing its end, and the moment three stars could

---

[15] 1 Samuel 21:9.

be seen in the night sky, the next day would have officially begun. Glancing upward at an overcast sky, he sighed again. There would be no stars visible this night.

Abiathar waited beyond the courtyard entrance. When he spotted David, he hurried over. He glanced at the bread and sword, and other than a tightening of his lips, he said nothing of David's new possessions, but he radiated disapproval. "Do you require anything else, my lord?" he asked in his deep voice.

"Nay," David said, "the king's business demands that I leave at once."

The young priest frowned. "The Sabbath is not yet finished. You would travel?"

"It is a matter of war," David said, moving past the priest. He didn't really want to explain himself. He'd told enough lies for one day. "The Philistines care not for our holy days."

Abiathar nodded. "Aye. Go with God then."

"I thank you."

David took three more steps before coming up short by a raspy voice that sounded like a stone scraping against harden clay. "Is this not David, son of Jesse, servant of King Saul?"

Anger surged through David like a lightning strike. He turned and fastened his eyes on the red-headed Edomite, Doeg. "What do you here, Edomite dog?"

Doeg's mouth tightened and his eyes narrowed, but he dared not respond in kind. Doubtless, he had learned a harsh lesson the last time he had tried to antagonize David. "I am detained before the LORD," he growled out.[16] "Is this not the Sabbath?"

"It is, and you would do well to heed our laws, dog."

Though running to fat, Doeg was still a powerful man, and his thick hands slowly curled into fists as his face flushed red like his beard and hair. David turned to face the Edomite more fully, taking an easy stance, but one that Saul's herdsman couldn't fail to notice. Slowly, the man's hands uncurled, and he executed a low, if clumsy,

---

[16] 1 Samuel 21:7.

bow. "Aye, it is why I wait here. But I find it curious that you are here, come this Sabbath."

It wasn't a question, but David felt the implied inquiry like a blow, and he flinched guiltily. He noticed Abiathar watching nearby, curiosity written all over his face. Feeling somewhat trapped, he stepped close to the herdsman and dropped his voice. "Do not presume to question me, herdsman. I am about the king's business."

"I would not," Doeg said, stepping back to gain space. He eyed the five loaves of bread and the huge sword slung over David's back. David saw recognition and cunning spring to life in the other's eyes. Those eyes shifted, unable to meet David's squarely. Finally, the herdsman said, "I too am a loyal servant of King Saul's, so perhaps I may be of service?"

"Abide here," David hissed, angry and frustrated. "Your aid is not required for what I do. Say no more."

"As you command," Doeg agreed, bowing once again.

With a last look at the Edomite, David hurried away even as worry replaced his anger. He did not doubt that Doeg would inform Saul of David's passing through Nob.[17] And knowing the herdsman as he did, David did not believe the man would wait long before running to the king.

He came to an abrupt stop as the temptation to return and kill the Edomite nearly overwhelmed him. He shrugged off the feeling, knowing that, as justified as he felt the killing would be, doing so in the city of priests would cause more of an uproar and upheaval than leaving the cur alone—at least for the moment.

Glancing back, he saw Doeg staring after him. With a silent snarl of rage, David pushed on, heading north. He stopped only to take a hooded robe lying near one of the Gibeonite huts. The owner bowed low in resignation, offering no protest. The Gibeonites could not forbid anything to a Hebrew. He felt guilty taking it, but he would need something to help hide his features. He knew Doeg was

---

[17] 1 Samuel 22:22.

— 68 —

still watching, so hopefully, by looking like he was heading back to Gibeah, he would stall the herdsman's report.

But once outside the city and away from any prying eyes, David turned toward the west. Shadows wreathed the land in shades of gloom, matching the way David felt. He'd already decided upon a direction and a destination. He did not relish it, but he would go to Gath and King Agag's court. If need be, he could always pretend to serve Agag. Nodding to himself and praying he wasn't making a profound mistake, he hurried along into the falling night.

7

Gath rose up like an evil blot on the eastern edge of the Shephelah plain. The Philistine city was an affront to David, representing an old failure that continued to haunt Israel to this day. When the people of Israel had first entered the land under Joshua, they had easily conquered every city and every people around them from the Jordan River to the Great Sea—except the Philistines.[1] There were still nations to the north, south, and east that had remained free of the Hebrew invasion, but Israel was a unified nation with clear borders—except to the west where the Philistines continued to reside on the Shephelah plain.

Joshua had been unable to conquer them, and they continue to remain a thorn in Israel's side, a blight upon the land as far as David was concerned. Many had come to believe that Jehovah had chosen to keep the Philistines specifically to test future generations of Israelites, to determine if His people would obey Him.[2] Perhaps, but David silently vowed that if he ever had the chance, he would drive the Philistines into the sea and forever break their power.

David stood upon a rocky promontory that overlooked the fertile plain that the Philistines controlled. Five key valleys ran from the mountains of Israel to the plain, one of which was the Elah Valley where David had slain the giant Goliath. The valley, because

---

[1] Joshua 13:1-3; Judges 3:1-3.
[2] Judges 3:1-3.

of its fertile farming land, was more populated than the hills and mountains, so David had kept to the wilderness parallel to the valley as much as possible, making the journey in two days while living off the bread he had been given by Ahimelech.

Gath overlooked the entrance to the Elah Valley, providing a natural defensive position against an army moving down the valley. It also served as a staging area for the Philistine armies when they wished to invade Israel. The Elah Valley provided a natural pathway that led almost directly to Bethlehem. For the Hebrews, the city of Gath represented the leading edge of Philistine dominion. Of all David's victories over the Philistines, none of them had come from a successful siege against one of their key cities. Many thought Gath impregnable with its towering walls and massive gates.

And for the moment, David was grateful for that fact. If there was any place Saul would be unable to reach him, it would be within those thick walls.

David started down toward the city. Like many of the cities of the region, Gath had been initially built on a hill, but the outgrowth had spilled out down the slopes, and the lower city was sprawled around the main hill upon which the city stood. A towering wall at least fourteen cubits thick surrounded the entire lower city. Guard towers reared up above the wall and David could see vague movement atop them, evidence that soldiers kept watch over the approaches to the city.

He took a moment to consider what it would mean to besiege a city of such obvious strength. Rumors of people far to the east spoke of engines capable of hurling massive stones and giant arrows great distances, but that hardly seemed feasible to David. Even if such things existed, how could they even put a dent in the massive walls surrounding Gath?

The story of Joshua and Jericho came sharply to mind. If the walls of Jericho were anything like the walls around Gath, then it was no wonder that Joshua needed Elohim's help to defeat the city. Any army attempting to breach the walls around Gath would need to climb ladders in the face of a withering storm of arrows and burning oil. The gates looked sturdy enough that a battering ram would need time to breach it, and all the while the men working the ram would be subjected to arrow bombardment, hurled rocks, and fire.

David shivered. No, he would not want to besiege Gath. Without Elohim's help, he would need a ten to one advantage—twenty to one would be better.

Knowing he was probably being observed, David trudged slowly down the sparsely wooded hill to a worn, dirt road that ran to one of the lower city gates. A week's worth of growth had given David's hair and beard a shaggy appearance, hiding his facial features and obscuring his identity. He fervently prayed that it would be enough to prevent discovery. As far as he knew, the Philistines still had a price on his head worth his entire head weight in gold. The last thing he needed was for some greedy Philistine to recognize him and call down the entire city upon him.

Hopefully, no one would believe a sane man in David's position would ever show up at the gates of Gath.

"You there," shouted a farmer in the guttural Philistine language when he spotted David trudging through his fields, "get you gone from my crops!" He brandished a sickle at David, warding him away.

David bobbed an apologetic bow and hurried on until he reached the road, where he joined the flow of shepherds and farmers that were moving either toward or from the city of Gath. Carts full of the autumn harvest moved sedately toward the city, pulled by weary or indifferent oxen. Philistine shepherds, some of whom were women, watched from small rises off to the side of the road, keeping a keen eye on their flocks of sheep and goats.

David had never been this close to Gath before, and he was annoyed to note that it far surpassed any city that the Hebrews possessed in sheer terms of population and industry. David had never seen so many people, and he wasn't even in the city yet!

He was both gratified and angered to note that he wasn't the only Hebrew making his way to or from Gath. Other Hebrews, some of them obviously farmers or merchants, were doing a brisk business with those moving along the roads. No doubt the city had several markets within, but some enterprising merchants had learned that there was profit to be made from those who were traveling to and from the city, so before David had even reached the gates, his ears were assaulted by hawkers, shouting at him and trying desperately to arrest his interest in their wares.

He ignored them all, keeping the hooded, outer robe that he had taken from Nob pulled low over his face. Most Hebrew men wore a turban when trying to keep their head covered from the elements, and many of the women's robes were hooded—such as what David now wore. Enough men wore something similar that he figured it would not elicit comment, but the hood provided him with the needed obscurity. But he would not be mistaken for a woman. His tunic came to just beyond his knees, unlike a woman's tunic that always fell to the ankles. That, plus the sword would not hide his gender.

Over the centuries, much of the Hebrew and Philistine cultures had mixed enough that David's dress caused no stir whatsoever. For this, he was grateful. He merged with the flow of traffic heading into the city and tried to match his pace to those around him, careful to avoid calling attention to himself.

At the looming wall, a squad of guards carefully watched those entering and leaving the city. Occasionally, they would stop one of the travelers and demand to know their business or to check what goods might be carried in the back of a cart. And if David hoped to avoid scrutiny, he was sorely disappointed.

"You there," a burly Philistine guard shouted, pointing at David as he attempted to slip unnoticed through the gate. "Halt and be known!" He spoke his native language, which David had learned, but the thick guttural tongue made it difficult for David to understand every word.

David stopped and turned slowly, trying to behave as if he didn't understand at all. He had to be careful. He was clearly a Hebrew, so trying to pass himself off as another race was out of the question. Deciding that flattery would not do any harm, he bobbed a bow and said in Hebrew, "Aye, Captain? I am your servant, ask what you will."

The guard wore a colorful headdress, painted red, as did all Philistine warriors in Gath. His ribbed leather armor had been studded with iron knobs meant to turn away the edge of a sword, though David knew from experience that a hard stab would pierce the armor easily enough. Many Philistine men shaved, particularly the warriors, so the man facing him was cleanshaven and sported an impressive number of scars, giving his face a crag-like aspect. David suspected some disease and not battle was the culprit of those scars.

The guard looked David over, his eyes narrowing as they lingered on David's sword strapped to his back. "You be a Hebrew, be you not?" he asked, switching languages easily enough.

"Aye, Captain."

"You be no farmer. What do you here?"

Apprehension rose as David noted three of the other guards moving to surround him. He thought quickly. "I am a warrior," he admitted. "I seek employment."

The guard spat to one side and said a word that vaguely translated to mean one without loyalty or home, a wanderer of sorts who sells his sword to the highest bidder. There was no direct word for it in Hebrew. "Your sword be of an unusual size," he added, running his eyes over the large hilt that poked up over David's right shoulder.

David shifted the sword on his shoulders self-consciously. "It suits me. Know you of a worthy merchant who may need a sell-sword to escort his goods to another city?"

The guard shrugged. "I know not. But seek such a one in the central market." He pointed into the interior of the city. "Though I doubt anyone would trust a Hebrew." His eyes narrowed. "Cause no trouble, Hebrew pig, while you be within our gates. You will find little tolerance and less love for Hebrews here."

Bowing again, David moved quickly away, knowing that suspicious eyes would linger on him until he had disappeared. He didn't make it far before the ringing sounds of hammers striking metal brought him to a halt. He looked for the source and stared in wonder.

A temple had been built near the gate, and next to the temple was a large iron mill. A score of smiths worked in a central yard, hammering on long iron rods. Never had David seen such a sight—so much iron at one time. Curious, David moved closer.

The smiths were clearly divided into three groups. One group worked on weapons. Racks of swords, spears, and iron tipped arrows lined one of the mill's walls—more weapons than David had ever seen in one place when not carried by an army. Another group worked on farming equipment—plows, hoes, scythes, and much more. Grinding wheels sent sparks shooting into the air as apprentices carefully sharpened the instruments. A third group worked on more delicate items, though David could not for the life of him figure out what they were doing.

A bell sounded, startling David, and his eyes went reflexively to the temple between the gate and the iron mill. The doors swung open and a priest dressed in a red robe stood forth, his hands dripping blood as he raised them over his head. His voice rang out as he shouted, "Praises be to mighty Dagon! He has accepted our blood sacrifice and blessings will be upon the people of the sea!"

Everyone stopped what they were doing, turned to face the priest, and bowed deeply. The priest surveyed the crowd meaningfully, until his eyes came to rest upon David—the only person standing upright. The priest frowned, and David's heart skipped a beat. He turned and hurried away down the street, refusing to look back, but knowing that eyes followed him even as the crowd returned to their activities.

So much for remaining inconspicuous.

The priest of Dagon didn't lose his frown as the Hebrew walked quickly away. That a Hebrew would be so profane as not to pay homage to the great god Dagon was mostly expected, though most of the Hebrew pigs who came to Gath knew better than to be so obvious about their lack of piety to the gods of the Philistines.

The Hebrew was headed into the heart of the city. The priest, admittedly somewhat lazy, would have been inclined to ignore the irreverent man, but something about the way the Hebrew carried himself or perhaps it was the unusual size of the sword strapped to his back had raised the small hairs on the back of his neck, a sure sign from his god that something was amiss. Over the years, he had come to rely upon such signs.

He looked around and motioned for the heavily scarred soldier who commanded the guard detail at the gate. The warrior hurried over.

The priest pointed after the hooded Hebrew, blood dripping off his hands to splatter in the dirt outside the temple door. "Follow that Hebrew. I would know where he goes, who he talks to, and what he does. I would know his purpose here in Gath."

"As you command!" the craggy-faced man said. He bowed, turned and barked some commands to his fellow soldiers to remain vigilant during his absence. He then scurried after the Hebrew.

The priest's frown deepened as he watched the bobbing hood of the receding Hebrew in the distance. It was likely nothing. At worst, the man was probably a spy for King Saul, but that would be nothing new. Spies abounded everywhere and were like cockroaches. You couldn't exterminate them all. But still, something about this particular Hebrew bothered him.

He glanced up to the top of the hill where the main temple to Dagon overlooked the entire city. He wondered if he should take the time to report this incident to the high priest or even to one of King Achish's many functionaries, but his natural laziness imposed itself, and he turned away. He could always do it later—if something truly needed reporting. If nothing else, he could simply order the Hebrew's death. That would solve the problem without having to bother the high priest of Dagon.

Turning, he retreated into the temple, but his mind lingered on the huge sword strapped to the Hebrew's back. He'd seen that sword somewhere else, he was sure of it, but the memory eluded him. The only other ones like it were wielded by the descendants of the giant Anakims. Not many of the giants remained, and each generation there were fewer and fewer. The Hebrew must be unusually strong to wield such a sword.

The stench of blood and burning flesh tickled his nose as he moved deeper into the temple, and all thoughts of the Hebrew fled his mind. He smiled in satisfaction as he gazed upon the body of a young woman lying upon the altar, her heart carved from her chest and offered to the fires of Dagon. The idol of the fish-god sat behind a firepit, its features illuminated by the flames that continually rose before it. The aroma of the burning heart filled the air. Such was the requirement of Dagon. What greater sacrifice than human life? The devotion would bring blessings upon the Philistines.

He had no idea who the girl had been, likely some slave purchased from a neighboring country for this very purpose, and he didn't care. The girl had fulfilled a greater purpose in death than she ever would in life. Her sacrifice would be honored, and her spirit would satisfy Dagon's hunger.

He turned to another priest. "Burn the body."

The young priest addressed bowed in deference, showing the top of his bowl-like haircut that left the sides of his head completely shaved, a mark of the priesthood that all the priests of Dagon bore.[3] "As you command, O hand of Dagon."

Dismissing the younger priest from his mind, the elder priest moved to a basin of water to scrub the girl's blood off his hands, pleased with the day's results. He would need to report to Ahuzzath later, but the high priest of Dagon rarely bothered with the doings

---

[3] Something like this may have accounted for the command in Leviticus 19:27 not to round the corners of their head or beard.

of the lower temple. As long as the fires remained burning and the sacrifices were made, Ahuzzath would be pleased.

More importantly, Dagon was pleased, and that is all that mattered.

8

David pounded on the stout door. It had taken time, but he had learned of a house near the outer wall where the resident woman would lend out a room for a few shekels. Such women had horrible reputations, often being named harlots and more.[1] In Israel, there was no need for such places where hospitality toward strangers was both part of the law and a way of life. No Hebrew woman would ever need to do as this one did.

The door opened, and the plain and hooded face of a woman peeked out. "What do you here?" she demanded, speaking the Philistine language.

David tried to assume an unthreatening posture. "I seek lodging. I hear tell you have a room that may be purchased for a night or two."

The woman looked him over, her brow furrowing when she spotted the sword hilt over David's shoulder. "What manner of man are you? Why do you obscure your face?" she asked.

"I am a warrior," he explained, lowering the hood of his cloak. "I seek employment with a merchant who may need a sword to

---

[1] Likely Rahab was such a woman (Joshua 2:1). It is not certain that Rahab and others like her would have sold their own bodies, and many think it likely that they acted more as mistresses of an Old Testament inn than as a prostitute. Both may be true, however, as prostitution would have meant more income for a single woman, but it is uncertain that they would always have engaged in both activities.

protect his goods while in route to another city. But the hour is late, and I know not where the merchants gather."

"A silver shekel a night," she said, her eyes narrowing in obvious greed.

David sighed. "A silver shekel for two nights," he countered.

The woman's eyebrows furrowed. "Two shekels for three nights."

"Done," David said, "though you must feed me well." He reached into his purse and extracted two silver shekels, handing them over to the woman.

She examined the coins. "These are Hebrew coins," she pointed out.

"Aye. I am a Hebrew."

She looked him over again and finally grunted, stepping back and pulling the door all the way open. "Take off your sandals. You may wash your feet there by the door. I will prepare your room."

She turned away in an ungracious huff, leaving David to decide where best to set down his equipment. He found a stool to sit upon and unlaced his sandals. Looking around, he wondered what sort of society would allow women to lend out rooms to complete strangers. Doubtless, the woman was a widow, her husband likely killed in some battle—perhaps even in one against David himself. To make a living, she had turned to lending out rooms and possibly even lending out other physical pleasures. But why had not some male relative taken her into his house?

In a city like this, harlots were not uncommon, and a woman left alone to make her own way soon developed a reputation, particularly if she could not quickly find another husband. The woman of this house might not rent out her body, but it would not stop the gossips from speculating when men came and went from under her roof.

He then thought about Michal, left alone when he had fled their house. In her case, her father would see to her needs. And if not he, then David's father would do it. No woman in Israel should ever be uncared for—though he knew of situations where a Hebrew woman had no family to turn to. Prostitution was not unheard of in Israel, for there always existed those who allow greed and lust to dictate their behavior. The laws of Jehovah were meant to make such desires unnecessary and to discourage the greed.

David finished unlacing his sandals and washed his feet free of the accumulated dust and dirt. He stared at his long toenails, wishing for a sharp knife to pare them down. Thinking of that led him to feel his somewhat scraggly beard. Since fleeing Gibeah, he had not had the chance to trim it. His present condition would, however, make for an effective disguise.

The woman of the house returned and stood silently nearby. The silence became uncomfortable, so David spoke first. "What are you called, woman?"

"Tirzah," she supplied, her face revealed by the light from the still open door.

David studied her. Her face seemed honest enough, despite the hardness that seemed permanently branded into her gray eyes. Perhaps in her thirties, her skin appeared worn already, like beaten leather. A wisp of raven black hair escaped her hooded garment, and she absently tucked it back into place with a heavily calloused hand.

"Well met, Tirzah," David said. "I am at your service."

She snorted. "No one serves Tirzah." She waved at him to follow. "Come. I will show you your room."

The room was tiny, consisting of a rickety stool and a short straw mattress that had been placed in one corner of the hardpacked dirt floor. A small window gave David a splendid view of the dirty stone-gray wall of the neighbor's house about two cubits away. He could almost reach out the window and touch the other wall. The room had no door, but someone had long ago hung a sagging curtain across the doorway to afford guests some measure of privacy.

The woman seemed to be waiting for something as she stood silently in the entranceway, one hand holding back the thin curtain. David nodded. "It will do. My thanks, good woman."

She grunted. "You may break your fast at dawn. All I have is bread and cheese." Without waiting for anything further, she

— 81 —

1 Samuel 21:10-15

disappeared, leaving David alone in the small room. He looked around at the brick and mud walls, feeling more alone than at any other time of his life.

For two days, David did nothing. He huddled in his small room, keeping to himself and avoiding Tirzah as much as possible— a mutually agreeable arrangement, it seemed. The one time he had looked out the front door of the house, he had spotted a soldier lurking in the shadows down the street. The craggy-faced man looked familiar, and his features put David in mind of the guard who had questioned him at the gate when he'd first entered the city.

He was being watched, and he didn't know why. His response was to huddle all day in his small room. The air in his room began to turn ripe with the smell of unwashed flesh, and if anything, his beard became even more unruly, and his eyes turned bloodshot from lack of sleep and the strain of uncertainty that gripped him.

He hadn't thought his way through what he'd do once he reached Gath. He felt safe from King Saul for the moment, but if the Philistines ever discovered who he really was, he would quickly find himself bent over one of Dagon's altars and his heart carved from his chest.

And he was now being watched.

He could think of any number of reasons for this scrutiny. Perhaps the Philistines watched every Hebrew or stranger who ventured into their city. Perhaps the watcher was only curious, or perhaps he was watching Tirzah. Perhaps the whole thing was David's imagination.

Being watched or not, he needed to decide on what to do next. He could not live here forever. His money would soon run out and with it, Tirzah's hospitality. She had but to lift up her voice, and the place would be swarming with soldiers. David doubted that a Hebrew's word would count for much in Gath.

He could travel south. The Amalekites had little love for Saul, a hatred born from when the Hebrew king had nearly wiped the

— 82 —

Amalekites from the face of the earth.[2] The remnant that remained eked out a poverty-stricken nomadic existence, forming bands that often turned to raiding. And they would just as soon kill any Hebrew who crossed their paths.

Still further south lay Egypt. It would be a long journey, but it was possible to find work and refuge in the land of the Pharaohs. The Hebrews had done so before.[3] But David's heart rebelled at the thought. If he went down to Egypt, he would likely never return. And despite everything else, David fully meant to return to Israel, his home.

He needed a plan that went beyond simply hiding from King Saul. He knew one thing, a truth that he now clung to like a lifeline: Jehovah had anointed him to be the next king of Israel.[4] He didn't know how or when, but he knew this to be true. He had finally accepted it, so whatever he did, he could not stray too far from Israel.

His acceptance of this truth brought sadness and a heaviness that draped over him like a heavy tent. For despite everything Saul had done, David still loved his king. He loved Jonathan, the king's son, and he loved the king's daughter, Michal. He would forever be tied to the house of Saul, and that understanding carried weight— weight David could not easily set aside.

No, he would not rebel against Saul directly, but neither would he permit Saul to kill him. He would stay out of Saul's reach until such a time as God smote him or removed him from being king. But whatever happened, he vowed it would not come by his hand. He would not lift his hand up against the LORD's anointed.

But he was still left trying to figure out what to do now. He stood to his feet and bellowed, "Tirzah!"

A moment later the surly woman pushed aside the curtain, her nose wrinkling at the smell that rolled over her. "What?"

"I wish to explore the city. When I return, I want to bathe. Please have water ready."

---

[2] 1 Samuel 15:7-8.
[3] Genesis 45:9-13.
[4] 1 Samuel 16:13.

1 Samuel 21:10-15

She snorted softly to herself, and David couldn't tell if she was pleased that he would finally clean himself up or if she was irritated over having extra work to do. She'd need to make at least two trips to a nearby well to fetch enough water.

"There is a bathing pool two streets over," she replied, turning away. "Bathe yourself."

David blinked. He had grown up bathing atop the roofs as was often the custom in Israel as it was an easy place to gather rainwater. Some villages had communal bathing pools where men and women would plunge into the water fully clothed, but generally, Hebrews preferred bathing in private—or as much as rooftop bathing would allow.

In Israel, bathing was often a religious ritual as much as it was an effort to be clean. The picture of washing away the sin of the flesh in preparation to serve Jehovah Elohim was a major part of every Hebrew's life.[5]

Shrugging, David strapped on his sword and walked out the room and house. The early evening cast dark shadows across the streets. Several men walked by, laughing coarsely, and David stepped away, trying not to be noticed.

He moved down the street. Tirzah hadn't been all that explicit about where the bathing pool was located, so he decided to start by walking deeper into the city. Now that he had decided to get out of the room and into the open, he felt rejuvenated, despite his uncouth appearance.

He found the bathing pool two streets over just as Tirzah had mentioned. The pool was built into an excavated part of the hill, lined with coarse sand, and then filled with water. A woman emerged, her clothing dripping wet and the skin of her arms and face glowing reddish in the late sunlight.

The woman carefully wrapped another garment around her and bound up her wet hair before moving on. A man stood waist deep in the water, scrubbing his face with sand. David understood. The

---

[5] Leviticus 15.

— 84 —

sand would scour the skin, scrubbing away the dirt and filth. The sand would also act like a drain of sorts, allowing the dirt to settle below, leaving the water on top clean. David suspected that at least once a week, the pool would need to be drained, cleaned, and then refilled.

Or perhaps a natural spring fed the pool. Regardless, the water looked inviting, if cold. He unslung his sword and bent over to undo the laces of his sandals and froze. The man he had spotted loitering around the street of Tirzah's home was leaning casually against a wall not far away, watching.

So, I am being watched, David thought. He straightened, all thoughts of the bath forgotten. He stood for a moment, undecided as to what to do, and that was his undoing.

A dirty urchin, a boy from the brief glance David had, bumped into him, and rebounded, his eyes wide and staring. "Apologies, master," the boy muttered in a heavily accented version of the Philistine language.

Distracted, David hardly noticed the boy, until the urchin scampered off. He followed the boy with his eyes as suspicion gnawed at the edges of his mind. Quickly, he patted himself down. His purse was missing!

"Come back here!" he shouted after the boy.

The boy glanced over his shoulder, squeaked, and darted off like a rock shot from a sling. Muttering all sorts of wishful mayhem he intended to bring down upon the thief, David took off in pursuit.

A cry of alarm sounded from behind. David glanced over his shoulder and saw the soldier who had been watching him emerge more fully into the street, followed by two other soldiers. They all shouted something and ran after David.

By the beard of Abraham! Without meaning to, he'd incited a chase. David looked forward and saw the boy dart down a narrow alley between buildings. Turning, David ran after, now more interested in losing his pursuers than in catching the boy, but the boy would doubtless not allow himself to be caught in some blind alley, so David figured to let the thief be his guide for the moment.

— 85 —

He had to turn sideways to slip into the alley, the pommel of his sword banging against the clay bricks of one of the walls. He shuffled as quick as he could down the short alley and burst into the next street, his eyes scanning up and down. He saw the small urchin darting up the road, climbing deeper into the city.

David didn't hesitate. Years of combat had taught him that hesitation was often a greater mistake than making the wrong decision. He ran after the boy, plunged through the crowd who, though hardly noticing the boy, took exception to the large Hebrew barreling through their midst, and shoving those aside not quick enough to jump out of the way. Many of the Philistines walking the street carried baskets or clay pots—last minute shoppers from a nearby market.

An idea came to him. He purposely ran into those carrying goods, spilling baskets full of clothing or foodstuff, knocking off clay pots that shattered as they struck the street, splashing water and mud everywhere, and knocking some of the men off their feet. Angry cries and curses followed David has he plowed through the crowd. The pursuing guards couldn't help but know where David was going, but hopefully the confusion left in his wake would slow them down.

He risked another glance over his shoulder and saw the guards struggling to get through the angry crowd, who was pushing back against the soldiers worried that they might trample the spilled goods.

The thief, eyes wide at the trail of destruction that followed in David's wake, panicked and ran down another alley. David tried to follow, but this one was even narrower than the first. The sword strapped to his back would not allow him entrance.

Growling in anger, he ripped the sword out of the sheath and tossed away the leather. Then holding the sword in front of him, he turned sideways and scooted quickly through the narrow passage and emerged into yet another street.

Women screamed and scrambled to get out of the way as David burst into their midst, huge sword held aloft, his bloodshot eyes glaring from a filthy, harrowed face. Men scurried aside as the sword-wielding Hebrew turned this way and that, looking for the thief, his impromptu and unwilling guide. Shouts and curses from the alley behind told him he didn't have much time.

He turned around frantically, trying to find the thief, and the crowd rippled as everyone tried to keep out of the sword's reach. The boy was gone, disappeared into the crowd like smoke on a foggy day.

Whirling around, he took a step back to the alley entrance. He could easily defend the narrow opening as his pursuers could only come at him one at a time. The leader was the guard that had questioned David when he had first entered Gath. The crag-faced man froze when he realized David's intent.

"Hey now!" he bellowed. "What are you about?"

David waved his sword. "Stay back!" He didn't want a fight. If he killed someone, he would doubtless be executed. He needed time. "Stay back!" he yelled again.

From behind the crag-faced guard, another soldier warned, "He's mad!"

David feigned a strike at the men in the narrow alley. Startled, they tried to back up, but got tangled in each other's feet and only succeeded in wedging themselves tighter in the alley.

Seeing his chance, David turned to flee and came up short as two giants—nearly as big as Goliath had been—strode toward him, the crowd parting like the Red Sea had done for Moses. Both carried giant spears, and they towered over everyone.

"What is this?" the slightly larger of the two rumbled, his voice sounding like an avalanche.

"A Hebrew, I think," answered the other, his voice deep and raspy as if his vocal cords didn't work quite right.

The two giants studied David who whirled toward them and flourished his sword in a futile attempt to keep the two behemoths back. He felt a spike of fear. The giants could skewer him with their huge spears as easily as spitting a trapped pig.

The eyes of the larger one narrowed. "Saph, know you that sword?"

1 Samuel 21:10-15

The one named Saph studied David's sword. "'Tis Goliath's!" he hissed. "Where did you come by that sword, little man?"

The two giants were dressed for battle in a similar nature as Goliath had been, lacking only the helmets. They wore more traditional mail coats to protect their larger torsos. Their arms, looking twice the size of David's legs, had metal braces that looked thick enough to turn aside a sword. They wore greaves around their calves to protect their legs.

The one called Saph bore a striking resemblance to Goliath, and David knew that he was looking at a brother or possibly a cousin to the giant he had slain with naught but a stone and sling. The giant's wide face and small, dark eyes glared at David from beneath a bristling black beard.

Saph took another long step toward David, forcing the Hebrew to retreat quickly. "Answer me, Hebrew! Where did you come by that sword?"

Ready to panic, David belatedly realized that bringing Goliath's sword into the dead giant's home city was a profound mistake. He might be able to explain his presence in the city, but there would be no way he could explain why he had the sword of one of Gath's more renowned champions.

Lacking any alternatives, he threw the large sword as hard as he could at Saph, turned, and ran frantically away. The sword clanged off the giant's mail shirt and fell to the dusty street. The giant didn't even so much as grunt at the impact.

"Get back here, ye little coney!" the giant roared, referring to a rodent like creature known for inhabiting clefts in rocky areas.

David made no more than a dozen strides when the giant's huge legs caught up to him. The giant kicked him in the back, sending David sprawling painfully into the dirt. He slid for a dozen cubits before stopping painfully in the middle of the street. Never had he been kicked so hard, not even with his father's cantankerous mule had kicked David in the side years ago.

He gasped for breath and wondered if the giant had snapped his back. He couldn't feel his legs to move them, and his arms refused to cooperate. He felt nothing but pain.

The giant's long shadow fell upon David, and a huge hand grabbed him by his tangled hair and yanked him into the air. He gasped as tears filled his eyes and created muddy streaks down his dirty cheeks. He finally found the use of his arms and grasped the giant's hand, trying to tear the fingers loose, but the giant's grip was like iron.

He dangled fully a cubit off the ground, kicking futilely while the two giants regarded him as one would a curious-looking bug. Saph's nose wrinkled when he caught a whiff of David, and he held the smaller man out at arm's length. His scowl, however, looked thunderous. He demanded, "Where did you come by that sword?" He pointed to the large blade that the other giant now held.

9

"Break his neck," the other giant suggested, his eyes gleaming. "Surely he happened upon the sword, for he is no warrior."

David said nothing, but squirmed violently, trying to break Saph's grip on his hair before the giant pulled his entire scalp out. Finding the use of his legs, he kicked out, hitting the armored stomach of the giant. Pain blossomed in his foot, and his eyes began to water even more. He likely broken a toe on the iron mail links.

The cragged-faced soldier who had been chasing David finally arrived. He took in the situation and grinned. "Seems our cur has been caught."

The two giants regarded the guard implacably. "What have you to do with this one?" Saph demanded, shaking David until his teeth rattled painfully.

The guard gestured at David while offering a respectful bow. "Saph, Ishbibenob, I was bid by a priest of Dagon to follow this stranger and see what he was about."

The giant identified as Ishbibenob scowled so that his eyes nearly disappeared in the folds of his face. "You think this man a spy?"

"We know not his purpose," the guard admitted. "I was bid to follow him and see."

"And what did you witness?" Ishbibenob asked.

"'Tis most strange. He arrived two days anon, claiming to be a warrior seeking employment with the merchants. Yet he spent days in a harlot's house, neither coming nor going until this evening. Then at the pool near the high street, he stops and regards the water as if he might bathe, but then he ups and flees like a madman. We gave chase, and you witnessed his insanity. He menaced the people with his sword as if he would slay everyone."

During this speech, David continued to struggle. The pain had grown to the point where his entire world had become agony. He could hardly think. He began mumbling incoherently and spitting randomly, mostly they were desperate cries to Jehovah for deliverance.

Saph shook David again to quiet him, while he continued to regard the soldier. "He carries Goliath's sword," Ishbibenob explained, gesturing with the sword he had recovered. "We would know how this came to be."

Crag-face frowned. "Truly? Was not the sword taken by the Hebrew David, the son of Jesse? Do they not sing songs that he has slain tens of thousands? This David, I hear, is now the king of Israel. I hear he has slain his master, King Saul, and taken his place. But that is merely rumor. Perhaps David and this man are one and the same."

All three regarded David thoughtfully. "You think this may be the one who slew Goliath?" Saph asked, his voice dropping dangerously.

Despite his pain, David grew almost frantic. He had no doubt that the moment he was found out, they would either kill him or sacrifice him to their false gods. He had to be careful. He dared not confirm their suspicions.

They all looked doubtful. The guard shrugged. "Who else would have Goliath's sword?"

David suddenly laughed maniacally, his voice high-pitched and tinged with a bit of madness. He hardly needed to fake it. He knew what a sight he made, his blood-shot eyes, his dirty and ragged beard,

1 Samuel 21:10-15

his unwashed and fouled body. "Aye! Aye! I slew the giant! I plucked the sword from his vary grasp and slew him with his own blade!"

Saph grunted and shook David violently, causing him to bite his own tongue. Blood began to seep out of his mouth looking like red drool. "Goliath was slain by a coward with a sling!" the giant roared.

He threw David to the ground, where he struck painfully, the wind knocked out of his body for the second time. Never had David felt so abused. He ached everywhere from his broken toe to the top of his head. Still, he managed to laugh weakly and spit blood at his tormentors even as he gasped harshly for breath.

Ishbibenob waved a dismissive hand that could easily engulf David's head if he so decided. "Take him," he rumbled, turning away. "This man is no warrior. He may be a spy, but by your very words, I suspect he is a madman."

The crag-faced guard came to stand over David. "And what of the sword? I may need to show it to the priest."

Saph grunted. "The sword is mine. I am kin to Goliath and would not see his blade in another's hand. If the priest wishes to discuss it further, bid him seek me out."

Realizing he would gain nothing more, the guard bowed silently to the two giants as they strode away. Neither of the giants so much as looked back.

David began to laugh weakly. He had nothing to laugh about, but it struck him as ironic that he would flee from Saul only to end up being caught by a blood-kin of Goliath's. The sword had betrayed him, for surely if he had given it much thought, he would have never brought the sword to Gath. But he had. All his efforts, all his planning had been for naught. Despite everything, he was now at the mercy of his most hated enemies, the Philistines.

The Philistine soldier regarded him in disgust. He gestured to his two companions who had lingered off to the side. "Take him. We go to the priest."

They came over and hoisted David up between them, ignoring the smell of him. Together they dragged him off, and as they did,

David began to laugh even louder, his laughter rising in pitch and intensity.

Finally, Crag-face had enough. He rounded on David and slammed a well-worn fist into David's jaw. A flash of pain was followed almost instantly, and with no small sense of relief, by blackness.

"Who are you?" a voice, persistent but little more than a whisper, demanded.

David groaned and tried to roll over, but ungentle hands held him in place. His eyes flickered open to see a gaunt man wearing a blood-stained robe standing over him. The man had the sides of his head completely shaved as if someone had placed a shallow bowl on his head and then shaved everything else off. Designs of Philistine gods had been tattooed completely around the shaved parts.

David blinked and groaned again. This was a priest of Dagon— or perhaps one of the other false gods these heathen worshiped. He tried to sit up, but hands held him in place. Something wet seeped into his back, something sticky.

"Who are you?" the priest demanded once more. "Who are you to carry the sword of our champion, slain by Hebrew treachery those years ago?" The priest wielded a long-curved knife. He placed the point against David's chest and pressed ever so slightly.

David belatedly realized his tunic had been stripped away, leaving him bare chested on some sort of rocky table. He saw blood well up where the knife pierced his skin. He hardly felt it. He ached all over as if every part of his body was on fire.

The priest regarded David with a deep frown, and David remembered this priest as the one who had stepped forth from the temple to announce the successful sacrifice of another human life to their false god Dagon.

It dawned on David that he was being held down over an altar. A fire, the heat of which caressed his face and side, blazed behind where they stood. Drying blood from previous victims stained the smooth stone of the altar, sticky and smelling foul.

The priest's dark eyes bore into David's. "Are you David, the son of Jesse?" he asked in a sibilant whisper. "Has Dagon delivered our most hated enemy into our hands?"

That last question caught David off-guard. By coming to Gath, had he defied Jehovah? Had the LORD delivered him into the Philistines' hands for fleeing Israel? Had he made a profound mistake in coming here?

The irony of his situation was not lost on David. In his efforts to flee King Saul, he had simply walked into the den of enemies who would cheerfully carve out his heart and offer it to the fires of Dagon. Pure hubris had led him to believe he could hide from the Philistines in their very midst. The fear that stabbed at his heart mixed with the irony of his situation caused him to begin to laugh, his body shaking with fearful mirth.

The priest, if possible, frowned even deeper. He withdrew his knife and stood back, watching David with sober eyes. "Enough!" He gestured sharply, and David was hauled off the altar and dragged over to be held up before the angry priest. "You mock me? You mock our gods?"

When David didn't stop, the priest turned to another shorter priest. "Bring in the Hebrew traitor."

The shorter priest, with fewer tattoos, scurried away. He returned soon with another man in tow. A Hebrew. One David knew.

Maon, David's brother, strode over to confront David. The sight of his lost brother cut off David's laughter. Years ago, Maon had fled to the Philistines after conspiring against Israel and King Saul. Maon had lost his way, lost his faith in Jehovah Elohim, and had turned to the false gods of the Philistines.

His betrayal had made him a curse to Israel and his name stricken from the genealogical record. It was as if he had never been born. Indeed, their parents and family were even forbidden to mourn him. Maon lived in chosen exile—a Hebrew lost to his own people.

David had held out hope that his brother could be redeemed. And once Maon had saved David's life from an assassin, but that had been years ago. David had seen Maon only once more since that day, on the eve of battle when he had confronted three Philistine champions. Maon had fled that battle along with the defeated Philistine armies to his uncertain fate.

Maon stood about two fingerbreadths shorter than David. His small mouth pursed, and his brown eyes narrowed nearly to slits as he studied David. His hair had grown even longer and was tied back in the Philistine fashion. He now sported two tattoos on his face, tributes to the false gods of the Philistines.

The priest looked at Maon. "Is this your brother?"

Maon studied David's battered and bruised face. David had accumulated an impressive amount of scars over the years, the most obvious being the one that ran from his left ear and disappeared into his beard. David was filthy, reeked, and lack of sleep had given his eyes a dull, bloodshot appearance.

But David saw recognition in his brother's eyes along with reawakened pain. David understood. There were two different types of awakenings that people experienced—rightly or wrongly—when their values and beliefs shifted. The first kind created a sense of a higher purpose founded upon a higher value system that awakened a sense of inadequacy, of being lesser, and of being unworthy. In such an awakening, there existed a need to rise beyond oneself, to see sacrifice as a gift, and to become something more.

The other awakening invoked a sense of bondage and imprisonment. It translated the concept of a higher purpose into a perception of bondage. Such a one would invariably feel trapped and enslaved, seeking release. They sought a lesser value system, feeling as if they'd been robbed of certain pleasures and opportunities.

This last was Maon's choice. He had felt enslaved to the laws and commands of Jehovah Elohim. He saw the Hebrew law as nothing more than a means of manipulating his life. He languished under the holiness of Jehovah and had struggled against it until he'd finally broken free and fled to the gods of the Philistines.

But it was one thing to be born under the stricture and morality of the Philistine way of life and another to step down to it. For whatever Maon may say, the law of Jehovah promoted a higher morality, a higher value system than what existed for the Philistines. Those Philistines who never knew differently did not feel the burden of this descent. Maon did.

David could read it all in his brother's eyes. Something profound had changed in Maon's soul. It was scarred and injured. Maon bore the price of his abandonment of Jehovah. He was less, and even if he didn't recognize this fact, he carried himself as if he was less.

David had met a few men and women from other nations who had turned to Jehovah, the Hebrew God. For them, they had stepped up to a higher sense of purpose and existence. They didn't carry the burden of abandonment of their old way of life. They carried a sense of renewal and purpose unlike anything they had ever had before.

One of David's own ancestors, Ruth the Moabitess, was such a person. David had heard the stories—how Ruth had abandoned her old way of life, proclaiming that Naomi's God would be her God and Naomi's people would be her people.[1] She had adopted a stricter, narrower way of life, but one that promoted a higher purpose.

Ruth had been fully accepted into the Hebrew way of life. For all intents and purposes, she was a Hebrew. But for all of Maon's efforts, the Philistines would never see him as one of them. To them, he would always be the Hebrew traitor—never trusted, never fully accepted.

And Maon knew it.

David stared into those haunted eyes and saw despair. Maon flinched and looked to the priest of Dagon. "Aye, this is my brother. This is David."

---

[1] Ruth 1:16.

The priest's eyes lit up with fervor. "Blessed be the great god Dagon who has delivered our enemy into our hands! Have him over the altar! I will carve his heart out this moment!"

David stiffened, panic flooding his body. He tried to resist, but his body had been too badly abused. He lacked the strength, but then mental resolve asserted itself, forcing his fear aside. If he was to die this moment, then he would do so with a prayer to Jehovah on his lips. He would never give these dogs the satisfaction of watching him beg for mercy.

Maon stepped close to the priest. "Do not be hasty, O Hand of Dagon. Should we not bring him before the king?"

The priest spat to one side. "Even King Achish bows before Dagon, blasphemer!"

"Aye," Maon agreed softly, staring at David. "But would the king be so forgiving if you robbed him of the chance to watch as you rip out the heart of his enemy? And what of the high priest of Dagon? Would you risk the wrath of them both? Pray tell, what happened to the last man who defied the high priest?"

The under-priest hesitated. No doubt Maon painted a grim picture, though David could not completely comprehend it. But he could guess. If rumors were true at all, then neither the king nor the high priest of Dagon would be kindly disposed toward anyone who defied their will.

"Very well," the priest relented. "But I will be the one to present our enemy before our king." He turned and began walking toward the temple entrance. "Bring him," he commanded over his shoulder.

As the two soldiers began dragging him away, David began laughing again, weakly, but a laugh that still bore the edge of hysteria to it.

Behind him, Maon followed, his eyes troubled and haunted. Whether it was over David's plight or his own, David knew not. He wasn't even sure he cared. He realized now that coming to Gath had been a mistake. If he was to survive, he would need to keep his wits about him, but he couldn't help himself. He kept on laughing.

— 97 —

10

King Achish sat upon his opulent and padded throne, his rotund body looking decidedly out of place among a court full of beautiful women and muscular men. If the king felt any discomfort from being the only fat man in the room, he didn't show it as he greedily tore meat off the bones of some roasted fowl and ate nosily. Between large bites, he eyed David as the Hebrew warrior was dragged in before him.

But if there was one thing about Achish that stood out to David, it was the man's intellect. He had no doubt that the Philistine king was the most dangerous man in the entire city. The two had met only once, before the battle when David had slain the three Philistine champions on the Shephelah plain. But that one meeting had convinced David of the man's cunning and eloquence as he had pushed hard to turn David against King Saul.

David was thrown to the cobbled floor. Still exhausted from his ordeal, he lacked the strength to pull himself upright. He lay before the throne, breathing heavily. His toe ached, sending lances of pain up his leg every time it had brushed the ground. Cracked ribs protested every breath he took, and his spine felt bruised from the giant's kick.

The king paused in his eating long enough to look at the pathetic figure sprawled before him. He glanced at the smug under-priest who stood over David. "What is this?"

"This is your enemy, O king! Is not this David the king of the land of Israel? Did not the Hebrew women sing one to another of him in dances, saying, Saul hath slain his thousands, and David his ten thousands?"[1]

David remembered the song the women had sung of his praises. *How had the Philistines known of it? Had Maon told them?* David gnawed at his lower lip, fear hammering at the edges of his mind.[2] If he didn't do something soon, he would surely be sacrificed on the altar of Dagon.

Achish frowned at the pathetic figure sprawled before him. "Surely this is not the same man who slew our champions."

A desperate plan formed in David's mind. He returned the king's look, but as if seeing right through the man. He grinned suddenly and forced saliva into his dry mouth and then let it drool out the corner of his lips, stained with blood. The slobber seeped into his beard.[3] Slowly, as if finding his situation humorous, he began to laugh.

Achish flinched at the sound, for it was laced with hysteria and madness. "What is this?" the portly king demanded, rising to his feet, food forgotten.

The court fell silent except for David's laughter. Still prone, he began scratching at the cobbled stones, until blood left crude designs on the floor. "I killed them," he whispered through his laughter. "I am king. I killed them all."

The Philistine king looked at the priest of Dagon in disgust. "This man is mad! Why have you brought him to me?"[4]

The priest's face clouded. "This is surely David, my king." He pointed to Maon. "This man has testified this to be true and claims kinship with the man before you."

The king glanced inquiringly at Maon. David's brother nodded with a respectful bow. Achish then turned to the high priest of

---

[1] 1 Samuel 21:11.
[2] 1 Samuel 21:12.
[3] 1 Samuel 21:13.
[4] 1 Samuel 21:14.

1 Samuel 21:10-15

Dagon who stood behind the throne when the king held court. For while the high priest was the ultimate power when it came to things pertaining to their gods, the king held absolute sway over all other matters. In court, the high priest served as adviser and provided counsel. And Ahuzzath the high priest was not pleased. One look at the man's face proclaimed as much.

"What counsel do you give?" Achish asked the high priest.

Ahuzzath glared at the lesser priest who had presumed to bring the enemy of the Philistines to the king without first informing his superior. He let his eyes drift to the giggling man who scrabbled pitifully at the stones and then said to the king, "The man is touched by the gods, my king. If this truly is David, our enemy, then the gods have claimed him as their own, and we may not slay him."

Hope surged through David at these words, but he dared not let it show on his face. He whispered, loud enough to be heard, but not clearly understood, "Darkness came and feasted with the light, while shadow served upon a platter the sun and moon. They were brothers, these three. My brother!" he surged to his feet and leaped toward Maon who jerked away violently. "My brother!"

David fell back to the stones, giggling and scratching with bloody fingers at the stones, drawing crude designs of unfathomable meaning.

"Behold, my king," Ahuzzath proclaimed. "The man is mad. His mind belongs to the gods, and thus the vessel is holy."

The under-priest looked ready to eat a thorn bush. "Should we not sacrifice him to Dagon? Is this not your promise made before this assembly of Philistines?"

The high priest scowled, matching that of his underling. "Heed well your words, Kenaz! It may be *your* heart I carve from your body."

David's captor paled, but he clearly wasn't ready to give up on sacrificing David. "He carried the sword of Goliath. Call the giants. They will bring testimony. We must sacrifice this man to Dagon."

Achish sat back down on his throne, his face dark. "Have I need of madmen in my presence? Shall this man come any longer in my house?"[5] He pointed to the under-priest. "Take him away. Cast him into prison if you must but bring him no more before me."

The priest hesitated, obviously torn by the desire to kill David and claim the glory of bringing down Philistia's enemy and obeying the king. Ahuzzath, the high priest, nodded, his eyes alight with cunning. "This man belongs to the gods, and you, Kenaz, will attend him." With a gleeful grin, the high priest advanced on the under-priest. "The gods have brought him to you, so it will be you who sees to his needs. Every word uttered is word from the gods, and you will faithfully record them lest any mystery be lost. Do you understand, Kenaz?"

The under-priest bowed, his body shaking with anger, but his eyes never left the muttering, giggling Hebrew scrawling bloody marks on the stones. "This is your will?" he demanded, keeping his head bowed.

"It is. Heed carefully all the words spoken by this mad fellow, for in such words do the gods speak to us." The high priest paused as if thinking. "If the gods relent and restore his mind, bring him to me, and I will allow you to offer his heart to Dagon."

"I thank you, my lord."

Ahuzzath smiled tightly. "But until such a time, take heed to each word so that we may more closely know the mind of our gods. Who can say what we may learn?"

Kenaz bowed again. "I will obey."

"Truly," the high priest said, his voice bleeding ominous finality.

The priest Kenaz gestured to the two warriors who had escorted David to the palace. "Take him."

They jerked David back to his feet, where he hung limply between them. Drool dripped from the corner of his mouth and white spittle stained his beard. He giggled again to cement the notion that he was mad and wondered if he was truly insane for even considering such a scheme.

---

[5] 1 Samuel 21:15.

Kenaz looked at the portly king and bowed. "With your leave, my king."

Achish his mouth full, grunted and waved his permission for the priest to withdraw. David was dragged away, his laughter rising in pitch and intensity.

His captors threw David into a dark hole. He hit the ground and rolled over, smearing his body with mud and other refuse. He had never before seen a prison, but he'd heard of them. This one had been dug into the side of the hill upon which the city had been built. The walls and ceiling were all rocky dirt and a gate had been fixed firmly in the narrow opening. The pit reeked of excrement and, the floor was a morass of muddy dirt mixed in with things best left unmentioned.

The gate was lashed into place, leaving only a bit of light to filter through the cracks in the closely fitted wood. It was enough for David to make out some of his surroundings. It brought no comfort. There was only one way in and one way out.

He closed his eyes, trying to suppress his rising fear of tight places. He shuddered, trying hard to imagine himself back at his father's table, laughing and teasing his younger nephews. He wished for his harp and to hear the thrumming notes as the strings vibrated. And here, at his lowest, in a pit of slime and excrement that served as a prison of his enemies, he prayed desperately, his chest constricting in both pain and fear. Worse than any beating, worse than the threat of death was this lonely, shallow pit.

How long he prayed, he had no idea. Prayer served as his only barrier from descending into true madness. His body was torn, ill-used, and exhausted. His mind hovered on the brink of rational thought and sheer insanity. Nothing in his life had prepared him for this moment, and his only shield, his only refuge was Jehovah Elohim.

He clung to his God as to a lifeline in a stormy sea. Surrounded by enemies, hunted by a man he loved, and separated from his most trusted companion, he was still not alone. Something of Jehovah's presence began to fill the small prison, bringing peace and clarity, easing some of his pain, and driving back the fear. The LORD's presence was the only thing that helped him step away from the edge of true madness.

And with rational thought came hope. Somehow, he needed to escape this prison. But how? The only thing keeping him alive was the fact that the Philistines thought him mad. For the moment, he would need to continue the deceit, and hopefully, an opportunity would present itself.

David took a long shuddering breath, trying to calm his mind and prepare himself for the ordeal ahead. He would escape this small prison. He would return to his home and his family. Rolling over to hands and feet, he crawled through the muck to the gate. The faint light acted as a beacon to him, and he sought it hungrily. Searching, he found a crack bigger than the others, but when he put his eye to it, he could see little—only a hazy white that might be a building or a person for all he could tell.

He scratched at the crack in vain, trying to widen it.[6] Someone kicked the gate from the other side, causing David to jerk back, startled.

"Enough of that," came a muffled voice. So, someone stood guard without.

David effected a giggle for the benefit of the guard and sidled up to the gate. He began scratching and muttering under his breath. No one else would understand the inarticulate words—certainly, not through the gate—but in truth, David's muttering was a prayer to Jehovah, seeking deliverance and strength.

The guard on the other side kicked the gate again, and David laughed, scratching harder with already raw and bloody fingers. Cursing in disgust, the guard walked away.

David studied the gate with his hands. It was fastened in such a way that it fit into place over the hole to the prison pit. He could find no lock or hinges to get at from his side. The wood felt thick,

---

[6] 1 Samuel 21:13.

and David doubted he could kick or ram it open. Iron bands had been used to bind the timbers together, making it even less likely that it would yield to mere human strength.

His stomach rumbled, reminding him he had eaten nothing since that morning. His mouth felt like he'd been sucking on wool, and he knew he'd need water before food—and soon. But based on the sun's position before he'd been thrown into the pit, night would soon be upon the land, and he doubted the Philistines would care enough to bring him something to eat or drink before morning.

A groan from behind brought David around, his battle instincts rising. He wasn't alone in the prison! He heaved himself to his feet, muscles and joints protesting, toe screaming as he put weight on it. A wave of exhaustion and dizziness nearly sent him back into the mud, but he held his feet and waited for his head to clear.

Hidden within the darkness of the pit, he sensed someone else watching him. Perhaps more than one. He scanned the dark recesses of the cave, straining to see against the darkness, but if there was someone back there, he was shrouded in darkness.

Another groan came, and a faint whisper, "Water…"

David turned toward the sound and took a step in the direction he thought it may have come from. Three more steps, and he nearly stumbled over a huddled form half buried in the mud. Kneeling, David bent close, straining to see. The little light that remained revealed an old man covered in slime and mud. Only one other detail of the man gradually became evident in the dim light. The man's eyes had been burned out of his head.

David took a sharp intake of breath. He'd heard of this. The Philistines had done something similar to Samson many years ago.[7] Instead of immediately sacrificing Samson to their gods, they had made a spectacle of him by blinding him and then parading him in front of mobs of Philistine men and women.[8]

Some stories claimed that Jehovah had returned his strength to him even as the Philistines were preparing to sacrifice him to Dagon.

---

[7] Judges 16:21.
[8] Judges 16:25.

Others hinted that he was the entertainment at a great sacrifice to Dagon—but not the sacrifice himself. Whatever the truth, Samson had pulled down the building, sacrificing himself to slay nearly three thousand Philistines at one time.[9]

For the second time in his life, David was struck with the parallels between Samson and himself. Both had become enemies of the Philistines, and both had been captured. David wondered if they would put out his eyes as well. He shuddered. Death would be a better fate than living as a blind slave to the Philistines. Samson, at the end, had chosen rightly after living a life that sharply verged from the laws of Jehovah. David vowed not to become like Samson in either life or death.

Swallowing bile that had risen into his mouth, he addressed the old man, "Say again, old one?"

"Water..." the fellow croaked.

David stared at the man helplessly. "I have none." He glanced around in the hopes that their captors may have left some vessel, but he could see nothing. "There is none."

The old prisoner made sucking noises that might indicate he was trying to lick his lips with a swollen tongue. David bent close to hear. "Water...wall," the old man croaked out.

Water wall? Baffled, David sat back. What could the old man mean? He glanced around again. He could see nothing. Was there water by one of the walls? Getting up, he reached out until he found the nearest wall and then began working his way along it, feeling with hands and feet for a jug or pitcher—anything that might contain water. He froze when his hand slid across something wet. Growing excited, he moved his hands up, seeking the source of the damp wall.

It took time, but he found a small crevasse about head high where water seeped out and then ran along the wall. Returning to the old man, he fetched a long piece of straw he remembered feeling near the other prisoner. This he stuck into the crack at a downward

---

[9] Judges 16:27, 30.

1 Samuel 21:10-15

angle, and then he waited, hands cupped beneath. Finally, a drop of water hit his dirty palm.

Somewhere nearby, a well had been dug and the water had found its way into the prison cell. Most likely, the guards expected him to drink this. And he would do so gladly. Drops started falling from the end of the straw in a steady pattern. He cupped his dirty hands until he had enough to wash away most of the grime. Then, once he had another handful, he hastened back to the old man and gently poured water into the other prisoner's mouth, dribbling it in as slowly as he had gathered it. David could hear the old man's throat working violently as he tried to drink.

"Not too fast," he cautioned the blind man. "Slowly. Slowly."

He made several trips for the blind man and then took the time to gather enough water to satisfy his own immediate thirst. By then, darkness had fallen completely, and he had to make his way blindly back to the old man's side.

"I thank you," the blind man said in his raspy voice. From his accent, David judged the man to be an Edomite.

"You are far from home," David observed.

"Aye. Very far."

"How long have you been in here?" David asked, suspecting that the guards outside had completely forgotten they had a prisoner. He wouldn't put it past the Philistines to toss someone in here and then let the person slowly starve to death.

"Time matters little here," the man rasped. "I was once a merchant. Not prosperous, perhaps, but well off enough that my children lacked for little. I came here to trade." He swallowed. "My youngest daughter traveled with me to seek a husband. We'd heard there were many powerful and wealthy Philistines." His voice broke, and he fell silent.

David put a hand on the man's filthy shoulder. "Say no more, old one. I can guess the rest." Indeed, he could. The Philistines doubtless had seen the beauty of the man's daughter and had either taken her to be sacrificed to Dagon or one of their other abominable gods, or she had been sold into slavery. It was a common enough

— 106 —

practice, and a person had to be either wealthy enough or powerful enough to prevent it.

The old man had probably thought he was wealthy enough, but apparently this had not been true. When he had resisted, they had put his eyes out and thrown him in this prison.

The broken old man sobbed quietly for a time, and David sat silently beside him, wondering if he too would end up blind and broken.

David lost track of time. He sat there for hours, likely, with nothing to see and the only thing to listen to was the ragged breathing of the old, blind man as he slept fitfully at David's knees. In a way, the darkness was a blessing. He could not see the walls of his prison, so he could imagine it larger than it was. By this means, he kept a firm grip on his fear. But eventually exhaustion took over, and he fell into a restless sleep.

A shout brought David awake, his heart pounding violently. A light flared through the cracks in the gate, and David came to his feet, muscles and joints protesting. Disorientated, he crouched like an animal, his face twisted into a mask of feral anger and fear. Mud clung to him in clumps, weighing him down.

The gate was pulled away from the opening of the pit and David squinted, blinded by the brilliant light that filled the opening. A dark shape stood before the light, regarding the bedraggled creature crouched at the back of the pit.

"Come, my brother," the figure said.

David shaded his eyes with one hand. "Maon? Is it truly you?"

"Aye, David." Maon moved into the pit, picking his way carefully across the muck and grime until he stood over David. His voice dropped low. "Truly, this madness of yours is but an act." He studied David. "Then again perhaps not, for you have truly fallen to a low estate, brother. Tell me, why have you come to this city?"

David crouched even lower, conscious of his appearance. He considered telling Maon nothing, but then realized that if he truly wished to escape Gath, he would need help. Maon would be his best—no, his only option. He lost nothing by telling the truth. "I flee from King Saul. An evil spirit has beset him, and he is convinced I am his enemy. I fled here…seeking to hide until the king's wrath abated."

"Perhaps not the wisest of choices," Maon murmured, chuckling without humor. "Why would you flee to your enemies?"

"As you say, perhaps not the wisest course."

Maon's grin looked evil to David. "And where is your God now, my brother?"

David scowled, but the intended effect was lost upon his grinning brother. "He is still with me. It is not He who failed, but I."

"A truly humble answer. Well then, you should know, the Philistines believe their gods have delivered you into their hands. They also believe you have been touched by them—and such is their belief with all those who are mad. They will listen to your words but be warned—if they do not hear the voice of their gods in you, they will slay you without thought."

"I understand."

"Do you? Then you are more remarkable than I took you for. Come. We will clean you up for the priests have no wish to wallow in filth to hear the voice of their gods."

David gestured to the sleeping figure at his feet. The old, blind man hadn't awakened during the conversation. "What of this one? Can you not bring him some food?"

Maon glanced down at the still form. "He is dead. What need has he of food now?"

David looked at the old man and saw it was true. Sometime during the night, the old Edomite had died, and David hadn't even noticed.

Standing upright, David took a deep shuddering breath, knowing that the next few hours would likely determine if he would share the old man's fate.

11

onathan intercepted Doeg, forcing the scruffy Edomite to pull up short in surprise. He watched in amusement as the red-headed man's hand went instinctively to a nicked and rusty knife belted at his waist. "And would you draw a weapon on the king's son?" Jonathan asked in a low voice that nevertheless carried both real and imagined threats.

Doeg snatched his hand away as if bitten by a snake. "Nay, my lord!" He stumbled back, trying to offer an awkward bow.

They stood down the hill from King Saul's house, surrounded by small, narrow houses owned by the citizens of Gibeah. The hard-packed dirt road ran up the incline directly to the main gate of Saul's house atop the hill. Jonathan had seen the Edomite coming, and knowing that the surly herdsmen would not come before King Saul unless summoned or having obtained information he believed would earn him a reward, Jonathan had hastened to stop the man.

"What news brings you away from your duties, herdsman?" the king's son demanded.

Doeg's eyes shifted, refusing to linger long on Jonathan. "I have news of the son of Jesse," he said reluctantly.

Jonathan's heart began to pound. *News of David?* He instinctively knew he needed to hide this from his father. But how? And what did the Edomite know? The herdsman had been out of the city for quite some time, so it was doubtful that he had time to

1 Samuel 21:10-15

learn much of the latest news regarding David, but the city was alive with gossip. Doeg would have surely heard something of the strife that existed between the king and David. "And," Jonathan began, "you think it worthy enough to bother the king? How is it that you leave your herds to bring this news to the king? Could you not have sent a messenger? Perhaps you seek a reward?" He took slow steps forward, crowding the Edomite, who shuffled backward uncomfortably. "Answer me, O king of the fleas!" Jonathan barked.

Doeg stiffened at the insult, but he bowed again, hiding the anger that had lit his eyes. "Nay, my prince," he sniveled. "I have left the herds in capable hands—"

"Then you are needed no longer?" Jonathan cut in, filling his voice with scorn. "If there are others more capable, why are you chief herdsman?"

Doeg blanched. "I—I—"

"I know your heart, dog," Jonathan pressed, refusing to give the herdsman a chance to regain his equilibrium. "You seek to rise above your station. My father may have been mistaken to give you, a stranger in Israel, authority over cattle. Why should a dog be king over horses? It is unnatural."

Unable to stop himself, Doeg's eyes shot up to latch upon Jonathan's face. Hatred flared in those evil orbs. For just a moment, Jonathan wondered if he had pushed the herdsman too far, but no, a moment later, the other's eyes again slid away, hidden in another deep bow. "I beg your forgiveness," the Edomite said, his voice full of false humility. "I but thought news of the son of Jesse was of import. Perhaps I believed in error."

Jonathan folded his arms and sneered. "You believe much in error, I am sure. What could you know, Edomite?"

Doeg's body stiffened, keeping himself in a half bow. "I beheld the son of Jesse coming to Nob. He sought the aid of the priests there, and they did give him bread for a journey."

Jonathan affected a bored posture. "That is all? What of it? You think this news alone is worthy of abandoning your duty to bring word personally to the king? You are slothful, herdsman. Perhaps

— 110 —

this is what my father should learn. He would be well pleased to know of your dereliction, I am sure."

"Nay!" Doeg swallowed. "Word has reached my ears that the king seeks the son of Jesse. I saw him but four days ago. Should I hide this from the king?"

"Have you no underlings to send? This is not of such import as you suppose. Four days ago? The son of Jesse could be anywhere. You are lax, herdsman. Come. Let us tell my father of this laxity." Jonathan gave the now fearful herdsman his best cold stare. "He will be ill pleased to have to choose a new chief herdsman in these dark days. Come." Jonathan started to walk up the street, but only took two steps before turning back around. Doeg hadn't moved. The Edomite looked appropriately frightened, standing rock still, his eyes as wide as a coney's.

"Nay," the frightened man whispered, "I should not intrude upon the king. You are most correct, my prince—I am negligent. I must return to my duties immediately. I beg you, take my news to the king." He hesitated, a glimmer of greed creeping into his eyes. "I pray you, tell him who brought this news."

Jonathan shrugged. "As you wish. Begone, maggot. I have no liking for your face."

Fighting to keep his hatred from showing, the herdsman bowed again and scurried away toward the city gates. Jonathan watched him go, heaving a sigh of relief when the Edomite disappeared from view. That had been too close. His father would not like this news. He had sent scouts out across the land seeking to discover David's hiding place. No one had even thought to send someone to the priests at Nob. Saul kept the priests there somewhat isolated as if he didn't trust them, and Nob was too close to Gibeah to be a safe place for David to turn. In this case, it had worked to David's advantage. His trail was still hidden. Where he might have gone from there was anyone's guess, but it was good to know that he was safe, even if the news was four days old.

Turning, Jonathan started toward his own house. These days, his home felt foreign to him. His father's obsession with David weighed upon him, but recently, his mother had begun to exert pressure and questions as to why he yet had no child, no heir of his own. His wife had yet to conceive, and though that troubled her more than it did Jonathan, her anxiety and tension with his mother had begun to affect him in recent days. And he missed David— missed him with a yearning he had not believed possible.

Three people stood outside his door, talking softly. Well, two of them were talking while the third stood slightly away with his arms folded. Adriel looked up as Jonathan approached, his handsome face relaxing. "Perhaps you can talk sense into your sister," he blurted, gesturing sharply at Michal.

"What's this?" Jonathan asked.

"Merab and I have offered to take Michal into our house until such a time as David returns. But she is stubborn."

Nothing new there. Jonathan turned a steely eye on his sister, weary of more strife. "I know why you would forego such hospitality. A woman alone in the city is surely safe from scrutiny and bother. All women should cast off their family's hospitality."

Michal returned his look with one even more flat. "I am not staying in my home, my brother. Until my husband returns, I would remain in my father's house. My place is here."

Jonathan glanced at the third individual. Captain Phalti stood stony-faced, trying hard to pretend he couldn't hear the conversation. Jonathan didn't know him well. The man had proven himself in battle and recently had been promoted. He was a Benjamite, and that lineage was what mattered most to King Saul these days.

Phalti noticed the look and bowed low. "I await your brother, my lord. We have been tasked with discovering David's haunts and whereabouts." He spoke softly, clearly knowing the love that Jonathan bore for David. But despite the tense feelings that rose up at his words, Jonathan noted that the other man carried himself well. Nearing middle age and graying slightly at the temples, he projected strength and solidarity.

"This is why I must remain in my father's house," Michal interrupted. "I must stop this madness. My husband needs to be reconciled to my father, not hunted down."

Jonathan agreed. He eyed the shorter captain. "When did my father order this?"

"This morning," Phalti said. He bowed to Michal, looking contrite. "I apologize if I am the cause of your trouble, my lady. I but follow the command of my king."

Michal's lips firmed, and she declined to answer him. He was beneath her. Jonathan held no enmity against the captain. He was only doing his duty. Sometimes, however, duty weighed more than the world itself. But Jonathan liked little the duty placed upon the captain's shoulders. If he could, he would deliver David out of the captain's hands, and he suspected that Phalti knew this.

Jonathan was not completely convinced that his father's desire to kill David went deeper than the influence of the evil spirit that afflicted the king. He harbored a hope that it would pass, and David would be able to return in peace. But his friend would need to stay alive until such a time.

Adriel looked conflicted. "My sister," he said to Michal, "I beg you. Return to my house and join your sister, my wife. Your presence here will but remind your father of his anger toward your husband."

"Not so," she disagreed. "I must be here. This is my place." She gave no other reason, but Jonathan suspected that she had several hidden motives behind her decision.

"Your husband is a fugitive," Adriel snapped, irritated. "Would you watch as he is captured and killed before your eyes?"

"Were you not tasked with such a deed?" she retorted, eyes like two dark rocks.

Adriel recoiled, and Jonathan stiffened. He had heard what the king had ordered his friend to do. Though he didn't blame Adriel, a spark of distrust had been born between them.

"And what," Adriel said softly, "would you have had me to do differently? I did what I could."

— 113 —

Michal sniffed, turning away. "Your presence makes me unclean. I need to purify myself." She stormed away. Such storming was an artform she had perfected over the years.

Adriel looked after her sadly, but Jonathan gave his sister a silent cheer. Still, something about her insistence in staying near their father bothered him. He didn't believe it was because she loved David, and that was the core of the problem. He shivered.

Then Ishui marched up. His scarred face and hands reflected the sunlight, giving him the appearance of being all angles and lines. He frowned at his older brother, gesturing to Phalti. "Come, Captain, we must begone."

Jonathan stepped close. "To hunt David?"

Ishui didn't back down a hairsbreadth. If anything, he crowded even closer, their noses nearly touching. "Aye," he growled, "I go to hunt the treacherous dog wherever he may be."

"To what end?" Jonathan demanded, unimpressed with his brother's aggressive stance.

"To slay him, as our father commands."

"You are a leech, Ishui. You seek David to try your hand against him in battle. Speak. Is this not so?"

"And if it be?" Ishui shrugged, grinning. "I care not what the reason. The son of Jesse must die. I will see the deed done if I may."

Jonathan relaxed and a grin claimed his lips. "This should not be too difficult of a task for you, brother. David is surely easy prey. He but defeated four of the Philistine champions, three at once, the other but a small giant. And all do know that the Philistines choose mere fledglings to champion them, boys but days away from their mother's skirts. Aye, you will prevail with ease, of this I am sure."

Ishui's face was a study in conflict. All knew of David's true prowess in battle, and despite his bluster, Ishui didn't truly think he could match the son of Jesse in a fair fight. In truth, if David killed Ishui, Jonathan would lose little sleep over it. His only worry was that if such an end came to pass, reconciliation between Saul and his friend would be impossible.

Backing up in the face of Jonathan's confidence, Ishui turned away and snapped at Phalti, "Gather the men. We leave immediately."

Phalti bowed first to Ishui and then to Jonathan. "As you command, my lord." He turned and marched away, his face smooth, revealing little of what he truly thought. Jonathan marveled at the captain. Few would have been so calm in the face of the task set before him.

Ishui gave his brother a final sneer. "I will find David, my brother, and I will slay him. Mark my words."

"They are marked," Jonathan growled back. "And know, that should this come to pass as you say, there will be a reckoning…brother."

Ishui grinned wickedly. "I look forward to it."

12

The smell of death filled the prison pit. The Philistines had left the decaying body of the old Edomite, so David had tried to bury the old man by pushing as much mud as he could over the body. It stifled the smell somewhat, but he knew that unless someone took care of the corpse soon, it would only get worse, and his own health would be at risk.

But he dared not complain, for that would only prove his sanity, and the only thing keeping him alive was the fact that the Philistines believed him mad. So, he spent long hours in the prison pit talking to the dead old man, laughing at imaginary jokes and conspiring with no one, all to keep those who listened at the door convinced he was insane.

Maon had made an appearance each of the last three days. He and two others would drag David out of the cell and throw him into a pool of water where two men unceremoniously scrubbed away the filth from his clothing, hair, and beard. He would then be hauled away to the temple near the city gate where the priest Kenaz would pretend to listen to his ramblings.

David knew that the young priest only did so to appease the high priest of Dagon. That Kenaz feared his superior was obvious, and that alone kept the priest from carving out David's heart. But the moment someone determined David wasn't mad, he would die.

During these strange visits to Dagon's temple, Maon had said nothing, and David had dared not try to strike up a conversation with his estranged brother. Maon watched with frosty, suspicious eyes, but then he watched everyone that way. His brother's unhappiness radiated off him in waves. Whatever Maon had been looking for when he had gone over to the Philistines and their gods, he still hadn't found it.

Sighing, David picked at the mud beneath where he sat, pushing it one way and then another with his hand. Finally, he settled back against the driest wall and closed his eyes. Even insane people needed to sleep. His stomach growled, reminding him of his acute hunger. His toe, ribs, and muscles continued to ache and randomly shoot sharp stabs of pain through his body. He'd lost weight over the last three days, and his ribs had begun to show. If this continued, he'd not have the strength to attempt an escape.

And he still sought a way to escape. Each time they'd dragged him from the pit, hope surged within, thinking that an opportunity to flee would present itself. It never did. He had to continue to act mad, spitting, ranting, and laughing in an unnatural high-pitched tone, but for some reason, his madness only made his captor's vigilance even stronger.

The only thing he could do was pray. He spent long hours in prayer when his guards believed him asleep. He earnestly wished for a Hebrew priest, for he honestly didn't know if Jehovah would hear his prayers without first going to an intercessor. But something deep within hoped He did. So, he prayed.

He began another silent prayer, determined to pray until exhaustion tumbled him into another fitful sleep. He could see nothing in the pit, for night lay over the land without, and if any guards were beyond the prison gate, they hadn't lit any lamps or torches. The darkness was absolute.

Closing his eyes helped convince him the darkness was his own decision and not beyond his control. It also helped him to imagine the dark room larger than it was. He continually had to fight back his fear of enclosed places. Trying as best he could to even out his breathing, he began to pray, begging Jehovah for forgiveness and for aid.

Iron scraping against iron roused him from his reverie. His eyes snapped open. A beam of light moved erratically between the cracks in the heavy wooden gate. Then the door was leveraged aside, and David raised a hand to protect his eyes from the sudden brilliant light that flooded his cell.

He squinted against the glare, trying to see beyond to the dark figure holding the torch, but his sensitive eyes couldn't make out anything. A voice spoke, "Come, David, it is time to leave this place."

David rose slowly to his feet, keeping a hand outstretched to block out the stinging light. "Maon?" he asked in a hoarse whisper.

"Aye. It is I."

The torch moved aside as Maon stepped back from the entrance to the prison pit, revealing the sharp features of his brother. Maon looked determined, something David hadn't seen in his brother in a long time, and he wondered at it.

Belatedly, David realized he should be playing the role of a madman, but he didn't have the strength to continue the charade. He needed a respite. Even a madman could be overcome with exhaustion.

Maon took a step forward and gestured to the open door. "Come, we must hurry."

"To what end, Maon? I grow weary of you and of the priests of Dagon."

David spotted a tight smiled that tweaked the corners of Maon's mouth. "I knew your madness was feigned, brother. Your speech does now betray you."

"I am weary. If Jehovah has ordained this to be my end, then so be it." David let strength fill his voice. "But know that I shall never betray my God. If I go to the grave, I will await my salvation, for the LORD will not leave my soul in hell. My flesh shall rest in hope, but one day, I shall behold His face."[1]

Maon regarded him stoically in the lamplight. Finally, he nodded. "It is as I thought. Be of good cheer, brother. I seek not to take your life from you this day. In the stead, I seek to save it. Come. I will see you out of the city at once. From there, your precious God will need to sustain you."

David blinked at his erstwhile brother in confusion. "What is this you say?"

Losing his patience all together, Maon reached out and grabbed David by the arm and began dragging him to the exit. "We must hurry!"

David let himself be dragged out into the night. He instinctively glanced up at the stars, marking their current position. Three hours yet remained before the false dawn began a gradual lightening of the sky.

"Linger not!" Maon hissed.

The renegade Hebrew dragged his muddy, filthy brother down the street toward the same gate David had entered upon his arrival at the city days ago.

Light escaped from a few windows here and there, but only the stars and the three-quarter moon cast any light on their surroundings. Maon hurried him along, his flickering torch casting dancing shadows on the walls of the buildings as they descended toward the city wall and freedom.

Hope swelled in David's heart as he limped along on his still injured toe. Suddenly a suspicion rose, warring for supremacy in his mind. At length, he tore his arm from his brother's grasp and put a dirty hand on Maon's clean tunic, bringing his brother up short. "Do you seek to betray me?" he asked.

Maon snorted. "You are already a prisoner, my brother. Eventually, the priests will see through your feigned madness and then they'll carve out your heart."

---

[1] Psalm 16:9-10.

David frowned. "Then why? Why free me?"

His older brother huffed and pulled David along. "Do not stop. We can speak as we go, but do not raise your voice. I would not that people take notice of us."

David followed his brother, but after a moment, he repeated, "Why free me?"

Maon cast him a contemptuous glance. "It is not because of any misplaced love, my brother. This I swear. But I fear that once they finish with you, they will have no more use for me. The Philistines cannot see my true worth. They seek only to know you, their greatest enemy, through me. When you are gone, I fear they will have no place for me." He gave David a tight grin. "So, you must escape and live so that I can continue to conspire with the Philistines how best to bereft you of your life. They will need my knowledge of you."

David found no humor in Maon's predicament. "To what end? What will become of you once I am no more?"

"By then, they may have seen my true worth and given me a place of honor among them." He looked away as they continued through the quiet town. "You know not what I have endured. Here, among them, I am still a Hebrew. The Philistines trust me not, but they need me."

"As long as I am their enemy?"

"Aye. I need more time to prove my allegiance. In time, perchance, I will wed one of their daughters. In that day, I will have found my place."

"I envy you not, my lost brother," David said softly, looking sadly at the religious tattoos on his brother's face. "You had a place once. You had a family that loved you."

Maon snorted. "It was no place for me. I have made my choice, and I regret it not."

David sensed the lie. "Do you not?"

Maon looked away, but not before David could see the pain in those orbs. "I do not," he affirmed, but without much conviction.

David said nothing further, content to follow his brother through the streets. Once, they hid in the shadows, their torch hastily quenched, as a patrol walked by without seeing them, the guards careless in the security of their own city.

Eventually, they reached the main gates. Two watchmen lingered atop the walls to either side of the gate. Maon shoved David deep into the shadows of the ironworks. Together, they studied the guards and the gate. David noted that the sentries would frequently look both ways, out beyond the gate into the surrounding countryside and back below them to see any movement from the streets. The latter was likely more of a gesture of reassurance, laying eyes on something familiar and safe. The real danger would be beyond the walls. But it did present a problem for the two brothers. The gates were closed and barred, and David doubted they could walk to them without being noticed.

"Here," Maon whispered, handing David a bundle. "Change your clothing."

David complied without a word. He found a fresh tunic inside along with a flask of water and some bread and cheese. His stomach rumbled the moment his nose caught a whiff of the food, but he forced himself away from the tantalizing smells. He could eat later.

He changed quickly and noticed ruefully that he was now dressed in an identical manner as Maon. The tunic was cut in the Philistine fashion that allowed for the padded and ribbed armor that would be wrapped around a Philistine warrior's torso. From a dark recess near a water barrel, Maon produced the leather-studded wrappings and began wrapping them around David's body.

"You wish me to appear as a Philistine warrior?" David remarked.

"Aye, the watchmen will be less likely to decorate your body with their arrows if they think you are one of their own." Maon produced a colorful headdress and affixed it David's head. "In the dark, they will not be able to tell the color, which is to your advantage. They will not shoot lest they inadvertently slay a tribesman from one of King Achish's own tribe. Such an act would earn them death. Their hesitation will be your only window of escape."

"They'll see me?"

"There is no other way." He offered David a spear. "This is all I could find. I could not take a sword without notice."

Taking the weapon, David fingered the smooth shaft. "This is a foolish plan, Maon."

The older brother laughed lightly. "You never liked my strategies."

"With good reason."

Ignoring that last remark, Maon pointed toward the base of the gates. "What do you behold there?"

David studied the dark area. Slowly he saw the faint outline of a smaller door or gate next to the larger one. "Is that a sally gate?"

"It is." Maon looked around nervously. "I bribed one of the watchmen to leave that gate unbarred. He believes I seek an advantage with the merchants encamped without the gate. I have promised him a portion of my profits."

"Will he not say something when it is discovered I am escaped and you have no profit to share with him? Will he not betray you?"

"Nay. It would mean his death. He will keep silent. Have no fear for me."

David gave his brother a sharp look. "I have none."

"Then it is well," Maon rejoined bitterly.

David wanted to say something else, but a trumpet blast cut through the air. David spun around to look back into the city from where the trumpet had been blown. He knew an alarm when he heard one.

Maon cursed. "They have discovered your escape! You must go. Now!" He shoved David ahead of him. "Run!"

Still exhausted from his long ordeal and with is toe still smarting abominably, he nevertheless summoned forth enough energy to half run, half stagger toward the sally gate. Maon ran out after him and yelled up at the watchmen, "What do you see? Is an enemy at the gate?"

Both of the watchmen had instinctively turned toward the sound of the trumpet, but with an authoritative voice shouting at them to watch for danger outside the gate—their primary duty—they spun away from the two men charging toward them to peer over the wall into the darkness beyond.

"There is nothing," one shouted back after a moment.

"Stay vigilant!" Maon shouted. "We're sending a scout to investigate. Hold your arrows!"

They reached the sally gate, and Maon lifted the single iron bar that secured it from the inside. He shoved the gate open with one hand, and it swung ponderously open.

David grabbed him by the shoulder. "Come with me!"

Maon shrugged himself out of David's grasp. "Nay. I can never return. I have made my choice. This is my place."

A roar of anger froze whatever argument David meant to offer. Both David and Maon spun back around to see two giants charging at them from the edge of the courtyard. He recognized them in the dim light. They were the same two who had captured David. One carried a torch raised high, and he could see their contorted faces as they charged toward the two brothers.

Maon cursed again, spun David about and thrust him hard through the sally gate. David, his body still not recovered from his ordeal, fell, hitting the rocky ground hard and rolling over several cubits. He gasped for breath and leveraged himself up to his elbows. He had to move, or he would die.

He looked up and saw his brother framed in the sally gate, his back turned to the two giants racing toward them from within. He opened his mouth to say something, but whatever it was never came out. A spear point suddenly blossomed in Maon's chest, driven completely through his body from a mighty throw by one of the giants. The huge spear nearly cut Maon in half.

Maon's eyes bulged, and one hand came up to grasp the iron spear head, but then all life faded from him, and he fell forward. The bloody spear point dug into the ground, keeping Maon's body

— 123 —

1 Samuel 21:10-15

partially upright on his knees. In the darkness, he looked like he was bowing in reverence over the spear haft.

Shocked beyond words, David could only stare at his brother's lifeless body. No words came as his mouth worked furiously. He found himself on his feet then, and he took one step toward his brother as if he could somehow save him.

A shout from one of the watchmen above reminded David that he had best flee. Turning away from Maon, he whispered one last benediction: "This too was for the good."

He then fled into the night, knowing that the giants would never be able to fit through the smaller sally gate. By the time they opened the main gates, David meant to be a long way away.

Tears stung his eyes, and he angrily brushed them away. He had long ago mourned his brother, and the animosity that existed between them was complicated. Maon had saved his life several times now while continuing to aid the Philistines. But too, many Hebrew women were widowed because of Maon's advice.

Maon was dead, but whatever his reasons for helping David at the last no longer mattered. He had helped David escape Gath. It was for that act that David chose to remember his brother. There at the end, Maon had meant to say something, but only Jehovah knew what. Maybe, just maybe, Maon had repented at the end. David could only hope.

13

David studied his backtrail. Since leaving Gath, he had spent more time hiding than running. Surprisingly, the Philistines had been relentless in their dogged pursuit. David didn't understand. The way King Achish had acted upon believing David was mad had convinced him that the Philistine ruler would be glad to be well rid of the Hebrew.

But that had not been the case or perhaps Kenaz, the priest of Dagon, was the one responsible for why three of Gath's finest scouts were doing their best to hunt David down and kill him. The more he thought on it, the more this seemed likely. Escaping had put the lie to his madness, and doubtless the priest of Dagon had been made to look a fool in front of his superiors.

But David had assumed they would turn back once they had entered Israel, but they had not. From his hiding place among the shadows of some trees, David watched as the three leading scouts cautiously edged out of the tree line from the other side of the Valley of Elah. Perhaps half an hour behind them marched nearly a dozen Philistine warriors, all bent on one thing—to kill David—and led by one of the giants.

The scouts were good. David had tried everything he could think of to shake them from his trail, but they had persevered, spending hours, if need be, to pick up his trail if they lost it.

— 125 —

The lead scout, one David had dubbed Sniffer, seemed part dog. He bent over the ground, his nose nearly touching the soil as he studied the dirt. Not well trained in the skill himself, David nevertheless knew what the Philistine was doing. He was looking for displaced dirt or bent grass blades, anything that would indicate a human had recently traveled that way.

David had led them to the same region where he had killed Goliath those years before. A few of the trenches that the Hebrews had dug on the northern hillside was all that remained of the fortifications that had been built to repulse the Philistines. The small brook that flowed through the valley ran close to the hillside there—the same brook David had gathered the stones that he had used to kill Goliath.

David had run upstream for some distance, before cutting across the valley to his current hiding place near the crest of the southern hills. He watched as Sniffer edged out of the trees, descending the slope until he led his fellow scouts to the edge of the brook. Not much water flowed during this time of year, but enough did that David had been able to replenish his supply of water and make it difficult for the scouts to follow him by jumping from rock to rock in the middle of the shallow wadi.

The scouts squatted by the edge of the stream, consulting with each other and pointing in various directions as if in a heated discussion. Finally, one of them stood, surveyed his surroundings, and then ran back up the slope and disappeared into the trees, presumably to report to the squad of warriors following behind.

David clutched his spear tightly, considering his next move. He might be able to take the two remaining men with ease, but to get to them, he would have to run back across the entire valley. He'd be seen long before he could close with them, and at least one carried a bow. There would be no guarantee that the third scout and the trailing squad of warriors wouldn't catch up even if he could make the dash across and dispatch the two waiting scouts.

Closing his eyes, he tried to picture the terrain around him. Bethlehem, his home, lay less than a day's journey almost directly east of where he hid. If he could reach the city, he would be safe within its walls from the Philistines, but then he would need to worry about King Saul. The moment the king learned of David's whereabouts, he would send more than a dozen men to end his life. No, he dared not go home. But where then?

There were a number of good-sized cities to the north, cities where he wasn't that well known. Perhaps he could flee to Bethshan or Lodebar. Even the residents of Jabesh-gilead would be unlikely to recognize him. Going north was an option, but not one David relished. He would be leaving his traditional homeland of Judah, and if he had allies anywhere, it would be among his native tribe of Judah.

He seriously considered going southeast to Hebron or maybe even farther south to Beersheba, the southernmost city in Judah. He irritably shook his head. No, he could not go to any city, not yet. King Saul would have sent spies to all the likely places David would flee to, and if not spies, then surely a reward for his death, capture, or whereabouts.

Which meant that the frontier cities along the Israel and Philistine border would be out of the question as well. He would likely be welcomed in Lachish or Mareshah, for he had defended them against Philistine incursions and deprecations when he was captain of over a thousand men, but it would only take one greedy man to report back to Saul, and David would be undone.

And after his experience in Gath, he was not willing to leave Israel again—not unless he had no other choice.

He drummed his fingers on the spear shaft, his eyes narrowing as he considered his options and watched the remaining two scouts split up, one going east and the other west along the brook edge, trying to pick up where David might have crossed. He was certain that they would eventually find his trail. Sniffer was too good a scout to be thrown for long.

Where to go? He had heard of caves around Adullam,[1] a small village of farmers somewhat to the south of David's position. The

---

[1] 1 Samuel 22:1.

village was remote enough that the Philistines typically ignored it as it wasn't worth the effort of reaching it just to slaughter a few farmers and sheep herders, and there was little plunder to be gained from the venture anyway. But the caves would be a likely place to hide from both the Philistines and from King Saul.

Yes, the caves would be a perfect place to hide. He felt better for having a plan, but he would first need to deal with the squad of Philistine warriors trying to track him down. Attempting to take them all on in a fight would be foolish. No, he needed to stay ahead of them and make them believe he had fled to a major city in Israel. Only then would they break off the pursuit and return to their own lands. He would make it look like he was headed to Bethlehem. That would make sense, and once they broke off, he could double back to the caves near Adullam.

Having decided on a plan, he moved out quickly from his hiding spot and headed east. Night was falling, and the darkness would give him the opportunity to put some distance between him and his pursuers.

By the afternoon of the next day, David looked upon the walled city of his hometown, Bethlehem. Not as fortified as Jerusalem, perhaps, and precariously situated on a natural invasion route, the medium-sized town had done well to repel invaders over the years. For David, it was simply home. This was his city. Rachel had died here, and Ruth the Moabitess had made a home here. Many of the fields and flocks that David looked upon belonged to his father, Jesse, once owned by David's great-grandfather, Boaz.

Glancing back, he could see nothing of the squad of Philistines persistently dogging his trail. He knew they were back there, and by now, they had to know he was headed to Bethlehem. But subtle signs had convinced him that the Philistines persisted. They hadn't turned back as he thought they would.

David studied the city. Two main gates, one to the east and the other to the west, gave public access to the city. The western gate was open, and the few guards on duty did not seem overly vigilant.

The gates hadn't always been guarded, but these were troubled times. Running his hand through his overgrown beard and shaggy hair, he figured few people in the city would recognize him. It had been years since he last made any sort of lengthy visit, and now that he was here, he yearned to discover how his family fared. He feared for them. King Saul wouldn't hesitate to bring harm to David's family if he thought it would lead to David's capture.

He hadn't intended to go into the city. He just wanted to convince his Philistine pursuers that he was going to the city so that they would break off their pursuit. But the need to see his parents and his brethren rose up within him like gathering clouds in the sky above.

With a last glance over his shoulder, David began a slow walk toward the city gate, careful to not put a lot of weight on his healing toe. He used his spear like a walking stick and made no effort to conceal his approach. A single spear-wielding Hebrew would not create too much of a stir. He had long since shed the Philistine armor and headdress his brother had given him and wore only the tunic and a castoff turban he'd found along the way, so he felt confident that he would go unchallenged. He would not be the only one who wore clothing cut in the Philistine fashion, and hopefully it would reinforce his appearance as a stranger.

The hills of Bethlehem were strewn with large rocks and low trees. Fields had been carved out where they could around the base of the hills and even along the gentler slopes, creating tiers of flat area where fruit and nut trees and vineyards grew. The grain waved in a strong breeze, and David realized that summer was fast nearing its end and the harvest would soon be upon them.

He crested one of the hills and found himself among a herd of sheep, the animals bleating their objection and darting away from the foul-smelling stranger in their midst. This, naturally, attracted the attention of the shepherd who stood up from where he had made a comfortable perch atop a slab of white rock that jutted out of the nearby hillside.

"Who goes there?" the young man shouted.

1 Samuel 22:1-3

David stopped, trembling. He knew that voice. He turned to look at the young man who stood cocksure atop his rock. A sling was held loosely in one well-muscled hand and a knife was belted around the man's waist. It had been years since David had seen him, and he had changed from a boy into a man since.

"Joab? Son of Zeruiah?" Zeruiah was Joab's mother's name, David's oldest sister.

Joab jumped down from his rock, landing lightly and well-balanced upon the balls of his feet as if he expected an attack from the stranger. David nodded in appreciation. Surely, his nephew had grown into a warrior true.

"Aye," Joab said. His voice, though deeper than David remembered it, maintained that tone of command that he used upon his younger brothers. "I am Joab. By what name do you lay claim, stranger? And how do you know me? Speak or you will taste Flinger's wrath!" He brandished his sling, twirling it slowly. David knew that in a fraction of a moment, the sling could be up to full speed and launch a projectile that could easily kill him.

"I know you, son of Zeruiah, because it is difficult to forget a face I have repeatedly beaten—and with ease. Behold me, Joab, do you not recognize me?"

Joab edged closer, his frown swallowed up in a carefully cultivated, but young, beard. The beard did little to hide a flat face and square jaw that distinguished Joab even during his boyhood. The dark skin, an inheritance from his father, glistened in the sunlight as he moved with fluid grace toward David.

David stood easy, letting Joab take his measure, and after a long moment, Joab's light-brown eyes lit up. "David? Is it truly you?"

"Aye, son of my sister. It is I."

Joab dropped his sling and in two bounds slammed into David, embracing him fiercely. "You live! We feared the worst!"

Taken back by the sudden display of affection from a youth he hadn't seen in years, David was momentarily at a loss to say anything. Joab pushed away and stared at David, looking him over with new eyes. David knew what his nephew saw, and he self-consciously tried

— 130 —

to smooth his wild beard, keenly aware of how he must look and smell.

"You are well?" Joab asked, the question dripping with concern.

"Aye," David replied, brushing aside all the unasked questions that obviously filled Joab to overflowing. "What news? What of my father and mother?"

Joab looked around, ensuring they were alone on the hillside. A cloudy sky cast a shadowless gray over everything, and when Joab looked back at David, he could see pain in his nephew's eyes. "Your father and mother are well. They hide in the city from King Saul."

David started violently. "Has the king sought to harm them?"

"Who can say? Word reached us of the king's search for you and his command that you be put to death. No one here understands it, David. You are the king's most loyal servant, so why should the king wish you slain? The elders of Bethlehem disbelieve the rumors that you wish to be king." Joab studied David's face, searching for some sign of the veracity of this rumor. "Is it true?"

David grunted and shook his head. "King Saul is the LORD's anointed. I would not lift up my hand against him—even to save my own life. It is false."

Joab nodded once, but David detected a small measure of disappointment in his nephew. "I understand. The elders of Bethlehem have kept your family hidden from the king. We know every stranger who comes to the gates of the city, and your father and mother are moved from house to house as necessary. They are not found by Saul's men."

David clapped a hand on Joab's shoulder, surprised at how his nephew had filled out. The young man fairly rippled with muscles, and David had no doubt that he was well practiced with both his sling and a sword. Joab had ever desired to be a warrior. "Will the sheep abide? If so, please take me to my father and mother."

Joab nodded and clapped David's shoulder with a free hand in return. "I will. The sheep will not stray if I return soon."

Turning, David's nephew raised his voice and called sharply to the sheep. The startled beasts snapped up their heads and stared at Joab, their easily frightened eyes wide. Joab called again in a warbling cry that David recognized as a danger signal. The sheep began to bunch together, bleating their distress.

"That should keep them from straying far until I return," Joab said. He shook his head as he picked up his sling. "Can't be forgetting Flinger."

"You've named your sling?"

"Out here," Joab said, gesturing to their surroundings, "it gets lonely. I bring my companions." He hefted the sling and his shepherd's staff. "Meet Flinger and Basher."

David gave his nephew a peculiar look.

Joab noticed and grinned. "I know what you're thinking. But you know how many times I've had to bash one of those stupid sheep to get it going in the right direction?"

"You're a horrible shepherd, Joab."

"Aye. But then I've never wanted to be a shepherd, David."

"I know. But we all do what must be done."

They started walking toward the city gate, and David had to force himself to walk at a steady pace, though every muscle in his body quivered to sprint to the gate and find his parents and brethren right then. The city remained much as David remembered it. Rachel's well still stood outside the main gates, and David longed for a drink of its water. Much of the water in Israel was brackish and had to be cut with wine to make it drinkable, but the water from that well was clean and the very thought of taking a drink from it brought back many of his childhood memories.

Shivering, he forced himself to walk at an even pace. "What of my brothers and sisters?" he asked.

"All here. Even Abinadab. He forsook his captaincy when it became clear that even he had become suspect. He too hides in the city."

"What of the flocks and fields? Who is caring for them?"

"We do what we can. My brothers and I help, as you can see, and we are getting by, but it is precarious. Twice have I been questioned by the king's men." His chest puffed out. "I told them nothing."

David nodded, understanding his nephew's boast. The family was in danger, and only the kindness of the townspeople had succeeded in keeping everyone safe. Inter-tribal politics was only ever truly set aside when an enemy threatened all of Israel. Your tribe meant something, and David belonged to Judah—as did most everyone who lived in Bethlehem. And the king, despite being king over all Israel, was still a Benjamite. But David doubted this cat-and--mouse game could last, and the longer he was here, the more he put his family in danger. "Let us hurry," he urged.

"But not too much," Joab cautioned. "The guards are from the garrison. They are not Bethlehemites or of Judah. I cannot say if they would recognize you, so we must not draw their attention."

David agreed. "I will be guided by you, then."

Joab threw a startled grin David's way as the pair approached the gate. The two began an earnest, but completely contrived, conversation regarding the shepherding techniques best used in the hilly surroundings of Bethlehem. As they approached, neither of the guards gave them more than a quick glance and a frown for the spear David carried.

Doubtless, they had been ordered to keep an eye out for David, but whatever they imagined the son of Jesse to look like, David's current appearance apparently did not match their expectations. The sentries didn't challenge the two arguing shepherds as they made their way into the city.

With a covert glance over his shoulder, Joab steered David swiftly down a narrow street. "Do you remember, Elhanan, the son of Dodo?"

David frowned slightly. Dodo was a common Hebrew name, and one of David's lieutenants, Eleazar, had a father by that name.[2] "His father is the carpenter?"[3]

"Aye."

"I know him. His family is known for fashioning the weaver beams for the women, is he not?"

"Aye. People call Elhanan's father Jaareoregim."

"What of him?"

Joab continued to pull David through the streets, occasionally turning down another as he led him deeper into the city. "Elhanan and his father are keeping your father and mother safe. Your brothers are scattered throughout the city, but at least one of them stays with your parents at all times. Come."

Joab fell silent, but there was no need for further conversation. David knew exactly where to go. Dodo was one of the elders of the city and owned a large house at the edge of town, near the wall. His trade required a bit more space than others, so instead of one of the central compounds owned by the more affluent members of Bethlehem, he had elected to build his home against the wall of the city with easy access to the gates and the trees beyond.

Joab paused at the compound gate, looking first one way than the other before pounding on the worn wood with his staff. He waited. Shortly a voice from the other side called, "Name yourself, or begone!"

"Joab, son of Zeruiah," he said in a low voice.

"Joab, you wool-gathering mouse!" called the irritable voice from the other side. "Where is the sense Jehovah granted you? Surely you know not to come here in the day! Begone with you!"

---

[2] In fact, there are three Dodos in the Bible: (1) An Issacharan mentioned in Judges 10:1; (2) An Aholite, the father of Eleazar mentioned in 2 Samuel 23:9; and a Bethlehemite, the father of Elhanan, mentioned in 2 Samuel 23:24.

[3] Dodo of Bethlehem (2 Samuel 23:24; 1 Chronicles 11:26) goes by two other names in Scripture: Jair (1 Chronicles 20:5), meaning "forest," and Jaareoregim (2 Samuel 21:19), meaning "forest of weavers." Based on these meanings, Dodo may have been a forester or woodcutter, possibly a carpenter.

Joab's face reddened. "Open this gate, Elhanan, or by Judah's eyes, I'll chop it down and feed your toes to the wolves!"

David glanced around, his eyes narrowing, worried that the commotion would draw undo attention. He tried to hush Joab, but his nephew had the stubbornness of an ass, and he ignored David.

"You hear me, Elhanan! Open this gate!"

The voice on the other side laughed. "I'd like to see you try, sheepherder!"

David put a restraining hand on his nephew's shoulder. "Be at peace, Joab," he said softly. Then turning his attention to the gate, he raised his voice. "Grant us entry, Elhanan, son of Dodo. We have need."

"Who speaks?" the voice on the other side cried sharply. "Who goes there?"

"It is I, David, the son of Jesse." Both David and Joab glanced around, making sure they were not overheard.

David could hear the wooden board that secured the gate being removed, and soon the gate was pulled inward. The young man who stood in the entrance, brandished a spear before him, but his wide eyes betrayed the excitement he felt.

But one look at David produced a frown, and suspicion replaced eagerness in those brown eyes. Hands tightened on his spear shaft and the tip lowered toward David's chest. He glanced at Joab but couldn't keep his eyes from sliding back to the bedraggled figure of David.

"What mockery is this?" Elhanan demanded.

David held up his hands. "Be at peace, son of Dodo. There is no deception here. I am David in truth."

In a way, David was relieved. If Elhanan didn't recognize him, then perhaps he could come and go without the fear in the city. No, he would still need to be careful. It would be men he had fought alongside, men who he had crossed paths within Saul's household and armies that would likely not be deceived by a wild beard, tangled hair, and a plain tunic.

— 135 —

1 Samuel 22:1-3

Elhanan didn't seem totally convinced. His eyes narrowed to near slits on his wide face. David took a good look at the youth. In truth, everything about him was wide. Though short, Elhanan reminded David of nothing less than a massive, squat pillar. He looked immoveable. Even the young man's beard looked as if it grew horizontal more than any other direction. David remembered when Elhanan was a boy. He could never run like the other boys, but he nearly always won any wrestling match. Even at a young age, boys years older could not tumble him. Now he simply looked like a rock on stubby legs.

Elhanan finally relaxed when Joab nodded confirmation to him. "Well met, son of Jesse! Well met!"

They clasped arms in greeting, and David grinned. "You have a firm grip, my young friend."

Elhanan grinned back. He lost his smile almost immediately as something beyond David arrested his attention.

Spinning around, David saw the outline of a man watching from the shadows of a nearby building. The man's dark turban hid his hair, and part of the turban had been lowered to wind around the man's face. David could only see two eyes that studied the three men with an unsettling intensity.

Grumbling something about strangers, Elhanan quickly closed the gate and slipped the locking board into place. His face betraying his worry, he motioned for David to follow. "Come. I will take you to your father."

"Did you know that man?" David asked.

"King Saul has many spies in the city, David. We cannot be too careful."

Feeling ill at ease, David vacillated between going to see his parents and turning about to hunt down the stranger to be sure he posed no threat. The need to see his father won out, and he motioned for Elhanan to lead the way.

— 136 —

14

"My son!" David's mother fell upon his neck, weeping softly, her tears soaking into the fabric of his tunic. Greatly moved, he patted her shoulder gently even as his own tears threatened to overflow. Natzbet continued to weep, occasionally bestirring herself to kiss him on both cheeks. Jesse stood behind his wife, one hand on the small of her back, his eyes brimming.

David had only seen his parents on occasion over the last handful of years. His duties for King Saul and his fame after the battle of Elah had prevented him from returning home.[1] That had been five years ago.

He had so much to tell them, so much to ask. He glanced at his eldest brother, Eliab, who stood in the corner of the room, wearing a disapproving scowl. Eliab was approaching middle age with a fringe of gray touching his temples and wrinkles around his eyes. Despite that, he was still a tall and powerful man who had fought in many battles alongside King Saul. The difference in age meant that David had never been very close to his eldest brother, but they had never been at odds either. Eliab had mostly ignored David, often being gone from home for long stretches at a time.

---

[1] 1 Samuel 18:2.

He nodded to Eliab, a gesture of equals, and indeed, the last five years had hardened David's muscles and given him the grace and power of a lion. This, more than anything, was something Eliab could appreciate being a man of war himself. After a moment's hesitation, he nodded back.

"Father," David began when his mother pulled back, "we have much to speak of."

His father nodded and gestured to a low table set in the middle of the room. Like most houses, the room was opened to the other rooms around it. Elhanan and his family had politely left this area of the large house to give David and his family a measure of privacy.

They sat on the hard-packed dirt floor around the table. A bowl of fruit sat on top, and David's stomach growled the moment his eyes fell upon it. He eagerly reached out and snatched a few of the dates, popping them into his mouth all at once. While he chewed, he cracked open a pomegranate and began picking out the juicy seeds.

Jesse smoothed his long white beard and examined his son with worried eyes. "Why have you returned?" he asked finally. "As good as it does my heart to see you again, my son, it is dangerous for you to be here in Bethlehem." Unspoken was how dangerous it was for everyone else that he was in Bethlehem.

David bowed his head. "Forgive me, my father, but I had need to see you." He glanced around at his family. Joab sat in barely restrained anticipation, but everyone else regarded him with a mixture of worry and relief. "I know that I am endangering all of you by coming here, but the need is great—at least to me. King Saul is indeed hunting me, seeking unjustly to slay me. Why, I know not. I have been faithful to him and served him with my whole heart." His voice broke as he thought of Jonathan and Michal—friend and wife. "That you are already in hiding proves that the king will seek to use you against me. You must flee, Father. Take my mother and brethren and flee!"

Jesse's thick hands spread out. David blinked. Those hands seemed more swollen then he remembered. In a heavy voice, Jesse asked, "And where would you have us go, my son? Every city in

Judah is being watched against your return. All of Judah fears the king and his armies, and there are many sons of Belial[2] who will surely sell us to the king if they thought there be gain in the act. This is our home. Where else would we be safe?"

David ran a hand through his beard, tracing the scar on his left cheek. "Edom perhaps?" he suggested. The descendants of Esau were kin in many ways.

"The Edomites hold little love for us," Eliab said. "We would not be any safer there." He glanced at his father. "I fear we must fight. There is no other way for us to be safe." Leaning over the low table, he speared David with his cold eyes. "My brother, surely there are men who would rally to you if word was sent out. Surely you could rise up against the king. Judah is the largest of all the tribes. We would rally to you and how many others would come? We could meet the king on the battlefield army against army."

David stared at his brother. "You speak of treason."

"You forget, brother, I was there when Samuel anointed you to be king over Israel. Why do my words speak treason? You are the rightful king of Israel."

There it was, and from the last person David would have ever thought to hear it. For the first time, the dread that lay heavy on David's heart ever since Samuel had anointed him was mentioned aloud by someone who supported him. To become king, he would need to rise up against King Saul. No. He could not do that.

"I cannot lift my hand against the LORD's anointed," he protested.

Eliab's heavy eyebrow rose. "Are you not the LORD's anointed? My brother, how can it be treason when you but obey the command of the Great Seer? Besides, if we do nothing, then Saul will find us and slay us. We—all of us—are caught in this as surely as a fly in a spider's web."

"Father," David implored, "is this your mind as well?"

---

[2] The term "son of Belial" was a colloquial saying in the Bible that meant "evil, greedy person" or something equivalent.

1 Samuel 22:1-3

Jesse looked from son to son. "Elohim's will must be done, my sons. We must put ourselves in His hands. That is the most men may do in any case." He folded his hands atop the table and sighed deeply. "Yet, Eliab is persuasive, but his words carry both wisdom and danger. There may be yet a compromise. You must leave Saul in the LORD's hands. Jehovah will see His will done upon us all, but I fear that you cannot continue this alone. I remember when Saul became king. Many years ago, Samuel had called the people to Mizpeh.[3] Surely, I thought the Great Seer would doom us all. His words still echo in my mind: 'You have this day rejected your God.'[4] I always wondered why he had said that—right before choosing Saul to be our king. Maybe this is all because we long ago rejected God. I know not. But one thing I do know, my sons. Jehovah did not reject us. For when King Saul left that day to return to Gibeah, a band of men left with him—men whose hearts God had touched."[5]

Eliab nodded sagely, but David stared at his father in confusion. "I do not understand."

Jesse's dark eyes glittered in the light from the open window. "Do you not? Or do you refuse to recognize the truth? Your name is sung from the lips of thousands across this land. King Saul fears you, David. He fears what you will become and what that will mean for his sons."

"But I—"

Jesse lifted a hand. "I know you mean them no harm. But is that not the way of the kings of other lands? When a new king comes to power, what does he do to the dethroned king's sons?"

David knew as well as anyone. They were killed—to the last man, boy, and infant.

Jesse read the truth in David's eyes. "But you will not raise a hand against Saul, this I know. But, my son, think. How will you

---

[3] 1 Samuel 10:17. Not the same place David hides at in Moab. In fact, there may be three places called Mizpeh in Scripture.
[4] 1 Samuel 10:19.
[5] 1 Samuel 10:26.

— 140 —

keep Saul from hunting you down and slaying you? What will it take for him to stop seeking you?"

"I know not."

"It will take a band of men whose hearts God has touched. You must surround yourself with men who will fight for you—men who will die for you."

David gave a start. "Die for me?"

"Aye. Only when you are strong enough will Saul stop seeking you. He must be convinced that seeking you would be folly, perhaps even bring about the very thing he fears."

Eliab nodded. "Listen to our father, David. This is the only way. Saul will not stop hunting us until we force him to stop."

David shook his head. "I will not lift my hand against the LORD's anointed. It is not in me!"

Eliab threw up his hands in disgust. "Then you doom us all!"

Jesse put a restraining hand on Eliab's shoulder. "Be at peace, my son, and rein in your hasty words." Turning back to David, Jesse explained, "You do not have to lift your hand against Saul. You must only fortify yourself with men. When you are strong enough to slay Saul, that is when you show mercy. Mercy is what will turn aside Saul's hand. I know the man. Naught else will."

David considered. If his father's analysis was true, he would need to raise a large enough force to give Saul pause. It would be a fine balance between strength and threat. Gathering men to himself would make him an even larger threat in Saul's eyes, but he had to admit, it might be the only way to keep him and his family alive.

Mercy. Mercy can only be shown to the weaker. To do as his father suggested, he would need to become more powerful than Saul. He shuddered, trying to think it through. He would need to begin in secret. If Saul discovered what he was doing, he would not hesitate to march the full might of Israel's armies against him. Men would die. Die because of him. He swallowed and looked into his father's eyes. "Is there no other way? Could I not flee?"

"One man alone is easy to betray," Jesse said sadly. "Many men have done so for a few gold coins. But betraying an entire troop is altogether a different matter. If but one man survives to bring retribution, the betrayer may find his own life cut short. There are three kinds of men you must beware—the greedy, the loyal, and the one with hatred in his heart for you. It is the greedy we seek to sway with this plan, my son—and perhaps the loyal. Their loyalty to the king may cause them to see to the heart of the matter quickly and see the truth Saul seeks to hide."

"But I am loyal," David protested. Tears brimmed his eyes. "I know not what evil spirit is driving the king. He has no cause against me. None."

"We know, my son. As does most of Israel."

"But if I do this thing, then he will have cause."

Jesse looked sadly upon his son. "So be it. Call your band together, and you will have the power to prove that you truly mean the king no harm. It is all that can be done."

Joab pounded the table and spoke up for the first time. "Aye! Do this David. I will come!"

Eliab nodded as well, but he still looked disappointed. David didn't know why his eldest brother wanted to fight King Saul. Perhaps being brother to the future king was no small matter.

Looking from son to son, Jesse added, "Your brethren will rally to your call, David. All of them."

Shaking his head, David whispered, "Not all of them."

Jesse sat up straighter. "Of whom do you speak?"

"Maon."

Everyone around the table except David stiffened. "That name may not be spoken here," Jesse said, and David's mother abruptly tried to choke back sobs. "You have no brother by that name."

Maon's betrayal had forced Jesse to strike his name from the genealogies. It was as if he had never been born. But he had, and everyone around the table remembered him despite the formal words Jesse spoke.

"Your words are truer than you know," David whispered, slumping against the table. "He is dead—truly dead, slain by a Philistine spear as he helped me escape Gath."

A wail escaped Natzbet's lips, and she clutched at Jesse. David's father stared long at David, his eyes wet with unshed tears and his face pale, but the hardness around his mouth was unwavering. "He aided you?"

"Aye. He did." David knew the truth of the aid. Maon was only helping him to keep his precarious position among the Philistine elite. That alone had motivated him, but his parents need not know that. Let them think he had a change of heart. Let them believe he sought to return to the light of Elohim. It would not be enough to restore his name in the genealogy, but it would ease his parents' minds. That would have to be enough.

Eliab's eyes glittered as he bowed his head and said the benediction for the dead, "This too was for the good."

Jesse shot him a sharp glance but said nothing. Natzbet simply sobbed.

David caught Joab's eyes, and his younger nephew nodded in understanding. Clearing his throat, David said, "Father, my thoughts turn to the caves above Adullam. I was pursued by the Philistines, and I came here only to elude them. I thought that they would leave off once I entered the city. But it was to Adullam that I wished to go. There, I may yet hide from King Saul."

Jesse, his eyes lingering on his wife, nodded. "That is a wise choice, my son. The caves are extensive and impossible to search thoroughly. Even if Saul learns of you, you will have ample time to escape if he attempts to seek you out."

Eliab grunted. "You could easily hide an army in those caves."

David agreed, and thinking of what his father had advised, he might just have to. "Do you see another way, Father? I do not wish to be king. I want only to fight for my God and for my people."

"Elohim's will is not so easily undone, my son. You have been anointed. We know the end, but not the journey. It is His timing we now wait upon, but even with this knowledge, you must not be careless." He leaned back in his seat, one hand still rubbing his wife's shaking shoulder comfortingly. His eyes betrayed his own troubled soul. "Moses wrote of Abraham, the patriarch of our people. It is said that Abraham once changed the mind of Jehovah, arguing on behalf of the city of Sodom. One of his blood and kin resided in that wicked city, a city Elohim meant to destroy, and it was on his kin's cause that Abraham so argued. It is said that God's will bent because of Abraham." Jesse looked hard into his son's eyes. "But it may also be true that Abraham's argument was part of God's will. Who can say? It may be that no power on earth or in heaven can change what will be. But then why allow us the power of choice? Son, perhaps the only one who can alter God's will for your life is you. You must remain steadfast. You must believe. You must walk in Him. Only then can Elohim be a buckler and shield to you. If you choose to walk in darkness, there is no telling your end."

His father's words—words echoed by Samuel during his stay in Ramah—resonated deeply with David's soul. His father was right. If he but walked in Jehovah, there would be no power on earth that could bend God's plan for his life. The only one with the power to do such lay within David himself. He resolved right then to walk in the light. "I praise Elohim for such a wise and loving father. I will do as you advise. I will go to the caves above Adullam. Pass the word. Let anyone who is in distress, or in debt, or discontented resort there to me." That should get the attention of a few old friends at least.

Joab's eyes glittered with delight, and David knew instantly that nothing short of Elohim's hand would stop his nephew from joining him. He sighed deeply. He did not want his family to be ensnared in his troubles, but in truth, they already were. Where else could they go?

Eliab spoke, "Once this begins, there will be no turning back. Saul *will* learn of it sooner or later. Word will reach him. But when word does, let him doubt it. Let him wonder as to the truth of what he hears."

David leaned forward. "How?"

"Let your whereabouts be reported in all the cities of Judah. Let him hear that you are everywhere, then when word comes of where you truly are, he will doubt."

"You can do this?"

"Leave it to me, my brother," Eliab said, smiling. "In two days, word will begin coming to Saul that you are in every city in Judah."

"That is well considered," David acknowledged. "Let it be done."

Standing, Jesse looked upon David. Pride for his son shone in his aged face, and it gave David strength. He started to plan. The Philistine scouts should have turned back the moment they realized he'd gone into Bethlehem. If they wanted him now, they'd need to bring an army. It should be a simple matter to slip out and make his way to Adullam.

There was still the matter of the spies Elhanan had mentioned skulking about the city. The figure of the man watching him from the shadows came to mind. But Eliab's plan should surely confound Saul. Still, he needed to move fast. If Saul learned of David being in Bethlehem first, then he might come quickly. He could not be anywhere near Bethlehem when that happened.

Standing, he moved around the table to embrace his mother and father. Pushing back, he said, "I must leave. But let the word go forth. I must prepare. Tonight, I leave."

"I will go with you," Joab said, as David knew he would.

Turning, he laid a hand on his nephew's shoulder. "Be not hasty, Joab. It may be that we are destined to fight the LORD's battles together, but tonight I leave alone. You must look first to your father and mother."

Joab's eyes tightened. "I am a man, David. I am twenty years of age and able to draw the sword."

"Aye, you speak truly. But see to your parents. And more. Pass the word. This, better than I, is something you must do."

Joab seemed on the verge of arguing further, but he bit back his response. Straightening, he bowed to David. "As you command, my lord."

For some reason, those last two words carried the same effect as a trumpet announcing a royal arrival. Grimacing and somewhat embarrassed by the display, he said, "Now then, does anyone have a sword?"

15

Slipping out of Bethlehem proved easier than David expected. Since Dodo's house was built next to the outer wall, the family had access to one of the smaller, less-used gates that allowed for quick egress beyond the walls. And because of their trade, the family was well-known to the guards stationed there, so when David and Elhanan walked through the gate as evening fell, the only notice the guards took of the pair was a hearty warning to be back before the gate was closed for the night.

Elhanan waved jovially but kept right on walking. David walked at his side, a woodcutter's axe hefted over one shoulder and his new sword concealed under his cloak. The sword was a gift from Abinadab who had slipped into Dodo's house once word had reached him of David's arrival. It had been good to see his second eldest brother. Eliab was a warrior, but Abinadab was a leader of men. And if there was anyone David trusted to help him in the coming days, it would be Abinadab.

Half a league from the city, Elhanan stopped. "This is as far as I need go, my lord," he said, bowing awkwardly.

Curse Joab! Now he had Elhanan bowing to him. Forcing a smile, David handed over the axe and then placed his hands on Elhanan's shoulders. "Thank you, Elhanan, son of Dodo. Your help has been invaluable. Please convey my gratitude to your father."

— 146 —

"Aye. I will do that." The young man hesitated, fingering the shaft of the axe nervously. "And if my lord will permit, I will be joining you at Adullam."

David's eyebrows climbed nearly into his hair. "But why? You have it well here in Bethlehem. What need is there for you to leave your father and live in the wilderness—for as surely as the LORD lives, that is what we will be doing. I have no illusions about my fate. If Elohim allows, then one day perhaps...but until then, I fear, my life will be one of constant peril. I advise against this course of action."

The squat young man struggled with a response, and his wide eyes narrowed nearly to slits as he considered. "I do not believe I have a choice in this matter, my lord. The decision feels...right. I have no other way to say it. I am compelled, my lord."

David fought to understand. He had never felt that way—wait, yes, he had. The first time he had met King Saul a similar emotion had gripped him. The revelation shifted the world under David's feet. Ideas and truths reordered themselves in his mind, and for the first time, he truly understood what being anointed by the LORD meant. Jehovah had not forsaken him, had not left him alone. Men would come to him at Adullam as surely as sheep would heed a shepherd's call. When God called, there was a compulsion that resonated deep in one's soul. Satisfaction and peace could only come by heeding that call. That is what Elhanan felt—and likely Joab too. It is what David felt as well.

He had seen it before. Adino. Eleazar. Shammah. These men had been moved to supernatural feats because they had heeded the LORD's call. Adino's words, spoken soon after the meadow battle, came to mind with the force of a summer gale, *"I found something worth fighting for—and perhaps dying for. You."* The LORD had called David for a task, and it seemed Jehovah would bring into his life those needed to help him fulfill it. He would not be alone.

Focusing on the younger man, David said, "Then do what you must. But first, help Joab spread the word. What must be, will be."

— 147 —

1 Samuel 22:1-3

"Thank you, my lord. Thank you!" Energized, Elhanan bounced on the balls of his feet, a grin taking up the whole width of his wide face.

Watching him go off to cut down a tree for the benefit of the gate guards, David felt both exhilarated and sad. It felt good to know that he would not have to face the coming trials alone, but he was not deceived. Men would die. Perhaps even Elhanan. That, more than anything, ate at him, seeking to devour his resolve and courage.

Turning away from Bethlehem, his home, he circled the city until he was to the west, among the ridges that would lead him back to the southern arm of the Valley of Elah and to where the caves of Adullam would provide him with the safety he needed. A full moon cast enough light to see by, and he walked slowly, in no hurry. As far as he knew, Saul did not yet know where he was, and the Philistines were long gone.

A shadow moved in the distance, and David froze, adrenalin surging through his body. He was battle trained enough not to jump at random shadows in the dark, but what he'd caught out of the corner of his eye was neither an animal nor a swaying tree. Someone waited up ahead.

Joab! he thought sourly. His nephew was the impatient type, and David wouldn't put it past him to slip out of the city and await David. Some sense of warning, however, caused him to step deeper into the darkness of a few olive trees that loomed overhead to block out the moon's light. *Would Joab be skulking about in the dark?* Most likely, the young man would be making enough noise to convince a town guard an army was approaching. Something was wrong.

Moving only his eyes, David studied the landscape. Much of it was wreathed in deep shadow, a faint glow from the moon illuminated what he could see. Hills, dotted with large white rocks, rolled toward the west until forming the ridges and valleys that led to the Shephelah plain dominated by the Philistines. Wild trees often clustered more thickly at the base and lower slopes.

But over the centuries, the slopes closest to Bethlehem had been terraced into huge step-like tiers. The prevalent rocks of the

— 148 —

region had been gathered into the walls of each terrace, often creating sudden drop offs of more than a score of cubits to the next lower terrace. Husbandmen tended groves of olive trees or vineyards on the level areas. David stood on one such leveled step. The owner of this slope had planted rows of olive trees on the flattened parts, stair-stepping down to the base of the hill.

Frowning, he peered into the gloom, trying to catch sight of any movement. He was careful not to allow his eyes to linger long on one spot or to focus fully. Catching movement in the dark required the mind to pick it up peripherally. The brain could imagine what was not there.

After a moment of seeing nothing, he carefully reached up to place a hand on one of the gnarled, thick trunks of the nearest olive tree. *Perhaps I imagined it.* However, he saw no sense in taking chances and just bulling his way down the slope. So, moving slowly, careful of his injured toe, he edged to his right, cautious not to step on anything that would snap or crack under his sandaled feet. His leather-soled sandals allowed him to feel what he was stepping on before he put his full weight on it, and so moving thus, he slipped in and out of the olive trees, away from where he'd seen the movement.

He didn't get far. A whisper of cloth brushing bark was his only warning. He spun into a crouch as a black shadow leaped at him from higher up. An iron blade glinted briefly in the moonlight, and David threw himself to the side. But not fast enough. The dagger ripped through the cloth of his tunic and scored a long line across his chest and ribs.

He sucked in his breath as pain shot through him, and only training and adrenalin kept him from freezing fatally. Using his momentum, he continued his roll between two olive trees. Coming to his feet in a smooth motion, he darted around one of the trees, keeping low so as not to brain himself on the lower branches. He lurched into a run, dodging trees. He could hear his pursuer, trying to keep up and thought he heard muttered curses in the Philistine language.

— 149 —

1 Samuel 22:1-3

So, the Philistines hadn't left. They had laid in ambush, waiting for him to come out. But how had they known where he'd emerge? Abruptly, he spun to his left toward the rock wall that descended to a lower tier of the hill. His sword banged into his legs, and he had to use one hand to keep the scabbarded sword from tripping him. Blood dripped down his chest to coat his stomach. He couldn't see well enough to know how bad the injury was.

The pursuing Philistine scout kept pace. David was making enough noise that his pursuer had no problem following him in the gloom of the olive trees.

He spotted the edge of the rock wall ahead, a dim line of white with darkness beyond, and not knowing how far down the drop would be, he sucked in his breath even as he raced for it. At such times, he would simply have to put himself in the LORD's hand and trust Him to see him through. So, whispering a desperate prayer to Jehovah for favor, he flung himself at the edge, sliding the last few cubits to slow some of his momentum.

He went over the edge with a strangled cry. The retaining wall was slightly sloped so instead of a sheer drop, he slid rapidly down the rough stones, bouncing and jarring every bone in his body. He couldn't say how far he dropped in the dark, but when he hit the bottom, he shot forward into an awkward roll across rocky ground of the next lowest tier.

He rolled to a stop, and bounced to his feet, spinning around and drawing his sword in one motion. It was a wonder he hadn't bent it in the fall, or worse, gotten it tangled in his legs or wedged in the cracks in the rock wall. *Praise Jehovah!*

The pursuing Philistine didn't follow David's method of descent. Instead of sliding, he tried to arrest his momentum at the top, but in the darkness, he misjudged the distance and with a gasp, he teetered on the edge and then fell off, his arms windmilling desperately. The enemy scout crashed to the bottom, landing hard on his side.

Wasting no time, David darted forward and stabbed down, ending the man's life and agony. From the way the man had fallen,

— 150 —

he had broken at least one of his legs. Unfortunately, the man didn't die easily. His scream of mortal agony pierced the dark sky, acting as a beacon for any who heard.

When the man at last lay still in death, David crouched, looking around. Three Philistine scouts had been trailing him since he left Gath, and at least half a dozen more warriors, including one of the giants, followed them. Were they all in the vicinity or only this one scout? Thinking of the first shadow he'd seen move, he doubted this one scout was alone. *There are at least two more,* he thought. The warriors may have been sent back, for if they had been discovered, the Bethlehem garrison would have rallied in pursuit. The scouts, however, could likely hide in the area without ever being detected. So, at least two more men were hunting him through the night.

Eyes narrowing, he decided that he didn't like being hunted. Putting a hand to his chest, he felt the wound he'd taken. It didn't feel too deep and even now the blood was crusting over. A scratch then. He could live with that. His back ached from the slide down the rock wall, and he'd surely re-injured his right big toe, but he forced down the pain and stood battle-ready.

Time to take the fight to them, he decided.

He didn't have to wait long. Something shot past David's face, so close that individual hairs of his beard were moved by its passing, and thudded hard into the gnarled trunk of an olive tree. Startled, David stared at the quivering shadow before realizing he was staring at the dark fletching of an arrow that had barely missed him. With a yelp, he rolled backward, regained his feet, and darted behind one of the other olive trees. He gasped desperately for breath and put a hand to his beard in wonder. He could still feel the hairs move as the arrow had passed.

He clamped down on his breathing, holding his breath, his ears straining to hear any movement. Other than the frantic beating of his heart, he heard nothing—not even insects. *Two more, and they know where I am.* He needed to reposition, or he would be open to a flanking attack. One of the scouts could hold him while the other moved so that David would be caught between them. He didn't relish the idea at all.

He sheathed his sword so that the blade would not reflect the moonlight and give him away. Then lying flat on the ground, he began crawling, being careful to stay deep within the shadows of the olive trees. The effort cost him some pain as his toe protested the abuse, but it had to be done. The moon's position meant that the trees' shadows lay perpendicular to the terraces, so he crawled as silently as he could to the edge of his terrace and slowly looked over the edge of the rock wall. He waited, holding his breath.

Nothing. Still no sound.

He needed to get down there. He slithered over the side, using cracks in the wall to keep him from falling. He let his legs swing over until he was a spider, hugging the terrace wall. He could see more of the terraces below him, descending into more shadow. He estimated that there may be five more of the large steps before reaching the narrow ravine at the bottom. He hadn't planned on going that way, but with two more Philistines hunting him, he didn't have much choice.

Slowly, trying to make no sound, he edged down the wall. His hands found easy handholds in the unevenly placed stones. Old roots that had wiggled their way through some of the rocks aided his descent. But about a quarter of the way down, one of the rocks, worked loose perhaps by rain and roots, gave way under his hand and with a strangled yell, he slid down the rest of the way to the bottom in a loud shower of dirt and small rocks.

His hands and toes stung painfully from trying to stop the slide—particularly the broken toe—but he forgot all about that as he stared fearfully up. His fears took shape as a dark form seemed to blossom at the top of the wall. David could see something held in the man's hand and rightly guessed a bow. He flung himself to the side and something hissed by him to slam into the ground.

Fear gave way to anger. Snarling, he pivoted and ran behind another tree, but only to gain space. Turning, he darted back toward the rock wall. Where he had come down was not terribly high, maybe

— 152 —

a little more than twice his own height. With a little momentum and favor from the LORD, he should—he jumped, found one spot for his left foot about a quarter of the way up, and leaped up, stretching as far as he could.

His target was the ankle of the scout above. The man had stood calmly atop the wall, nocking another arrow to the string of his bow. But his placid pace cost him. Before he could draw back and shoot, David's fingers clamped around his ankle. With jerk and heave, he yanked the Philistine right off the edge of the terrace.

The enemy scout gave a startled shout that was cut off as he fell back and slammed his head against the rocks. Their combined weight sent them both tumbling down to the next terrace below. David hit hard, the breath knocked out of him. The scout slammed into the ground next to him and lay groaning. David rolled away and fumbled for his sword, struggling to breathe. The world spun around him in flashes of darkness as he sought to regain his feet and his breath. Perhaps it hadn't been the wisest decision to leap up drag the Philistine down.

He staggered some and nearly fell. The world would not stop spinning! He managed to draw his sword, but it fell from his fingers as he braced himself to keep from falling. It seemed to take forever, but eventually, the world returned to a normal rotation, and he blinked tears out of his eyes as he drew in deep ragged breaths.

When he could see, he realized that the scout he'd pulled off the terrace above was slowly regaining his own feet. Grunting, David reached down and retrieved his sword. The scout noticed, and though he looked to be in no better shape than David, he yanked out a sword of his own. The long, tapered blade flashed in the moonlight.

What took place next would have been comical to David if he didn't hurt so much. Like two drunken soldiers, they attacked each other. David's first overhand swing went way wide. His blade bit into the rocks, sending a few sparks up into the night. He righted himself, barely, and blinked, trying to decipher what the scout was trying to do.

— 153 —

1 Samuel 22:1-3

Mumbling to himself in his ugly tongue, the Philistine was weaving a meandering path to attack David, his sword swinging wildly. David braced himself to meet the attack, but his leg gave out; he collapsed to one knee. He tried to lift his sword, but his arms would not cooperate yet. He could only watch as the Philistine waved toward him, sword slashing the air.

But David knew it would not end like this. He knew that he'd somehow survive. As if the thought was a prophecy, the enemy scout overbalanced, and his swing sent his sword whizzing through the air above David's head. The man tripped over David, and they both sprawled on the ground, the scout's legs atop David's chest.

For long moments, they stayed that way until David found the strength to shove the legs aside and squirm his way to his knees. He knelt there, prepared to ram his sword into the Philistine, but saw there was no need. The scout was dead. The back of the man's head was a bloody mess, likely having occurred when David had yanked the man's foot out from under him. The wound had been mortal, but it had taken the Philistine time to die.

Still one more, he warned himself. Looking around, he saw nothing, but he was blinking so rapidly, he doubted he would see anything even if Goliath himself came striding up. Realization of his condition slowly seeped into his addled brain. He couldn't fight a child to save his life. His body was doubtless a mass of bruises and his toes and hands stung as if he'd stuck them in a bee's nest and teased the angry inhabitants with his tender skin.

He struggled to his feet, breathing heavily and trying not to cry out for the pain. It took him three tries to sheath his sword, and the blade felt like so much dead weight on his waist. It dragged at him as he took stumbling steps to the nearest olive tree. There, he leaned against the twisted trunk for a long time, trying to gather himself. If the third scout came upon him in that instant, David would surely die.

But no one came. Nothing moved in the deep shadows except for the branches of the trees swaying in a faint breeze. Taking another shuddering breath, he pushed himself away from the tree and looked around for the haversack he'd dropped somewhere along the way. There was some bread and hard cheese stashed away in it, and he needed something to eat. To drink too, but he had brought nothing with him, meaning to stop at a cistern several miles away.

The sack was gone, likely up on one of the higher terraces, and he didn't feel like searching for it, not with another one of those scouts skulking about in the darkness. He would just have to take his chances and head to the cistern. He'd gone days without eating before.

A bitter smile touched his lips. Nothing to do but to continue on. That seemed to be the story of his life. With a last look around, he shambled slowly along the terrace, looking for an easier way down to the bottom of the ravine than the way he'd come down so far. He prayed that the third scout was well away—elsewhere. And for good measure, he prayed for strength—at least until he could reach the cistern between Bethlehem and Adullam. With Elohim's favor, he hoped to reach the caves sometime tomorrow evening.

Some distance behind David, a shadow detached itself from another, deeper shadow. A man stepped into the moonlight, watching as David slowly made his way along the earthen terrace. He watched David go, not following. Long after David disappeared in the darkness, the man turned in a different direction. Having watched his companions die, he had no desire to tangle with David even injured. And as the only remaining scout, his duty was to report what he'd seen.

16

David knew of the caves only from the passing remarks of an Adullamite who had once come to trade with his father, Jesse. He had idly spoken of the limestone caves honeycombing the hills above the small, sleepy village. The caves were sometimes used as a dry place to press olives and grapes in years past or used as cool storage for wine.

Adullam once had a king,[1] but the original city had been razed during Joshua's conquest. The land, including the ruins of Adullam, had been given to the tribe of Judah as an inheritance.[2] Now it was a village that produced olive oil and barely in moderate quantities by farming the southern spur of the Elah Valley. It was otherwise unremarkable and unimportant.

The Philistines tended to ignore it other than to occasionally raze and burn it down. But the inhabitants would stubbornly return afterward to rebuild. David knew some of the people. During his time as captain over a thousand under Saul, he had defended the area and the people from Philistine depredations. He felt confident that he could hide in the caves, and the inhabitants of the small village would not betray him to King Saul. He hoped so anyway.

He stopped in the village only briefly the next day, his body weary, bruised, and sore from his battle with the Philistine scouts.

---

[1] Joshua 12:15.
[2] Joshua 15:20; 35.

But he, like the Adullamites, were Judean, and though they might not actively protect him if King Saul marched an army into the area, they were predisposed to give him food and water. Even if they did report him to the king, the information would be only one tale among many conflicting ones designed to confuse his whereabouts.

After leaving the village, he made his way into the foothills west of the southern arm of the Elah Valley. One particularly tall hill had been pointed out by an affable old Hebrew who knew the area, he claimed, like he knew every scar on his feet—and the man did have an impressive number of scars crisscrossing his feet. The old man hadn't volunteered how he had come by them, and David thought it polite not to ask.

After a careful search of half a day, he finally found a hole that looked like it led to a larger cave. He had to lay nearly flat on his stomach and poke in his head to peer into the darkness within. His jaw tightened when only a pool of light illuminated the cave floor below him. It looked to be about a two cubit drop before sloping sharply down into darkness. He couldn't see very far in, and an old fear of close and tight places rose up to clamp onto the edges of his mind.

He fought against his fear, knowing he needed shelter, some place to hide, and forced himself to worm his way inside. There, he sat for a long time in a pool of light from the entrance, peering into the darkness deeper into the cave. Nothing moved. But that wasn't what concerned him. Frankly, if the cave held an entire family of bears, he wouldn't have much cared. No, it was that he couldn't see how big the cave was. He didn't like small, enclosed places. Never had. But exhaustion finally overcame his fear, and he slid down the incline into the darkness where he found soft dirt to curl up on and promptly fell asleep, not caring if he shared the cave with less amiable creatures.

He woke up the next morning surprised that he was still alive. Every muscle in his body protested as if a blacksmith had gleefully used him for an anvil. His head pounded abominably as if the same

1 Samuel 22:1-3

smith had taken up residence inside his skull. Every time he moved, he winced at the stabbing pain.

He had some food and water still from the village, and he knew where he could get more, but he ate and drank sparingly, worried that his stomach might rebel. Even that effort wore him out. He lay back against one of the large boulders and closed his eyes. He just needed a moment. Maybe two. *I'll get up and....* He slipped into a deep sleep.

A stone clattering through the open mouth of the cave woke him. His eyes snapped open, causing him to grimace. His headache hadn't let up much. Blinking, he tried to fix his eyes on the cave entrance. By the dim light filtering through the mouth, he thought he might have slept most of the day, but a moment later, he realized something or someone was blocking the light.

He tensed and reached for his sword. For a panicky moment, he couldn't find it. He finally spotted it lying behind a boulder not too far away. He slowly crouched, every muscle screaming, and reached around to retrieve his sword. Another rock clattered as it was kicked into the cave opening.

Baring the blade, he waited. Finally, a head was stuck through the hole, the light behind obscuring any features. David froze, knowing whoever was looking in could not see beyond the pool of light.

"David? David son of Jesse, are you within?"

The familiar sounding voice echoed in the cave, and David realize the cavern was much larger than he could see. Some of the tension in his shoulders left him knowing that. Focusing on the voice, he tried to remember where he'd heard it before. The owner of the voice sounded eager, not threatening. And most certainly Hebrew.

Taking a chance, he raised his voice, "Who speaks?"

The head jerked, startled, and David thought the man would disappear altogether. But after a vain attempt to locate David in the darkness, the newcomer spoke, "It is I, Asahel, son of your sister, Zeruiah."

Asahel? The last time he had seen Joab's youngest brother had been—too many years ago. So, it hadn't been Joab who had followed him. It had been Asahel. He relaxed, carefully setting his sword down. He barely had the strength to wield it as it was. "What do you here, Asahel?"

The head disappeared to be shortly replaced by a pair of long legs that dropped lightly into the cave. Asahel then slid down to where David rested against a large boulder. Enough light filtered through that the young man could make out David sitting next to his rock once his eyes adjusted.

After repeating his question, his young nephew sat down near him and said, "Joab told me you were come."

David frowned. "When?"

"This morning." He grinned. "I ran all the way here."

David's headache only increased. *He ran the entire way?* He studied his nephew with intent eyes. The last time he'd seen Asahel, he had been but a boy. Now, long of leg and thin as a pole, he vacillated between boyhood and adulthood. He had a face like a stretched coconut, brown in color, and with a scraggly beard just beginning to form on his cheeks. *He must be nearly eighteen,* David thought.

"What do you here?" he asked Asahel again.

The young man had sense enough to look sheepish. His dark eyes slid away from David. "I want to be with you, David, to fight by your side."

"This is no place for a boy," he snapped.

Asahel's face tightened, and he began rubbing his hands together briskly. "I am no boy. I can fight as well as the next man, and no one can outrun me."

As tired as David was, he shifted to look more carefully at his nephew. He noticed a whip-like hardness to the young man. And even five years ago when David had left to serve Saul, few people could keep up with Asahel. He ran like a deer, and he had the quickest hands of anyone David had ever seen. No, Asahel was no longer a boy, and in the coming months, David would need everyone willing to help. He just hoped his sister would understand.

"It is true. You are a lad no longer." He put a hand on Asahel's shoulder to reassure him. "Be it even as the LORD wills. Abide here then if it pleases you."

The other's eyes lit up, and he snapped to his feet so fast that David wondered if there had actually been any motion from sitting to standing. "I brought more food, David." He scrambled up the hole as if it had been made for him and was back again before David could take five breaths, carrying a travel haversack that bulged with bread and cheese.

"You ran all the way carrying that?"

Asahel looked puzzled. "Aye. It was no great feat."

Perhaps not, but David doubted he could have done likewise even at full strength. Asahel didn't realize how special he truly was. He acted as if everyone could do what he did.

Asahel began unpacking the bags, eager to show David what he'd brought. David held up a hand to forestall him. "Be at ease, Asahel. There is no need of haste."

Asahel froze as if struck, his face turning red. "I-I'm at fault. Forgive me."

Staring at the young man, David shook his head in wonder. He thought he was being chastened. "There is no fault, Asahel. Please be at ease. I need to think."

His nephew fell silent, allowing David to close his eyes. He was nearing sleep when Asahel broke in, "What do we here in this cave, David? Do you know where King Saul is? Are you going to slay him before he slays you? What if he learns you are here? What if—"

David sat up straight, his eyes snapping. "Please," he begged, "I am in need of peace. Your questions can wait. There is no danger, so we can take our ease." He hoped that was true anyway, but he'd never get any rest if he allowed Asahel to continue his incessant questioning.

But Asahel couldn't resist. "What do we do now?"

"Now? We wait."

The young man looked confused. "On what do we wait?"

"Word is being spread that I am here, Asahel. Your brother, Joab, is seeing to that. Men will come. Men who support my cause."

Asahel's frown deepened, and he began rubbing his hands together fiercely. "Then we will slay King Saul?"

David's eyes narrowed, and his face clouded to the point where Asahel could see the anger even in the dim light. He recoiled from David. "King Saul is the LORD's anointed," David explained in a measured voice. "We will not slay him. I seek only to prevent falling into his hands for he would surely slay me. I seek no throne nor kingdom of my own."

Asahel looked abashed. "Forgive me, my lord. I spoke in haste. I seem to run that path too often." He offered a feeble grin.

Sighing, David waved a hand. "It is nothing. But if you are to follow me, then you must heed my every word. I have need of men I can trust in the coming days. I have no need of men who follow their own paths. Do you understand?"

Asahel nodded so quickly that it reminded David of a hammer swinging. "I will obey your every word, my lord! This I swear by the God of Abraham!"

David leaned back with a satisfied grunt. It would have to do. It would have to be enough. As eager as Asahel was, it was still a start. He didn't even correct Asahel for calling him "lord." He would need men such as he to serve him. And it felt good not to be alone. He had been alone too often of late, and that thought caused him to think of Michal. He hadn't seen his wife in some time, and he wondered how she fared. In truth, he didn't love her strongly. They had not been together long enough for that. But she was a connection to Saul. Their marriage made him the king's son-in-law, and that should have afforded him some measure of protection. But it had not. He only hoped Saul did not take his wrath out on her.

No, in truth, the person he most missed was Jonathan. He would do much, sacrifice much, for Jonathan. No man shared his thoughts and fears like Jonathan. A tear crept down his cheek. He feared less for Jonathan than he did for Michal, but he missed Jonathan more.

Asahel shifted uncomfortably, his eyes darting about, trying to peer into the darkness. Finally, they settled on David. "Why were those Philistines after you?"

The question took David by surprise. "What know you of that?"

"We found two bodies—and the food you'd dropped. It is one reason I came. To see if you needed aid."

David saw no reason why he shouldn't answer. "I fled from King Saul and took refuge in Gath. Surely that would be the one place Saul would not seek me. Surely, I thought, I would be safe. But it was not so. The Philistines discovered me."

His nephew's eyes widened in shock. "How did you escape?" He leaned forward eagerly to hear the story.

David pulled at his unkempt beard, remembering. He had feigned madness to escape, but in truth, the only thing he could subscribe to his victory was Elohim's hand. Nothing else made sense. His subterfuge of madness had not truly deceived anyone, so his escape had come despite his efforts. He thought of his lost brother, dead with a Philistine spear through his chest.

Softly, just loud enough for Asahel to hear, David began to sing. He couldn't rightly explain what possessed him to say the words he spoke…but they felt right. Holy even.

"I will bless the LORD at all times: his praise shall continually be in my mouth. My soul shall make her boast in the LORD: the humble shall hear thereof, and be glad. O magnify the LORD with me, and let us exalt his name together. I sought the LORD, and he heard me, and delivered me from all my fears."[3] He continued singing words that described the faces of the Philistines and his desperate prayer. But the angel of the LORD was at hand, and he said, "O taste and see that the LORD is good: blessed is the man that trusteth in Him."[4]

---

[3] Psalm 34:1-4. This psalm was written specifically regarding David's feigning of madness before King Achish (called Abimelech in the Psalm).
[4] Psalm 34:8.

David wasn't finished with his song. Words came easily. He sang of a warning to the children, challenging them to keep their tongues from evil—an apt admonition considering the youth listening to him—to depart from evil and to pursue peace. David could see how each word depicted a truth of his actions among the Philistines. Some of what he had done was not of the LORD, and he felt shame. But he sang, "The righteous cry, and the LORD heareth, and delivereth them out of all their troubles. The LORD is nigh unto them that are of a broken heart; and saveth such as be of a contrite spirit. Many are the afflictions of the righteous: but the LORD delivereth him out of them all."[5]

His heart sang just hearing those words. He knew the truth of them. He had lived it! But then a line of the song passed his lips that had the weight of prophecy upon it, and David's eyes widened in barely suppressed wonder, "He keepeth all his bones: not one of them is broken."[6]

Not one of his bones were broken? What could it mean? True, not one of his own bones had been broken during his time in Gath—well, perhaps he had broken his toe…maybe a rib or two—but he knew deep within that those words had nothing to do with him. They were reserved for something—no, Someone—yet to come.

He sang a few more lines and then his strength gave out completely, and he lay panting like a dog under a summer sun. He licked his lips and tried to swallow. *What just happened?* In his mind, he sang the words again. He could clearly remember every single one.

He lifted his eyes to look at Asahel and saw wonder on the young man's face. "That song—those words," he whispered, looking how David felt. "Was that how it was? Truly?"

David nodded.

"But I know those words. They yet sing within." Asahel swallowed. "My lord, I can recite each word. They have been engraved upon my heart."

---

[5] Psalm 34:17-19.
[6] Psalm 34:20. Very likely a prophecy of Jesus Christ on the cross (John 19:36).

David could only nod. He understood. The Spirit of the LORD had come upon him, and without harp or chord, he had sung a song that could only have come from the LORD. For long moments, they just sat there, each replaying the words over and over in their minds and hearts.

At length, drowsiness stole over David, and his eyes began to slide shut. He still needed to regain his strength. Asahel saw, but before he could slip into the comfort of sleep, the young man asked, "Do we still wait?"

"Aye. We wait," he replied before drifting off into a dreamless sleep.

17

A black mood combined with a throbbing headache conspired to make King Saul want to scream his throat raw. To feel pain elsewhere would be a relief! The reports that kept trickling in only increased the tension that consumed him. His house felt like a prison, and everything in it simply reminded him of David. He could scarcely look at his own son and daughter without feeling as if they were silently condemning him—condemning him for doing what he had to do, what he must do. They simply didn't understand. He had needed to be away from their frowns, their silent, but unceasing exchange of glances when they thought he wasn't looking. So, he had personally taken charge of the hunt for David after Ishui and Phalti had failed to find the renegade. Clearly, he could trust this to no one. He would not rest until he ran David to ground and killed him.

Increasingly, he had become convinced that the only way to rid himself of the evil spirit that plagued him was to kill David. It was obvious to him now that David was to blame. Thus, he drove his soldiers mercilessly, pouncing like a starving dog on a lame hare on every hint of where David may have hidden himself. But so far, the son of Jesse continued to elude him. And if the rumors were to be believed, David was everywhere.

He grounded his spear into the rocky soil, unmindful of dulling the point and brushed back loose strands of hair as a stiff breeze on

1 Samuel 22:1-3

a cloudy day played havoc with his hair. "What news of David?" he demanded of Ishui, his son.

Ishui scowled from where he stood next to Captain Phalti. The pair had failed to find David on their own, so his son had no cause to resent his king's tone. He impatiently gestured for his son to speak. Hardly trying to disguise his glare, Ishui said, "He has not been found in any city in the north. Though there are still reports that he has fled to the remnants of the Danites. Other witnesses claim he has fled to the Moabites or to the Ammonites."

"Nay," Saul spat, pushing his son roughly out of the way and storming off across the hard-packed dirt of the road. The only good thing about this day was that the clouds obscured the sun. With his aching head, the last thing he wanted was for the sun to beat down upon him. He could smell a hint of rain in the air. It suited his mood.

He sensed more than heard the men shifting to follow. Stopping at the top of the hill, he gazed south toward Jerusalem and Bethlehem beyond. Despite the clouds, he still squinted. "If he hides anywhere, it is in Judah." *Or in Ramah with Samuel.* He didn't say this last aloud because, of all scenarios, that was the one he feared the most and why he laid in wait outside that very city. Samuel had already proven his treachery and his power. Just the thought of confronting the old seer again sent a spike of fear down Saul's spine. "Only in Judah will he find those willing to provide aid." He was trying to convince himself.

Ishui came to stand at his father's shoulder, and just beyond him, the ever-implacable Captain Phalti followed. "Then we should march in strength," Ishui said, his eyes glowing. "Hang a few of the more rebellious of those known to favor the son of Jesse, Father, and the rest will give him up quickly." When his father said nothing, he muttered, "We are wasting time here. He is not coming back to Ramah."

Saul wasn't so sure, but he saw Phalti nod curtly from the corner of his eye. "It is so, my lord," the captain said softly. "It is unlikely that the son of Jesse will return here."

— 166 —

Saul glanced back over his shoulder at the town of Ramah. He had lain in wait about the city for over a week, sure that David would try to return. Surely, if anywhere could be considered safe for David, it would be with Samuel. It was the only thing Saul could think of, but it hadn't worked. For whatever reason, David had not returned to seek Samuel's aid—yet. Rumors of the son of Jesse's whereabouts persisted like swirls of snow and just as substantial. The rumor that David had been in Gath had persisted beyond all reason! As if David would go there! What nonsense!

Still looking off into the distance, he asked, "What of our scouts in Judah? Have they tidings of David?"

"Aye," Ishui growled, reluctance clearly lingering in his voice. Saul should have asked Phalti. "He has been reported everywhere. Jerusalem. Bethlehem. Hebron. Adullam. And a score of other places if the reports are to be believed." He struck his chest with a clenched fist. "I believe them not!"

Saul let out his breath in a long hiss. *More rumors!* It could all be a decoy to lure him to Judah while the son of Jesse sneaked into Ramah while he was gone. It could also be that David truly was in Judah. But which rumor held the truth? He fumed, his headache pounding at him like a blacksmith worried that his forge may go out before he finished. He rubbed at his temples, trying to think. What would draw out his enemy? What would force his hand? Imprisoning David's family was always an option, and if he could easily find David's brethren, mother and father, he would have, but he suspected that the elders and citizens of Bethlehem were hiding them. He could raze the town, but he worried that Judah would rise up against him if he did that. He could ill afford to have the largest and most powerful tribe angry at him.

And that was Saul's second greatest fear. He knew that most of Israel loved David, and if given time, David could rebel and perhaps most of Israel would rally to him. The son of Jesse could not be allowed to do that. He had to be found and killed.

A small plume of dust suddenly appeared from the hills to the south, from the direction of Gibeah. Saul waited, wondering if a scout was returning with tidings of David. A squad of men appeared on the next hill over, spotted Saul, and came on. Saul squinted, trying to make out the newcomers, and his headache spiked. He winced and rubbed furiously at his temples.

Ishui, his eyes younger, saw who commanded the squad and swore. Saul might have rebuked him, but before he could, Ishui said, "It is Jonathan, Father."

Saul straightened. His eldest son, coming here? He had intentionally left Jonathan in Gibeah, knowing he loved David. The blind fool could not be trusted in any matter that pertained to the son of Jesse. *What is he doing here?*

When Jonathan marched up, Ishui stiffened at Saul's side. Little love was lost between his two sons. Jonathan barely glanced at his younger brother. His weathered face was streaked with sweat, and his slicked hair glistened with oil—even in the dimmer light of the cloudy day. Saul's eldest son exuded strength. Not as physically strong as Ishui, he was still more skilled in combat than his brother. His quickness and ability to understand the ebb and flow of combat, to read an opponent, and then to predict what he would likely do next had done Jonathan well. Jonathan was popular with the people, and Jonathan was the one Saul wanted to succeed him one day. The only thing Jonathan lacked was ambition. He would allow David to take the throne without contest. This knowledge weighed upon Saul like an overloaded camel straining to rise to its feet.

Jonathan clanked to a stop, his bronze armor glinting dully. "Father, I come with tidings." His voice held an edge to it, like a knife used for sheering. It also held disapproval. His perfunctory bow was just within the bounds of propriety.

Glancing at Jonathan's men, he noted that Adriel was not among them. He would have sharp words with his newest son-in-law for failing to keep Jonathan at Gibeah. If the news was of such import, then Adriel himself should have come to deliver it, not Jonathan. Now he would need to deal with his deluded son face to face. "Then speak, my son. What news?"

— 168 —

"The Philistines stir, my lord. Scouts have been seen in the Elah Valley and around Bethlehem. Reports that the Philistines are gathering around Gath have come in from several scouts. It may be a prelude to invasion, my lord. You are needed in Gibeah."

Eyes narrowing, Saul studied his son. So, Jonathan would use the Philistines as an excuse to abandon his search for David. Could he not see his own transparency? Saul glanced at Abner, knowing he would see nothing in his general's face, but also knowing what his cousin would be thinking. But he could allow nothing to interfere with finding and killing David. "The Philistines lack the strength to invade again. They are of no concern."

Jonathan gave his father a level stare that would do a rock proud for its lack of emotion. Saul silently cursed himself. The only reason the Philistines could not invade with any real strength was because of the defeat they had suffered at David's hands. No matter where he turned, David haunted him.

"It would seem prudent to put a force of men near Gath to dissuade them, my lord. It would behoove us to see to our true enemies."

The blind fool! Could he not see that David was more dangerous than any of the nations around them? Saul snarled, taking a step forward and looking down at his son. "I know your mind, my son, and I like it not. You would take me away from hunting my enemy to chase conies!"

Jonathan backed up a step so he wouldn't have to look up so sharply. "Is this not your duty—"

"Speak not of duty!" Saul roared, his hands clenching his spear as if he would thrust Jonathan through with it. Jonathan eyed the spear askance, which served to only infuriate Saul the more. "I know my duty. It is you who should learn his! You are to do as I say!"

"I have ever been loyal, my lord."

"Your love of David speaks the lie of your words! You love him to the confusion of your mother. Nay, my son, I will do *your* duty as well as mine and end the son of Jesse. This I vow!"

Jonathan stiffened, his short beard bristling with indignation. "David is your son-in-law, my lord! He has ever been loyal to you!"

The reminder that David had married Michal struck Saul like a physical blow. He growled deep in his throat, and he might have attacked his son then, but a glimmer of inspiration came to him. He felt sure that David loved Michal, but that a deeper love existed between the traitor and Jonathan was no longer in doubt. He could use this. "Do you truly believe that David is honorable?" he demanded.

"Aye, he is."

Saul repressed a grin that turned into a wince as his headache expanded into a company of needles stabbing into his head. Teeth clenched tightly, he tried to think. Perhaps there was a way to draw out David yet. It was time he fulfilled his vow to his daughter.

He turned away from his son and faced his men who had edged cautiously closer to hear, knowing that any tidings likely involved them. He scanned them, his eyes falling on Captain Phalti. The man was nearing middle-age. His light-brown hair had been cropped quite close to his scalp, but gray showed around the edges and in his beard. Still a powerful man, his muscled forearms gripped his spear casually. He was short, not stocky, but with a slim waist and wide chest. His weathered and lined face looked curious as he waited upon his king. More importantly as far as Saul was concerned, Phalti was a Benjamite, hailing from the small city of Gallim.[1] He had been married once, but his wife had died young, if he remembered the story right. More importantly, the man had proven his loyalty these last weeks. Perfect.

"You are blind in this, my son," Saul said, watching Jonathan intently. His son stiffened. *Good.* Saul plowed on. "The son of Jesse has beguiled you and bereft you of all reason. That he seeks the kingdom is no longer in doubt. And what, suppose you, will he do once he has the kingdom? He will slay you. You believe he is honorable, but he conspires with Samuel. Men speak of him

---

[1] 1 Samuel 25:44.

throughout the land, Jonathan! He breeds rebellion in all whom he touches!"

Jonathan tried to speak, but Saul stabbed his spear down so violently that his eldest son was forced to step back. Leaning forward, Saul nearly spat in his son's face. "Nay, I will not stand idly by while he wrests the kingdom from your father's house." Straightening, he looked around, making sure he held everyone's attention. He had it. "I declare that David, the son of Jesse, is outcast. He is Hebrew no longer! Let his name be struck from the chronicles. He is dead to all, so let all who lay eyes upon him slay him without remorse or hesitation."

Jonathan paled and backed up, and the shocked murmurs that sprang up among the soldiers were gratifying. Jonathan opened his mouth, but a look from Saul shut it quickly. His son did not know how close he had come to death at that moment. If he would have defied Saul in this, the king would have no choice but to kill his own son. Fortunately, Jonathan retained enough wisdom to know he was beaten.

"Hear me!" Saul shouted suddenly, and all the whispers died as suddenly as they had sprung up. "My daughter, Michal, is widowed. He whom was once her husband is dead, and I would not see her so bereft in Israel. Therefore, I would give her to a worthy man among us." He looked Captain Phalti straight in the eye. "To you, Captain, I would give my daughter. You too have been bereft. The days of your mourning have long past, and it is time to take to you another wife. Will you take her?"

Underneath that stoic face lay a very emotional man. The captain's mouth worked soundlessly as he fought for an answer. Saul nodded. To him, it was as good as agreed upon. Having declared David outcast would certainly cause any man to hesitate in defying the king.

Impatiently, Saul moved to lay a hand on the captain's shoulder. "Then in the name of Jehovah Elohim, I proclaim it done. You, Captain Phalti, will be my son-in-law." He ran his eyes over the men, daring them to contradict him, daring any, especially his son,

— 171 —

to dissent. "Let the tidings be known throughout the land, and let all Israel rejoice."

Jonathan quivered in fury. Beads of glistening sweat had formed on his brow, matching the shine of his hair. Red-faced, he stared at his father in as close to a murderous rage as he'd ever seen in his son. But it had been necessary. The effort David had gone through to marry Michal only to have Saul give her to another would be motivation enough to drive the fugitive out of whatever hole he had hidden himself—once he heard. And hear he would. Jonathan would see to that.

"May I have leave to return to Gibeah, my lord?" Jonathan's words were clipped as if bitten off.

Saul waved a hand. "You may depart."

Turning on heel, Jonathan strode away. He gestured and his men formed up behind him. Saul watched until his son disappeared over the next hill. It had begun. Only Jehovah could know the end of it. But it had to be done. His head throbbed, sending jolts of pain and stabbing light behind his eyes. It had to be done.

18

Word spread, and men came. More than David believed would come, but well shy of what he had hoped for. If he was to force a peace with King Saul, he would need to do it from strength, but four hundred men[1] would merely be an irritant to Saul.

Looking around at the men coming and going through the extensive cave system, David saw both familiar and new faces. Leather-faced Adino, whom men called The Spear, lounged near the largest cave entrance; his thin frame resembled a reed propped up against a wall. He would occasionally spit out an Elah shell as he chewed absently on a mouth full of nuts. Shammah, his bald head polished like a bronze knob, walked by, his tongue lashing out at the men like whips as he organized and cajoled them into some semblance of order. The bronze beads woven into his braided beard created a chime-like sound whenever he moved his head. Eleazar, the finest swordsman David had ever seen, sat hunched over a clay bowl filled with dates, ignoring everyone and everything around him—like a rock with nothing to fear from a brush fire.

Those three, in particular, had served with David when he had captained the Indebted. Indeed, somewhat more than half the men

---

[1] 1 Samuel 22:2.

who had gathered to him had once been part of that mighty group of men. That alone had warmed David's heart.

But new faces were just as prevalent, and many of them were of David's own family.[2] Joab, his square face, set in something of disapproval, looked ready to chew sand for fun. He obviously expected more from the men who had gathered to David's cause, and he just as obviously didn't know what to do about it.

Joab's two brothers had come. Asahel, the youngest, stood nearby, vacillating from jumping to do whatever Joab barked at him to do and running to following Shammah's growled commands. The poor lad's face looked like he'd rather be sleeping in a den of vipers. Abishai, the middle brother, was around some place, but not currently under David's sight.

Many of his brothers had trickled in over the last few weeks, and Shammah, his third eldest brother—who incidentally looked nothing like David's lieutenant by the same name—had arrived and quickly set about establishing supply lines and organizing food distribution and other essential matters. Shammah wasn't much of a warrior, but he had a keen mind and a tenacity to get things done that would do credit to a stubborn badger.

New faces, some old and many young, made up the rest of David's growing army. He spotted Elhanan, the son of Dodo, wide and as solid as any of the boulders, and standing among the younger men who had rallied to David's cause as if he intended to grow roots. Certain names had engraved themselves in his mind as many of the younger men had been introduced to him: Benaiah the son of Jehoiada, Elika, Helez, Ira the son of Ikkesh, Abiezer, Mebunnai, Zalmon, Maharai, and more.[3] One very young man had already impressed David very much: Uriah the Hittite.[4] Not yet twenty and unmarried, the stranger had adopted Hebrew ways to the core, seemingly more Hebrew than most Hebrews. He clearly had a level

---

[2] 1 Samuel 22:1.
[3] 2 Samuel 23:20, 25-28.
[4] 2 Samuel 23:39.

head on his shoulders for one so young and unblooded in battle. This was a young man to keep an eye on.

But it was the women and children who bothered David most. Many of the men had brought their families, and among them David's own father and mother. There was no other choice in the matter. Saul would use their families if he could to snare David or any of the men who had chosen to follow him. Some of the women would've come even if they did have a choice, but he fretted about it anyway. He worried he was leading everyone to their deaths.

Something had to be done to keep the elderly, women, and children safe—and to free up David's men to do what had to be done. If they had to run and fight, they couldn't very well do it while trying to protect women and children. But anything he did would put too many people at risk. He sighed, frustration boiling his blood.

"Why such a sigh, David?"

David jumped nearly out of his skin. Turning, he swallowed his first impulse to scream at the newcomer and found himself wanting to smile instead at the prophet who had snuck up on him.

Gad's grin only grew as if he knew David's thoughts. "Did I not tell you that we would meet again? Did I not tell you that I would bring the word of the LORD to you?"

David felt a rush of eagerness. "The LORD has spoken? What is it that I am to do? Where should I go?"

But Gad was already shaking his head, his grin gone before David could blink. "I have come at the word of the LORD, but Jehovah has yet to reveal His will regarding your circumstances."

"You have heard nothing?"

Gad shrugged. "It is as I say." His grin reappeared. "But fear not. The LORD will speak when He does. Not before. Worry not about it."

That was hardly comforting, but then David had always found that Jehovah worked on His own timetable, not his. Why should this be any different? Regardless, seeing Gad did David good. He felt reassured somehow that the LORD was indeed with him. "You are welcome here, my friend, most welcome. How did you find me?"

1 Samuel 22:1-3

"It was not hard, and few will attempt to deceive a prophet."

David looked skeptical. If it was that easy to find him, then Saul would have descended upon him with the full might of his army. He would already be dead. "Nay, the LORD told you." He considered. "Or Samuel."

Gad spread his hands, his face looking innocent behind his black beard and boyish eyes. Those eyes twinkled with mirth. "Perhaps so."

David laughed. It felt good to laugh, and his spirits rose. "I am glad you are here, seer, but I tell you plainly, I wish it were Samuel that had come."

Taking no offense, Gad nodded. "Samuel will not leave Ramah. It is his home, and he intends to die there."

David had thought as much. The notion of the Great Seer dying sent a stab of pain into his heart. He cleared his throat and glanced around at the bustle of warriors and families. "But you are here, and I am glad of it. I am in need of counsel."

"Then I will apply my formidable wisdom to the problem, my lord. Pray tell me of this need of yours?"

David laughed again. Gad was a refreshing breeze on an otherwise stifling day. "Tell me, O wise one, what I should do. I have nearly four hundred men here, but some have brought their wives and children. Tell me how to keep them safe, for if Saul learns of me, he will not fail to seek my life or the lives of all here."

Rubbing his hands together, the seer quirked a smile. "Guide my understanding, my lord, if I stray. You seek a safe haven, a hold, to keep all here safe?"

"Aye."

"What options have you considered?"

"There are not many." David pondered the question a bit. "I could flee to the south of Judah. It is not as populated. Perhaps safety lies in that direction?"

"What problems do you foresee in doing so?"

Another good question. "Resources. Feeding so many in so sparse a land will be difficult. There are few to barter with and fewer

— 176 —

who would have need of our services—particularly that of four hundred men."

"Then where else?"

"North is beyond our power, I fear, unless the LORD intervenes. King Saul will doubtless know if we pass through Benjamin, and the Philistines will impede us if we attempt to swing around by traveling first to the west. That leaves only the east. Moab."

"Would Moab welcome so many?"

"Perhaps. The king of Moab has little love for King Saul. When Saul rose to power, I am told he clashed often with Moab.[5] I was there when the ambassador from Moab taunted King Saul." He didn't say that the man had used David to do his taunting. "I think they might reach an accord with us. My great-grandmother, Ruth, was from Moab. I can claim blood ties if need be."

Gad nodded, his face twisting in thought. "Very well, but where in Moab would you go? Where would you be welcome?"

"There is an abandoned watchtower left over from Saul's war with Moab. It is known as Mizpeh.[6] It is strongly fortified, and we should have little trouble making the place habitable. Saul would have no power there. The elderly, women, and children will be safe."

"For a time," Gad agreed, stroking his beard. "But the king of Moab will hear. Do you think he will be pleased?"

"He will not. But I will send messengers to him, seeking peace. I will make it known that his enemy is my enemy." He said this last as if biting into a rotten date. Saul was not the enemy as far as he was concerned, but he needed the Moabites' help. "I think I can prevail upon him to lend us Mizpeh for a time."

Gad looked doubtful, but he didn't disagree. "How will you get there?"

"We can go by way of Hebron into the wilderness and swing around the Sea of Salt to the north." David paused, trying to

---

[5] 1 Samuel 14:47.

[6] 1 Samuel 22:3. The name means 'watch tower.' This is not the same place Samuel had called the people together in 1 Samuel 10.

1 Samuel 22:1-3

consider all the consequences, trying to foresee both the good and the ill of such a decision. Finally, he nodded emphatically. "Aye. To Mizpeh of Moab we go." He glanced at the seer watching him. "That is unless you have other counsel to give?"

"Nay. You have tapped into my vast store of wisdom rightly."

"Then I must take my leave of you, seer. If we are to do this, then we must do so quickly before Saul learns of us here."

Gad's grin returned, but even broader than before. "It seems you have wisdom of your own, my lord."

Chuckling, David left to begin overseeing preparations to leave. Only later did he realize that Gad had not actually advised him on anything. Clever that. Asking questions that helped David solidify what needed to be done. It was then that David learned of another, less pleasant truth—not everyone who had come to him was as understanding as Gad.

"Surely it is not true!" roared a thick man only vaguely familiar to David as he strode toward him, his hand gripping the hilt of a short sword so tightly that his knuckles showed white. "Tell us truly, David, mean you to take us to Moab?"

David's eyes narrowed in anger and surprise. How had word spread so quickly? Joab, who had tagged along with David, stiffened at his side. The man hadn't come alone either. A score of hard-faced, rugged men stood in a ragged group behind their spokesman. Each bore a frown plastered upon an angry or disapproving face. He had seen these men about in the last few days. He had welcomed them, knowing he would need every man willing to aid him, but he liked not the looks of this one or of his companions. He had often seen this man in the company of another, a tall, rat-faced man who always looked as if he were eating something sour. But he didn't see the fellow in the crowd before him. Likely, the fellow had fled. Well, David wasn't requiring any man to stay who didn't want to, but if the man had truly gone, then it was time they all left as well. It was only a matter of time before Saul discovered them or someone betrayed his location.

— 178 —

David suffered these men as long as they carried their own weight and didn't cause trouble. He didn't have time for troublemakers. "And who are you?" he demanded.

The stocky man pulled himself up straight, apparently with effort, his beard bristling and his close-set brown eyes trying to bore a hole in David's head. His face looked as if someone had spent a considerable amount of time throwing small stones at it, and David idly wondered what disease had so transformed him. "I be Shobal," the man bellowed. "By what right have you to take us to Moab? It is a heathen land where every sword and spear will be against us. It is folly!"

Echoing murmurs reached David's ears from the Shobal's followers. David's eyes shifted to them, and they instantly fell quiet. Looking back at the ugly brute, he said, "You may leave at any time. None here will hinder you, save that you take no more than a day's provisions." He looked at the group. "Each."

"Do we then not have a say in this? It is said that you are not truly wanting to be king, but that you wish Saul to remain so. Are these sayings false? Do you then intend to rule us as a king? You are not alone in sharing King Saul's wrath." The man stepped forward menacingly. "We should be seeking a way to slay the king afore he finds us—not fleeing like cowards to hide in rocks."

Growling in irritation, David took his own step closer to the large man. Shobal's eyes widened as if he just realized who he was facing down and reflexively he tried to bring a spear to bear, but with astonishing speed, David slammed the spear aside, gripping Shobal's fist in a hand of iron. Slowly he squeezed, causing wrinkles of pain to form around the brute's eyes and mouth. "Stay or go," David said softly. "I care not. But know this. If you follow, you will obey my command and the command of those I appoint. To do else will invite a swift death."

Angry now, he shoved the man away. The brute stumbled back into his group of astonished followers. That should have been the end of it, but Shobal possessed either more courage than intelligence or he was looking for an early grave. Rubbing his hand, he glared at

David. "And what of King Saul? Do we always flee before him? What will you do about the king?"

And that was the core of the problem. If King Saul found them—any of them—they would die. Doubtless, Shobal was a son of Belial, perhaps hoping David would plunder towns and villages or because he was himself a criminal fleeing the king's justice. Some men flocked to trouble like maggots to a corpse or sought refuge from justice. And Shobal wasn't the only such man who had flocked to David's cause. David had let it be known that any man who was in debt or discontented could join him. He should have known that criminals and baser men would see opportunity in that. Regardless, he would use them as long as they followed his command.

More men had gathered at the confrontation, including Adino and Shammah. They watched passively, waiting to see what David would do. Questions of his leadership and authority needed to be laid to rest, or in a very short time, David would find himself dealing with a full-blown insurrection—or betrayal. It would only take one disgruntled man to send word to King Saul.

"Fetch me a harp," he said, never taking his eyes off Shobal.

The son of Belial looked confused, but Joab took his meaning instantly. "Aye, my lord!" he said as he dashed off.

David waited, staring at Shobal and his followers without so much as blinking once. His face, though expressionless, promised retribution and pain. The whisperings fell silent even as more men gathered around. Even the women and children, sensing something important, began to congregate, climbing higher on the hillside to get a view of David or clambering atop rocks and standing like carved statues, waiting.

Soon enough, Joab returned carrying a harp. Where he had gotten it was beyond David, but he had heard music in the camp over the last few days, so he knew one could be found. When the harp came into his hand, he broke his cold stare with Shobal and stroked the strings on the instrument. They sounded right to him. Closing his eyes, he began playing a simple melody to get himself in the right frame of mind. He needed to let go of his anger. More and more lately, he had found it hard to keep his irritation in check, but a good commander couldn't let his feelings rule him. More than one general had watched his men being slaughtered because of his anger.

Once before, after he had killed a lion, men had demanded answers of him. And as before, words had failed him. He couldn't explain then what he'd done—not in simple words. He'd done so in song alone. Opening his eyes, he fastened them on those gathered all around. "Do you all then fear?"

A ripple of murmured assent washed over David, and he sighed deep in his soul. He shared their fear. It had settled over his heart like dust on honey. He knew the struggle to cleanse such fear. He needed the men to know his source of strength. He was in God's hands. If they believed that and if they believed that God would see him to safety, they would follow.

He gave a nod to the crowd. "Then hear my prayer spoken while alone in the cave when naught but I stood against the wrath of a king. Tell, if you are able, if the LORD will hear or not." Strumming his harp, he closed his eyes and sang his prayer, "I cried unto the LORD with my voice; with my voice unto the LORD did I make my supplication. I poured out my complaint before Him; I shewed before Him my trouble. When my spirit was overwhelmed within me, then Thou knewest my path. In the way wherein I walked have they privily laid a snare for me." David played on, caught up in the spirit of the song, his prayer. His voice throbbed with conviction, with need. "I looked on my right hand, and beheld, but there was no man that would know me: refuge failed me; no man cared for my soul. I cried unto Thee, O LORD: I said, Thou art my refuge and my portion in the land of the living. Attend unto my cry; for I am brought very low: deliver me from my persecutors; for they are stronger than I. Bring my soul out of prison, that I may praise Thy name: the righteous shall compass me about; for thou shalt deal bountifully with me."[7]

---

[7] Psalm 142:1-7 (the entire psalm).

He let the strings of the harp fall silent. Taking a deep breath, he opened his eyes and cast them upon the gathered crowd. All looked upon him in wonder. They had felt what he had felt. The words, more than simply a song, had rung with the power of the Spirit of the LORD. It was like standing too close to a lightning strike. Energy and power coursed through the crowd, brought to life by the song. David had no doubt that even the smallest child present could have repeated the prayer back to him word for word.

Shobal licked his lips, his eyes alight with fervent heat. He started when he realized that David was looking at him. Waiting. He bowed deeply. "Forgive me, my lord. I spoke in haste. Now I know that the LORD is with you. We will go where you think we ought. You are indeed the LORD's anointed."

A wave followed as each man bowed to David, pledging themselves to him. He stood gravely, unmoving, until the last man had straightened. Then he spoke, his voice easily carrying to the farthest man, "Prepare then. We go to Moab, and there we will discover what the LORD will do for us."

The crowd dispersed then, each moving to his task like men with renewed hope. There was one man, though, that David hadn't seen watching him, and from that man alone he was most anxious to get approval for his decision to go to Moab.

David found his father standing on the hillside above the cave entrance, staring toward Bethlehem. When David approached, the old man turned to face his youngest son. "We are leaving." It was not a question. "Where to?"

"Moab, Father. By the blood of Ruth, we can claim kinship and thus sanctuary."

Jesse's haggard face didn't so much as twitch, but his eyes seem to sadden. "I like it not, my son. I have never left the lands of my nativity. I remember the stories told by my mother's mother. I fear the land of Moab is not a hospitable place to those who trust in Jehovah. Did you know that Ruth was once married to another—before Boaz, your great-grandfather?"

David had a vague recollection of something like that. His memories of Ruth were sketchy. She had died when he was very young.

Not waiting for a reply, Jesse continued. "She married a Bethlehemite by the name of Mahlon.[8] In those days, there was a great famine in the land when Mahlon, his father Elimelech, his mother Naomi, and younger brother Chilion sojourned in the land of Moab. But the famine lay long upon the land, and in the process of time, Mahlon married Ruth, a Moabitess." He looked square into David's eyes. "A heathen woman of an idolatrous and uncircumcised people."

David blinked, taken aback. "But I thought she—"

Jesse smiled, making him look years younger. "She did. She wholeheartedly adopted our God and our way of life, but only after Mahlon died and Naomi wished to return to Bethlehem.[9] You must understand, my son; some within our family believe Mahlon and Chilion were destroyed[10] because they took Moabitish women to wife in violation of the law that Moses gave."[11] His eyes grew distant again. "They sojourned too long in Moab. It is not a place we should resort to lightly."

David had never heard that part of the story before—not like that. Most of the stories revolved around Boaz and what he had done for Ruth. Rarely had he considered who Ruth may have been before she met Boaz. She would have been reared as any other Moabitish girl, believing in false gods—heathen in every way of life. He swallowed. "We are in the LORD's hands," David said, hoping to alleviate his father's fears. "It will be only for a short time—until I know what God would do for me."

Jesse nodded in acquiescence, but his eyes continued to look doubtful. "Very well, my son. We will go." He looked off into the distance again, and then so softly, David had to strain to hear it, he

---

[8] Ruth 4:10.
[9] Ruth 1:16.
[10] Ruth 1:4-5.
[11] Deuteronomy 7:1-3.

whispered, "And pray that our sojourn is not as Elimelech's and Naomi's."

David turned to try and offer some assurances, but a voice crying his name frantically, pulled him around. Asahel was charging up the slope, trying to get David's attention. His long legs chewed up the ground, and in a matter of moments, the young man came to a puffing stop, his chest heaving and his eyes wide, almost frantically so.

"What is it?" David demanded, grabbing the young man by the arms. "Is it King Saul? Has he found us?"

Asahel nodded furiously. "The king—" He gaped at David, his mouth working soundlessly.

"Where?" David snapped. Everything rested upon the direction from which Saul was coming. David had mapped out several escape routes, all dependent upon Saul's movements and how many men he had brought. "Out with it, man! Where is the king?"

"Where?" Asahel looked confused. "I know not, my lord. I bring tidings. Tidings you will must hear!"

David relaxed, letting a long sigh escape, and he didn't care if that made him look weak. Saul was not about to descend upon him. Disaster had not found him. He refocused on his anxious nephew. Something had the young man all riled up. "Then speak on."

"Your wife, my lord. The king...the king—" he broke off, his face turning pale.

"What of Michal?" David asked uneasily. The way Asahel looked, he wasn't sure he wanted to know. Had the king punished her for her part in his escape from Gibeah?

His nephew swallowed. "She has been given to another man to wife, my lord. Two men bore word of it."

Cold fury swept through David, freezing his face into a stone, chiseled out of anger. *No.* Michal. His wife. Given to another man. This was beyond all propriety. How could this be? How could Saul do this?

Asahel wasn't finished. "There is more, my lord. The king has declared you outcast, cut off from the Hebrew people. Your name is to be stricken from the chronicles and your inheritance forfeit."[12]

Those words shattered David's cold facade. Images of his brother, Maon, flashed through his mind, also outcast and dead with no name, no part in Israel. Anguish mixed with anger bubbled up and burst forth. He fell to his knees and screamed in primeval rage, trying to shatter the sky with his pain. And it seemed Jehovah was unheeding to his cry.

[12] 1 Samuel 26:19.

19

King Saul placed his scarred hand on the bark of the tamarisk tree. Such trees were rare in Israel, but often grew to prodigious heights and shaded a significant area with their long branches and dense foliage. The tree stood at the pinnacle of the hill around which the small community of Ramah had grown. Hence the origin of the name, as Ramah meant "height" or "high place." His other hand clutched his spear tightly as he regarded the tree, greeting it silently like an old friend.[1] For of late, Saul had been feeling sorely used, and the tamarisk tree held no judgment. It simply was.

With a deep sigh that did little to negate his anger, he turned and struck the butt end of his spear into the dirt beneath the tree. He did this twice more, and his soldiers, Benjamites all, turned to regard him. A few other servants and retainers necessary to keep an army in the field waited behind the soldiers, but the troops were sons of Benjamin, his family.

"Harken, my brethren," he said to the warriors, "and attend, for the son of Jesse has fled this place, and is not here." *And would likely not return, curse him.* Saul had encamped another two weeks around the city of Ramah, expecting David to sneak back or even to seek a confrontation with him once he had heard that Michal had

---

[1] 1 Samuel 22:6.

been given to another. But nothing. The man had simply disappeared. Saul's eyes tightened. "Why is this so? Where has he fled?"

Saul carefully kept his eyes from the small encampment situated at the base of the hill. Two men stood at the edge of the city of tents, looking up, watching him. The centermost one was old, with long flowing hair of a Nazarite. Samuel.

Trying to put them out of mind, he focused on the men standing around, men of his elite guard, soldiers of high caliber and sons of Benjamin, the only men he felt he could fully trust in these dark times. Word of David's whereabouts came like a slow drizzly rain. Apparently, the son of Jesse was everywhere. It was clearly a ruse, but the subterfuge showed organization and manpower. One man alone could not have been so thorough. Not only was David still out there, he had help. He was no longer alone.

Saul growled something inarticulate and struck the tree with the flat of his hand. He ignored the splinters that gouged his flesh. He rounded on his warriors, furious.

David's trail began and ended here in Ramah. *Curse the prophets!* He glanced down the hill where the two prophets stood calmly, watching him. He wanted to attack them, to slaughter the whole lot of them. For that Samuel had conspired with David was clear.

But the last time he had attempted to attack the city of prophets, it had backfired. He shuddered as he recounted the embarrassment of that failed plot. He had lain near naked on the ground for a day and night, prophesying. Worse, he had known what he was doing, but it was as if the Spirit of the LORD had consumed him. He could no more stop it than he could uproot this tamarisk tree barehanded. He had been trapped in his own mind and body.

No, as much as he wanted to do so, he would not renew his attack against Samuel. But if he ever discovered anyone else who had a hand in David's escape, woe be unto him!

A Benjamite scout who had only just returned to Gibeah stood impatiently next to Abner. Saul could see that the man wished to speak, but Saul had forbidden him, fearing he would reveal more of

— 187 —

those frustrating rumors. But then he remembered that this man had been sent on a special mission. "What word?" he asked the anxious man.

"You are most right in your suspicions, my king," the scout began with a deep bow to his king. "As you suspected, those who would be counted with the son of Jesse have fled. They are gathering somewhere, but none would tell me. And as you commanded, I sought out Jesse, David's father, but his household has abandoned their inheritance. His house stands empty. I searched the city and saw many strange things. Men cloaked and hidden coming and going within the city. The elders behaved most oddly and refused to speak to me. Others have also left their homes and inheritances."

Saul frowned. "What others?"

"Many families are void of their sons, sent away on some pretext or other. I searched other cities and discovered that Adino, whom they call The Spear, along with other captains who once fought beside David against the Philistines are also missing."

Saul scowled at the scout. So, no good news at all. "Do you know where they flee to?"

"The rocks, my lord. They hide in the wilderness, moving in small groups. We've found one or two of these and, as you have commanded, slain them to a man. Except for one—one eager to tell what he knows. He claims loyalty to you."

Saul blinked. Why hadn't the scout led with this? "Bring him."

The scout turned and gestured. Two soldiers dragged a bedraggled fellow with a rat-like appearance before him. The man had been battered some, and blood ran from a cut on his forearm. The scout shoved the man down to his knees. "You are before your king, man!"

The man put his face in the dirt. "Mercy, O king! I am your loyal servant! Mercy!"

Eager for news of David, Saul drew the man to his feet. "You are given leave to prove your words. What is your name?"

"I am Jether, a Zebulanite."

"And what news of the son of Jesse, Jether?"

The man's eyes slid sideways, much like a rat, and Saul wondered if the man could be trusted at all. Clearing his throat, Jether said, "I came to the camp of David." He swallowed. "To spy him out, my lord—for you."

Liar. But it didn't matter if he lied as long as he told the truth of David's whereabouts. "Where is he, my son? Tell me. You will be well rewarded if your words are true."

Avarice glinted in the man's beady eyes. "He resides in the caves near Adullam, my lord, the king. This I swear upon Jehovah."

"You have been there? You have seen?"

"Aye."

Suspicion and hope warred in Saul's soul. "How is it that you know of this?"

The man looked confused. "All of Israel knows, my lord. Word has come even to Zebulun. All men who would fight for David against my lord the king may come to Adullam. It is spoken everywhere."

Rage filled Saul like nothing he had ever felt before. A flood paled in comparison. How could all know and yet not a man who stood with him knew? It proved what he had suspected. David had help, and he was gathering an army. Two names came to the top of conspirators: Samuel and Jonathan. "How many," he snarled, "how many have gathered to the son of Jesse?"

Jether flinched. "Hundreds, my lord! Perhaps thousands!"

Saul trembled with unspent rage. He would need more men than the hundred or so currently with him. Rounding on his men, he let his anger fly. "Hear now, Benjamites! Will the son of Jesse give every one of you fields and vineyards and make you all captains of thousands and captains of hundreds?"[2] His servants looked away, refusing to meet his eyes.

Infuriated all the more, he glared at his men. "All of you have conspired against me. None of you have shown me that my son has made a league with the son of Jesse." The men around him shifted

---

[2] 1 Samuel 22:7.

uncomfortably. "There is none of you who is sorry for me or willing to show me that my son has stirred up my servant against me, to lie in wait as at this day?"[3]

Fearing that Jonathan had indeed thrown in his lot with David, he had left his eldest son in the city of Gibeah to attend to the household while he took his most trusted troops into the field to hunt down David. Had that been a mistake? Had Jonathan helped David while out from under Saul's eyes?

"Speak!" he shouted at them, irritated that no one had reaffirmed his loyalty to him. He knew David was loved, even by his own servants.[4] But these here should be among the most loyal to the king.

Then a voice did speak up, a raspy voice that sounded like rocks shaken in a clay vessel. "I saw the son of Jesse."

The recognizable voice had come from behind the warriors where the other servants of Saul stood. "Stand forth, Doeg, and be known. Cower not behind others."

The redhead pushed his way through the crowd of warriors and fell on his face next to Jether, his mass of reddish curls flopping around like reeds in a twirling wind. "I am your humble servant, my lord!"

Feeling disgust, Saul bid the man to rise. "You saw David? Where?"

The man's eyes shifted back and forth, refusing to lock onto a single object. "The son of Jesse came to Nob, to Ahimelech the son of Ahitub."[5]

An avalanche of fear rammed its way into Saul's mind. He had never considered this possibility. If the son of Jesse commanded the prophets and the priests both, then Saul was truly lost. "Wherefore did David go to Ahimelech?"

---

[3] 1 Samuel 22:8.
[4] 1 Samuel 18:5, 16.
[5] 1 Samuel 22:9.

"The high priest enquired of the LORD for him, gave him victuals for a journey, and gave him the sword of Goliath the Philistine."[6]

Goliath's sword? Saul rocked back on his heels, stung. The sword of Goliath was a symbol of Israel's victory over their enemies to the west. Worse, it was a symbol of the LORD's favor upon David. If David lifted up that standard, Hebrews would flock to him. In a matter of months, David could raise an army to rival Saul's. And the priests had conspired with the son of Jesse!

The king took two steps and grabbed the filthy Edomite by the throat. "Tell me truly, Edomite dog, is there ought else that your eyes beheld?"

Doeg's hands came up but stopped short of trying to pull the king's hands aside. To do so would mean instant death, and he knew it. Sweat sprung to life along his brow. All knew of the king's fits. And if this was one such, then Doeg's life could be measured in moments. He struggled to speak against the pressure on his throat. "I—I saw him flee north toward Gibeah. I...I sent word of this, my lord!"

Saul let go and pushed the herdsman away. "To whom did you give word?"

"Your son, my lord, Jonathan."

Saul went cold. *So, it is true.* His son was truly conspiring with David. The king glared at Doeg. "You have failed me, Edomite. You should have reported this to me with haste. In person."

The Edomite's face drained of all color. "Be not so hasty against your servant, my lord. Command me, and I will obey in all things!"

"Silence!" the king roared.

Doeg fell instantly silent, cringing away from the enraged Hebrew king. Rounding on the scout who had first given his report, he ordered, "Hasten to Nob and to the high priest Ahimelech, the son of Ahitub. Bid him and his whole house to present themselves

---

[6] 1 Samuel 22:10.

to me at Gibeah. I would know why the priests of the LORD are conspiring against the LORD's anointed! Go! Now!"[7]

The man started to turn, but Saul held up a hand to stop him as Abner stepped forward to speak. The stalwart general looked troubled, a rare emotion on the normally unreadable face. "My king," Abner said, "we know where the son of Jesse is. Let us go there in haste and make an end of this."

Saul wanted to do so more than anything, but if the priests were aligned with David, then they were the more pressing threat. If they were not dealt with quickly, they could easily warn David. The priesthood was the most extensive network in Israel, with priests present in every city throughout Israel's border. He couldn't think of a better vehicle to spread the disinformation that had plagued him. It made sense. His rage spiked until he was heady with it. "We need to gather the army, Abner, afore we seek out David. In the meantime, I would know the meaning of this treachery." He stabbed the scout with a glare. "Go, but tell the priest nothing of the reason. Tell him only that I command him and his household to present themselves to me at once. Understand?"

"Aye, my king! It will be done."

"Very well. Take what food and water you need, but hasten."

"My thanks!" Bowing low, the scout straightened and took off. He might stop to get water, but he could reach Nob before dark if he hurried. Saul would deal with the priests first and then see to David. Nob was on the way to Adullam. Little time would be lost.

King Saul turned back to the cringing Edomite. "I am wroth with you, herdsman. You have much to atone for."

Doeg's eyes widened. "I am your faithful servant, my lord. I will not fail you again!"

"See that you do not." He gestured to Jether. "Stay with this one. I trust him not."

Jether's eyes shifted about like a rat looking to escape a hunting cat. But he bowed, remaining bent over with his face to the ground

---

[7] 1 Samuel 22:11.

and saying, "I speak truly, my lord. I will lead the way if you command."

"Aye," Saul agreed in a flat voice, "you will." He turned to Abner. "Return to Gibeah and gather the army. I will return to you anon and when I do, we march for Adullam."

With those ominous words, Saul turned away and looked down the hill where Samuel and the younger prophet stood looking up. Some days ago, another young man had been with them, but of late, only Samuel and this other had come out to watch the king. *The priests will pay for this treachery,* he thought to himself. *But what can I do about the prophets?*

The prophets worried Saul. But Samuel had had the chance to do away with Saul while he had lain helpless before him in the throes of prophecy. If the old seer had truly wanted Saul out of the way, he had passed on the opportunity. But David had spared him too. Why this was so baffled the king. Maybe David hadn't dared since the Spirit of the LORD had so clearly been upon the king. Or perhaps Samuel had held him back. If the roles had been reversed, Saul would have surely killed David without mercy.

But David hadn't done that, and Saul suspected that Samuel was the reason, so whatever his anger against the old seer, Saul owed the old man and would not, at this point, confront him directly. He fervently hoped that day never came, and he longed for the days of old when Samuel would walk by his side and offer counsel.

Turning his back on Samuel and the city of prophets, he beckoned to his remaining men. "Let us depart. We will meet the priests upon the road and uncover this conspiracy. Then we will find the son of Jesse and end this."

Taking the lead, he began a rolling walk designed to eat up distances without bringing fatigue. The scout sent on ahead would run the entire way to Nob to deliver his message and would be there by nightfall. Sometime tomorrow, he would know the minds and hearts of the priests and if they had conspired against the LORD'S anointed to bring the kingdom to David.

Saul watched silently as the priests drew closer over the dusty, lonely road between Nob and Gibeah. He estimated that over eighty priests had answered his summons. His eyes narrowed. *Only eighty?* Clearly, they had not all bothered to obey their king. He knew that more than eighty lived in Nob, and he had expressly commanded that every priest at Nob to come to him. Anger at this disobedience charged his muscles, and he could feel them tensing in anticipation.

His eyes sought out Ahimelech. The high priest walked with a staff, not quite in the vanguard of the troop of priests. He was a middle-aged man, who had held the office of high priest for the better part of Saul's reign as king. The two men had never been close, but neither had they been enemies—*until now*, Saul amended.

He could not conceive what would possess the priests to betray him and conspire with David, but he would know the truth of the matter shortly. Saul glanced over at Doeg who watched the approaching priests with something akin to hunger. The Edomite was an ambitious man, a wretched cur who would lick the feet of anyone who he thought would fuel his ambitions. He was like a tick, clinging to power and leeching off as much as he could, while never becoming a true power himself. Saul despised the man, but the herdsman had his uses. He stood near Jether, watching him closely. Saul felt he could trust the Edomite that far—or more precisely, the man's capacity for greed.

Returning his attention back to the priests, he waited until they drew nigh, and then without any greeting, King Saul stepped forward and confronted Ahimelech. "Hear me, son of Ahitub."

The priest bowed his head, moving to the front. He had to be wondering why Saul had chosen to meet him on the road instead of his home in Gibeah. "Here am I, my lord. Speak."[8]

"Why have you conspired against me, you and the son of Jesse?"

The high priest started at this, his eyes widening, and he took a guilty step backward. "How so, my lord?"

---

[8] 1 Samuel 22:12.

Saul continued, his words dripping with venom, "In that you have given him bread, and a sword, and hast enquired of God for him. Do you not know that he has risen against me, to lie in wait for an opportunity to wrest the kingdom from me?"[9]

Murmuring sprung up among the priests, and several began to eye fearfully the soldiers who had subtly taken up positions around the knot of priests.

Ahimelech never removed his eyes from Saul, his expression one of feigned puzzlement. But Saul could see the fear in the other's eyes. The priest spoke, "Who is so faithful among all your servants as David, which is the king's son-in-law? Does he not go at your bidding, and is he not honored in your house? Truly, I enquired of God for him. Why should I have not? He claimed to be about the king's business. Be this error far from me, my lord. Let not the king impute anything unto his servant nor to all the house of my father, for your servant knew nothing of all this, less or more."[10]

"You did more than enquire of the LORD for him," Saul accused. "Did you not give him food? Did you not give him the sword of Goliath?"

The priest hesitated; guilt was plastered all over his face. That was all the proof that Saul needed. The conspiracy ran deep, and the priests—all of them—were part of it.

"David claimed that your business required haste and that he had not lingered to equip himself properly. That sword was the only one in Nob to give him."

Saul drew himself up. "Did it not occur to you, son of Ahitub, that such a sword could be raised to seed rebellion throughout the land? What symbol is greater than Goliath's sword? The son of Jesse has but to lift up that sword and the discontent and rebellious will flock to him. Already this has begun, and you allowed this. You have lifted up your hand against the LORD'S anointed."

"Not so, my lord!" Ahimelech protested, wringing his hands.

---

[9] 1 Samuel 22:13.
[10] 1 Samuel 22:14-15.

1 Samuel 22:6-18

"You should have told me of this the moment he came to you! You hid his coming and going! Had I known, David would have fallen into my hands, but I had to hear of this through an Edomite! Why have you betrayed me?"

The high priest began backing away, and the other priests began shuffling about, fear rising like a dark cloud among them. Ahimelech tried to protest, to explain further, but Saul would have no more excuses.

He snarled and pointed his spear at the high priest. "You will surely die, Ahimelech, you and your entire house!" Standing up to his full height, which was easily head and shoulders above everyone else, he gestured to his soldiers. "Turn, and slay the priests of the LORD, because their hand also is with David, and because they knew when he fled, and did not shew it to me."[11]

His men stared at him aghast, but though some shifted their weapons around, they did not fall upon the priests and obey. One by one, the soldiers dropped their eyes, refusing to look at their king. He knew what they were thinking—to slay the LORD'S priests would surely invoke the wrath of Jehovah. But they were wrong. The priests had forfeited any right to God's protection the moment they had turned against the LORD'S anointed—the rightful king of the land.

Despite his rage, one fact was clear. If he forced his men to kill the priests, he would lose them. Looking from face to face, his gaze finally fell upon Doeg the Edomite. "Son of Edom, you claim to serve me. If there be any truth to your words, turn and fall upon the priests."[12]

Doeg's eyes widened, and Saul detected a hungry light that sprang into existence in those dark orbs. The foot-licker saw opportunity here, and he acted without any further hesitation. He sprang to the side of one of the soldiers and stripped away the man's sword. The warrior thought better of protesting after a single look at Saul's face, and let the Edomite take the weapon.

---

[11] 1 Samuel 22:17.
[12] 1 Samuel 22:18.

— 196 —

The priests were milling about in a circle. For though the soldiers were not attempting to kill them, they did hold them back from escaping. Cries for mercy and cries to Jehovah Elohim went unheard, and more than anything, that justified Saul's decision. For if God would not spare His own priests, then surely they were guilty.

With a raspy battle cry, Doeg sprang upon the first priest, a man still wearing the linen ephod, the mark of his office. With one stroke, the Edomite cut him down. The man fell with a gurgled cry of protest and pain, blood staining the rocky ground.

Most of the priests panicked and tried to run at that point, but Saul's men kept the group bunched together with spears.

Doeg, like a wild man, began flailing about him without skill or precision. Soon the man was covered in blood, and the groans of the dying filled the air. Saul watched dispassionately until the red-headed herdsman came to stand before Ahimelech. A moment's doubt intruded into Saul's mind even as Doeg raised his sword to cut down the high priest. The king tried to speak, to stop the high priest from being killed, but no words came forth, and the sword descended.

Ahimelech met his death without flinching, indeed without moving. He had shed his fear and so made no effort to evade Doeg, his eyes staring at King Saul with incrimination that bore into Saul's very soul. The king could not look away as the sword fell, slicing through the high priest's neck. The eyes never wavered, even as the high priest fell to the side, his head nearly severed from his body.

The body hit the ground at an awkward angle, but the eyes, open and staring, seemed to continue to look upon Saul's soul. The king swallowed and tore his eyes form the spectacle, blinking rapidly. Soon it was over. Eighty-five priests lay dead on the bloody stretch of lonely road.[13]

When the only sound was the heavy breathing of Doeg, Saul turned back to witness the horror that the Edomite had perpetuated at his command. For a moment, he had a terrible feeling that he had made a grave mistake, and he staggered, only catching himself by

---

[13] 1 Samuel 22:18.

1 Samuel 22:6-18

planting his spear into the ground. But then anger, anger at the priests' betrayal, anger at David, anger at Samuel took control once again.

He looked upon his men who stood uncomfortably around the slaughter. He ignored the blood-soaked Edomite who alone stood in the midst of the dead priests. He saw fear and pain in the faces of his men. Uncertainty and doubt were building in their hearts, and in a moment of clarity, Saul realized he had made a mistake—not in slaying the treacherous priests, but in not justifying it properly. His men needed something much more.

An idea, undoubtedly inspired by Elohim came to him. It would mean a detour a delay in running down David, but there was no help for it. He stepped forward until he was standing over the body of the high priest. "I know your fear, you Benjamites, but the guilt of this is not on you. It is laid at the feet of the son of Jesse, but—" he stabbed his spear down into the blood-soaked ground "—not on him alone. Harken to me, my brethren! Harken and hear a tale of corruption! Know the history that made this slaughter necessary. Since the time of Joshua, the Gibeonites have been the servants of the priests. Joshua made them hewers of wood and drawers of water to atone for their treachery and deception against the people of Israel,[14] but in this, Joshua erred! In keeping them alive, descendants of those deceivers even now pollute the priesthood and contaminate the LORD's tabernacle in the holy city of Nob."

Saul paused to gauge his speech's effect on his soldiers and saw that he had their attention. They needed an excuse, a reason for this butchery. Raising his voice, he thundered out, "What should have been done years ago must now be accomplished. We must go to Nob and destroy that wicked city. Behold!" He stooped down and yanked the linen ephod off a fallen priest and held up the blood-stained garment for his men to see. "This is the mark of our priest, our intercessors before our God. Why did Elohim not harken to their pleas? Why did Elohim not withhold my hand? Because the

---

[14] Joshua 9:3-27.

— 198 —

Gibeonites have tainted the priesthood, for doubtless their blood has mingled with the Levites and corrupted their service to our God.

"We must cleanse the land of their evil and purge ourselves of their influence to reclaim Elohim's favor! We are called, brethren, to right an ancient wrong and to reclaim the priesthood and purge it of the taint that has defiled it. Hasten to Nob, my servants, and slay man, woman, and child! Only in this can we reclaim Elohim's favor, for too long have the Gibeonites been a stain upon the priesthood and upon the land God has given to us!"

This was an excuse his men could rally around. This made sense. All knew of the Gibeonites' service and how they had come to that service. Tonight, they would all die.

20

Abiathar paused outside the tabernacle gate and regarded the night sky. The clouds of the day before had moved on, leaving the ground damp from a light rain. The moon had yet to rise, so the sky was ablaze with stars. He had mixed feelings about the chaotic shimmer of stars overhead. He liked order, symmetry, and the stars above seemed to be placed randomly, splattered across the sky like a novice archer unable to hit his mark. Yet, there was something majestic about the night sky, something that spoke to him and reminded him of the power and might of Jehovah Elohim. The vastness of the heavens dwarfed everything, and he couldn't help but feel small beneath this great canopy.

The light tread of sandaled feet brought him out of his musings. He looked over at an aging man, one of the many Gibeonite servants. "My lord," the older man said, bowing his head in deference. "Our duties are finished for this day. May we retire?"

"Of course, Jabin," Abiathar said, smiling. The man had made a ritual out of reporting the ending of the Gibeonites' work each day. Normally, he would have reported to Abiathar's father, Ahimelech, but since his father had left to meet with King Saul, the older man had turned to the high priest's son instead.

"Has our labor this day pleased, my lord?"

"Aye, old friend, it has. You may take your rest and ease this night. We will call upon you again in the morning."

"It is our pleasure to serve," the stately old man said, bowing his head and then moving off toward the crude house he called home. The old man had thirteen grandchildren in the camp, each learning his or her role in the service to the priests.

Abiathar moved away from the tabernacle into the large open area that fronted the structure. This was where the men of Israel would meet twice a year to present themselves to the LORD, and the feet of thousands of people had trampled it flat. The young priest glanced upward to the stars again and then bid them goodnight.

But a flicker of movement from the nearby hills to the north caught his attention, and he stopped to stare into the inky blackness. Abiathar had been sure he'd seen something. Perhaps a wild animal skulking about the edges of the city seeking easy food...but something about the movement tickled the edges of his mind and the hairs on his arm rose.

He frowned and unconsciously smoothed his robes with one hand. In his other, he carried a linen ephod. He wasn't old enough to wear the priestly garment, as the typical age of service for the priesthood began at thirty.[1] He was yet only twenty, but his training had begun in earnest this very year. He would be ready to carry out the duties and follow his father as a priest of the Most High God. He would not be the high priest, of course; that honor was reserved for his eldest brother. But he would still serve as a son of the current high priest.

He stood for a long moment, staring at the spot in the distance where he'd seen that movement. It came to him then that only men would move in such a way. But who would be skulking around in the night? Bandits? Nob was situated close to the seat of power in Gibeah, and Saul had kept the priest's city free from harm for decades, and it was one of the primary reasons for moving the tabernacle from Shiloh to here. It was safer.

There! He saw more movement. A flash of darker shadow crossing over the ridge to the north, coming toward the city.

---

[1] Numbers 4:3, 23, 30, 35, and 39.

1 Samuel 22:19-20

Abiathar squinted, trying to see more, and his face puckered in worry. *Why would men be sneaking around Nob in the darkness?*

A chill of certainty stole over him. *Danger!* "Up!" he roared. "Up! Rouse yourselves, Levites! We are undone! Evil is upon us!"

Startled cries and questions greeted his warning, but it was too late. Men in armor, wielding spears and swords, burst into the city as if springing from the ground. They moved in silence, the typical battle cries of true warriors absent. A priest stood forth from the door of his meager house and was cut down. The priest screamed as the spear pierced his body, driving him back into his house. The murderous warrior followed the dying man in, and more screams erupted from within—screams of a woman and children.

Sickened and with adrenalin pounding in his veins, Abiathar spun around and began to run. He had to escape and warn his father! He had to seek out King Saul and return with help!

Another warrior loomed up out of the dark night and the young priest threw himself to one side, barely avoiding being skewered by the man's spear. He rolled, came to his feet, and dodged away through the scattered houses.

Fear gathered like a lump in his throat, threatening to cut off his breathing. He forced himself to take long shuddering breaths, but he could hardly control his body. He had recognized the warrior who had tried to kill him. The man was a Benjamite in service to King Saul!

Like a kicked anthill, the city of Nob erupted into chaos. People dashed about, seeking to escape. Men huddled protectively over wives and children, but the Benjamites had no mercy, and cut down everyone—Levite or Gibeonite.

Another warrior caught sight of Abiathar and shouted something to his fellows. Three of them started after the young priest. He ran as hard as he could, dodging bodies, struggling men, pleading women, and crying children.

A spear cut through the air at his side, cutting his arm. The impact knocked him sideways, and he tumbled against the side of one of the Gibeonite's tents. The tent collapsed under his weight, and for a moment, Abiathar was sure he was to be killed, but the pursuing warriors saw the tent come down to reveal a Gibeonite husband and wife huddling protectively together. The Gibeonite servant was no fighter, but in desperation, he launched himself at the three Benjamites, trying to give his wife that precious moment needed to flee, but she could only watch in stupefied horror as her husband was killed before her eyes. The three Benjamites then advanced on her.

Abiathar didn't wait around to see what happened next. He crawled away until he was certain he was out of the murderers' line of sight, struggled to his feet and staggered away, still clutching the linen ephod to his chest.

Fires began to spring up around the small city and for one heart-stopping moment, the young priest feared for the tabernacle, but a quick glance showed the holy structure untouched, and since it lay alone in a large enough clearing, Abiathar hoped it would be isolated enough from the other fires. For surely, the Benjamites even in their madness would not dare set fire to the LORD's house!

But then he caught sight of a tall figure striding through the city, his body illuminated by the fires. King Saul! The king was here! Abiathar stopped at the edge of the city and stared helplessly at the slaughter that continued to rage around him. What could he do? He was no warrior. He'd be cut down quickly by the least of the men attacking his home.

Father! he thought, latching on to the word as a starving man would the smell of fresh bread. He had to find his father! Whatever madness had consumed the king, his father and the rest of Israel needed to be warned!

Turning, he started blindly away from the slaughter and into the night, tripping over bushes and the uneven ground. The fires would rob the Benjamites of their night vision and hinder them from locating him as he ran into the darkness.

Saying a simple prayer to Elohim for protection, Abiathar stumbled on, heading into the wilderness, away from his home, away from his friends and family. His mother and three of his brothers were back there still, but he could only hope that his warning had come in time to give them a chance to escape.[2] The realization of his impotence stung him, and the likeliness that his brothers and mother would die tore at his heart like a lion tearing at his prey. Tears came unbidden to his eyes. He stumbled, fell, ripping his once pristine robe. Groping blindly, he clambered to his feet and stumbled on, the screams of the dying following him as he fled into the night.[3]

Abiathar didn't know how long he ran. He was covered in cuts and scrapes from repeatedly falling down and cutting himself on the rocks and thorny bushes. He felt none of it. He stumbled along, numb, his eyes wide with shock and his breath coming in gasping gulps he could not control.

He was a Hebrew, and the Israelites were surrounded by enemies, so he was no stranger to death and hatred, but what he had witnessed, what King Saul had done—to the priests of the LORD no less—defied reason. He didn't understand. He couldn't understand.

He stumbled on, jabbing his toes into rocks he couldn't see in the darkness, but he didn't know where else to go. His father had gone to Gibeah, so it was there the bruised and battered priest was trying to reach. Saul must've called his father and the other priests away from Nob so that he could attack the city without them being there. Why this might be so, Abiathar had no inkling. But it was the only reason that made any sense to his addled and exhausted brain.

He trudged wearily on, desperation to reach his father driving him forward.

By some miracle, he stumbled upon the worn cart path that connected Nob to Gibeah. He paused for a moment, trying to catch his breath, and looked around. A quarter moon had risen while he had been staggering about, and in the distance to the north, he could see the lights of King Saul's hometown, Gibeah. Somewhere to the southeast lay Nob. The two cities were not that far apart. A strong man could run the distance between them in an hour.

---

[2] 1 Samuel 22:20.
[3] 1 Samuel 22:19.

A cold shudder ran up his spine. Saul and his men could be coming back this way at any moment. Abiathar had been running around the hills almost blindly and had wasted a lot of time. He had to reach Gibeah before Saul returned, for doubtless, the king would not want any witnesses to his atrocities.

Turning toward Gibeah, Abiathar trudged forward as quickly as he could. Not long after, he tripped over something lying in the road. He fell with a strangled gasp, adding more scrapes to his arms as he landed. Gritting his teeth, he pulled himself back up and turned to see what he'd fallen over.

It was a body.

He went cold, for in the faint moonlight he could see that the man lying at his feet wore an ephod. Slowly, he looked around, knowing of a certainty what he would find and dreading it. In a crude circle that covered the road, he made out more bodies, the darkness hiding much of the bloody wounds he knew he'd find if he looked.

He stumbled forward in stupefied horror. He found his two older brothers first. Both had been hacked to death, not cleanly, but as if someone without experience had flailed about him with a sword, hardly caring that his strikes would kill or maim. Swallowing bile and revulsion both, he looked for that one body he knew must be there, but so desperately hoped would not. He found his father at the edge of the circle of dead, his head nearly severed from his body. With a hoarse cry, he fell to his knees and wept uncontrollably, his hand upon the cold brow of his father's head. All the pain he felt for the loss of his brothers, his mother, and now his father came pouring out.

Ahimelech's eyes were still open, and it was as if he was staring at his son, warning him. The former high priest hadn't died in fear or even in anger. He didn't even look surprised. It wasn't a look that Abiathar had ever seen on his father before. Gulping, he reached down and closed those eyes, his tears dripping off his chin to spatter darkly in the dirt and blood near his father's head.

After an indeterminable time, he gathered himself and stood, his knees wobbling with fatigue. King Saul would doubtless be

— 205 —

1 Samuel 22:19-20

coming back this way soon, and if Abiathar didn't want to share the fate of his father, he would need to be a long way away when they came through.

But where should he go?

David. The thought jumped at his still bemused mind, and he clung to it as a dog did a favorite bone. He must find David, the son of Jesse. Despite David's attempt to assure him and his father that all was right between him and the king, everyone knew better. The stories of the strife between the king and the mighty son of Jesse had spread far and wide. It was why his father had been so fearful when David had appeared alone to ask for provisions for the road.

David would know what to do.

Abiathar seriously doubted that David was in Gibeah, but where? Bethlehem? Would even that city be a refuge from King Saul?

But without any other direction to go, Abiathar's exhausted mind clung to the faint hope that David would be there. He would go to Bethlehem and seek out David's family. Surely, they would know where the son of Jesse would be. But first, he would need to avoid Saul.

He couldn't follow the road as that would be the most likely route Saul would take on his return to Gibeah. Looking off into the darkness, he decided to head due west. Another track that led from Gibeah to Jerusalem was off in that direction. If he could find it, he could head south, avoid, King Saul, and reach Bethlehem sometime tomorrow.

He looked down at his father one last time. He couldn't help but feel as if what had befallen his family was a result of the curse that had come upon Abiathar's great-grandfather Eli. Stories whispered in the night spoke of Eli's son, Phinehas, Abiathar's grandfather, as being an evil man who had died in battle when the ark of the LORD had been taken by the Philistines.[4] The curse, first uttered by a stranger unknown to Eli had been a closely guarded

---

[4] 1 Samuel 2:22-25, 4:17, 14:3 (Ahimelech is also called Ahiah).

family secret for years, but the words were burned into Abiathar's heart: "Behold, the days come, that I will cut off thine arm, and the arm of thy father's house, that there shall not be an old man in thine house."[5]

Ahimelech was not an old man by any consideration and now he was dead, and Abiathar's older brothers were now dead in the flower of their youth. Even his uncle, Ichabod, had died at a young age when Abiathar had been a child. He shuddered. *Is such a fate in store for me?*

Looking down at his father, he uttered the benediction of the dead, "Blessed is the True Judge who will embrace you this day, my father. This is also for the good." Those last words rang hollow in his ears, particularly as he now realized that by all rights, he should be anointed as the next high priest of Israel.

And who would now do service in the tabernacle? Priests around the country would be called upon, but would they come knowing what had happened to their predecessors?

One thing at a time, he decided. Looking to the west, he started a slow, but steady walk. And none too soon. He reached perhaps a few score cubits westward when he heard the clanking of armor and the heavy tread of weary troops. He fell flat on his stomach behind a good-sized boulder, trying to breathe evenly even as his heart pounded in his chest. Faint moonlight and flickering torches illuminated nearly a hundred warriors as they moved up the road toward Gibeah.

One man walked in the vanguard, head and shoulders above the rest. When they came to the bodies littering the road, they stopped. For a long moment, Saul regarded the bodies. Finally, he turned to his men. "Bury the priests of the LORD, for though they conspired against me with my enemy, David, and were beguiled by the Gibeonites, they were still Hebrews, and I would not leave them for dogs and ravens to devour. Let them rest with their fathers."

---

[5] 1 Samuel 2:31-33.

1 Samuel 22:19-20

Abiathar grit his teeth. He hadn't been a hundred percent sure Saul had killed his father, but now he knew, and somehow David was indeed a part of it. *But what was this about the Gibeonite servants?*

A warrior saluted Saul. "It will be done, my lord." The man hesitated. "What of Abiathar, the son of Ahimelech? We found not his body among the slain in Nob. We fear he has escaped."

Abiathar, listening not that far away behind his boulder, held his breath.

"The Gibeonites' corruption must be purged for our people to regain the LORD's favor. The line of Ithamar, Aaron's son, must be purged, and Eleazar's line must ascend.[6] That Abiathar fled is evidence that he too has fallen and been taken with the corruption of the Gibeonites. We must find him and slay him. Doubtless he has fled to David. Bury the dead quickly. We must resort to Gibeah and meet Abner. Then we must catch David before he flees again."

Hardly crediting his own ears, Abiathar nearly forgot to breathe. How could this be? If he'd remained in Nob, he would be among the dead. How could fleeing murderous soldiers prove his guilt? He realized then that the rumors of Saul's madness were true. Something had possessed his king and turned him against his own people. Saul was a murderer now, not just of Hebrew men, but of Hebrew women and children. He had no concept of why the king believed the Gibeonites had somehow corrupted the line of Ithamar, from whom Abiathar was descended, but one thing was clear: Saul was surely mad.

Israel needed a new king, or all would be lost. Moving as silently as he could, he crawled away into the night. Soon he was far enough away to stand without being noticed. With one last look at the distant torches—the lights being all that he could see—he headed west toward the Jerusalem road.

Saul thought he would flee to David, and so he would. But he had to be careful, and first, he needed to find the son of Jesse.

---

[6] 1 Chronicles 24:1-6.

21

King Achish let a deep scowl bombard the under-priest, trying to inflict as much disapproval upon the one they called Kenaz, assuming he remembered the man's name right, as possible. The man didn't notice. He would not give over, would not let go of his foolish notions. Ahuzzath watched from his place off to one side; the aged high priest of Dagon seemed even more stooped with age than normal. He leaned heavily on his staff, frowning at his subordinate, but making no effort to rein in the man.

Kenaz lifted both hands toward the sky and raised his voice as he continued his diatribe. Perhaps he was finally getting to a point in all that rambling. "The gods have spoken! We must retrieve David! He must be brought back!"

There it was. Finally. Achish frowned, which caused his close-set dark eyes to narrow to near slits. "Why? He is gone, hunted, if our scouts are to be believed, by King Saul. He has nowhere to turn. Nowhere to go. He is no use to us anymore." Strictly speaking, that wasn't true. Achish could envision any number of ways he could use David against Saul. The young warrior was a firebrand that only needed to be tossed in the right direction to set Israel aflame. He deeply regretted that David had escaped. He suspected that the man's madness had been feigned from the start—an intelligent stratagem, that. It had certainly saved him from the fires of Dagon

— 209 —

and had raised the young warrior much in Achish's esteem. He fully approved of such cleverness.

Kenaz flung an emaciated hand toward Ahuzzath. "The high priest has spoken. It is *he* who proclaimed that this David, the son of Jesse, was touched by the gods."

Glancing at the high priest of Dagon, Achish thought he noticed the man's mouth tightening, creating spider webs of wrinkles that spread across his tattooed cheeks. No one liked having his own words thrown back into his face. For this reason, Ahuzzath held his peace. He would not contradict his own words, and that meant that Kenaz could pretty much say what he wanted on the subject. The portly king sighed. So much for a relaxing day of eating and sinking his portly body into the sweet embrace of his large harem.

Turning back to the under-priest, Achish sat back, tapping his fingers on the arm of his throne as he considered his response. Kenaz, his eyes alight with fervent heat, watched him with a triumphant smile. Achish nearly shuddered. He hated fanatics of any kind. Fanaticism got in the way of more practical paths to power. As far as Achish was concerned, nothing was sacred, and anything could be bartered if it gained him more power. Surely there was a way to turn this to advantage, to use Kenaz and even David.

"How do you propose to capture him?" he asked the gaunt-cheeked under-priest.

"We know his whereabouts. He is near Adullam."

"Aye. But of the three scouts sent to spy on him, only one returned."

"This is so. The scouts erred in trying to kill him. He is touched by the gods and is not to be harmed. The voice of Dagon has spoken. Only on the altar of Dagon may his life be bereft from him."

Naturally the ugly priest would exempt himself from the burden of capturing the Hebrew. "So, your answer is to send an army?"

"Doubtless, King Saul will seek to keep us from David, but nothing should stop us from this sacred duty."

The man was without wit—or was cleverer than Achish imagined. Sending an army into Israel would stir up King Saul against the Philistines and certainly take his attention away from hunting David. Achish was content to let Saul do the hunting and let them all do the dying.

But wait. Maybe there was something to be gained here. An army laying waste to the Hebrew countryside while Saul was distracted did have merit. If handled right, Achish might be able to annex entire swathes of land before Saul could react. It would take time, though. Autumn was approaching, and before long winter would put a halt to any invasion plans. But the preparations could still proceed. Adullam, if he remembered right, was on the southern arm of the Elah Valley. If he timed things right, he might be able to gobble up every city in the valley all the way to Keilah.[1] He tapped his fingers together, thinking. Nothing major could happen until spring…possibly summer, but if David could remain elusive long enough, Saul would waste time and resources that Achish could easily exploit. *Yes, it might work.*

Standing with effort, Achish looked over the crowd who watched silently. He spotted his general. "Gather your army, general. You will seek David, the son of Jesse, wherever he may be and in whatever cave he may be hiding. You will root him out and bring him to me. Alive."

Kenaz's triumphant smile nearly consumed his face. "A thousand thanks, my king," he said.

Achish pursed his thick lips in thought. The man was an annoyance, one he could easily do without. He turned to Ahuzzath. "It strikes me that such a venture will do well to have spiritual guidance. Would it not be wise to send a priest with the army? Perhaps a priest of Dagon's presence will tip the scales in our favor. Perhaps Dagon will smile upon what is done."

Ahuzzath's grin could be called nothing less than predatory. His eyes gleamed as he nodded to the king in respect. "This is so,

---

[1] 1 Samuel 23:1.

— 211 —

my king. A man should be sent." His eyes swept to Kenaz. "You, Kenaz, will go. You will see to it that David is brought before this assembly, alive."

Kenaz paled, his own smile disappearing as if wiped away. His eyes reminded Achish of a hart being chased by wolves. "But, my lord, I—"

"Say no more," Achish interrupted. "It is settled. I think Kenaz is an excellent choice. The Voice of Dagon has spoken. It is for the Hand to obey."

Kenaz snapped his jaw shut, but his chin trembled.

"Indeed," Ahuzzath said, his voice slipping through his teeth like a serpent's. "And if he does not return with the son of Jesse, then his life will be forfeit."

If possible, Kenaz grew even whiter. Achish grinned. He loved it when his manipulations brought forth such delicious fruit.

Saul waited impatiently as his men slipped into position around the hill. He had elected to execute his attack on the Adullam caves during the dark of night with only a partial moon to provide enough light by which to see. He hoped to catch David by surprise. Jehovah had shown favor when a man had come to him from out of David's encampment. A son of Belial if there ever was such, but even the wicked could be used by the LORD. The man was greedy and sought a reward. Well, if David was truly in the caves above the small town of Adullam, he would give the man enough riches to sate any man's avarice.

Three thousand men moved stealthily through the night, ringing the hills where the caves were reputed to be. The man who had brought word of David's whereabouts stood behind Saul under the somewhat watchful eye of Doeg the Edomite. Saul didn't trust the redheaded Edomite all that much and had refused the man permission to take part in the raid against David. Still, the man had followed his orders in killing the evil priests when all else had refused. That meant something.

The spy had taken an instant dislike to the fawning Edomite and stood as far away as he could without seeming to be trying to escape. Jether was a tall man, dark of complexion, and possessing a face like a rat. He acted like a rat too.

According to him, David had hundreds, maybe thousands, of men, but after much reflection, if there was more than a score, Saul would be shocked. Throwing your lot in with David was a death sentence, so unless you had no choice, who would dare? But he was taking no chances. He had brought the bulk of the Gibeah garrison to deal with the fugitive.

He grounded the butt of his spear into the dirt and twisted the hilt of his sword impatiently. How long could it possibly take to encircle the caves? He wanted this done. He wanted David's head on a spear point. Soon enough, however, a high-pitched, almost cricket-like, call of a sparrow floated through the air. The sound meant that Ishui and Abner were in position.

Stepping up to a rise that overlooked the hill and the cave system where David's men were hiding, he uncovered a shuttered lamp and dashed it violently upon a bush soaked in oil. The bush roared into flame, sending a beacon none could fail to notice in the darkness. Like the burning bush of Moses' day, Saul envisioned the beacon to herald his inevitable victory. And like the Hebrews before the falling walls of Jericho, his men, led by Ishui and Abner, let loose with a roar that seemed to shake the heavens, and charged.

Straining, Saul tried to see what was happening in the dim light. He could hear men yelling and cursing, and even the occasional clash of arms. His blood pulsed through his veins, throbbing in his ears so loudly he could hear little else. *At last! David is mine!*

"Did I not say so," Jether cried, his eyes shining brightly in the light of the burning bush. "Hear, my king! The sounds of battle!"

Saul ignored him, and Doeg darted near to kick Jether hard. "Hold your tongue," the Edomite hissed. "Speak when spoken to!"

Saul's hands twisted over the haft of his javelin, his eyes peering into the darkness beyond, snapping toward any shout or clash of metal. He envisioned David standing before him, and he saw his hands ram the javelin deep into his enemy's chest. He could almost smell David's blood as it poured from his mortal wound. He could almost picture David's agony and shock.

Torches sprang to life all around the hill, some disappearing as if swallowed by the darkness. Those must have entered the caves. There would be no escape.

After some time, it dawned on him that he was hearing nothing further. No more shouts. No more clashes of weapons. He frowned. "Something is amiss," he whispered, straining to see.

"All is well, my lord," Doeg said in what must have passed for soothing tones but sounded more like tree bark being rubbed over stone. "Your enemy is cast down. Soon your foot will lie upon his neck."

The image pleased Saul, but he couldn't shake the feeling that everything was too quiet. If even a score of men were in those caves, it would not have been over so quickly—least of all if there were hundreds as Jether claimed. Could David have truly been alone?

The sound of sandaled feet marching up the gentle slope to where Saul stood watching grabbed his attention. He stared as a dark figure loomed out of the night and into the pool of light cast by the still burning bush. Another trailed after, and Saul recognized Ishui and Abner.

"It is done?" the king demanded, stepping forward. "Where is my enemy? Where is David?"

Abner shook his head and bowed to his king. "He is not here, my lord. No one is. The caves are abandoned."

"No!" Saul roared. "This cannot be! I heard the clash of arms! Shouting!"

"Some of the lads blundered into each other, my lord, and two stepped wrong in the darkness and suffered injuries. The caves were indeed inhabited, my lord, and not long ago. By the sign I saw, several hundred people—probably more—were living in the caves. But no longer."

Snarling, Saul reached out and snatched Abner to him by the neck of his armor. "Treachery! You allowed him to escape, Abner!"

Abner never showed emotion, but a hint of fear darted across his eyes like debris carried down the rapids of a river. Then it was gone. He reached up and clasped Saul's hand, ignoring the other one poised to ram a javelin into his side. "Not so, my lord. I have not."

Ishui came to Abner's rescue. "It is so, Father. No one inhabits the caves, though clearly some did." He cast a dismissive look at Abner. "Though I doubt more than two score were ever present at one time."

With a roar of rage, Saul thrust Abner away. The stern general staggered back a few steps before regaining his footing. He stood there impassively, his face betraying nothing, but he watched Saul like one would watch an asp that suddenly had crawled too close.

His fury unsatiated, he spun to face Jether, who flinched violently when the king's eyes fell upon him. The greedy man must've sensed Saul's intent. He flung his hands up and tried to back away. "He was here, my king! I swear it! Upon the lives of my son and daughter, I swear it!"

Saul was beyond hearing. He took two rapid steps toward Jether and rammed his javelin deep into the man's chest. The shock stood the spy up on his toes for a moment, and his mouth worked in soundless denials. He tried to bring a hand up to grip the javelin, but blood fountained from his mouth, and his eyes were already glazing in death.

The infuriated king kicked the body away, jerking his bloody javelin free, his rage hardly diminished. Doeg fell to his face beside the corpse as if driven to the ground by a hammer. He began blubbering about his loyalty, his nose and mouth in the dirt.

Disgust replaced fury. He turned away so he wouldn't have to look at the groveling, sniveling Edomite. He fixed his eyes on his son and general. "Find him," he commanded in a hoarse whisper. "Find where he has gone." He pointed at Jether's corpse. "This was treachery. He knew David would be gone from here—if he ever was here. By this deception, the son of Jesse could be anywhere. But if he was here, then I would know where he has gone."

Abner and Ishui both bowed low. "As you command, my lord," Abner said. He spun around, his face hard enough to crush rock. It didn't matter to Saul if his general agreed or not. Just that he obeyed.

Ishui remained, studying his father. He didn't bother to give the dead man even a single look. "Let me find grace in your sight, Father, and let not your anger be turned upon me, for I have ought to say, but my words may be displeasing."

Saul's eyes narrowed. "Say on," he ordered, promising nothing.

"If David is to be found, we must see to his friends, my lord. None be closer to the son of Jesse than Jonathan, as my lord does surely know. Abner will doubtless scour the countryside, but he will find the son of Jesse not. But if any do know, it would be Jonathan, your son."

The truth of those words struck Saul like hammer blows. He felt his strength draining out, and he staggered, barely righting himself before falling. His son made no effort to help. He simply studied his father as a jackal would a wounded animal. Saul noticed and visibly righted himself, trying to project strength. He needed to be strong in front of his son. "What do you propose, my son?"

"Let me spy upon Jonathan. Let me shadow him. Sooner or later, he will lead us to the son of Jesse. We have but to wait."

Saul didn't want to wait. He didn't want to spy upon his son. But right then he didn't have another plan. David was like an eagle. He soared out of reach at every turn, and if Saul wasn't careful, those talons would slam into him from on high. Perhaps there was something to be said for Ishui's plan. Maybe.

"Very well, my son. Do so." He lifted a closed fist. "But bring no harm to your brother. I would have your oath on this."

Grimacing like a man tasting rotten meat, Ishui bowed. "I swear not to bring any harm to Jonathan. I would only learn of David and the places he haunts."

— 216 —

There was a lie hiding in his son's words, but Saul could not determine what it might be. "Then it is well. Go. Do as you have said and bring David's head to me."

"On my life, my lord!"

Saul watched as Ishui turned to leave. He hoped he had made the right decision, but everything else had failed. Muttering under his breath, he started down the hill, following his son. He forgot entirely about Jether and the groveling Doeg.

22

David peered over the broken wall at the advancing army of Moabites, his feelings on their approach were dubious at best. A banner lifted high in the vanguard proclaimed that the king of Moab had finally come...and not alone. There were enough Moabites to easily overrun David's five hundred men. "Why didn't any of our scouts see them?" he demanded.

Adino spit out a shell of one of his ever-present Elah nuts. Where he had gotten them and how he still had a cache of the nuts after six months was beyond David. Shammah grunted and muttered something about skinning the lazy sentry once he laid his hands on the culprit.

Adino shrugged and stifled a yawn. "They know the passes around here better than we do. I doubt they had much trouble slithering by our sentries. That or they killed them."

David hoped not. These men had followed him blindly into Moab. That had been nearly six months ago. He scratched at his beard. "By the number of soldiers, the king of Moab has brought here, he is less than pleased at our presence."

Eleazar's rather plain face looked somewhat satisfied. "Did I not say they would come? Did I not warn you all that the king of Moab would be displeased that that we have invaded his country?"

"We've invaded nothing," Shammah rumbled. "We've paid for any food or livestock from the locals—stolen nothing. Threatened

— 218 —

no one." He sounded disappointed about the last. He gestured with a huge hand at the ruined fortress they had inhabited. "Even this place was abandoned."

"I wager the king of Moab has an altogether different view of the matter," Eleazar muttered. "I warned you. All of you."

That he had, but then the vain swordsman gave dire predictions about everything whether or not he was consulted on the matter. Despite the bickering from his captains, David felt at ease having these three men with him. They had faced much together, and the bonds they had forged would not be easily broken. This was true for any of the Indebted who had rallied to his cause, which fortunately, was the bulk of his small army.

The only other man with David yet to speak was the prophet Gad. He was stroking his black beard, his grin belying the seriousness of the situation. "What say you?" David asked, wondering still why the prophet had chosen to follow him all the way to Moab. The man kept his own counsel most of the time.

"What is there to say? We are here. The king of Moab has come. Is this not what you wanted?"

Not precisely. David hadn't really thought that an army would be sent against him. He swallowed a sarcastic retort and gestured to his friends and to the prophet. "Come, let us meet the king of Moab and discuss terms." As David turned away, he noticed Joab lingering nearby, his eyes looking expectantly at David. Since leaving Adullam, Joab had been like an extra set of hands. The young man had followed him everywhere. His two brothers were not much better. He nodded to his nephew. "Join us, Joab." Excitement brightened his nephew's eyes, and without a word, he fell in behind the other four men.

The once strong walls of Mizpeh had long since been worn down by war, weather, and the locals needing stone for their own villages. The few buildings within the perimeter had been repaired over the last few months as best as could be, but enough to have had provided shelter from the more frigid cold of winter in the higher mountains. The abandoned fortress lay in northern Moab and sat on

— 219 —

a small plateau of the mountaintops that overlooked the Jordan valley. On a clear day, David could see the Jordan River sparkling in the sunlight and spot the Salt Sea to the southwest. The rugged, rocky and mostly barren mountains of Moab leveled off to the east, and it was from the southeast that the Moabite army was advancing.

David didn't much care for the mountains here. Most of it was shattered rock, with brush growing in crevices and the lonely tree clinging precariously to the mountain sides. Barren and rugged, David couldn't help but compare his surroundings to the more fertile mountains of his homeland.

The six men made their way onto the plateau some three hundred cubits from the broken wall of the fortress. David then took a half dozen more steps out beyond that of his companions and folded his arms in the universal sign that he came in peace, without weapons in hand.

Northwestern Moab was not a rich land. The arid mountains rose from the hotly contested fertile Jordan valley, and little grew on the heights. In recent years, Moab had been pushed back by both Israel to the west and Ammon to the north, forcing them to abandon any claim on the Jordan valley. They had pulled back to the more fertile hills to the east of the Salt Sea. In doing so, they had forsaken some of their forward outposts, one of which David and his men had occupied. Forsaken, however, did not mean forgotten.

Once, long ago, the tribe of Gad had occupied these lands, but constant waring and being separated by the Jordan River from the rest of the Hebrew tribes had made it impossible to keep the Moabites from gradually pushing the Gadites out. Apparently, that had been easier than waging war against Edom, Moab's southern neighbor.

David found it interesting that the Moabites favored Egyptian-style armor and weapons. Most of the men marching toward him carried the typical spear, but the swords swinging at their sides were known as sickle swords, a curved single-edged blade meant for hacking and slashing, a weapon favored by Egyptian infantry. Officers wore bronze or iron scale armor, a robe-like suit made of overlapping metal scales that fell to the knees. But the majority of the infantry were bare-chested, wearing linen or leather skirts, leaving the thighs bare. Each carried a shield over which a helmeted head peered.

In contrast, most of David's men were armored from head to thigh, and many wore metal greaves on their calves or forearms. Each man carried a spear and most even had a straight sword or iron dagger. A squad of archers waited behind the walls, ready to rain death down upon the Moabites if necessary. David hoped it wasn't necessary. He was outnumbered three to one, and he suspected that a company of Moabite archers lurked behind the marching soldiers, ready to reciprocate.

A horn sounded, a piercing note that echoed off the slopes of the mountains. The Moabite soldiers came to a crashing stop, right outside effective bow range. Schooling his face to show no emotion, David waited. He didn't wait long. From the ranks of the Moabites emerged a stout man wearing a dark robe. His head was shaved all around, leaving hair only on the top of his head. His beard was shaved bare from both sides and from the upper lip, but it grew long at the chin, falling nearly to his chest. A belt cinched the robe tight against his waist, showing the man wasn't all fat.

He strode forward like a man ready to do single combat, ignoring every soldier, both Moabite and Hebrew. His dark eyes, set close to his nose, were pinpoint focused. If a gaze could start a fire, David would've been a charred heap in moments. He came perhaps a score of cubits from David and stopped. David recognized him. He was the Moabite ambassador who had set King Saul into such a rage over his question as to who ruled in Israel that David had to flee for his life. This was the man who had set all the recent events in motion.

A flash of rage shot through David, and his eyes narrowed to match that of the ambassador's. Without taking their eyes from each other, the Moabite herald lifted his strong and resonating voice and proclaimed in Hebrew for all to hear, "Who comes to the land of Moab like cowering dogs? Why do the Hebrews invade our land?

1 Samuel 22:3-5

Give answer, one of you, or taste the wrath of our mighty army and the power of our gods!"

As if David hadn't stepped forth to give such answer. David had to fight down his growing fury—not at being called dogs; insults were expected in a situation such as this from the stronger position. This was merely the first stages of negotiations. No, David still couldn't shake the picture of the ambassador goading Saul into a rage that had turned David into a fugitive—a fugitive, an outcast, and bereft of his wife.

Taking a shuddering breath, David smashed his anger flat and silently prayed for aid from Elohim. He would need to rely upon the LORD here. His words would determine the fate of all who had followed him to this land—not all were soldiers either. Old men and women, wives, and children were counted among those watching from the broken walls of the old fortress.

"I am David, the son of Jesse, a Hebrew," he began, being sure his voice reached as many as possible. "I seek sanctuary with the king of Moab. I and my family."

One of the ambassador's eyes rose faintly, and he broke his stare to glance at the people lining the walls behind David. "Is your family so large then?"

"These others have followed me. We are fugitives from King Saul who seeks our lives—*all* of our lives."

"And by what right do you come here?" the Moabite ambassador demanded.

"The right of blood."

Now the ambassador's face did crack as both eyes widened. "What is this?"

"The mother of my father's-father was Ruth, a Moabitess. She came to our land and became the wife of a Hebrew. I and my father are her sons. We come seeking refuge, a haven. We mean no harm. Indeed, we have taken nothing, paid for our food, and treated the people of Moab with honor."

The ambassador pursed his lips, frowning. His voice fell soft so that only David could hear. "It is so," he agreed. "And it is why we have agreed to speak first. What is it that you want, David, son of Jesse?"

"It would behoove us to ask the king of Moab to join us," David said. "I perceive that he is here." He pointed back toward a towering banner that flapped in the slight spring breeze.

The ambassador nodded. "Abide here. I will inquire if my king will have words with you." Turning, the ambassador left. David set his arms again and waited.

Minutes passed, and finally a small troop of guards emerged from the ranks of Moabite soldiers. In their midst walked a powerful-looking older man with iron gray hair and a mass of wrinkles that scarred his weathered, but still strong face. In many ways, the king resembled the barren landscape—rugged, hard, and uncompromising.

David bowed as the king approached. It did no harm to honor the king of the land, especially when one wanted favors.

The ambassador, walking a step behind his king, lifted up his voice so that all might hear. "The king comes! The king comes! Let all the earth do reverence! King Pahath the Mighty is come!"

"You do me honor, great king," David said as smoothly as he could. Flattery wouldn't do any harm here either. "I am David, son of Jesse, son of Obed, son of Ruth, the Moabitess woman who returned to Israel with Naomi and became wife to Boaz of Bethlehem."

The stately-looking king gave a respectful nod of his head. "I have heard of you, son of Jesse." His deep voice carried like a drum, deep and resonate, surprising David with the ease by which he spoke the Hebrew tongue. "Your name, it seems, is spoken by all. It is said you are king of Israel."

"Nay, O king. I am but a humble servant of Elohim, my God. King Saul is the LORD's anointed, and while I yet live, neither I nor any of mine will lift a hand against him. Saul remains king of Israel."

1 Samuel 22:3-5

"A pity," Pahath murmured, half to himself. "I have no love for King Saul. He has caused me grief in times past."[1]

David kept his mouth firmly shut. Moab had not shown itself to be a friend either. The wars Saul had fought against Pahath were to drive the Moabites back across the Jordan. But saying so would not be wise. Instead, David said, "It is why I have come, O king. I seek sanctuary from Saul, and my hope is that the blood we share in Ruth the Moabitess will grant us favor in your eyes."

But Pahath was already shaking his gray head. "It cannot be," he said. "You must be gone from our lands." He gestured to the soldiers lining the walls. "You come armed and reside in one of our strongholds. It does cast the appearance of an invasion. If you do not leave, I will have no choice but to attack and treat you like invaders." The king's eyes narrowed. "Your troubles with King Saul are none of our affairs. You would do well to look to them yourself and not to bring trouble down upon our heads. What would you have me do if King Saul learns you are here? We are not strong enough to impede him if he comes looking. We have problems enough with the Edomites. I seek no war with or occasion against Saul."

David's heart sank a little bit lower with each word. He had known this was a possibility. He knew of the bad blood between Saul and Pahath and had counted on capitalizing on it, hoping it would be enough to overcome any fear of retribution from Saul. But he didn't know the true political state of Moab. He knew they had border issues with Edom, but not the extent of the troubles. Clearly, Pahath worried about being embroiled in a two-front war.

However, the idea of trudging through the wilderness with the elderly, women, and children worried David. He had nowhere else to go. He must come to some sort of accommodation with the king of Moab. Smoothing his fears and anger, he tried to look humble and contrite at the same time. He bowed again. "I hear your words, O king. I understand. However, I would seek a favor yet."

---

[1] 1 Samuel 14:47.

Wariness entered Pahath's eyes, but he nodded. "Say on."

Turning, David lifted his hand and gestured, a predetermined signal. Soon Jesse and David's mother, Natzbet, appeared walking toward the parley.[2] When they came, David presented them to the king. "This is my father, Jesse, son of Obed, and his wife Natzbet, my mother. Let my father and my mother, I pray, come forth, and be with you till I know what God will do for me."[3]

Jesse, leaning upon his staff, bowed as deep as his aged body would allow. "I am honored to meet the people of my grandmother," he said in his raspy voice.

Pahath looked Jesse over and returned the bow, a gesture of respect for the elder's age and blood ties. "I too am honored, son of Obed, son of Ruth. I would be pleased if you return with me to my city and people. You may continue with us for as long as you need." He then returned his eyes to David. "But you, son of Jesse, must take your men and leave this place."

Now that he had wrung a concession from Pahath, David thought he might be able to push it farther. "What of the old men, women, and children yet with me? If any seek to abide here, would they have your protection, O king?"

Pahath frowned and turned to his ambassador. "What advice have you for your king?"

The ambassador had not once looked away from David, but he did so now to bow to his king. "I can see no harm in this, my king. They would be hostages against David's behavior and to see that he does truly leave our lands."

The king nodded. "That is so. Very well, son of Jesse. Be it even as you ask. The old men, women, and children may return with us, to my city, Dibon."[4] Dibon had once been built by the tribe of Gad soon after they possessed the land in Joshua's day.[5] The

---

[2] 1 Samuel 22:4.
[3] 1 Samuel 22:3.
[4] Jeremiah 48:16-18. Likely the capital of Moab in David's time.
[5] Numbers 32:34. Likely rebuilt by Gad after its destruction in Numbers 21:30.

— 225 —

1 Samuel 22:3-5

Moabites had displaced Gad and taken the city. It was where the kings of Moab resided.

David bowed again. "I thank you, O king. May I consult with my advisers?"

"As you wish," Pahath answered with a wave of a leathery looking hand.

David turned, and taking his father and mother with him, returned to his friends and the prophet Gad. "You heard?" he said softly.

"Aye," Shammah rumbled, "but I see no reason to flee this place." He gestured to Eleazar. "We three stood upon the fields of barley and lentils, remember, and slew the Philistines with a great slaughter."[6] He poked a thick finger at Adino. "Remember, my lord, the great victory that The Spear won with but his namesake.[7] If the LORD be with us, these dogs cannot stand before us. Let us drive them from the field and claim this land for Israel."

Adino merely grunted, looking disinterested. He would do whatever David wished and worry about the consequences later. Eleazar was another matter. "You speak foolishly," he shot at Shammah. "This is not the same, you ox. Who is to say the LORD is with us in this? What would we gain by making the Moabites our enemies? Would you have every hand against us? Forever vagabonds?"

Shammah's face went flat, and his body quivered, an avalanche straining to begin. David thought that Eleazar should take care with his words, but that would be like trying to hold back the wind with your finger. David lifted a hand to forestall the argument and looked to Gad, the prophet. "What say you, prophet?"

The grin had yet to disappear, and it had only grown wider as the tension grew between Eleazar and Shammah. His eyes went from one to the other as if he relished to see what would happen next. "Abide not in the hold," he said, finally turning to David. "I say depart and get you into the land of Judah."

---

[6] 2 Samuel 23:9-12; 1 Chronicles 11:12-14.
[7] 2 Samuel 23:8; 1 Chronicles 11:11.

"Judah!" Eleazar exploded while Shammah shouted, "Madness!" They broke off and eyed each other, probably worried that they had actually agreed on something.

But David's curiosity fought against his unease. "We have but fled Judah. Why do you counsel us to return?"

The prophet shrugged. "The LORD has chosen you to be the next king of Israel, not of Moab. If you truly wish to see what the LORD will do for you, return to Judah. Put yourself in the LORD's hands. If the LORD is on our side, what fear have we of what man does?"

The words must have been Spirit-filled because they strummed all the chords of David's heart and soul at once, and he knew of a certainty that he had to return to Judah. Indeed, troubling rumors and evil tidings had reached the ears of all. It was said that all the priests of the LORD were dead, killed by raiders—no, killed by King Saul. David could hardly credit this last, for the same rumors said that Bethlehem had been burned to the ground, and he was sure that wasn't true. But then Doeg had been present when David had turned to the priests at Nob for help. Doubtless he would have spoken of it to Saul if given the chance. And the word from Israel was that Nob had been destroyed. Could the two events be connected? David had mourned for the priests and for Israel as well.

Events were getting away from him. Returning to Judah might be the best move. Turning away from his friends and family, he walked back to the king of Moab and bowed once more.

"We will leave," he said, "even as you desire. But according to your word, my father and mother, and any of the old men, women, or children who wish to remain may return with you to Dibon."

Tension seemed to seep out of Pahath. Clearly, he had no relish for fighting David. He had heard the stories too, and he had to be wondering if the army he brought would truly be sufficient if David chose to fight. "My word is law. It will be as I say. They will remain safe with me until called for."

David felt tension leave his muscles too. "Then we have an agreement. We will leave on the morrow."

1 Samuel 22:3-5

Looking thoughtful, Pahath gestured to David. "Walk with me. I have more to say, but these words must be for your ears alone."

Curious, David fell in step with the king. The king, though aging, was still a powerful man, a mighty warrior without a doubt. A warrior did not live to such an age without wisdom and cunning. They walked far enough away so that they could not be overheard. The others watched them, wondering.

"I have word from Israel and Philistia," he began. Translation: spies had brought word to the king of Moab. "Saul seeks your life still."

David looked suspiciously at the king, but the Moabite continued, "There have been deaths in the search of you. I do not know the details, but Saul has slain many in his pursuit. I think him a desperate man and thus a dangerous man. I think him quite able to invade Moab if he learns you are here, and I cannot afford the distraction. Edom is stirring, and I must see to my southern border."

"You said something of Philistia?"

"Aye. The Philistines seek to take advantage of Saul's obsession. They mobilize, but what is most peculiar is your name being on the lips of every man there. You have stirred a great hornet's nest."

"I have done them much harm," David replied slowly. "They doubtless seek my life as well."

"Perhaps. But not every word we hear speaks of such. Some believe you have made an agreement with the king of Gath. They say you have allied yourself with him."

Now David understood. Pahath worried that if such rumors bore any measure of truth, then with both David and the Philistines allied, Israel would surely fall quickly. What then would stop them from expanding toward Moab?

"Fear not, O king. I am not allied with the king of Gath. I would not ally myself with the Lord's enemies." Left unspoken was the fact that the Moabites served false gods and by any definition of the nations, this meant they were enemies. Moab shared similar gods with the Philistines, but only Israel held to a single God.

— 228 —

Pahath took the omission with good grace. He inclined his head slightly to acknowledge the unspoken words. "Then we leave in peace. I do not necessarily wish you well, David, son of Jesse, but I do wish you peace."

"And I you, king of Moab."

"I will leave a suitable escort to see that all those who wish to remain are brought safely to me in Dibon."

And doubtless to be sure that David truly left.

"Again, you have my thanks," David replied.

Pahath beckoned to his ambassador and honor guard and strode briskly away toward his own lines. In short order, except for a contingent of several hundred men, the Moabite army began to turn and retreat back the direction that they had come. Dibon was not all that far from Mizpeh, so it would only be a matter of a day or two before David's father and mother were safe under Pahath's protection.

He prayed fervently that it would indeed be protection. He sighed. He had to bid his family farewell and begin preparations to return to Judah. The hunt was still on, and he wondered how much longer he must remain a fugitive.

23

Jonathan ran the honing stone down the edge of his iron sword. The harsh scraping sound filled the small room—tried to fill him so that he could ignore the only other person in the room. But she would not be ignored.

Like a persistent hound, Michal planted herself in front of his chair and gave him such a look with her blue eyes that he should've been fried to a cinder or frozen solid. He couldn't decide which. "Please, Brother," she said, her rich voice reaching Jonathan despite the honing, "I seek your blessing in this."

With a sigh, Jonathan put the sword and honing stone on the tiled floor and stood. He needed at least some height advantage when it came to dealing with his wily sister. Her tongue could skin a foul-tempered snake from a hundred cubits away, and he already knew this conversation would not go well.

"I cannot give it," he said as gently as he could. "You are David's wife, not Phalti's. What Father has done is wrong, and you know it."

Michal never showed much emotion unless it was anger, and that usually came out in a bitter tongue so that everyone within earshot knew. But her face looked untypically worried, and she bit her lower lip hard enough that she must have felt some pain. "I have no choice in this, Brother. Father has chosen this path, and my duty is to obey. What would you have me do?"

"Duty? Why did you not go with David when he fled? Should that not have been the duty of a wife?"

She recoiled, her face turning pale, though Jonathan suspected it was more from indignation than from shame. "You know why I could not. He could not take me and evade the men Father sent to apprehend him. I did my duty. I helped him escape."

"And then lied to Father," Jonathan snapped, his own anger rising. This was a sore point between them. "We both know that David would never threaten you."

She shook her head. "What was I to do? Father sees enemies on every side. Jonathan, you have made yourself into such an enemy. Father no longer trusts you as he once did. You must repent of this foolishness. The kingdom is more important than any one man. No matter the man. This is what Father has taught us. We must preserve the kingdom, and David has become a threat to the wellbeing of the Hebrew people." Michal gathered herself, wrapping indignation around herself like a cloak. "I did my duty to my husband and to my father. I regret not one decision. Father has proclaimed David as an outcast. He no longer has a name or inheritance; he is as dead. I am as widowed. Why then should Father withhold me from another man? It is his right! And I would have your blessing. Phalti is a mighty captain, a good man."

Jonathan fell silent for a time, marveling. His sister had gone from loyal wife to loyal daughter within the space of nine months. When it became evident that their father would not relent on his desire to kill David, she had quickly turned her back on her husband, much to King Saul's delight. When the silence grew uncomfortable, he said, "Aye, Phalti is a strong warrior and a good man, but I cannot bless this—not while David yet lives. It is not right."

She regarded him as if he were but silk in the market that didn't have the right coloring or quality to please her. "I would have felt better with your blessing, Jonathan. You are to be the next king after Father, and I do not want your face to be turned away from me, and you will need Phalti in the days to come."

1 Samuel 23:1

Suddenly, Jonathan knew where all this was truly going. He sucked in his breath and ran his hand through his slicked hair. He then tugged at his short beard, trying to think. She was trying to charm him into accepting Phalti, possibly as an advisor or commander, when he became king after his father. Michal was the daughter of a king. Her entire life had been surrounded by the affairs of the kingdom. She knew nothing else. The thought of living a quiet life somewhere with a husband and children was foreign to her.

She had already accepted the loss of David and was trying to ensure that she stayed in the center of power. No doubt she thought this her duty. For as long as he had known her, duty—her duty as she saw it—was paramount in her eyes, even over what was right.

Before he could say more, the door burst open and Adriel strode in, followed closely by his wife, Merab, Jonathan's eldest sister. With them came the subject of his conversation with Michal, Captain Phalti. "I have news of David," Adriel announced. "His men were spotted near the ruins of Jericho, not two days ago."

Jonathan's eyes snapped to Phalti. He knew what the man must be thinking. His marriage to Michal was to take place in a week. Yet David lived. And as long as David lived, Phalti would likely never feel that she truly belonged to him. "Has my father been told?"

"I was commanded to report immediately," Adriel drawled.

But instead he had come to Jonathan first. The eldest son of the king raised an eyebrow in question.

"Is not reporting to the king's son the same as reporting to the king?" his brother-in-law asked mildly.

Jonathan suppressed a grin. "Indeed."

Phalti looked troubled. His lined face could not hide his feelings. The man had grown more emotional over the recent months that he had been invited to join the king's household as the newest member. "What troubles you, Captain?" Jonathan asked, as if he didn't know, but the older man surprised him.

"Word has come to Abner that the Philistines march. They even now move through the Elah Valley. The scouts believe they are heading toward Keilah."

The summer crops had not done well, and Philistine raids throughout had left a swath of land burned or pillaged. Keilah, though, had a successful wheat harvest, and this time of year in early autumn, the threshing floors would be filled with grain. Jonathan instinctively knew that the Philistines were intent on robbing the threshing floors.

"Then we must tell the king," Jonathan said, rising to his feet. He tied the sword to his belt—he never went unarmed these days—and strode past both Adriel and Phalti, pausing only to give Merab a kiss on both cheeks. His sister demurely lowered her head, her jewelry making a soft tinkling sound. He smiled at her and threw a dark look at Michal who returned it with one just as fierce and swept out the door without another word, leaving by a different direction.

Adriel and Phalti heeled him like two well-trained dogs. He walked down the hallway toward the door at the far end. His father, as he had done for much of this last year, sat beyond, brooding. He had not taken well the news that David and his men had disappeared last year, seemingly without a trace. He had spent considerable time in the field seeking David to no avail. Not even Jonathan knew where David had gone, but this report by Adriel said much.

Taking a deep breath, he pushed the door open and walked into the dimly lit room. Saul cared not for light these days, desiring darkness to hide his shallow cheeks and sunken eyes. His father did not look well.

Only Ishui was with father, a constant companion that worried Jonathan mightily. His younger brother was like a leech, sucking out their father's spirit and feeding on the darkness that was Saul's constant companion. He paused to let his eyes adjust to the gloom and dismissed his younger brother from his mind. "Father, the Philistines march. They will rob the threshing floors of Keilah."

Saul had his head in his hands when Jonathan and his companions had come in and had not raised his face to see who had intruded, but at these words, he lifted his head slowly to peer at his eldest son. "Is this so?" he asked quietly, almost listlessly.

Jonathan swallowed. "It is, my lord."

— 233 —

1 Samuel 23:1

Saul snarled softly. "What care I for this? Keilah is in Judah. Let them pay the price of their treachery for they hide David yet and have not told me where."

Ishui added his own scowl directed toward Jonathan. Jonathan wanted to snap an angry reply, but he fought against the impulse. He needed to tread lightly here, or he would sink in the mire of his father's vengeful heart. But it was Adriel who spoke up. "Not so, my lord. David has been found. He is not in Judah."

"What!" Saul roared, coming to his feet so swiftly, that Jonathan and his companions took involuntary steps back. "Where?"

"Near the ruins of Jericho, my lord."

Jonathan shot Adriel a furious glance. He had thought that his friend would keep this from Saul for Jonathan's sake. Everyone knew of their friendship. Not that Jonathan believed that this would be kept from Saul; it just hurt to hear it coming from his friend.

Saul spun to Ishui. "Gather the men. We march within the hour!"

Jonathan blinked. "But the Philistines, my lord—"

"I care not!" Saul barked. "Judah will pay the price for their treachery. They knew David had fled elsewhere and told me not." Grinding his teeth, Jonathan searched for a suitable reply, but found none. His father ignored him the moment he spotted Phalti. "Captain, it is well you are here. Go with Ishui and gather the men. David must be seeking to return to Judah. If he was near Jericho, then he has been hiding in Moab all this time!" He cursed harshly, his face a mask of rage. "No place else would be safe. If we hurry, we can intercept him and finish this at last!" He held his fist high as if crushing an egg.

Jonathan's heart fell into his stomach. His father saw instinctively what David must do and how to counter it. If nothing else, his father was a brilliant commander. "By your leave, father," he said, "I would take a small troop and set watch over the Philistines to ensure they do not turn their eyes toward Benjamin." He now

— 234 —

needed to lace the request with plausible motive. "I do not wish to be part of this hunt for David."

Saul waved an impatient hand, frowning. Ishui shot a suspicious glance at his brother but held his peace. Saul said, "That is well. But no more than five scouts. That would be sufficient to send warning if there is need. I require the rest to spy out David's movements."

Jonathan nodded, bowing and not trusting himself to speak. In truth, they had no further words for each other. Jonathan nearly bolted from the room, Adriel on his heels. Phalti and Ishui came out together and followed them into the courtyard. Jonathan turned away from Ishui and headed to his own house, while his brother and Captain Phalti left the courtyard together to rouse the men for a forced march.

He had nearly reached his home when he realized Adriel was still following him. He rounded on his friend. "I am most displeased with you, Adriel!"

Merab's husband nodded. "I know, my lord, but heed your servant this once. You seek to warn David, do you not?"

Jonathan schooled his features into passivity. His former armorbearer was entirely too perceptive, curse the man. "I am worried about Keilah. The king should not abandon them. It is wrong."

Adriel took a deep breath, looking around to be sure they were alone. He dared not openly agree with Jonathan as that would likely mark him. Saul was not known for accepting disagreements lightly. "It comes to me that if the king will not save Keilah, then there is another who may."

Jonathan stared back at his friend uncertainly. *Does he mean David?* "Say on."

"If you seek for David, know then that he will not be found near Jericho. That report is four days old. King Saul will doubtless find evidence of his passing and pursue, but by this time, in Judah is where the son of Jesse may be found."

1 Samuel 23:1

Jonathan blinked. He knew that Saul had put his brother-in-law in charge of the scouts, so it would not surprise him that Adriel knew truly where David was—or would be. But if Saul ever found out about this deception…but no. They would take this chance. He placed a hand on his friend's shoulder. "You have the heart of a true king," he said softly. "You do credit to your father's house and name."

The well-muscled, good-looking man nodded soberly. "My father was truly named after an ass, my lord."

Jonathan roared with laughter, eliciting an excited grin from Adriel. "Come," he said, still chuckling. "We must be about Keilah's salvation. And we can take our ease doing it, for doubtless Jehovah will keep the Philistines from Keilah until David can arrive and send them running home with their tails between their legs."

Adriel's smile faded, his face sobering so that Jonathan frowned in response. "But, my lord," Adriel said urgently, "David has not his sling!"

Jonathan laughed again. It felt good to laugh. He hadn't done so in a long time, seemingly since David had fled King Saul. "Then perhaps we should take one to him."

Both men were veterans of sudden, forced marches where the enemy may be waiting for them at the end of their journey. They quickly gathered what they would need, bid farewell to their wives, and set out, confident that they could locate David somewhere in Judah.

Slipping out of Gibeah proved no problem. King Saul had already given them permission to leave, and the Philistine army *was* in the direction they were heading, so their departing should not be the least suspicious. They took none of the scouts, however. For what they had planned, secrecy would serve them best.

It was good to be out in the wilderness with Adriel. Once, long ago, he and Adriel, then his armorbearer, had set out to attack a Philistine garrison and won a great victory for Elohim. This, in many, ways felt like that time. It felt impulsive, but right. And to see David again after such a long time would bring great joy.

The two men spent the better part of the day walking south, camping just north of Bethlehem and with the walls of Jerusalem visible to the north. Jerusalem was a true fortress, and Jonathan had always thought it would make a better capital for Israel than Gibeah. But it was still inhabited by the Jebusites, and it lay within the boundary of Judah, not Benjamin. His father would never live outside his tribal family land.

The early autumn night brought a chill, and puffy clouds obscured the half moon, leaving the land plunged into darkness, except for the few pinpricks of light from the walls of Jerusalem and the occasional star from overhead.

The next morning, the two discussed if a stop in Bethlehem would garner any useful information about David's exact whereabouts. Adriel doubted it, and after a somewhat heated debate, Jonathan conceded the point. It was unlikely that anyone loyal to David would give them any real information.

Still, they had a good idea where David might be. The easiest place to hide a large body of men was either east of Hebron in the wilderness or in the valleys and hills west of Bethlehem. Choosing on instinct, they skirted Bethlehem and moved into the hills to the west, moving slow and cutting back and forth to look for sign of a troop having moved through the area.

Jonathan suspected that David would need to be constantly on the move, remaining in place only if it was safe to do so. He would likely employ spies to stay informed of Saul's efforts to find him, and he would just as likely be wary of larger towns and cities. It would take only one person to betray David.

By the third day, Jonathan was growing frustrated and worried. The Philistines would be getting closer to Keilah, and his father would have learned that David was not near Jericho. The Philistine attack could come at any time now, and he worried that he would not be able to warn David in time.

But that afternoon, Adriel came running toward him from where he had been scouting some distance off upon one of the hilltops. "I've found them!" he cried, his breath coming in short gasps. "They are encamped in the wood of Hareth."[1]

Jonathan did a quick calculation. "That is within a couple hour's march from Keilah! Jehovah be praised!"

"Aye, my lord."

"Come! We will give warning, and if it be God's will, we will fight with David and send these uncircumcised dogs back to Philistia like the curs they be!"

Jonathan started westward. Hareth was a small wood less than an hour's run from where they now stood and not too far from the Valley of Elah. Keilah was located at the end of the southern arm of the Elah Valley, where they did most of their farming, and if the Philistines were marching on Keilah, they would likely be heading right down the valley.

Loping into a ground-eating run, Jonathan began envisioning the battle to come. He knew that David's men would be outnumbered, but that was of no concern. The LORD was with David, and Jonathan seriously doubted there was an army on earth that could withstand his friend.

Three men emerged from the trees ahead of Jonathan and Adriel, moving down into the grassy area at the base of the ravine. They stood in Jonathan's way. He slowed as he came closer, and then he heard Adriel gasp from beside him. "That's Ishui!"

Jonathan flinched and crashed to an abrupt stop so quickly that Adriel ran past for a few steps before pulling up. *What under everything holy is my younger brother doing here?* He was supposed to be with their father, hunting David up around Jericho!

The two groups stood about a bowshot away from each other, but even at that distance, Jonathan could see the satisfied smirk etched into his brother's features. Ishui leaned over to one of the two men flanking him and whispered something. The man bowed and loped off up the ridge, heading in the direction of Gibeah.

---

[1] 1 Samuel 22:5.

— 238 —

Jonathan pulled Adriel close. "He has been following us," he hissed. "He knows where David is!"

Adriel was a quick thinker. "He sent that fellow to report," he agreed.

Jonathan looked into Adriel's eyes. "You must stop him. These sons of Belial cannot reach my father!"

Adriel paled. "But my lord!"

"Stop him. Slay him if you must but stop him."

Adriel gave Jonathan a long penetrating look, knowing full well what such an act would cost. "What about Ishui?"

Jonathan smiled grimly at his friend. "Leave him to me."

Nodding, Adriel ran off, hefting his spear. Jonathan did not doubt that Adriel would prevail. Taking a deep breath, he turned his attention fully to his younger brother.

As if by mutual agreement, the two brothers started toward each other at the same time. Jonathan loosened his sword and took a firm grip on his spear. Ishui, whip-thin, seemed to glide across the brown grass like a dancer. He didn't carry a sword but used a heavy spear that he could twirl with blinding speed. Only one man could better his brother with the spear, and that was Adino, the one they called The Spear. Ishui's thin frame belied tremendous strength and speed. The sun highlighted the many scars accumulated over a lifetime of battle. His long hair was held back by a leather cord about his head, but even so, streaks of gray had already begun to mar his brown hair. Battle had aged his brother, making him seem older than his years.

They stopped just outside of a spear thrust from each other. "What do you here, Ishui?" Jonathan demanded. Anger simmered within.

Ishui laughed. "I follow you, my brother. I knew you would lead me to the son of Jesse. Your love for him will be his undoing." He stretched, muscles rippling. "When I saw Adriel come running, I knew." He looked toward the west. "David must be near for such haste."

1 Samuel 23:1

Jonathan snorted. "You know nothing. We seek evidence of the Philistines."

Now it was Ishui who snorted. "You know as well as I that the Philistines would not be this far east if they truly seek to rob the threshing floors of Keilah. Nay, it is David whom you seek and David whom you found. I will tell Father, and soon the son of Jesse will be dead. And you, brother, your treachery will not be overlooked this time. As the LORD lives, you are worthy of death."

Ishui knew too much. He would not be dissuaded. "Then, come brother," Jonathan hissed, "let us discover whom the LORD favors!" Jonathan crouched, his spear angled up and toward his younger brother.

Ishui's eyes lit up with a mad glee. "I swore to Father not to harm you, but I think he would repent of such an oath. Nay, I wink at such foolishness. Come, Brother, I have waited long for this!" So saying, he leaped forward, spear spinning, and the battle was joined.

24

Jonathan nearly died in that first moment. He should've anticipated Ishui's mad, reckless attack. The man had no regard for his own safety! The spear, like a viper, seemingly struck everywhere at once. Jonathan had no time to draw his sword and barely managed to block the attack with his own spear.

Never before had he fought such an opponent. He and Ishui had often sparred as children, and much of what Ishui knew he had learned from Jonathan, but this...this was a whole new level of fighting.

Twisting in near circles, like a dog chasing his own tail, Jonathan retreated across the dying grass, driven back by the pure fury of Ishui's attack. He took two wounds on his arms in that first furious moment, scratches, but they bled, making his hold on the spear shaft slick.

Ishui suddenly stopped his spinning attack, and lunged forward, trying to impale Jonathan and end the fight quickly. Even if he could draw his sword, the spear's much longer reach would have kept Jonathan on the defensive. To win this fight, he needed to get in close. Twisting to one side, he let the spear slice through the air where his chest had been, bringing Ishui forward enough for Jonathan to reach him.

But even this move Ishui had anticipated. The moment the spear struck through empty air, the wily fighter slashed sideways,

1 Samuel 23:1-4

reangling the spear point so that it would carve a grove through Jonathan's chest as he brought the spear back toward him.

Jonathan had only one chance to avoid a likely fatal wound. He dropped his spear and caught Ishui's right behind the spearhead with both hands.

Ishui grunted as his spear came to a dead stop, his eyes widening. Jonathan wasted no time. He yanked his brother closer, and keeping both hands on the spear shaft, he twisted abruptly elbowing Ishui across the left cheek. His brother grunted in pain and went sprawling to the ground, leaving his spear in Jonathan's hands.

Jonathan could've killed his brother then, but he didn't. Something inside him forbade it. He feared that losing Ishui in this way would break his father and would send him over the edge of whatever sanity he desperately clung to. In all likelihood, Saul would blame David for it, and any chance of reconciliation would be shattered forever. No, Ishui must live, but he must also be stopped before he could betray David.

Jonathan used his foot to flip his own spear into the air and catch it with his free hand. He then spared a glance at the soldier who had accompanied Ishui. The man watched him warily, saying and doing nothing. At least he had enough sense to stay out of the fight. Turning, Jonathan heaved first one and then the other spear as far away as he could.

Ishui climbed to his feet and sneered, rubbing at the angry welt forming on his cheek. "Do you mean to slay me in dishonor?" he demanded, his voice dripping venom.

Jonathan drew his sword and brandished it at his brother. "You have never fought with honor, Ishui. You'd as soon stab someone in the back as face them. You love bloodshed too much."

"So, you would kill a man unarmed and defenseless?"

"I'm not going to kill you, Ishui, not unless you force me to. Nay, I will teach you a lesson in the stead." So saying, he pointed the sword at Ishui's companion. "Disarm yourself or die where you stand."

— 242 —

The soldier, his forehead beading with sweat, bowed. "As you command, my lord." The soldier cast his own spear toward where Jonathan's had landed, drew an iron dagger and flung it in the same direction. He then dropped his shield and stood atop it, folding his arms in the universal gesture of peace.

Nodding, Jonathan turned back to his brother. "You have interfered in my business, brother, and it is time we had a discussion about your manners."

"You're holding the sword," Ishui growled, "so you have leave to do the talking."

Jonathan spun and flung his sword away. Ishui watched it fly, his eyes alight with a perverse joy as he realized that Jonathan was giving up his advantage in order to fight him hand to hand. He should've been watching Jonathan. His brother's full-armed punch took him right in the nose, splattering blood and mucus over his face.

Ishui's groan turned into a grunt as he hit the ground. But Jonathan had never met a man more capable of ignoring pain than his younger brother. Ishui bounded to his feet, a grin taking up most of his thin face. He ignored his shattered nose and the blood running down his face. He breathed heavily through his mouth and spat out the blood that ran into it.

He charged.

Jonathan wrapped his brother up, pulling him close with his powerful arms, but not before Ishui's forehead smashed into his own face, missing his own nose by a hair and nearly knocking him unconscious. They both fell to the grass, rolling over and over, each trying to gain the necessary leverage to pound the other senseless.

Jonathan shook off the pain and pushed his brother away. They came to their knees, not a cubit apart and swung mighty blows at one another. Ishui flung his fists in wild abandon, striking Jonathan multiple times, but his attacks were uncoordinated and random. His brother was trusting to chance and the sheer number of blows to do the job.

— 243 —

Jonathan was more calculating in his attack, striking where he could infuse as much power as he could. He took several strikes to his chest and head, but as Ishui pulled back for another wild punch, Jonathan saw an opening. His uppercut took Ishui on the chin, driving him over onto his back.

For a moment, Ishui's eyes glazed over, and then he blinked rapidly as consciousness, if not sanity, returned. Jonathan wasn't through. Ignoring the many bruises and cuts of his own, he shoved himself to his feet, reached down and yanked his brother up by his leather tunic. He then measured his brother and punched him hard in the stomach.

Ishui doubled over, breath wheezing through his mouth. Jonathan stood him up again and proceeded to give him a beating that Ishui would doubtless never forget.

When it was over, Ishui lay senseless on the ground, and Jonathan wondered if he hadn't broken a few knuckles in the process. Both hands throbbed, and his lacerated knuckles bled in no fewer than three places.

His face hurt, and his cuts still bled. But the fight was over. He stood over his brother, breathing hard. He'd not been in such a fight in many a year. He looked over to the remaining soldier who watched impassively. "Fetch water and wine. Your master will need care. Tend his wounds, let him eat, and move him to shade." He sighed, realizing he himself was in not much better condition. He would need to see to his own wounds and soon. Tiredness swept over him, and he barely kept his feet.

The soldier bowed. "As you command, my lord." He unslung a wineskin and went over to Ishui, knelt beside him, and began to tend the unconscious man's wounds.

Taking a deep breath, Jonathan went to fetch his own wineskin from where he had left it. Water often required that it be cut with a bit of wine to make it drinkable, but the wine would help clean out the wounds as well, preventing infection. And he sorely needed a drink right then.

Not an hour later, Adriel returned at a jog. His face was set, and he didn't look happy. "The scout is truly fleet of foot. I could not catch him. He will likely reach Gibeah today and King Saul tomorrow."

Jonathan's scowl bounced off Adriel with no effect, and he had to fight down the urge to scream at his friend. Once Saul learned of David's whereabouts, he would be coming with an army as fast as he could. "You should have slain him before he could escape," Jonathan muttered. Adriel's eyes lowered at the rebuke. Both knew that Adriel might have been able to bring Ishui's scout down with a good toss of the spear.

The remaining soldier heard and looked up fearfully at this talk of killing, but Jonathan ignored him. Adriel's short bow was just short of mockery, saying nothing. He didn't have to. Jonathan was just angry. Adriel had done the right thing in not killing the scout. Saul would have seen the slaying as an act of treason. Adriel couldn't be blamed for not crossing that line.

Adriel glanced at Ishui, still senseless on the ground. "Did your discussion not go well?"

Jonathan grunted, taking a deep calming breath. "We had a quiet exchange of opinions."

Adriel raised an eyebrow. "Looks to me as if neither of you got the other's point."

"Not so. We got it all too well." Jonathan pulled Adriel out of earshot of the soldier. He found his legs wobbly, and Adriel had to assist him lest he fall. "Heed me, Adriel. I must stay and attend to my brother, but David must be warned." He gave his friend a feeble smile. "In truth, neither I nor my brother is fit to travel. You must take word to David. Tell him that my father still seeks his life and will come upon him soon but tell him of the Philistines. He must stop them at all costs."

"Doubtless your father will be following hard. Will David have time to defeat the Philistines and evade your father?"

— 245 —

"Jehovah willing. It must be. Do this, Adriel, and slack not. When you are done, return here." He glanced at his brother and the remaining soldier. "I will have need of you."

Adriel gave a curt nod, his disapproving face dark enough to cast its own shadow. "As you command, my lord."

"Someone comes!" the sentry shouted from atop his assigned hill.

David looked up, his conversation with Adino and Joab forgotten. "Does he come in peace?" he shouted back, concerned. Thus far, Saul had not found him or picked up his trail, but he knew it would only be a matter of time before that all changed.

"He runs!" the watchman replied. "He runs here!"

So, whoever he was, he knew where they were. "What manner of man is he?"

"He is arrayed as a man of war."

"King Saul's man?"

A slight hesitation. "Aye!"

David looked grim. "Joab, take a squad and detain him. Do not let him escape, but harm him not. Bring him to me. I would speak to him and know why he runs with such haste."

"Yes, my lord!" The muscular youth seemed to flow across the ground as he began barking out orders. David made note of it. Joab had natural command ability, and he could make use of that in the coming days.

When Joab returned, he had in tow the very last person David ever expected to see. "Adriel!" he exclaimed, suspicion and anger surging up in him. The last he had seen of Adriel was when the man had sought to kill him at Saul's orders.

Adriel must have seen something of David's intentions, for he held out his palms in a gesture of surrender. "I am sent, my lord, by Jonathan. I bring tidings."

Instantly, David's mood changed. "Is all well? Is Jonathan well?" Adriel took a deep shuddering breath. He had clearly run far. David snapped a hand toward Joab, anxious now. "Fetch water!"

"In a moment, my lord," Adriel said, but he made no move to stop Joab as the younger man darted off on his errand. "I am come on a matter of great importance. First know that Jonathan is well and sends greetings in the LORD God Jehovah, but he bids you to gather your men and come to the rescue of Keilah. The Philistines even now seek to rob the threshing floors."[1]

David's attention was riveted. "How is this known?" He gave his former friend a suspicious look. "And how knew you to find me here?"

"I swear before Jehovah; I am not about the king's business. In this, I am Jonathan's man. I am yours."

David frowned, uncertain, but he had nothing to lose from hearing Adriel out. "Say on."

Nodding, David's former armorbearer continued, "The king has made me captain of the scouts, my lord David. They brought me word of your passing by Jericho some days past. Jonathan and I knew you would seek refuge in Judah. I sought until I discovered your camp."

"Does Saul know?"

"He seeks for you even now near Jericho. It will not take him long to discover his error and follow your trail." He hesitated. "Even now, word runs to him of your whereabouts. He will come, my lord; look for him soon." Adriel's hands twitched as if he wanted to put them upon David's shoulders in the familiar gesture of friends, but he restrained them. David still stood in a battle pose, his body tense. Instead, the former armorbearer said, "The king will not save Keilah. If the city is to be saved, you must do it."

And do so while evading capture by Saul at the same time, David mused. Indecision warred in David's soul. If Saul was coming, he needed to move soon. Saving Keilah would be a beacon for Saul that

---

[1] 1 Samuel 23:1.

— 247 —

he could hardly keep the king from noticing. But Judah would need the grain from Keilah. Already the Philistines had ruined or stolen much of the crops from the Elah Valley. Such depredations could not continue. He tugged at his beard, his jaw clenching so hard that his teeth ground together audibly.

Turning, he ran his eyes over the men who had gathered around, searching. Joab returned with a wine flask which he handed to Adriel, but news of the newcomer had spread fast, and many had gathered around, curious. Muttering had already started up, for obviously, Adriel was a king's man and an officer besides.

He found Gad standing toward the back of the crowd. He had to shout to be heard. "Seer, attend, I pray you. I have need of counsel."

Gad, grinning, wove through the crowd, taking no notice when he bumped into someone or of the muttered curses left in his wake. He ambled up to David and bowed. "You seek counsel, my lord? Very well. I perceive the man before me is a king's man. A spy, surely. Behead him and let us begone."

Someone muttered agreement, and Adriel paled. David's eyes narrowed as he glanced at his former friend. *Former?* He considered. Adriel had risked much to bring him this news and had diverted Saul for a time. Perhaps friendship still existed. Carefully, he replied, "Adriel is a friend."

"Then why seek you to slay him?" Gad asked, his grin taking on a quizzical cast.

"I do not."

"Then why do you seek counsel?"

David had to reign in his temper, but the smattering of laughter from the men quenched it absolutely. Gad was making sport, trying to ease the obvious tension in the air. Taking a breath, David returned Gad's grin. "I seek to enquire of the LORD. Keilah stands in peril of the Philistines. Should I go and smite them?"[2]

---

[2] 1 Samuel 23:2.

It was rare to see Gad so sober faced, but he lost his smile almost instantly, even as he straightened. He eyed David and the men watching. Finally, he nodded. "Go and smite the Philistines and save Keilah."

"This is folly!" a voice shouted. David turned to see pock-faced Shobal shoving his way to the forefront of the crowd. The man looked ready to chew thorns, but David could sense a spirit of fear about him and from the men who stood behind him. "We live in dread every day that Saul will find us. We flee before him on every hand, and now you want to fight against the Philistine armies?[3] Madness! We must flee this place before Saul falls upon us!"

A sense of unrest broke out among the ranks of men watching. Few relished the idea of taking on the Philistines. David had a force of nearly six-hundred men now, and many were untested. He had spent the last year avoiding battle, not engaging in it. A few, such as Joab and his brothers, longed to test their skills in battle, but for the most part, David wanted no part in Hebrew killing Hebrew.

But the Philistines were an entirely different matter. He would not hesitate to slay them, and Keilah was a Hebrew city. However, if he forced the men to go, would they turn and flee before the first arrow flew? Would these abandon him?

Turning back to Gad, David hoped an answer could be found with the prophet. "Enquire of the LORD yet again, seer. Shall we go and fight the Philistines?"

Gad was not a big man, but he seemed entirely at ease, not bothered by the fear radiating from the men around him. He merely fixed David with his eyes and repeated, "Arise, and go down to Keilah." Despite the evenness of his voice, it carried to every ear around. "Go," he added, "for I will deliver the Philistines into your hands."[4]

There could be no doubt who the "I" was in this case. David licked his lips. This was different than when a priest spoke with God's voice while using the ephod. Gad's voice hadn't changed. His

---

[3] 1 Samuel 23:3.
[4] 1 Samuel 23:4.

demeanor did not take on a different aspect. He didn't seem taken by the Spirit of God. Yet confidence in his announcement bled from the prophet so strongly that David took heart from it.

Trust. He would have to have faith in the prophet's words. He would need a lot of it. He would be risking the lives of every man here upon that faith. Failure here would not mean that he would need to start over. No, failure meant death. If he didn't defeat the Philistines and stay out of Saul's hands, he, his family, and his followers would all die.

His mind went back to another prophet, standing over him with a horn of oil and anointing him the next king of Israel. Trust. Faith. God had yet to fail him. And he remembered Samuel's warning. He alone could thwart God's will. Jehovah had granted man the power to defy Him, to disregard His will. But if he put his life in His hands and yielded to His will, then God would see him through any problem.

Straightening, he turned to face the men warily watching both him and Gad. "The LORD has spoken through His seer. There can be no doubt. We are going to Keilah and deliver them from the hands of the Philistines. Let any man here who doubts depart. I would not have that man stand with me."

His words rang like a challenge through the troop. Shobal grimaced, his mouth tightening, pulling the hairs of his beard tighter around his lips and nose. He might have said something, might have taken up that challenge, but Joab with water flask in one hand and spear in the other, thrust his spear into the sky and shouted, "As the LORD lives, we will save Keilah!"

Another spear rose into the sky, and someone David couldn't see shouted, "We will save Keilah!"

"Save Keilah!" a chorus of voices replied, shattering the heavens.

Shobal winced as if the voices were personal attacks. David eyed him, waiting. If the man brought further dissent, he would need to be dealt with. But the stocky man nodded, saying nothing. David sighed gratefully. It would have to do.

Raising his arms into the sky, David took charge. "Break camp. We march on Keilah. Let no man remain and let all else follow as they are able. Haste is the word; let every man heed to it!"

The men scattered as if blown apart by a whirlwind. Shouts of excitement filled the air. They were marching to fight the LORD's battles, and not a man there but could not feel the energy building. After all the running, they were running no longer.

Adriel looked around in approval. He knew many of the men, having served with David as his armorbearer while David had commanded the Indebted. "I wish I could go with you, my lord. But Jonathan urgently requested that I return to him on a matter of importance."

David felt a lump form in his throat. He wished above all else that Jonathan could join him. His friend's steady nature was like a rock he could lean against in a gale, but what had to be, had to be. They embraced and any grievance between them was forgotten. "Go with Jehovah, Adriel. Keep Jonathan safe."

He purposely didn't mention Michal, his wife, and Adriel seemed to understand. His eyes turned sad, but he too refrained from bringing up the sensitive subject. Word of Michal's pending marriage to another man had reached David's ears, and it had been all he could do to stop himself from marching on Gibeah the moment he had heard. In his way, he loved Michal—but he loved more about what she represented. Marriage to her meant he was the king's son-in-law but being outcast had changed all that. Faith. He needed to keep faith.

Without another word, Adriel turned and left. He would seek water and food, but he would leave quickly. David had a funny feeling that this would be the last time the two would meet on friendly ground. The next time he saw Adriel, his friend would be standing with King Saul. For he too was the king's son-in-law. Unfortunately, the next time they saw each other would likely be all too soon. Saul was coming, inevitably, irrevocably, like winter. Saul was coming. The bitterness of the moment threatened to spoil the enthusiasm building in the camp.

— 251 —

1 Samuel 23:1-4

Taking a deep breath, he forced a smile on his face and began urging his men to greater speed. His men needed him. They trusted him. He would trust the LORD God. "Move your lazy, good-for-nothing carcasses!" he shouted. "We march to battle!"

25

The walled city of Keilah sat atop a hill along the southern arm of the fertile Elah Valley about a half day's journey south of Adullam. Part of the tribe of Judah's inheritance, the inhabitants of Keilah consisted half of Hebrews and half of Canaanites, descendants of those who had survived Joshua's invasion. Hebrews owned the land, while the Canaanites worked it as servants.

The normally placid and forgotten town was peaceful no more. An army of Philistines surrounded the walled city. Drums beat out a rhythm of death as the enemies of the LORD attacked the city. David, lying flat on his stomach to avoid being seen, watched as another assault on the walls began. The Philistines first shot arrows at the wall to keep the defenders occupied while squads of men bearing wooden ladders rushed to place them at the base and hold them as other soldiers tried to scramble up and force a breach on top of the wall.

The defenders fought back fiercely, exposing themselves to arrow fire to topple the ladders and repel the invaders. But it was obvious to David that they could not hold out much longer. The threshing floors had already been pillaged, and the barns burned to the ground. He could see grain-laden wagons behind the Philistine encampment, ready to begin the journey back to Philistia. Only the Philistines looked set on destroying Keilah first, which was somewhat unusual. Raids rarely bothered with laying siege to a walled city. It consumed too much time and too many lives. David wondered what had changed.

Regardless, it was time to put a stop to it. "Shammah," David said to his lieutenant, "what say you? How would you go about punishing the Philistines?"

The large man rubbed his bald head. As his wide face moved, the bones of a rat woven into his beard made small knocking sounds. The bones were a bizarre affection that David had never really understood, and it had become something of a comforting superstition with the men. Strange what men would believe. "I think your plan is as good as any," the warrior replied, frowning.

"I thank you," David replied dryly.

"They surely outnumber us seven to one," Adino, laying on David's other side, added. "But we have overcome such odds before."

Eleazar had not even bothered to look at the Philistine siege. He wore a grimace as comfortably as another wore a well-worn pair of sandals and sat below David looking the other direction. "This is a mistake," he warned. "Mark my words well. We should be fleeing afore Saul falls upon us."

"Have you and Shobal become companions then?" Shammah rumbled.

Eleazar's vain face twisted in disgust. He spat to prove his point. "Do not pair me with the son of Belial."

"Then speak not of despair," Adino added with an amused grin. All knew of Eleazar's penchant for pronouncing doom. But come what may, the expert swordsman would stand in the battle.

David placed a hand on Eleazar's arm. "The LORD fights for us this day. Be at peace."

The swordsman nodded, his face softening, but he couldn't help but mutter, "Be at peace? We're about to do battle. Where is the peace in that?"

David beckoned to Joab who stood at the base of the hill out of sight of Keilah. The young man waved back in acknowledgement

— 254 —

and darted off. He would pass the word. They would begin the assault as soon as everyone was in position. This would be Joab's first action in combat, and he was eager, too eager by far. David couldn't refuse him, however. He was of an age, and David would need everyone, including his family.

Only one of David's brothers had come with him from Moab. The rest had remained behind with their father and mother. Abinadab, however, had chosen to come with David, and he now commanded a company of two hundred spears. A warrior true, David trusted his brother to fight well, and it lightened his heart to know that his stalwart brother was near.

"See to your men," he ordered his lieutenants. "You know what to do."

The men scattered, each to his command. David now had just over six hundred men—not nearly enough to take on the army besieging Keilah, but with surprise and the LORD's help, they would prevail. Only he hated the haste with which all of this must be done.

The fighting below intensified. The Philistines sensed victory at hand and were pressing their advantage. This was good. Hopefully, they would be too occupied to notice the hostile force to their rear until it was too late.

A sense of urgency gripped David. He had to win this fight quickly. If Saul came upon them too soon, they would be trapped. And if that happened, David would have to retreat into Keilah itself. Saul would simply pick up the siege where the Philistines had left off, and Hebrew would shed the blood of Hebrew. That had to be avoided.

Looking to his left and then to his right, he studied his men. They looked nervous and scared. This would be their first true test of both their faith and loyalty. Truly, David didn't know how much of each they had. He would need to lead them. They would need to see him in the forefront of the battle. More than that, they needed to see David's faith. They would believe if he believed.

He did. At least he hoped he did. Doubt was the enemy of faith, but years of experience had taught him that faith never existed without doubt. Faith wasn't the absence of doubt; it was overcoming one's doubts. Taking a deep breath, he steadied his hands which had begun to shake. He stood slowly, and every eye snapped to him. It was time. Time to overcome his doubts.

Hefting his shield and sword, he walked to the crest of the hill, standing in plain view of the enemy besieging Keilah. He noticed for the first time a red banner bearing an image of the fish god Dagon. That meant a high-ranking priest had accompanied the Philistines. David nearly cursed. This was likely the reason for the siege. A priest would cajole the Philistines to fight beyond their normal inclinations. The priest would need to die and die quickly.

That would be David's task.

Lifting his sword high in a prearranged signal, he began a steady, seemingly unhurried walk down the hill toward the Philistines. He never looked back to see if his men followed. But he knew they would. He had faith in them, even if many lacked faith in themselves.

Silently, like spirits, his men flowed over the crest of the hill and descended toward the bottom. They gave no war cry, no shout, and came with little haste. Unless someone looked back, the Philistines would not know they were in danger until it was too late. At the base of the hill, David broke into a jog. The sound of jingling armor intensified as his men picked up their pace to follow.

The Philistines had spread out on the opposite slope, moving steadily upward toward Keilah and oblivious to what approached from behind. Their drums beat out the sound of death, a mocking sound that echoed the insulting taunts shouted up at the defenders. It enraged David, and without thinking, a battle cry roared forth from his lips even as he lurched into a full sprint.

One or two of the Philistines waiting in the rear turned at the sound. Their colorful headdresses waved in a smoky breeze, and the sudden smell of charred wood and blood assaulted David's nose.

The nearest of the Philistines to notice David reacted as true warriors, spinning around to meet the assault, a cry of warning rising from their lips, but it did them little good. Arrows fell among them, decimating the back rank, causing no small amount of confusion. Shammah had seen David's sudden charge and had ordered his archers to open fire.

David saw nothing else. He slammed into the Philistines' rear, his sword swinging in powerful arcs as he literally cut his way through the shocked Philistines, his shield bashing them aside when they slipped too close. He had a goal firmly in mind. He could see the Philistine banner standing tall in the middle of the enemy army. There he would find the Philistine leadership. Cut the head off the snake, and even though the rest of the body continued to writhe for a time, it would eventually die.

An enemy spearman turned toward David, spear darting like a scorpion's tail. The son of Jesse deflected the spear point to the side with a twist of his shield and stepped within the arc of the spear, slashing downward, sword cutting through the Philistine's banded leather armor. He kicked the dying man aside and continued his implacable advance on the red banner. Something inside drove him toward that standard like a herdsman driving cattle.

He faced a swordsman, this one using lightning fast lunges that kept David at bay. They exchanged blows, David taking a few of them on his shield. But at the next lunge, David used his shield as a ram and bashed the Philistine to the ground where he easily dispatched him. He continued his advance as chaos erupted all around.

To his left, the bulky figure of Elhanan drove everyone before him like a battering ram. The young man's face was twisted into a grimace, a mixture of fear and rage. He wielded an axe like a woodsman would chopping wood. Beside him fought Benaiah and young Abishai. Abishai's brothers, Joab and Asahel, fought to David's right. The brothers twisting around each other in a dance of death that befuddled the Philistines and left a trail of slain and wounded enemies in the pair's wake.

Beyond them, Adino whirled through the enemy like a scythe through wheat, and Eleazar still farther away, his sword a blur as he

— 257 —

fought with a grace David envied. The rest of David's troop followed these mighty men, pushing hard to keep up.

But then a cry went up from behind the Philistines. The voice was edged with hysteria, but it was one David knew. The priest of Dagon, the one who had demanded David's heart be carved from his chest and thrown into the fires of his false god. Kenaz. "'Tis the son of Jesse!" the priest shouted shrilly. "Lay hold of him! Bring him to me!"

David turned toward that voice. Kenaz stood beneath the red banner that waved over a chariot and doubled as the Philistines' headquarters. He wore no armor, but he gripped a spear tightly, if clumsily. The moment their eyes locked, the priest's face paled, and his dark eyes bulged. The priest's tattoos stood out sharply in the daylight, curling up his face to encircle the shaved part of his scalp. The priest entirely forgot his command to capture David. He jabbed a finger at David, shrieking, "Slay him! Dagon demands his blood!"

A snarl curled David's lips, and he took a step toward the priest. All around him, men struggled, screamed, bled, and died. The battle had disintegrated into a general melee that favored David's smaller army. The Philistines caught between the fortifications of Keilah and David's men made all too tempting targets for the defenders atop the wall. Arrows rained down upon the enemy who had turned to meet the new threat from behind.

The fight reached a breaking point. All David needed to do was kill the priest, and the Philistines would likely flee. The priest stood but a score of cubits away, his eyes bulging in terror, knowing that death stalked him. But then a shadow loomed up over David, and he jumped back in time to avoid the head of a gigantic spear as it smashed into the ground where he'd been standing.

Stumbling back, David's eyes traveled up and up to meet the enraged eyes of a giant. Not quite as large as Goliath had been, this giant's wide face was still marred by a ferocious scowl and tattoos that reminded David all too much of Goliath. Worse, David recognized him. Like a recurring bad dream, he saw again the spear that had skewered Maon mere cubits from freedom. Saph. That was his name. Saph had killed Maon.

In that moment, it didn't matter to David that Maon had turned his heart away from his people and his God or that his name had been blotted from the genealogies. Maon had once been his brother, and this giant had killed him.

Growling, David stepped forward and swung his sword. The giant snorted in disdain as the blade clanged off the bronze armor protecting the giant's thighs. "Puny coney," the giant spat, stabbing at David with his huge spear.

David danced aside, mindful of the damage even a glancing blow could cause him. He darted in and used his superior speed to land a handful of blows against the giant. Most glanced off the armor. Only one drew blood, but hardly enough to matter. The cut only enraged the giant more, and he swung his spear in short arcs trying to catch up to David.

David danced in and out, avoiding the spear and knowing it couldn't last. He wished desperately for his sling. Fighting close in with this behemoth was hardly the wisest thing he'd ever done. He landed a dozen more strikes against the giant, producing two more shallow cuts, but little else. The giant's face reddened, taking on a cast of intense concentration as he tried to spit David on the end of his spear.

"Stand ye still!" the giant roared. "Fight me!"

As if David was not! The effort of avoiding that colossal spear was draining David's energy. If he didn't do something soon, he would be easy prey for the giant. He backed away, forcing the giant to take a lumbering step after him.

The battle wavered on the edge of a stalemate. The Philistines were recovering from their surprise. Officers rallied their men, forming new battle lines and halting the advance of David's smaller army. Slowly, almost ruthlessly, space opened around David and the giant. No one, even the Philistines, wanted to come within reach of the giant's mighty spear.

"I will avenge the blood of Goliath upon your head," Saph rumbled as he stalked after David. "You have witnessed your last sunrise, son of Jesse!"

The priest of Dagon still stood upon his chariot, surrounded now by shield bearers to protect the priest from arrows. David's archers tried to reach the priest, but the man crouched down behind the shield wall and managed to avoid taking any damage. The priest was shrieking at the giant, urging him on, calling upon his false god to aid the giant's already massive strength in killing David.

David sucked in great gulps of air. His strength was flagging. Keeping out of range of that spear took an incredible amount of energy. His chest heaved and sweat soaked his head and beard. He tried to push the attack, but the giant refused to give ground. When he could not strike with his spear, he kicked and stomped with his massive feet. David knew from experience that one blow would likely cripple him, so he dodged, rolled, and leaped just to avoid even a glancing strike.

But then the head of another giant loomed up from behind the Philistine lines. Two giants! The second giant, likely the companion who had helped kill Maon was lumbering toward the pair. If he joined in, David would be doomed.

He had to act now. Calling upon the LORD God of Israel, David leaped to one side, dropping his useless shield. When Saph twisted on his ponderous legs to follow, David dove forward, right between the giant's legs. The spear smashed into the ground behind him, striking sparks against the rocks. He rolled quickly to his feet, shedding more of his armor as he rose. He needed quickness and speed.

Darting away from the giant, David charged the chariot where the priest stood surveying the battle. Strength flooded into his muscles as the Spirit of the LORD enveloped him. Like before in desperate times, Jehovah answered by giving strength to the man answering His call and purpose.

Focused now, David launched himself at the men surrounding the priest of Dagon. He ignored the lumbering steps of the giant

— 260 —

trying to catch him. He ignored the panicked screeches of the priest. He ignored the plight of his men. He knew what he had to do.

He slammed into the first shield, bowling the man over and providing a small gap in the defenses around the priest. He lost his sword in the process, but he hardly needed it. He bounded to his feet and shoved aside another of the shield bearers, creating even more space. He then plucked a discarded spear from the ground and rammed it into one of the other guard's side. The man's face drained of blood, and he slumped over, his eyes already glazing toward death.

That left David facing the priest atop his horseless chariot. The priest gaped incredulously at the son of Jesse, his mouth working soundlessly. But David merely stood there, unarmed, looking at the priest who had so wanted to carve David's heart from his chest and offer it to his false god.

"You're dead," he told the priest in a quiet voice that reached only the priest's ears.

"Nay!" the other shrieked, "it is you who shall fall this day! Dagon has claimed you—" Two arrows streaked by David's head to slam into the priest's chest, cutting off the man's rant.

The priest looked down at the shafts protruding from his body. He reached up and tugged at one as if to draw it out. "Nay," he whispered. "Nay, this cannot be."

"But it is," David replied. "Your false god is a lie. Prepare yourself to meet the wrath of the living God of Israel."

A look of pure terror spread across the priest's face, but then his body realized it was dead, and he flopped over backward out of the chariot.

A groan rose up from the ranks of the Philistines upon the death of their priest. With the priest dead, they believed their god had abandoned them. It was true. Dagon was no match for the true God of Israel.

Sensing an attack from behind, David, placed his hands on the edge of the chariot and vaulted over it, landing lightly on the dead priest's chest. A spear the size of a weaver's beam slammed into the chariot, driving all the way through both sidewalls and stopping a hair's breadth from penetrating David's back.

Saph cursed David, yanking frantically on his spear which seemed stuck in the heavy chariot. The entire vehicle shook and was dragged sideways, twisting and trapping the spear. Arrows began to pepper the giant, most glancing off his armor, but several found flesh, and the giant yelled in anger and pain.

Finding yet another discarded spear, David snatched it up and cast it like a javelin. The barbed spear point found part of the giant's unprotected bicep and drove through. Saph roared in pain, stumbling away, his eyes wide with shock. He stared at the spear sticking out both sides of his upper right arm, and clapping his other hand around the shaft, he turned hate-filled eyes upon David.

David stood his ground, unarmed. He knew the Spirit of the LORD was upon him. The giant was nothing compared to the power coursing through his body. Perhaps the giant sensed something of this, for he turned and began lumbering away, his giant steps quickly taking him to the north.

The bulk of the Philistine army crumbled then, and David's men commenced to destroy the fleeing army with a great slaughter.[1] The second giant, having seen what had befallen his fellow, was already fleeing after his companion. Within the space of a quarter of an hour, not a single standing Philistine could be seen from the walls of Keilah.

Slowly, the groans of the dying Philistines were cut off as their agony was ended with the edge of the sword or the tip of the spear. No respite would be given to the enemy. They would be destroyed without mercy. Their false god had presumed to invade Israel. David had no tolerance for such evil.

David had, surprisingly, lost only a few men. He needed to commend the archers. Whoever had shot those arrows that had killed the priest had done remarkably well. Both arrows had come within a hand's span of his head and neck before striking the priest.

---

[1] 1 Samuel 23:5.

Upon further consideration, David felt a cold chill run down his spine. *That was entirely too close.* Still, he would commend those bowmen.

A young Hebrew man stumbled up to him. The man was not dressed for battle, though he looked to have fought in one. He wore clothes that had not been washed often. His beard and hair were long and unkempt as if they had not been trimmed in a long while. David peered closer at the man and realized the other carried something reverently in his hands. An ephod. He was a priest, and David recognized him.

"Abiathar?"[2]

The priest nodded, looking more exhausted than David felt. The young man could barely stand on his feet, but David's elation at finding at least one of the priests from Nob alive could not be concealed. He had thought them all dead.

"Here, sit," he ordered the young priest. David helped the man to the ground.

"I have found you at last," the other whispered. "I pray that it is not too late."

"What mean you?"

"King Saul follows hard on. He will be here on the morrow by daybreak."

David's face froze. *Saul? Here?* And closer than he'd dared believe. "How know you this? How do you come to be here?"

"Last year in his zeal to hunt you, King Saul slaughtered the priests of the LORD."

David sucked in his breath. So, it was true then. Saul had done the deed. Sadness filled him. "Tell me. What happened?"

Abiathar slumped over his knees, clutching his stomach. David steadied him. The young priest's face aged before David's eyes. What had happened to the fastidious young man he had met those many months ago?

---

[2] 1 Samuel 23:6.

When the young priest spoke, his deep voice sounded raspy, parched as if he had not used it much in a long while. "A messenger from King Saul commanded my father to present himself with all his house before the king. I alone of my father's house was left behind to tend the tabernacle of the LORD." David could see the haunted look on the young man's face. "All were slain by King Saul. My father. My brethren."

David trembled, each word wounding him deeply, but he needed to hear this. He needed to know. "This by King Saul's own hand?" he demanded.

"I know not. But the king came to Nob." Abiathar's lower lip trembled and tears filled his eyes. "They slew everyone—men, women, sucklings…even the animals. Why would the king do this? He spared not even the Gibeonites but slew all."[3]

Strength left David, and he fell to his knees next to the young priest, tears clouding his vision. Since David had heard of the rumors, he had known in his heart this was a possibility, but to have it confirmed…desperately he sought to disbelieve, to lay the blame at another's feet. Then he remembered Doeg the Edomite. It seemed like an age ago, but the Edomite was the only one who would have told Saul about David's visit to Nob. His hands clenched into tight fists, and his breathing came in short ragged breaths.

Men had noticed the exchange and were slowly gathering around. Whispers of a priest come to them were already spreading. And Saul would be here soon. When David had himself under control, he reached out and clasped Abiathar's head with both hands, pulling the distraught young man to his breast.

"I knew it that day—when Doeg the Edomite was there—that he would surely tell Saul. I have occasioned the death of all the persons of your father's house."[4] The young man broke down into sobs, clinging desperately to David, and David let him weep, trying to offer what comfort he could. A year had passed since the slaughter, but some wounds did not heal so quickly. Guilt racked

---

[3] 1 Samuel 22:20-21.
[4] 1 Samuel 22:22.

him. *I should have long ago killed that Edomite dog.* But how could he have known that Saul would go so far? How? "Abide with me, Abiathar, and fear not, for he that seeks my life seeks your life. Abide here, with me. I will keep you safe."[5]

Somehow, he had to see to it that Abiathar survived. He owed the young priest that much. And if chance ever put Doeg in his hands, he meant to see the treacherous man dead. And not just for what had happened to the priests or the entire city of Nob. The redheaded herdsman had much to answer for.

With an effort, Abiathar pulled himself together and sat back, surreptitiously wiping his face with a cloth he produced from a worn haversack. Something of the finicky man yet remained, and it made David feel some better. "My lord," the priest said, gaining control of himself. "You must flee. I have sought you since the day my father was slain, hiding in rocks and caves. When I could, I spied upon Saul, and I have seen his army. Word has spread of Keliah's plight, and I knew you would rescue them if any would, so I came here. Thanks be to God for delivering me into your hands. But Saul comes even now. He will destroy the city and everyone in it if he must. He will stop at nothing until you are delivered into his hands. All Israel does now know of his hatred toward you."

David did not doubt the young disheveled priest. Adriel had warned him this would likely happen. He had only hoped for more time. David turned to look at the walls around Keilah. His men were weary, worn from battle. A forced march at this point might break them. Could he hide within the city? Would the inhabitants protect him? Men lined the walls, watching David's men in silence. They watched David, neither cheering nor jeering. They were glad of deliverance, assuredly, but would they betray him to Saul?

He looked at the ephod in the priest's hand. Reaching out, he stood up, pulling the young man along with him. "Bring hither the ephod then. You now stand in your father's room, and I have need of you."

---

[5] 1 Samuel 22:22-23.

1 Samuel 23:5-13 & 1 Samuel 22:20-23

The young man visibly straightened, and determination filled his eyes. "Aye." He stood before David, more solidly, more steadily than when he had first come. Purpose often did that to a man. Unsaid was what both knew. There yet remained another line of high priests, another line of Aaron's sons. In one of the villages to the north, David had heard of a young man, Zadok by name, son of Ahitub and descended from the line of Eleazar.[6] Still a lad yet, but it was said that the hand of the LORD was already upon him. With Abiathar's absence, Saul may have already appointed Zadok as the next high priest.

Bowing his head, Abiathar took a deep breath and visibly gathered himself. He donned the ephod, the garment settling around his shoulders. Then looking up, he said, "Ask what you will of the LORD, son of Jesse."

Sucking in his breath, David felt the presence of the LORD's Spirit descend. The blood-stained ground upon which he stood was now holy. Quickly, he bowed himself to the ground. More of the men ceased what they were doing and gathered around. Soon, David's entire army was arrayed in a circle around David and the young priest.

A stillness fell upon the battlefield. Not a silence, but a stillness as the men awaited word from the LORD. David, on his knees, asked, "O LORD God of Israel, Your servant has heard that Saul seeks to come to Keilah, to destroy the city for my sake. Will the men of Keilah deliver me up into his hand? Will Saul come down as Your servant has heard? O LORD God of Israel, I beseech You, tell Your servant."[7]

A vast presence, almost like a tangible weight felt by everyone within earshot fell upon Abiathar. The young priest's brown eyes grew intense as if a light grew behind those orbs, and when he spoke, the raspy, parched tongue had been replaced by something deeper,

---

[6] 1 Chronicles 6:8; 2 Samuel 8:17.
[7] 1 Samuel 23:10-11.

something supernatural. The words were simple: "He will come down."[8]

"Will the men of Keilah deliver me and my men into the hand of Saul?"

"They will deliver you up."

The weight departed, and Abiathar blinked rapidly, his face slumping. He collapsed to his knees, breathing heavily. He looked apologetically at David. "That is the first time the LORD has used me thus."

David rose to his feet and placed a hand on the priest's shoulder, nodding. Beyond, he caught sight of the prophet Gad, smiling and nodding in satisfaction. Comforted some, David turned back to the priest. "It is well. And I know what we must do." He turned to look at the men gathered around. "I know you are weary. I know that we have won a great victory, but there is no time to celebrate. We must flee. King Saul comes with a vast host, and we dare not be here when he arrives." He hesitated, looking at Keilah. There was still a chance Saul would sack the city simply out of spite. He needed to do something to turn the king's wrath away from the city.

An idea came to him. A very dangerous one. But it would likely deter Saul from attacking Keilah and would bring a just recompense upon a deceitful tongue. He found young Joab standing near. "Fetch your brothers, Joab. I have need of you all."

Adino and Shammah stepped close. "What is in your mind, my lord?" Adino asked, using his bloody spear to prop up his lanky frame.

David grinned. "Nay, I do not wish to spoil the surprise. Take the army. Flee to the wilderness of Ziph. We will yet be delivered from Saul's hand."

Adino gave him an unreadable flat look, but he shrugged. "So be it."

---

[8] 1 Samuel 23:11.

Epilogue

Doeg squinted into the night, absently brushing crumbs from his reddish beard. His eyes had gotten worse lately. Things that used to be clear now appeared fuzzy, particularly those things in the distance. It was a common ailment, particularly as one aged, but he liked it little.

He thought he'd seen movement out in the darkness, shadows moving furtively in the dim starlight, disappearing behind rocks and shrubs. He squinted harder, seeing nothing. Pulling out an iron knife, brown with rust, he began peeling his long fingernails, trying to pretend that he wasn't listening to the conversation taking place under the nearby tent.

King Saul stood with stern-faced Abner, his head nearly brushing the goat-haired tent above. He stared down at his shorter cousin, their faces glowing from the light of a nearby fire.

"God has delivered him into my hand," the king whispered fiercely, clenching one fist before him. "By entering into a city that has gates and bars, he is shut in.[1] He is mine."

"What if Keilah will not turn him over?" Abner asked. He might have been enquiring about the weather for all the emotion he showed. Doeg had never liked the general and had tried to stay clear when he could.

---

[1] 1 Samuel 23:7.

"Then we will besiege it."[2] Saul snarled, snatching a spit from the fire and tearing off a hunk of meat from the end with his teeth. He chewed violently, his eyes refusing to stay still. "He will be mine at last."

Doeg hoped so. He'd earned much favor with the king, but he doubted he'd be able to capitalize on it until David was dead, but soon, when the king remembered his service, he could expect great rewards. Already, the king trusted him more than ever. It would only be a matter of time before he would be welcomed under that tent.

Abner said nothing. All knew of the king's obsession, and all knew that he would not be dissuaded. Nearby, also just outside the tent stood the scout that had brought word of David's whereabouts. Somewhere out in the night Jonathan and his brother Ishui lurked along with that hateful man, Adriel. Doeg hated them all. He despised them and would gleefully rejoice—not where Saul would see—if any of the three died.

He would be content to know if the two brothers had come to blows. Doeg cared little for the Hebrews in general. He was an Edomite, exiled from his own homeland and trying to find employment where he could—preferably next to the seat of power. Chance had brought him to Nob that night to see David slinking about. Informing Saul of this had elevated Doeg in the king's eyes. And rightfully so.

He spat on the ground and began picking his teeth with the rusty tip of his knife, trying to decide what to do next. He had been Saul's chief herdsman for many years. He yearned to be more. But how could he ingrate himself into Saul's good wishes further? Could he bring evidence of Jonathan's collusion with David? Perhaps he could prove Abner's incompetency? *There must be something.*

Saul turned to the scout. "Refresh yourself and then seek out my sons. Bring them to me here or at Keilah."

The scout bowed low and left. Abner also bowed low. "My lord, I will see to the disposition of the army."

---

[2] 1 Samuel 23:8.

Saul gave a curt nod, and Abner left. The general glanced once at Doeg who carefully averted his eyes. It would not be good to bring unwanted attention to himself. *Not yet.* But soon, he would have the power of life and death over men like Abner and then…a slow grin spread across his face.

"Edomite," Saul called, "attend me."

"Yes, my lord," Doeg replied, quickly sheathing his knife and bowing as he moved to stand beneath the open tent.

The king continued to eat the half-cooked meat as he studied Doeg. Finally, he leaned forward and placed a hand on Doeg's shoulder. "You have served me well," the king said softly. "It will not be unrewarded. I swear this by the God of my forefathers."

A surge of pleasure shimmied its way down Doeg's spine. "I am your faithful servant," he said in return. "I seek only to serve."

"Would that you were a Hebrew," Saul said somewhat pensively. "Tell me, Edomite, do you remain uncircumcised?"

Doeg shifted uncomfortably. "I have, my lord." But when Saul's eyes darkened, he hastened to add, "But I would most gladly perform the circumcision, my king." He lied, of course. He didn't give two bronze coins for the Hebrew God or their religion. But he would say and do anything to be at the center of power.

Saul relaxed. "That is well. I will have need of loyal servants in the coming days. We are surrounded by enemies. Everywhere I turn, my enemies circle like vultures. David is the most troublesome, but he will soon be in hand." The king's eyes glazed as he looked into the dark night. "I don't truly know how these things came to be. Where did I go wrong that Samuel betrayed me so? I took David in, made him as my own son, and he has joined in conspiracy with Samuel. Why?" His eyes focused on Doeg. "Am I not a good king, Edomite? Do I not care for the people of the LORD? Have I not fought the LORD's battles?"

"You are a great king, my lord. A mighty warrior."

Saul sighed. "Then where went the Spirit of the LORD from me?"

Doeg had no answer for that. In truth, he didn't care. There were many gods. If the Hebrew God had abandoned King Saul, then why not pick another? To him, it was that simple.

"Leave me," Saul muttered, waving a hand at Doeg. "I wish to be alone."

All too glad to comply, Doeg bowed and hastened away. The king's moods changed so rapidly anymore that he was becoming unhinged, unpredictable. True, this made the man easier to manipulate. All you had to know is what such a man wanted and tell him where to get it—even if it wasn't true. Because the mind wanted to believe, it found reason enough to believe.

The crickets chirped in the distance, and the hoot of an owl as it glided by the encampment of Saul's men momentarily caused Doeg to glance up. The sky was partly obscured by low clouds, and a wind sprang up only to die moments later. A strange night.

Doeg's tent lay on the outskirts of the encampment, near the herd that followed behind. He was still chief herdsman, even if he wanted more, and no Hebrew would willingly allow his tent among their own. Pigs, every one of them. But he would tolerate them if he must. The smell of power was strong in his nostrils. Soon, he would be Saul's most favored servant. Then he would be feared.

Cattle stomped their hooves and snorted in the grassy meadow used to keep them from wandering too far. He found the dark shadow that was his tent and marched up to it, suddenly feeling sleepy. He should probably check on his herdsmen, making sure they were doing their tasks, but that could wait until the morning. If those lazy fools didn't know what to do by now, they would never learn.

He pulled back the tent flap and, crouching, slipped inside. The light of a single candle illuminated the interior. It smelled faintly of mold and spoiled food. *Strange*. He hadn't lit a candle before he'd left.

Something crashed into his head. Blinding pain exploded behind his eyes, and he found himself lying on the rocky soil of the tent floor. He blinked, finding that even that movement sent waves of agony stabbing into his head.

— 271 —

Roughly, someone tied his hands and feet and stuffed a wad of dry cloth into his mouth. Doeg blinked again, desperately trying to focus, trying to understand what was happening to him. Was he under attack? Surely, he was safe near Saul's camp! Who would do this?

His vision cleared enough, and he made out the features of two men standing over him. The first man was unfamiliar. Young, but with hard eyes. The second man nearly made Doeg's eyes pop out of his head.

David!

The powerful Hebrew warrior sat down beside Doeg. "You know me then?" he said in a near whisper.

Doeg trembled. Of all men, Doeg most hated and feared the son of Jesse, but David's next words sent a spike of panic deep into the Edomite's soul.

"You are going to die this night," the son of Jesse said.

Doeg tried to roll away, but a kick in his side caused him to grunt into the cloth and sent him back toward David. The other man stood over the Edomite, watching in silence, but prepared to keep Doeg from escaping.

David's eyes glittered in the light of the single candle. They seemed to take on weight and power even as Doeg watched. When the son of Jesse spoke next, his words carried something more than mere authority. An element of the supernatural gave each word an edge, like that of the sharpest sword.

"Why boastest thou thyself in mischief, O mighty man?" David whispered, the words settling upon Doeg with the strength of inevitability. "The goodness of God endureth continually. Thy tongue deviseth mischiefs; like a sharp razor, working deceitfully. Thou lovest evil more than good; and lying rather than to speak righteousness. Thou lovest all devouring words, O thou deceitful tongue. God shall likewise destroy thee forever, he shall take thee away, and pluck thee out of thy dwelling place, and root thee out of the land of the living. The righteous also shall see, and fear, and shall laugh at him: Lo, this is the man that made not God his strength; but trusted in the abundance of his riches, and strengthened himself in his wickedness."[3]

Doeg was helpless before those words. He wanted nothing more than to leap to his feet and flee, but his muscles refused to obey. It was as if the words themselves had bound him tighter than any physical ropes.

David shook himself, seemingly to come out of a trance. There was a fervor in his eyes and awe in the face of Doeg's other captor. "I can remember every word," the young man whispered, "as if I've always known them. What power is this?"

The son of Jesse smiled tightly. "It is the Spirit of the LORD, Joab. Know the power of our God."

The one named Joab nodded and gestured to Doeg. "And what of this one?"

"He has heard the LORD's pronouncement of his guilt. He dies." Still, Doeg could not move. His muscles were paralyzed. He couldn't even take his eyes off David's face. "His death will be a message for King Saul. He will know that I am not in Keilah." Looking at Doeg, David said grimly, "You will do something good at last, Doeg of Edom. The blood of the priests of the LORD are upon you, for you have occasioned their death. I pronounce your life forfeit and pray that your death will serve to save the lives of others."

The last thing Doeg saw was the knife falling toward his heart. He felt a spike of pain, and then he knew nothing else until his spirit awoke in torment.

The End

Thus ends book three of the Davidic Chronicles. In book four, *Delivered*, David looks to end his struggle with King Saul before all is lost, but to do so, David must confront evil men within his own company and deal with betrayal from within his own tribe.

---

[3] Psalm 52:1-7.

Additional Biblical and Historical Explanations

Facts Versus Interpretation to Discover Truth

Stating a fact and interpreting the fact are not the same thing. By themselves, facts don't represent truth. They are merely facts. Truth is a fact that has purpose and meaning—often what we call a philosophy—that gives the fact a means to interact with your life and become relevant to you, meaningful. This then becomes a truth for you.

For example, take a fact: dinosaur bones. This fact coupled with either the philosophy of evolution or creationism will give two entirely different and opposing truths. Each side considers theirs to be true and their opposite to be false. But the core "fact" is still a bone. It is the interpretation of that fact that leads to one's perspective, views, understanding, and ultimately truth.

Jesus said that He is truth. This means that when we see life through His eyes, we find purpose and meaning that cannot be found unless we can view that perspective. Jesus is indeed truth. My truth, and I trust your truth as well. But even among Christian circles, that perspective varies enough that our "truths" are often not quite aligned with someone else's. Welcome to individual soul liberty.

I say this to explain that, though I try to incorporate *all* the facts that the Bible speaks of in these stories, I am still going to interpret what those facts mean for the characters and events described. Not everyone will agree with my conclusions. For example, a fact: Michal, David's wife, lied to her father about David's supposed threat to kill her if she did not aid in his escape. This is the fact. Why she did this is supposition. We can likely extrapolate that she did not want to face the wrath of her father and so lied to protect herself from him. But is that an accurate interpretation of the facts? Perhaps not. And that is the dilemma of interpreting the facts. We cannot know with certainty why someone did something unless God explains it.

When you interpret the fact, your "truth" of the event shifts. Your understanding of it changes. And how you relate to the fact and how it becomes meaningful to you also changes. This becomes your truth and understanding of the stories mentioned in the Bible. Preachers do this all the time.

These novels represent my interpretation of those facts into a cohesive and, hopefully, noncontradictory story that will entertain but also spark your fascination for the Bible, the characters, God's interaction with men, and ultimately your own relationship with Him.

I do not expect everyone to agree. But I do hope these novels will inspire you to delve into God's Word in a much more personal way and to see that the characters in the Bible had real lives and that it is those lives God wanted to introduce you to.

Gods and Religions

The Hebrews of David's day had only the first five books of our Bible to guide them—and possibly whatever Samuel wrote. This, along with cultural influences from the nations around them, would have shaped the Hebrew view on the pantheon of deities that existed in the various cultures they came in contact with.

Yes, most of the Hebrews of David's day believed that there was more than one god because the power of other gods was a fact of life to them. The difference between a Hebrew and someone from another culture was threefold:

First, the Hebrews were commanded not to have any other god before Jehovah Elohim (Exodus 20:3). This did not preclude the belief in other gods, but that Elohim was to be placed above all other gods, that He alone reigned supreme above any other existing power. This was unlike the other cultures that worshiped multiple gods and believed that the power structure of these gods could change, with one god being supreme for a time until his power was usurped by another god. This made Israel monotheistic instead of polytheistic. While other nations could bounce from god to god, the Hebrew was not allowed to do such a thing. They had one God.

Second, the Hebrews were commanded not to make images of Jehovah or of any other god (Exodus 20:23). This is significant on many levels. For the Hebrew, the Ark of the Covenant was the closest thing they had to a physical object that represented the very presence of their God. The nations around Israel had images and idols that represented their gods. These idols would be a focus for the indwelling of the spirit of said god and so became the object of their worship and devotion. For the Hebrew, there existed no such image. Jehovah interacted with the Hebrew in entirely different ways than how other cultures interacted with their gods. Instead of infusing an object with power, the Spirit of the Lord infused men and women directly. This made Israel stand out, and it created a larger barrier between the Hebrew and the non-Hebrew.

Third, the Hebrew was chosen by their God and not the other way around. While the theology of other nations sought out their gods, inventing them to help explain phenomena beyond their understanding, Jehovah claimed Israel as His people. Dagon, Ashtaroth, Baal and other false gods found worship among many people. But to worship Jehovah, one had to become part of the Hebrew culture. Ruth did this and so did others, such as Rahab, but in general, one did not have to be a Philistine to worship a false god such as Dagon. This was a huge distinction in the Hebrew culture.

Deuteronomy 4:35-49 explains the supremacy of Jehovah and attitude of the Hebrew to other gods: "That thou mightest know that the LORD he is God; there is none else beside him." However, other passages hint that there are other powers, other forces, that exist: "Thou shalt make no covenant with them, nor with their gods" (Exodus 23:23). Was there actual power in these false gods? There likely was. Some have theorized that these false gods were in fact evil spirits or, as some would say, demons. We know, for example, that Pharaoh's magicians had power to do some of the miracles that Moses did. These magicians likely believed their power came from their gods, and this was probably so. They were worshiping demons.

The average person living in that day and age was surrounded by supernatural phenomena. Some of this could be explained away with science not yet discovered, but some of it was truly supernatural, demonic, and oppressive. David would have likely believed in the power of the false gods of other nations, but he would have believed more in the greater power of Jehovah, his God.

The Philistine response to David's madness is another indication of their belief in how their gods interact with mankind. Whereas the Spirit of Jehovah can fall upon a person and work through that individual to do great supernatural feats, the other nations would have believed that such an interaction would have driven a man insane. They created idols to house their deities' spirits, fearing such a touching of the gods upon themselves. Based on New Testament evidence of how demonic possession affected people, we can see why they might have believed such a thing (Mark 5:1-5; Matthew 4:24, 17:15).

Fictional Characters and Events

I try to use characters that the Bible already speaks of. The story is already in place, and I believe the main characters should remain the main characters of the story. Where possible, I use characters the Bible already mentions.

But there are still several fictional characters introduced into this story. Shobal, one of David's followers, is entirely made up. We know there were men of Belial, evil men who followed David to escape justice or were out for personal gain. Their names are never given, so I made him up. Jether is another such. The king of Moab's name is never given, so I gave him one, and invented the Moabite ambassador.

Many of the real people mentioned in the story also performed fictional roles. In effect, they constitute my best guess as how a person could logically get from point A (a biblical fact) to point B (another biblical fact). The fictional part is often what happens between point A and point B.

Adriel again has a significant role to play in this story, but the Bible only mentions that he married Saul's daughter Merab. Phalti is in a similar situation. He is given Michal as his wife after David flees, but that is all we really know about him. I believe he was important to Saul in some way to gain such a reward, so I gave him a place of importance in the story. Gad is only mentioned once in Moab, telling David to return to Judah. He is not mentioned again until well into David's reign as king. I introduce Nathan and Gad both as pupils of Samuel, though this may or may not have been true. There is evidence that Samuel started a school of prophets, and I feel it is natural that both these prophets may have spent time with Samuel, but that is a guess.

Ishui is only mentioned once in Scripture as having died with his father. I made him a villain in this story, but his role is entirely fictional. Doeg the Edomite is only ever mentioned as having been at Nob when David was passing through and telling Saul of this. Scripture does describe his role in the slaughter of the priests, but his other roles in these novels including his death is entirely fictional.

Most all the characters mentioned take on some form of fictional role to explain how the story may have played out based on what is told us in Scripture.

Timelines and Timeframes

The biblical account is often vague on the actual timeline of events presented in this novel. Perhaps if there is any area that I take the most liberties, it would be with the timeline. For example, there is no indication whatsoever of how much time elapsed between when David fled Saul's javelin for the last time and the victory at Keilah. I imagine that fleeing to Moab took time, so I inserted some.

All we know for a fact is that David was thirty-eight years of age when he was crowned king over all Israel and that he became king over Judah eight years before that (2 Samuel 5:4). If David was roughly seventeen or eighteen years of age when he killed Goliath, then there are roughly twelve years that must be accounted for.

The only other timeframe given is found in 1 Samuel 27:7, which states that David was in Philistia for a year and four months when he was hiding from Saul.

I leave it to the reader to decide what is right and pray you have mercy on my decision.

Violence and Warfare

Life was cheap in David's day, and violence a part of everyday life. The early kings of Israel did not maintain prisons as we understand them today. In many cases, an infraction resulted in a physical punishment—the eye for an eye, the tooth for a tooth principle. More serious infractions or violations often resulted in death. Saul and then David often executed people for even minor violations of disloyalty. The Indebted, the men David commands in this novel, is an example of minor infractions being punished in severe ways. Many Hebrews were enslaved because of debt (though there were provisions to free them at the year of Jubilee). However, many of these men represent what we would consider petty criminals or rebels in our day. These are the type of men who came to David later because they saw a way to become free (1 Samuel 22:2).

But as stated, life was cheap. King Saul, for example, killed all the priests of Nob for the simple fact that they had helped David. Saul felt that such a drastic action was well within his rights as king, and no one chastised him for it either. David killed an Amalekite man who had admitted that he'd helped King Saul commit suicide. The man was lying, but David didn't take the time to find out the truth of the matter. He let the man's mouth be his judge and ordered him killed. On another occasion, David set out to kill every person associated with Nabal because he felt slighted and insulted by the man. Only Nabal's wife, Abigail, succeeded in turning away David's wrath just in the nick of time. When Nabal died a little later, David felt no remorse and saw it as vindication of God's favor.

These examples were not exceptions. They were the norm for that period. Violence and death were common bedfellows, and a simple way to eradicate malcontent was to kill the malcontented. I tried to keep this aspect of common society in the story. David was a bloody man according to God, and death and violence followed him.

Warfare was also part of everyday life which I tried to portray in the story. I studied the arms and armaments of the period along with common tactics and strategies. I did my best to keep them as accurate as possible in the story.

Sources and References

Much research goes into a novel like this. I wanted to stay true to the biblical account but also stay true to the era and times. This meant I had to learn how they built their houses, what their clothes were made of, and many other customs and facts. The sources below represent the majority of the information about customs, manners, and geography that I incorporated into this novel. Those not mentioned only corroborated what I found in the sources below.

Disclaimer: Undoubtedly, there are many facts about ancient life that I missed or didn't learn, and so the astute reader may discover historical and geographical errors. Feel free to write me about them, as long as you corroborate them with sources, and I will attempt to incorporate them into future editions of the novel.

Sources:
- The King James Bible
- www.biblicalarchaeology.org
- www.ancient-hebrew.org
- en.wikipedia.org/wiki/Salix_viminalis
- www.gci.org/bible/hist/weapons
- www.haaretz.com/archaeology/.premium-philistine-city-of-gath-walls-found-1.5382808
- gath.wordpress.com/about/gath-in-the-bible/

- www.livescience.com/51737-goliath-city-gates-uncovered-israel.html
- www.thattheworldmayknow.com/the-philistines
- www.bible-history.com/geography/ancient-israel/ot/adullam.html
- www.biblestudytools.com/dictionary/adullam/
- www.gotquestions.org/Jehovah.html
- www.theoldtestamenttimeline.com
- www.israelbiblicalstudies.com& blog.israelbiblicalstudies.com
- www.jewfaq.org
- www.bible-history.com
- www.biblewalks.com/info/trees.html
- www.netours.com/content/view/241/26/
- www.biblehub.com/timeline/psalms/1.htm
- www.bibleatlas.org
- www.bibleresources.americanbible.org/resource/inns-and-innkeeping
- www.biblegateway.com/resources/encyclopedia-of-the-bible/Bath-Bathe-Bathing
- www.biblestudytools.com/encyclopedias/isbe/bath-bathing.html
- Jan H. Negenman, *New Atlas of the Bible* (New York: Doubleday & Company Inc., 1969).
- Rand-McNally Bible Atlas- Published in 1910.
- Smith Bible Atlas - Designed and edited by George Adam Smith, 1915.
- Fred H. Wight, *Manners and Customs of Bible Lands* (Moody Bible Institute of Chicago, 1953).
- A. Van Deursen, *Illustrated Dictionary of Bible Manners and Customs* (Grand Rapids, MI: Zonderzan, 1958).
- Boyd Seevers, *Warefare in the Old Testament* (Grand Rapids, MI:Kregel Publications, 2013).

- Chaim Herzog and Mordechai Gichon, *Battles of the Bible– A Military History of Ancient Israel* (Barnes and Noble Publishing, 2006).

Commentaries and Dictionaries:
- James Orr, M.A., D.D., General Editor, *International Standard Bible Encyclopedia.*
- John McClintock and James Strong, *Cyclopedia of Biblical, Theological and Ecclesiastical Literature* (1895).
- Canne, Browne, Blayney, Scott, and others, with introduction by R. A. Torrey, *Treasury of Scriptural Knowledge* (1834; public domain).
- *John Gill's Exposition of the Bible* (1746-1766, 1816; public domain).
- *Jamieson, Fausset and Brown Commentary - A Commentary, Critical and Explanatory, on the Old and New Testaments* (1871; public domain).
- *Adam Clarke's Commentary on the Bible* (1810-1826; public domain).
- *Joseph Benson's Commentary on the Old and New Testaments* (1857; public domain).
- *Albert Barnes' Notes on the Bible* (1847-85; public domain).
- *Matthew Henry's Commentary on the Whole Bible* (1708-1714; public domain).
- W. Robertson Nicoll, *Sermon Bible Commentary* (1888-1893; public domain).
- *John Wesley's Notes on the Bible* (1755-1766; public domain).
- F. B. Meyer, *Through the Bible Day by Day – A Devotional Commentary* (1914; public domain).
- W. Robertson Nicoll (Editor), *Expositor's Bible Commentary* (1887-1896; public domain).

About the Author

Greg S. Baker has been writing novels for over twenty years. His books are widely read and enjoyed. His primary focus lately has been on his stellar Biblical Fiction novels and his engaging young adult adventure novels. He has written a number of other helpful books for the Christian life. He has a passion for expanding the Kingdom of God within the kingdom of men.

He lives in the southwest with his wife, Liberty, and their four boys. Much of his writing has been for them, desiring to provide entertaining stories that teach and inspire.

He attended Bible college in the late 1990s, pastored a Baptist church in Colorado for thirteen years, and now works as a writer, a freelance Christian editor, and a programmer from his house. He remains active in his church, serving God in a variety of capacities, but focusing mainly on teenagers and young single adults.

He loves chess, playing sports, and rearing his teen boys.

You can connect with Greg through his website GregSBaker.com. He loves hearing from people and engaging them as an active part of the writing process for his future books. If you love reading, then stop on by.

Printed in Great Britain
by Amazon